# Betting on the Bad Boy

## BAD BOYS OF NEWBRIDGE SERIES

**DYLANN CRUSH**

Published by Tickled Pinkest

www.DylannCrush.com

# CHAPTER 1

*Faith*

I COULD HAVE PLAYED it either way: waltz into the library like I owned the place, or go in full incognito. I'd always sucked at dancing, so I stood in front of the self-checkout in a bulky sweatshirt and dark shades, with a LA Dodgers baseball cap tugged low over my eyes. Hopefully, I'd find something in one of the books to inspire the final sexcapade in my manuscript before submitting it to my agent.

Receipt in hand, I pushed through the heavy glass doors into the unseasonably blustery September afternoon. As soon as I stepped outside, a gust of wind ripped my hat off, and I rushed to snag it. The hat bounced along the sidewalk, and I lunged as it tumbled toward rush hour traffic.

I grasped the brim, my sunglasses slipped, and the books fell out of my arms, scattering across the sidewalk. I snatched "Cunnilingus: An Oral History" and "Love Knots: A Beginner's Guide to BDSM" and tucked them under my arm. The last book sat open on the pavement two feet away. Before I could reach it, a large hand closed around the spine.

Six-plus feet of prime male crowded the sidewalk in front of me in suit pants, polished dress shoes, and a hint of a five o'clock shadow. His starched white oxford had the top few buttons undone, revealing a tight white t-shirt underneath.

My heart flip-flopped in my chest as his fingers casually flipped through the pages of "The Illustrated Kinky Kama Sutra."

"Whoa, I didn't know the library had books like this," he said, his deep, husky tone vibrating through me.

I held out a shaky hand. "It's for a class I'm teaching."

His lips quirked into a crooked smile, and he let out a deep laugh. "Sounds like I took the wrong classes."

His laughter rolled over me, making my stomach clench. I hadn't made a man laugh in a long time. Would it be completely out of line if I pressed my palm to his chest so I could feel the vibration ripple through him? I fisted my hand instead.

He pushed his glasses up on his nose, drawing my attention to his teasing blue-green eyes. "What class is it?"

The bones in my legs turned to jelly under his probing stare. I stumbled forward, convinced I'd end up splayed across the sidewalk.

His hand flew out, catching me by the elbow. "Careful there."

Even through the thick jersey knit of my sweatshirt, I could feel the pressure from his fingers. Dammit, I should have just googled the info I needed, although last time I'd done that, my laptop had been infected with a slew of viruses.

"Thanks. Sorry, I'm not usually quite this clumsy. The class is women's studies," I lied. "Can I have my book back?"

He held it out, pointing at an illustration on the open page. "You should check out the Lotus Blossom. It's one of my favorites."

My eyes widened, and I opened my mouth to speak, but no words came out. The sound of brakes squealing to a stop next to me pulled me out of my stupor. I snatched the book out of his hands, snapped it closed, and stuffed it into my backpack. "I've got to catch my bus."

I brushed past him and took off down the sidewalk.

"Hey, wait!" His voice pulled at me as I flung myself through the doors to the city bus.

The doors whooshed closed behind me while I stumbled down the aisle and slid into a window seat. As the bus rumbled past, he lifted his hand in a wave. Pulling my hat even lower on my head, I hunkered down in my seat, my cheeks on fire.

I should have known better than to go to the library, even the cavernous downtown branch. But I'd promised my next manuscript to my agent in less than a week, and I had to do something to get past my debilitating case of writer's block.

Hopefully, the books would help. Next time, if I wanted to keep my side gig a secret, I'd have to be more careful.

The bus wound through crowded downtown Newbridge, Indiana. An hour from now, the streets would be deserted. A group of business owners and city officials had been trying to infuse the downtown district with nightlife over the past few years, but it hadn't paid off yet.

I glanced out the window as we passed a slew of warehouses that had been recently renovated into loft apartments and some trendy restaurants and bars that had popped up along the riverfront.

My cheeks still felt hot from my incompetent interaction with the suit on the street. I closed my eyes and leaned my head back against the seat. Within minutes, my breathing stabilized, and my heart slowed down. That was too close of a call. I'd never seen the hottie from the sidewalk on campus, and he dressed much better than my colleagues, so he couldn't be a student or member of the staff.

But what was with the comment about the Lotus position?

I made a mental note to check it out as soon as I got home. Not that I should waste any time or energy on a stranger. Especially a stranger with a searing gaze and a laugh that could literally make me fall flat on my face. No, I didn't have time for that.

I opened my eyes, pressed my nose against the glass for a final lingering moment, then turned my thoughts to all the prep work I had to fit in over the weekend.

My phone pinged with an incoming text alert.

> You're going out w/ us tonight. Pick you up at 9.

Jess just wouldn't give up. She'd pestered me earlier in the week about going out with a couple of friends, but I kept putting her off. I was way behind on my lecture notes and needed to focus.

> Can't. 2 much 2 do. Have fun!

Before I tucked my phone away, Jess's response lit up the screen.

> Robin's bday. 9pm be ready!

Nice touch. Of course, I'd have to go out if Jess made it all about birthday drinks.

> Fine. One hour!

> We'll see about that!

I smiled to myself. Thank God for Jess and Robin. If left to my own devices, I'd probably only venture out of my apartment to travel the short distance back and forth to work.

We'd met at a happy hour hosted by the English Department a few years before. Someone had the bright idea to set up some party games so the three of us teamed up and spent all night holding onto the Pictionary champion title.

Now we all had real jobs—Jess and I as adjunct professors and Robin working at a local insurance company. I rarely joined them on their weekend excursions, but sometimes appreciated the distraction from my class prep and self-imposed writing deadlines. Unfortunately, tonight was not one of those nights.

The bus slowed to a stop on the corner by my complex and I filed off behind a handful of students. I'd lived in my apartment for just over a year, but still didn't recognize any of my neighbors.

Unfortunately, with a desire to live close to campus, I had to pick from the complexes that appealed to many of the undergrads. I kept to myself, avoiding the raging keggers and late-night parking lot parties that took place most weekends. Partying wasn't really my style. I'd rather spend my evenings getting my reading done or dreaming up steamy scenes for the erotic romance novels I penned.

I unlocked the apartment door and set down my backpack. Mr. Darcy wound around my legs then hopped onto the kitchen table. Nudging his head into my stomach, he prompted me to run a hand along his silky back.

"You're not supposed to be up here." I slid a hand underneath his belly and lifted him up so he could nuzzle the top of his head under my chin. He rumbled a purr of satisfaction, then leapt to the ground and sashayed over to the couch where he took up the never-ending task of grooming his unruly fur.

I tossed the baseball cap onto the counter and unzipped my bag. My hand closed around the books I'd picked up at the library. My interest was piqued about what exactly the

Lotus Blossom entailed, so I flipped through the pages, past images of couples, trios, and entire groups of men and women engaged in various acts of pleasure.

As my gaze scanned over the intricate illustration of the position in question, warm tingles marched down my cheeks, flushed my neck, and made color bloom on my chest. The Lotus Blossom itself wasn't so shocking. I'd written about experiences much more risqué than that.

But my breath hitched as I pictured the dark-haired, mass of man from the sidewalk and what he might look like sitting cross-legged and bare-assed underneath me.

# CHAPTER 2

## *Dante*

IF THAT CHICK'S cheeks had turned any redder, she might have spontaneously combusted on the sidewalk right in front of me. I smiled as I shifted the briefcase to my other hand. I'd enjoyed teasing her a bit. Probably more than I should have. But she'd been so embarrassed, it had been too easy to make her blush.

I shook the vision of her out of my head. Too bad I hadn't caught her name. It might be fun to follow up with her and find out what she thought of her new reading material.

I passed the entrance to the library and turned the corner, making my way toward the riverfront a few blocks down. I didn't mind the short walk from my office to my apartment, especially at this time of year. I'd lived in northern Indiana all my life, and fall could be a fickle season in the upper Midwest. May as well get the fresh air before the snow started to fly.

As my shoes thudded on the sidewalk, my thoughts turned back to the blushing redhead. Women's studies, really? Throughout my undergrad program and into grad school, I'd never heard of the Kama Sutra being required reading material, especially at a conservative school like Tempest. I'd only become familiar with the position during a weekend fling with a particularly limber yoga instructor. My lips twitched at the memory of exactly how flexible she'd been.

I ducked into a doorway and pulled on the large brass handle of a massive wooden door. It had been a while since I'd seen any action. Newbridge was pretty much a college town and tended to shut down over the summer. Now that classes had started up again, Tapped ought to be hopping.

I'd only been working at the bar for a couple of weeks. Maybe during my shift tonight, I'd try out a few lines on one of the eager female grad students. They always seemed to be making eyes at me and leaning over the bar in their low-cut shirts to ask for a free drink—one of the few perks of my new part-time gig.

"Hey, Dante. Can you stock the cooler and help me switch out a couple of kegs?" Wyatt, the owner, stood in the door-way, hands on his hips, a half apron with the Tapped logo on it tied around his waist.

We were both from the same small town of Hinkley, Indiana. Wyatt had been a couple of years ahead of me in high school. Now he and his new wife, Lindsey, had made the move to Newbridge to try their luck with the bar.

"Just let me run up and change." I cruised through the empty high-top tables to the staircase in back.

Tapped had barely been open a month. I'd lucked out when Wyatt offered me the job. Located a little farther from campus in the riverfront warehouse area of downtown Newbridge, Tapped drew more of the grad student crowd as opposed to the car-less, beer-sloshing, sloppy-drunk undergrads.

The fact that Wyatt discounted my rent on the second-floor apartment in exchange for working the late-night shifts had been the primary attraction of the gig. Although, the ability to get a head start on my massive student loans ran a close second.

As I opened the door to my place, my cell rang. I glanced at the screen and smiled. No matter how busy I was, I'd always make time for my grandmother.

"Did Bingo get canceled this afternoon, and you needed someone to entertain you?" I teased.

Meemaw's voice crackled through the phone. "They ran out of prizes. That Irene never gets enough prizes when they put her in charge. Why, if it were me, I'd make sure I had extra. And she calls the numbers way too fast. Half the poor folks couldn't even keep up. I ought to just take over the Bingo—"

"That's all you need, Meemaw... to be in charge of one more thing." I kicked off my shoes and made my way to the bedroom. I might put in twelve-hour days at the office, but I could guarantee that between all of her volunteering, my grandmother had me beat.

"Well, it gives me something to do all day. I can't just sit around here and twiddle my thumbs now, can I?"

"Nope, no twiddling. You don't sit still long enough for that." I could feel her grin through the phone.

"I just wanted to make sure you can still come down for dinner on Sunday. Bugsy finally killed that hairy, old hog and I'll have a nice pork roast with potatoes and gravy."

My mouth watered at the thought of a home-cooked meal. "I'm counting on it. Any chance you'll have time to make one of your famous apple pies?"

"Rolled out the crust this morning, my boy. What time can I expect you?"

I chuckled. She knew me better than anyone. "Should be there by two." I was scheduled to close Saturday night. That would give me time to sleep in and get a little bit of work done before making the ninety-minute drive back home to my grandmother's farm.

"I'll see you then. You know it's always okay with me if you want to invite a friend. I've got plenty."

Here we go again. "I think Murph's got plans. Plus, then I wouldn't have as many leftovers."

Meemaw clucked her tongue. "I meant a lady friend. It's high time you start thinking about giving me some great-grandbabies. I'm not gonna be around forever, you know."

A lady friend... that would be the day. The only girl I'd ever invited over for a Sunday dinner had played me for a complete fool, and I had no interest in ever putting myself out there like that again. "Just me this time."

"Sugar, you know I love seeing you. Just wish you'd find a smart, sassy, young woman to spend some time with."

I cleared my throat, my signal for an immediate change in topic.

Having raised me all my life, my grandmother picked up on it right away. "Oh, all right. Think you'll have time to help me put up some Halloween decorations at the center while you're here?"

I pinched the bridge of my nose. No such thing as a free meal where Meemaw was concerned. She'd always figure out a way to get some manual labor out of me. It was worth it, though. If I could spare the time, I'd be willing to work all weekend just for a few bites of one of her melt-in-your-mouth pork roasts.

"You bet. Nothing too spooky, I hope. Don't want to give Mrs. Blake a coronary."

"Oh, pshaw. That's not funny. You know she gets bouts of the angina. She's taking two different kinds of pills."

"Sorry, Meemaw. I was just kidding."

"I know. You stay out of trouble now and drive safe. I love you."

"I love you, too."

At eighty-two, my grandmother should be taking it easy, not single-handedly running the senior center in town. With a seemingly endless supply of compassion and energy, she seemed a helluva lot younger than most of the people who frequented the place.

She always said she felt sorry for them. "Those poor old folks, no family around to look after them." Pretty ironic seeing as how she was older than all of them and didn't have any family left to look after her. "I have you," she'd tell me. I just felt bad that I didn't get back to see her often enough. She was a spunky ole gal that was for sure.

It was about time she stopped bothering me about settling down, though. I'd told her a million times—my focus needed to be on my career for the foreseeable future. But Meemaw had always had ideas of her own where I was concerned, especially after we attended my cousin's wedding in Tennessee awhile back.

For a split second, I wondered about the woman from the sidewalk. Who would she be practicing all those moves on? What lucky guy or girl would be on the receiving end of all that newfound knowledge? Whoever it was would definitely have a better start to their weekend than me.

I tossed my phone on the bed and changed into some jeans and a flannel shirt. Much better. I didn't mind dressing the part at the office, but would much rather live in a pair of worn-in jeans.

After shoving my phone into my pocket, I locked up and made my way back downstairs, ready for whatever another Friday night behind the bar might have in store.

# CHAPTER 3

## *Faith*

I DRAPED my jacket over the back of the tall barstool. Sandwiched between Jess and Robin, I pasted on a smile and vowed to at least pretend to have fun. When was the last time I'd taken a break from work and writing deadlines to enjoy a Friday night out? Already three weeks into the fall semester, I hadn't so much as gone out to dinner yet.

"Check out the sex-on-a-stick behind the bar. Are you going home with him, or am I?" Robin nodded toward the bartender.

As if he could hear us from across the room, he looked up and made eye contact with me. A wave of heat washed over my cheeks as I took in the dark hair, five o'clock shadow, and wire-rimmed specs.

Of all the guys who could be working behind the bar, I would have to get stuck facing down Mr. Kinky Kama from earlier today. I looked away first, desperate to get out of there before he recognized me.

Twisting around on my stool, I put a foot on the ground, a slew of excuses on the tip of my tongue. "You know, I'm suddenly not feeling very well. I'll just catch the bus—"

"Like hell you will." Jess's hand wrapped around my wrist, holding me in place. "You were fine two seconds ago. Unless you're actively puking, you'll sit right here and have a drink with us."

I rolled my eyes and pulled my arm away. "Some friend you are. Wouldn't you be more comfortable at a table?" I pointed across the room. "Like one of those over there?"

Jess leaned close. "What's with you tonight? We usually sit at the bar. Besides, I think Robin likes the view." She nodded at Robin, who was busy eyeing the bartender like he was one of the happy hour specials.

"Fine. One drink. That's it." I slouched down on my stool. Mr. Kinky Kama probably wouldn't recognize me anyway. My schlumpy disguise from earlier was a world away from the snug V-neck and skinny jeans I'd squeezed my ass into for an evening out with the girls.

"Wait a sec, it's the bartender, isn't it?" Jess eyed me with suspicion.

I looked at my lap. Dammit, how could she read me so well?

"Do you know him?" Jess put an elbow on the bar and leaned toward me, encroaching on my personal space.

I shook my head and lied through my gritted teeth. "No, I'm fine. Just a moment of panic, thinking about all the work I have to do tonight."

"All work and no play makes Faith a big-ass lame-o." Jess leaned across me and swatted at Robin. "Go for it, girl. Jake and I are back on again so no competition from me. I know I've met your sex-on-a-stick before. What's his name again? Starts with a 'D.'" She put her hand to her forehead. "Damon, David...screw it, I forget. He seems like a nice guy, but I've heard he's kind of a player."

Robin wiggled her eyebrows. "Happy birthday to me. Playing is exactly what I have in mind."

I snorted. "Could you be any more obvious?" Subtlety was definitely not one of Robin's strong suits.

"Hey, I'm not afraid to go for what I want." Robin shrugged her shoulders.

"You should have told us that's what you wanted for your birthday." Jess winked and lifted a hand to beckon the bartender over. "I would have wrapped him up with a bow."

"Oh yeah? Which part?" I put my elbows on the bar and rested my head in my hands. The odds of him recognizing me had to be super slim. My hair had been pulled back in a ponytail, and I'd had shades covering my eyes during most of our exchange.

Tonight, I actually looked somewhat presentable. I'd even swiped on some lip gloss and dusted some powder across my nose in an attempt to downplay the light smattering of freckles that popped up every summer. I took in a deep breath, flipped a wavy lock of hair over my shoulder, and told myself to relax.

The object of their ogling walked over and put a few napkins down in front of us. "What can I get you, ladies?" He never took his eyes off me.

"I'll take that wheat beer you've got on tap," said Jess.

"MGD for me." Robin leaned forward, putting her ample cleavage on full display.

He nodded, not even glancing at her. "And for you?"

I swallowed the lump in my throat. Those eyes. Behind the glasses, his eyes reflected the most incredible shade of aquamarine, just like the ocean. Jess nudged my arm.

"How a-b-b-out a Honeyweiss?" I squeaked out.

One side of his mouth curled up in a half-smile. "Beer, huh? I didn't figure you as a beer kind of girl."

Was he flirting with me? "What kind of girl did you figure me as?"

His eyes twinkled. "You kind of look like you might enjoy a Sloe Comfortable Screw."

Jess erupted into a fit of giggles next to me. "He's got you pegged. If anyone could use a good screw, it's you, Faith!"

I elbowed my former bestie in the side. "Thanks, but I'll just take a beer for now."

He shrugged. "You sure about that? Maybe a Red Lotus Cocktail instead?"

"Mmm, that sounds good to me." Robin put her arm around my shoulder. "I think I'll switch to that."

Dammit, he did recognize me. I sat up straighter and cleared my throat. Even though I wrote about erotic romance, I hadn't experienced much of it myself.

I resisted the urge to fan myself under the heat of the bartender's scorching gaze. "Just the beer will do."

"That's too bad, Faith." He winked at me, and a shiver ran through my core. "One Honeyweiss coming right up." He moved away and grabbed some glasses from the overhead rack.

Jess swiveled toward me on the stool, her blue eyes wide with interest. "Are you sure you don't know him? That's the most I've ever heard him say."

"I may have seen him around town or something." My face flushed. At least he hadn't outed me in front of my friends.

I didn't have time to think about men. Between teaching the maximum number of classes I could, aggressively pursuing publication to get on a tenure track, and keeping my steamy side career a secret, I barely had time to brush my teeth, so I definitely didn't have time to play around.

"Hey, I already called dibs. And it's my birthday. That Sloe Comfortable Screw should be mine!" Robin stuck out her lower lip in a playful pout.

"Not this time. He's got the hots for Faith." Jess poked me

in the arm and taunted in a sing-song voice, "Somebody's gonna get some tonight."

"As if." I shook my head and waved my hands in front of me. "Don't worry. He's all yours, Robin."

"Yeah, you know Faith won't mess around." Jess let out a loud sigh. "She doesn't have time for that."

I'd received more than my fair share of teasing from the girls about my lack of a love life. There would be plenty of time for that later. I wasn't even two years into my six-year plan. I'd be on a tenure track to full-fledged professor while my friends were still comparing dating stories.

"You and your stupid rules." Robin shook her head. "Still haven't caved?"

Before I could respond, Jess answered for me. "Nope. Not once. No dates, no sexting, no hook-ups. Not since what's-his-face—"

"Brad. His name was Brad." I played with the edge of the flimsy paper napkin.

"That's right, how could I forget Baller-Brad?" Jess rolled her eyes.

I groaned. "I never should have told you about that."

Jess ignored me and leaned toward Robin. "Did she tell you he cheated on her during her grad school formal?"

"What's up with that?" The bracelets on Robin's wrist jangled as she lifted her hand to flip her braids back behind her shoulder.

I sighed. I'd confided in Jess in a weak moment over a bottle of Cabernet last winter. May as well get Robin caught up on my failed love life.

"The formal was in Chicago, so we had to stay at a hotel. Halfway through the dance, I got a horrible headache. When I couldn't find him in the ballroom, I went back up to get some Tylenol. I walked in on him screwing my roommate."

"Ouch." Robin grimaced.

At that moment, the bartender returned with our drinks. "Here you go." He set two giant frosty mugs down on the counter then slid a fancy tall glass filled with a dark pink liquid toward Robin.

She squealed and took a sip. "Wow, this is really good. You should have gotten one of these, Faith."

He leaned down on his elbows in front of me. "It's not too late to change your mind about the Lotus, you know."

"No thanks." I gave him a wary smile and took a sip. "Mmm, yep, this really hits the spot."

He returned the smile. "That's my specialty."

"What, delivering drinks?" With his full attention focused on me, I was surprised I was able to speak without stuttering.

"No, hitting the right spot for beautiful girls."

# CHAPTER 4

## *Faith*

I HAD JUST TAKEN another drink and spurted a mouthful of beer into my hand.

He pushed off the bar as he laughed. "I'm just messing with you. Do you ladies want to start a tab?"

I wiped the edge of my mouth with a napkin and looked over at Jess. "No, just the one for me—"

"Of course we do." Jess handed him her credit card. "We'll figure out how to split it up later."

He walked away with the card, and Jess raised her glass. "Ladies, a toast. To the men we love, to the men we screw... hell, forget the men, here's to me and you!"

We clinked our glasses and took a gulp of our drinks.

"So, back to Bastard Baller Brad." Robin set her glass on the bar as she narrowed her brown eyes at me. "That was what, a couple of years ago now?"

I fiddled with the handle of my mug. "Yeah." Actually, it still stung like it happened yesterday, but I didn't need to share that.

"Were you two serious?" Robin asked.

"I thought so." Hot pinpricks danced across my cheeks as

I remembered the sight of Brad's hairy ass bouncing in the air as he pounded into my roommate doggy-style on the big king-size bed.

I could have sworn he was The One. The chemistry was there—we couldn't keep our hands off each other. He was finishing up his degree in journalism, and I was getting my master's in English Lit. We'd been compatible in every way, and after four years together, he could still turn my insides to mush with a kiss. I'd entrusted him with my heart and soul, and he'd—well, he'd tossed it aside for a quickie on what should have been one of the best nights of my life. I really knew how to pick them.

Robin's voice pulled me out of my memories. "Don't you think it's time you cast out a line again? He's not the only fish in the sea."

"Yeah, you see, I don't really have time to go fishing. I prefer being landlocked. Just keeping up with teaching my classes is killing me. I don't have any extra time to try to reel in a big one."

"Ha, very funny," Jess said. "She's right, Faith. These are supposed to be the best years of our lives. Live a little!"

If only they knew. I was a regular vixen on the pages of the ten books I'd authored under my pen name, Chastity Austen. But I hadn't told anyone about that. The only one who knew about my alter ego was my agent, Steph, and she was sworn to secrecy. If my mom and stepdad, the poster couple for Christian family values, found out... I shuddered at the thought.

My eyes cut to the hottie and the way his shirt stretched taut across his broad shoulders as he switched out a keg. I didn't usually regret my uncompromising stance on the no-flings rule. But a boy toy like that gave new meaning to the term global warming and could cause even the most frigid ice queen to defrost.

I lifted my mug to my lips as he stood and raised his gaze to mine. Was that a challenge in his eyes? My front teeth caught my lower lip as I considered the possibility of making an exception.

Dammit, who was I kidding? I couldn't afford the time for a distraction like him. I tilted the mug to take a sip, and cold beer sloshed over the edge and spilled down the front of my shirt. Crap. I'd completely missed my own mouth.

"You okay?" Jess handed me a napkin.

"Yeah. Can't take me anywhere, right?" I hopped off the stool. "I need to find the bathroom. I'll be back." As I turned to walk toward the sign for the ladies' room, I allowed myself a final glance his way. He hadn't moved. His gaze still rested on my face, and a gorgeous teasing smile played across his lips.

---

### Dante

I BALANCED the stack of empty boxes in my arms as I pushed through the swinging door and headed to the box crusher in back. In my short time behind the bar, I'd already discovered a major flaw in design. No one should have to schlep empty boxes through the hallway and past the bathrooms to get to the storeroom. I'd almost taken out a few customers already. Once this place really got humming, there'd be no passing through the hall during operating hours.

I turned the corner and smacked into something hard. "Shit!" The tower of boxes fell out of my arms and crashed to the floor.

Faith stood in the middle of the hall.

I raised an eyebrow. "Are you okay?"

"I'm sorry." She rubbed her hand over her shoulder. "I

don't know how I didn't see you." Then she leaned over and tried to stack the boxes back up.

"No, I'm sorry. I shouldn't have tried to make it in one trip." As I bent down to grab a box, her shirt rode up in the back, exposing a sliver of skin right above the waistband of her jeans, along with part of a dark swirly tattoo. Hell, I was a sucker for ink. What did the rest of it look like?

I crouched down to help. "You sure you're okay?"

"Yeah, I'm fine. Where do these need to go?" She picked up half the boxes and stood.

"Here." I pushed a door open behind her. "They just need to go in the supply room." My hip brushed up against her thigh as she walked past me into the room, and my dick pulsed at the brief contact. Obviously, I was out of practice if a single bump could send a rush of blood to my crotch. The whiff of something flowery and sweet drifted up to my nose as she passed.

I almost hadn't recognized her as the frumpy chick I'd run into outside the library this afternoon. The bulky sweatshirt was long gone. Her snug t-shirt clung tight across her chest, the deep V-neck promising her bra contained more than a handful. She'd had her hair pulled up before, but now it flowed over her shoulders and down her back. Red, like the deep, dark color of the paprika Meemaw generously sprinkled over platters of her deviled eggs.

I stepped into the room after her, the door closing behind me. My finger flicked the switch, although the bare bulb hanging from the ceiling didn't provide much light. "If you just set them here, I'll come back later and break them down. Thanks for your help." I moved to the back corner and tossed the boxes next to the box crusher.

"No problem." The boxes fell from her arms, and she turned toward the door. She flipped her hair out of her face to back behind her shoulder, and the girly scent tickled my nose again.

What the hell was that? Shampoo? Perfume? Whatever it was, it sure smelled good. Usually, the girls I ended up with doused themselves in body wash, body spray, perfume, hairspray, and all kinds of other crap, so I couldn't tell what they were supposed to smell like. I shook my head to clear the scent away and noticed she'd almost reached the door.

I raced ahead of her and twisted the knob. "Let me get it."

I pulled, but the door didn't open. "Seems to be stuck."

I pulled harder, but it didn't budge. "Um, yeah, we might have a little problem here."

# CHAPTER 5

## *Dante*

CASES OF WINE, beer, and hard alcohol lined the room.
The locked door in front of us was the only way out, except
for a tiny window about eight feet off the ground. I banged
on the door a few times, then backed away and ran my hands
through my hair.

"So, we're stuck in here?" Faith asked.

"Looks that way. Do you have a phone?"

"No, I left it in my purse on the back of my chair. How
about you?"

"Nope. Mine's under the bar. Damn."

"They'll miss you up front though, right?"

"Um, yeah. Well, maybe. We're a little over staffed tonight,
so they might not notice right away." Her eyebrows knit
together, and for some inexplicable reason, I felt the need to
reassure her. "I'm sure someone will come looking for us
soon, though."

"Great, just great." She slid down to sit on the ground and
leaned up against a tall stack of boxes sporting a sheaf of
wheat on the side.

Putting myself through school as a bartender, I'd met lots

of girls over the years. Most of the time, I had to fight them off. I'd been told I was pretty easy on the eyes and rarely failed to take advantage of my good looks when a girl was involved, especially a hot one. This chick threw me off my game a bit, though. She'd bantered back and forth earlier but hadn't taken the bait.

I squatted down next to her. "Hey, we never really intro-duced ourselves earlier today. I'm Dante Bishop." I thrust my hand toward her for a handshake.

"Faith Wainwright." Her soft, warm hand felt way too good in mine. I tightened my grip, and she pulled away.

"Dante? Like Dante Alighieri, the famous poet?"

I studied her face. Not much makeup. That was a good thing. Damn, she smelled even better up close. Something about her pulled me in. She didn't look like the man-eaters she'd been sitting by at the bar. And what had she really been doing with those books outside the library this afternoon?

She must have mistaken my silence for ignorance. "You know, the poet who wrote *The Divine Comedy? The Inferno*?"

"Sure, I've heard of Dante's *Inferno*." I stood up, stretching out my legs. "But I was named after Dante's Pizzeria in South Bergen, Jersey. My parents hooked up in the backseat in the parking lot, and nine months later I appeared. Ever been there?"

She stared up at me for a moment, her eyes wide, then looked away. "Um, no. Can't say that I have."

Damn. I didn't mean to make her uncomfortable. My lack of a conventional upbringing was a sore spot, one I didn't broach during an initial conversation... or any conversation, actually.

"Yeah, I haven't either. But it's on my list of places to visit someday." I slid down and sat across from her, my back against the wall. "So, Faith, I take it you're a student at Tempest?"

"Adjunct professor. And you?"

"Got my MBA a few years ago and now work for Crosby Consulting. I'm mentoring a group of undergrads, so I'm on campus quite a bit. Let me guess—you teach Women's Studies?"

Faith shook her head. "English Lit."

"So, the spicy reading material is for…?"

"Um, research for an article I'm submitting to a literary journal."

"Huh. I'm surprised Tempest wants you working on that kind of stuff, being such a conservative university and all. You sure you don't hand out English Lit homework like that? Or maybe group projects?"

She appraised me with narrowed eyes and a half-smile on her full, pink lips. "No. It's all self-study."

Maybe I'd misjudged her. "Well, that could be pretty interesting, too. I'm available if you decide you need a research partner."

"I'll keep that in mind." Faith cleared her throat. "So, what kind of consulting do you do?"

"Mostly mergers and acquisitions, but on the marketing side of things." I shrugged. "I'm hoping to land a gig with one of our divisions out east. How about you?"

Management had their eyes on me. I'd love to make a big move to one of their higher-paying, higher-profile divisions. That would make it possible to pay off my student loans and maybe do something nice for Meemaw to thank her for everything she'd done for me over the years.

Faith stretched out and crossed one foot over the other, drawing my attention to her long, denim-clad legs. "I'd like to stay here at Tempest and earn tenure."

Smarty pants. "I thought all English professors wanted to take sabbaticals and write the great American novel."

"Writing isn't as easy as it might look."

"Yeah, I wouldn't know about that. But you sure as hell don't look like any English teacher I've ever had. You're missing glasses and a cat."

Her eyes narrowed. "What's wrong with cats?"

Great. I'd pissed her off again. "You have a cat, don't you?"

She drew her legs up and rested her chin on her knees. "Mr. Darcy doesn't really know he's a cat. He's more of a roommate."

"Mr. Darcy? Seriously? I take it back. I guess you do look like some of my English profs. I just didn't have a chance to meet them when they were still hot."

A splash of red spread across her cheeks. "Look here, Pizza Boy—"

"Hey, how about a beer or something while we wait for someone to rescue us?" I stood up and walked around the room, taking note of the stock.

Faith shook her head. "No thanks, I'm not a big drinker."

Great, what to do with the gorgeous green-eyed girl? If she hadn't already shot me down, I'd be able to come up with a few ideas. Although, she didn't really look like one-night stand material, and for the past six years, that's all I'd been interested in. No commitment, no one gets hurt.

By the looks of the red-headed beauty in front of me, she'd definitely fall into the long-term category—major ball-and-chain. I hadn't always been so hell-bent against commitments. But that was one lesson I only needed to learn once.

I walked back to the door and put my ear up against the cold metal. The muffled sound of the band filtered through. Maybe when they took a break, I could make enough noise to attract some attention. I looked at my watch. It was only nine-forty. Since I'd just restocked the main fridge, it could be quite a while before someone had to come back to the stockroom. Damn.

## Faith

I CHEWED on my bottom lip. Only fifteen minutes had passed. How long was I going to be stuck in here with Pizzeria Dante? I hadn't wanted to go out tonight in the first place. If I'd only listened to my gut, I'd still be at home in my pajamas, knee-deep in grading papers about Nietzsche's *Human, All Too Human* with Mr. Darcy nestled on my lap.

Maybe that was too optimistic. If I were at home, the Nietzsche papers would probably be laying on the floor, and I'd be snoozing on the couch. The man was brilliant, but not one of my favorites.

Still, I had work to do and those final scenes I promised Steph. I needed to get home and get busy if I wanted to turn everything in on time.

I studied the gorgeous bartender. What did he have against cats? Jess could be right, he might be kind of a player, but still... Dante... that would make a good name for the bad boy in my next novel.

I could probably just base the whole character on him. Thick, dark hair, nice build. He'd have to lose the glasses, though. The bad-ass biker I'd planned for my next steamy romance definitely wouldn't wear glasses.

The eyes could stay. It was too dark to see them in the storeroom, but I'd noticed them right away earlier. Somewhere between blue and green. An interesting match with the scruffy, dark stubble covering his face.

I filled out a character sketch in my head. Yeah, Dante it would have to be. He might have to be beefed up a little bit. Although, peeking over at him from under the fringe of hair that had fallen across my face, I reconsidered.

Underneath the unbuttoned flannel shirt, his tight white

undershirt hinted at a rock-hard chest. He pushed his sleeves up, and the muscles of his forearms flexed. If he lost the tad too baggy jeans, that bod would probably be pretty close to perfect.

How hard would his biceps feel under my hand? How dark might his happy trail be? I pondered the answers—all for character research, of course.

He paced the small room like a caged tiger, then walked back over to where I hadn't moved on the floor. "Are you sure you don't want something to drink? We may be here a while."

I shook my head while my stomach twisted into knots. "No thanks. I've got to get out of here. I told the girls I could only stay an hour." Surely, they were getting worried about me by now.

"Well, I could use a drink." He walked around the room, shifting stacks of boxes to see behind them. "Nothing's cold. I guess that means the hard stuff."

Hard stuff. That's right, where had I been in my mental inventory? I shook my head, sending all thoughts of Dante's potential hard assets scattering. *Focus.* If I was going to get any work done tonight, I needed to figure a way out and pronto.

I stood up and walked over to the door. Raising my fists, I pummeled the metal. "Hey! Anybody out there?"

Dante came up behind me and put his hand on my arm, sending a course of goosebumps down to my wrist. "Nobody can hear you. Come sit down."

I shook him off. "You don't understand. I have a ton of stuff to do and need to get home. Isn't there something we can use to pry the door open?"

"Gotta get back to your books? That self-study project, huh?" He eyed me over the rim of his glasses.

I put a hand on my hip and backed away. "Do you have something against women's studies?"

He moved close, crowding into my personal space. Close enough for me to smell the mix of fabric softener and male muskiness hovering around him. "Quite the opposite, Faith." His voice dropped a notch, and he lowered his gaze to my mouth. "I make it a point to study everything about women."

Oh. My. God. He was making a play. My hoo-ha tingled, gearing up for some long overdue attention. I squelched the sensation and put my hands on his chest—his granite hard, chiseled chest—and pushed him away. "It's creeps like you that give good guys a bad name."

"Ha! You're the one reading about getting it on. By the way, was that a BDSM book I saw you holding earlier? Your girlfriends know you're into kinky shit?"

My hands went to my hips, and I glared at him.

"Easy there, Ginger. I won't blow your cover. To each her own."

I sighed. "Can we just work on getting out of here? I've got a lot to do... reading... writing an article..."

He rolled his eyes. "I think someone's taking her work a little too seriously. It's only Friday. You've got all weekend."

"Yeah, and all weekend won't be long enough."

Dante scanned the room. His eyes stopped on the window. "Well, if you're really desperate..."

# CHAPTER 6

## *Faith*

I LOOKED up at the small rectangular hole in the wall. I could probably fit through there. Hell, I'd suck it all in and squeeze myself through if it meant getting away from the distraction with the cut pecs and amazing blue-green eyes.

"Fine. But you're going to have to give me a boost. I'll never be able to reach it on my own."

Dante made a basket out of his hands. "Come on, let's give it a shot."

I put a hand on his shoulder. His muscles tensed under my touch. I could feel him flex, and my thoughts shot forward to consider what might happen if we didn't get out of the storeroom. At the rate I was going, I might jump him if I couldn't force myself through the window.

Placing my foot in his hands, I pushed myself up as he lifted. My fingers grasped at the lever on the window, desperate to unlatch it.

"Dammit, I'm not high enough."

He lowered me back to the ground. "Time for Plan B. Here, get up on my shoulders."

I hesitated.

"Come on, I'll be a perfect gentleman." He squatted down low so I could climb onto his back.

A gentleman… he didn't seem like the kind of guy who'd ever done anything gentle. I threw a leg over each of his shoulders and grabbed his hands, sandwiching his neck right between my thighs.

Oooh. A pulsing sensation hummed through my core as I made contact through my jeans with the back of his neck. This was the closest I'd come to any kind of sexual interaction in well over a year, and my inner thighs clenched in anticipation.

"Whoa, easy there." Dante grabbed onto my legs, his hands wrapping around my calves, before he stood up and moved toward the wall.

I squeezed his neck between my thighs like my life depended on it and fumbled with the lock.

"Got it!" I pushed the window open. A cool rush of air blew past me into the room. "Now I just need to get through." I grabbed onto the window ledge and tried to hoist myself up.

Dante put his hands under my thighs in an effort to boost me higher.

"Just a little farther." I grunted with the effort as his hands roamed over my legs. Shivers cascaded through me, like a stampede of tingles that needed to be squelched pronto.

"Can you see anything yet? You don't want to jump into the dumpster."

I searched the ground. "Yeah, it's right under the window, but I think I can avoid it. Can you lift me just a little higher?"

His hands scrambled under my legs. As I wriggled to get a foot up on his shoulder, he moved me closer to the window, and his palms slid to my butt. He pushed, one hand on my ass and the other making contact with the apex of my thighs.

"Oh, my god." Heat pooled between my legs. His hand,

oh crap, his fingers were applying pressure in exactly the wrong spot. Okay, it was the right spot, but definitely the wrong spot considering the company and the situation. "Get your hand off my—"

"Sorry!" Dante yelled as I made it through the window.

I didn't care where I landed. My top priority was to escape. A metallic thud sounded as something crunched underneath me. In my rush to relieve my thighs of the pressure of Dante's fingers, I'd miscalculated my landing spot. I'd had to do something to get away from him. We'd just met, and already he'd touched me in places I'd been trying to ignore for over a year. Thanks to that boost, I wasn't going to be able to ignore them anymore.

Stumbling to my feet, I trudged through the garbage bags to the edge of the dumpster. The scent of rancid grease mixed with decaying produce assaulted my nose. I hoisted a leg over the side and jumped down to the pavement. An unrecognizable layer of slime covered my lower half, and some sort of liquid smeared through my hair. I couldn't go back in the bar looking like this.

I tried the handle of the back door. Thankfully, it opened with a loud creak. I crept down the empty hallway to the storeroom. As I turned the knob and pushed it open, Dante moved toward the door.

"Thanks." He looked me up and down. "What the hell happened to you?"

"You sent me sailing into the freaking dumpster. I don't know what this is on my pants, and there's crap in my hair, too."

"I told you to watch out." Stepping back, he took in my matted hair, slimy jeans, and the grease spots dotting my shirt. As he walked in a slow circle around me, a giant smile spread across those damn kissable lips.

I pulled my shirt away from my skin. "There's no way Jess is going to let me in her car like this."

"Don't take this the wrong way." He crossed his arms over his expansive chest. "I live over the bar. Why don't you come upstairs and wash off a little?"

"Seriously?" I focused on the tiny tic pulsing in my jaw. "Look, I appreciate the offer, but I just want to get home. Just because you had your hand up my—"

"Hey!" He put his hands up, palms out, in an effort to stop the words from sailing out of my mouth. "I was just trying to be a nice guy." He smiled. "By all means, go back to the bar and finish your beer. I'm sure your friends will enjoy the ambiance."

As he turned around to head toward the door to the bar, I looked down at the goopy mess covering my clothes. I really couldn't get in the car like this. Jess would kill me. The smell of grease would linger on the cloth seats for months.

"Fine. Yes, a shower would be good."

He stopped and whipped around to face me. "I'm glad you've decided to prioritize your personal hygiene."

I rolled my eyes. "It's not like I have much of a choice. Can I make one thing clear?"

"What's that, Stinkarella?" Dante cocked a hip, obviously waiting for me to make a slew of unreasonable demands. His gaze swept over me, warming me from the core like one of those molten chocolate lava cakes I loved. Liquid heat flowed through my veins as a smile settled on his lips.

"I'm showering alone."

"If you're sure that's the way you want it, your wish is my command. Follow me." He chuckled, then pushed through the back door and walked around the building to a set of stairs.

He led me up the wooden steps to the second story and opened the door. As I entered the apartment, I took in the exposed pipes and beams running across the tall, two-story ceiling. Red brick walls complemented the shiny wooden floors. For a moment, I forgot about the dumpster gunk covering my body and let myself absorb the warmth of his apartment.

"This is awesome." I slowly turned around in the giant open living space.

"Yeah, the guy who owns the bar gave me cheap rent in exchange for pulling the late-night shifts no one else wants."

"I bet you get tons of natural light." I ran my hand over the rough brick wall. A tall bookshelf caught my attention, and my eyes skimmed over the titles on display. Hemingway, Keats, Faulkner. *Hmmm, the hottie bartender likes to read.*

"The bathroom's back there." He pointed to the only room with a door, then pulled a clean towel from a cabinet and handed it to me. "Make yourself at home."

I made my way to the bathroom, taking in the details of his cozy personal space along the way. Tons of books, lots of comfy seating. The kind of space I'd like for myself. Too bad he wasn't my type. I could get comfortable in a place like this.

I shook my head. Comfort ought to be the last thing on my mind. I was about to get naked in a stranger's shower. The thought sent an army of nervous butterflies on a tirade through my stomach. *I guess there's a first time for everything.*

"I'll just be a sec." I clasped the fluffy towel to my chest and disappeared behind the closed door before I could change my mind.

# CHAPTER 7

## *Dante*

A NAKED FAITH stood in my shower. I ran my hand over the scruffy whiskers on my chin and contemplated my next move. I never brought girls to my place. What the fuck was I thinking? She was probably soaping herself up with my bar of Dial right now. Sliding it across her stomach, around her ass, and over that stretch of twisty, curly black ink. I shook my head. Enough of that.

I scrounged around, trying to find a pair of sweats that might fit her, so she'd have something clean to put on. As I walked by the bathroom door, I heard the water running and hitting the bottom of the tub. Damn lucky water, probably coursing down her thighs right about now. I pressed the bundle of clothes against my crotch and gave myself a little adjustment. What the hell was wrong with me tonight?

With the threat of my rising attraction temporarily held at bay, I walked into the kitchen. What do I do while I wait? A white tea kettle sat on the stove. It had belonged to my grandmother. She always offered her visitors tea. Girls liked tea, right? I ran some water into the kettle, set it back on the burner, and flipped on the gas.

The shower turned off, and I grabbed the stack of clothes I'd found as I walked toward the bathroom.

"Hey, Faith?"

"Yeah?" Her muffled voice floated through the closed door.

"I've got some clean clothes here you can put on."

She opened the door and stood in the doorway a few feet away, wrapped in my large tan towel. Her hair hung in long wet strands, and water droplets sprinkled across her face like giant wet freckles.

As I moved toward her, she pulled the towel tighter across her chest. What was it with her? It wasn't like I'd rip her towel off or anything... at least not unless she asked me to. Reaching up with one hand, I wiped a particularly large water droplet off her cheek with my thumb and fought the urge to pop it into my mouth.

"You sure you don't want to, uh, stay for a while?"

"Um, thanks, but I need to get back." She grabbed the clothes from under my arm and shut the door in my face.

Fuck. Shot down how many times now? I'd been going through a dry spell lately and hadn't been that close to that much skin in way too long. I adjusted myself again, walked back to the kitchen, and turned off the burner. No tea. I needed to get her out of my place... and fast.

Faith opened the door a few moments later, letting the steam that had built up during her shower escape into the room. My giant T-shirt hung off one of her shoulders, and the sweats pooled around her bare feet as she padded over to where I stood at the stove.

Looked like someone didn't put on a bra.

She must have noticed where my eyes lingered and crossed her arms over her chest. A wave of pink crept up her face from her neck to her hairline. If she hadn't looked so embarrassed, I would have laughed.

"Thanks for the clothes. Any chance you'd be willing to go get my friend and ask her to meet me out front by the car?"

"Yeah, um, sure." My conscience precariously balanced between wanting to invent some excuse to make her stay and rushing her out of my apartment as fast as her well-toned legs would carry her. I forced my feet to move toward the door. "Just give me a couple of minutes."

Outside, I paused on the steps. What just happened? I was losing my touch. Usually, when I had a half-naked girl in my general proximity, we both ended up sated and satisfied.

Hell, the high-strung redhead had probably never even had a one-night stand. The way she held herself... it was like she'd never lost control once in her whole life. What a waste. Body like a Victoria's Secret model and apparently the sex drive of a paperclip.

Those books probably *were* for some stupid professional research. She must be smart—the uptight scholarly type. Definitely long-term material, which meant off-limits for me.

I hadn't just been burned. My one attempt at a relationship had gone up in a five-alarm blaze of flames, and nowadays, I preferred the short-term, hot and heavy kind of fling. Even if I *was* interested, I didn't have time to get involved. Only a couple of weeks into the fall semester, and I could tell already it would take every ounce of energy and patience I had to mentor the group I'd been assigned to in the Entrepreneurial Leadership seminar.

No way would I blow my chance at earning a glowing recommendation from the chair of the department. It would go a long way to getting me out of Newbridge and to making bank out east; didn't matter how fine she was.

Between the mentorship, my grueling day job, and the part-time gig at the bar, I didn't have time for more than the occasional one-night stand. Refocused, I moved down the steps and located the two girls still sitting at the bar.

---

### Faith

I STOOD next to Jess's car, my gunky clothes stuffed into a plastic bag I'd found under Dante's sink. The walk of shame from his apartment to the parking lot had me on edge and eager to get home.

"What happened to you?" Jess asked as she tossed me my jacket and purse, then beeped the key fob to unlock the doors.

I shoved my arms into the sleeves of my coat, then climbed inside and pulled the door closed behind me. "You don't want to know."

"Like hell I don't. You disappear to go to the bathroom and an hour later I find you braless in some guy's clothes?"

I drew my coat tighter around me and crossed my arms over my chest. "Why didn't you come looking for me?"

Jess glanced my way. "Seriously? I thought maybe you were getting some. That bartender walked out right after you, and I had my fingers crossed he was delivering that sloe comfortable screw he offered."

"Is that the only thing you can think about?" I growled through clenched teeth. "We got locked in the storeroom together. Nobody could hear us banging on the door—"

"Wait a minute." Jess put her palm out toward me to silence me. "He was banging you up against the door? Maybe you're not hopeless after all."

I swatted her hand down. "Really? He pushed me through a window, and I landed in the dumpster. I stunk to high heaven, so he offered to let me take a shower in his apartment over the bar. Can you please take me home now?" How many times would I have to relive the sheer embarrassment of the evening? I never should have come out tonight.

Jess let out her signature laugh. It fell somewhere between a laugh and a snort, leaning more toward the snorting side.

"Only you, Faith, only you."

"Only me what?"

"Did you even notice how hot he was?" Jess turned the key in the ignition. "He totally made a play for you. Lock me in a storeroom with someone like him, and you'd have to break down the door and rip me off him to get me out of there."

Jess was absolutely right, but I would never fully admit the effect he'd had on me. "I suppose he *was* kind of cute." I relented a little, twirling a strand of damp hair around my finger.

"Kind of? Robin was ready to jump over the bar after him. And you end up in his shower? Are you sure you're into guys? It's okay with me if you're not—"

"Really?" I rolled my eyes.

Jess shook her head. "I'm just sayin'—"

"Okay, he was hot... freakin', smokin', panty-melting hot." I cradled my head in my hands. "And his hands... first on my butt... and they slipped, and he... agh." My body reacted as if his hands still cradled my ass. Goosebumps popped up on my arms, and a tremor quaked through me. I shook it off. "Are you happy?"

Jess stared at me for a silent moment, then turned her head to face the road straight ahead, a giant grin plastered across her mug.

"I just don't have time for this."

"For what?" Jess glanced over at me. "For a night of sloe comfortable screws? Delivered by a guy who obviously knows how to please?"

"Dante, his name is Dante."

"That's right. See, told you it started with a 'D.' I was right about that, and I'm right about the fact that you seriously need to get laid. Surely, even you, with your friggin' six-year plan, can take one night off?"

"You said yourself he's a player. He's probably loaded with STDs."

Jess blew out a long breath. "I give up. You're hopeless."

I slumped further down in my seat. No nights off. That's how I'd lose focus. A guy like Dante didn't fit into my plans, no matter how my traitorous body responded to him. There would be plenty of time for that later when I'd secured a tenured teaching job in a well-respected literary program.

A part of me knew I'd be better off if I never laid eyes on his hot bod again. The other part of me knew I wouldn't be able to get him out of my mind until I laid a lot more than eyes on him.

I gazed out the window and wondered—when it came to the sex-on-a-stick bartender, which part of me was going to win?

# CHAPTER 8

## *Faith*

I SAT near the back of the room, zoning out on the department's mandatory all-staff meeting while sipping on the caramel latte I'd splurged on earlier. I hadn't slept well over the weekend. My encounter with Dante kept playing through my mind, and I was operating in a sleep-deprived haze. Assuming I could survive the next hour, I'd have two hours to myself before I had to teach my next class. If I high-tailed it to my car and went straight back to my apartment, I might be able to fit in a forty-five-minute nap.

I let my mind wander to the brief period of time I'd spent with the buff bartender. Letting out a sigh, I relaxed against the back of my seat. Behind those nerdy rims, his eyes pulled at something inside me, something I thought I'd shut down a long time ago.

I spent a good portion of my time thinking and writing about romance. But I'd convinced myself that the kind of love I wrote about in my novels didn't exist in real life. I thought Brad and I were on the right track...until our relationship completely derailed.

According to my mother, my parents had it, at least until

my dad walked out. My mom was happy enough with Clem, her second husband, but theirs was a relationship based more on shared interests (the church) and shared preferences (low-fat, low-cal diet, early to bed, early to rise) as opposed to unbridled passion.

As far as I was concerned, I'd have to pick one or the other —sparks or long-term compatibility. It seemed impossible to find both with the same person. With Brad, I thought I had it all. But just like my dad, he turned out to be too good to be true. Common goals, similar family values, those were the things that would last. As soon as I got tenure, I'd find someone who looked good on paper and start to build a family. I'd never let myself go based on passion alone. Incredible chemistry and grand romantic gestures belonged to the heroines in my books. Those lucky bitches. The last one, especially.

The protagonist of my latest release, *Carnal Knowledge*, the one Steph was so excited about, was a journalist who got swept off her feet by an accountant who'd been hired to do an audit on the newspaper she was working for. He was like a Clark Kent kind of guy by day and morphed into a superhero at night. He delivered mind-blowing orgasms multiple times a day and also knew how to cook. If only I could find a guy like him in real life, maybe I'd change my mind about true love.

Professor Cornish clapped her hands, pulling me away from my thoughts. "With Professor Middleford's retirement, we'll need someone to pick up his classes for next year. Of course, first preference will go to those of you already established within the department. Adjunct faculty is encouraged to apply."

My ears perked up. I'd been living in my own little world for the past couple of weeks, feverishly typing on my keyboard every available spare moment, so I hadn't heard anything about Professor Middleford's retirement.

Picking up a few more classes would certainly help me out. My book sales had been modestly successful, but I still had thousands of dollars in student loans. My mom and stepdad had offered to pay my tuition, but I'd turned them down. I didn't want to be dependent on them or feel obligated to follow in my mother's footsteps. My mom wouldn't hold it over my head, but I'd seen Clem use whatever he could to his advantage, and I didn't want to take any chances.

The bell rang, and Professor Cornish officially adjourned the meeting. I gathered my papers and stuffed them into my backpack.

"Faith, do you have a second?"

I stopped next to her on my way out. "Sure. What do you need?"

"I hope you're planning on applying."

"I'd like to, but I'm not sure I'll have time—"

"Make time. I know you're paying your own way. This could really help, not only with your loans but also your career."

I nodded. "You're right. Of course, you're right." Revisions on my manuscript, plotting a new novel to submit to Steph, and taking on a few more classes next fall? A wave of panic cramped my gut.

I still hadn't beaten away my crippling writer's block. For every word I typed on the screen, I seemed to delete two. My shoulders tensed in anticipation of how much sleep I would miss out on over the next several weeks.

No time to think about that now. I'd do what I had to do like I always did. I wouldn't let anything or anyone throw me off track.

I joined the crush of faculty pushing through the doorway and into the crowded hall. I stepped to the right to get around a couple of undergrads who didn't appear to be in any sort of hurry. My foot slipped out from under me, landing me flat on my ass. Coffee flew into the air, and the stack of papers I'd been holding spread out all over the floor.

"Smooth, Faith, real smooth." A hand reached out to help me up onto my feet, then someone crouched down and started sweeping my soggy papers back into my bag.

"Thanks, Murph," I said. "I guess I didn't see the cone."

"Ya think?" He smiled at me. Tall and lanky, seeming to be made up of nothing but limbs, Patrick Murphy's bright red hair made him hard to miss in a crowd. He had friendly green eyes and freakishly white teeth, which was nice since he usually had a giant smile plastered across his face. He and I even shared a tiny office. We'd probably be good friends too, if he'd ever stop asking me out.

"Damn, my coffee. I really need the caffeine this morning." I picked up my empty cup and tried to sop up the puddle on the floor with a flimsy napkin.

"Come on, I'll buy you another cup," Murph said.

"I think I'm the one who owes you."

"Hey, I'll take a date any way I can get one."

I rolled my eyes. He'd been asking me to go out with him since we met back in grad school. "It's not a date, just a cup of coffee."

"You say to-may-to, I say to-mah-to." He shrugged.

I shook my head. "Come on, let's caffeinate."

He held the door for me as we walked out onto the quad.

"It's gorgeous out here," I said.

"Yeah, hard to believe that in a couple of weeks this place will be knee deep in snow," Murph said.

"I don't care. I love it." I spread one arm out in front of me, gesturing to the masterpiece of Mother Nature's canvas that was fall in the upper Midwest. The trees were on full display. Bold oranges and yellows played against a back-ground of deep green pines and a brilliant blue sky.

"Did you knock your head when you fell down? You sound a little loopy."

I stuck my tongue out at him and pulled open the door to the student center. We walked inside and joined the long line of sleepy-eyed students looking for their morning jolt of java.

"You grew up out west, right?" Murph asked.

"Yeah. Orange County, California."

"Why the hell did you come here?"

"My dad's from the Midwest. I wanted to experience what it would be like to live here for a while. Besides, the program here is one of the best."

"Why not Berkeley? They have one of the top programs in the country, and you could have done your reading assign-ments at the beach." Murph shook his head in mock disdain.

"Believe it or not, even the beach gets old. I was ready for a change of scenery."

"I bet. Sand in all the wrong places. Too much sun? Must be a horrible place to grow up."

Actually, I'd enjoyed growing up in California. It would always be home base for me. But my mother was there, and it had been time for me to get out from under her wing and see if I could fly on my own.

As far as I could tell, none of my classmates had figured out yet that my mother was Claire Kepner, a well-known Christian author and wife of Clem Kepner, a famous local televangelist. It helped that we didn't share a last name. I'd kept my dad's name when my mother got remarried.

At least my mom's sphere of fame and fortune hadn't caught up with me yet. It was just a matter of time, but I vowed to enjoy my anonymity as long as it lasted.

We reached the counter, and I placed my order. "What can I get you, Murph?"

"Just a large cup of coffee. None of that frou-frou stuff for me," he said.

I paid for our coffee, and we stepped aside to wait for our drinks.

"So did you have a good weekend?" he asked.

"Yeah, pretty low key. I stayed in and worked on putting together a few assignments." Assuming *assignments* was a fair way of describing my latest manuscript.

"That explains why I didn't see you at McGovern's."

Quite a few of my colleagues had a standing Saturday night get together at a local pub. McGovern's was a little classier than the beer-sloshing dive bars the undergrads frequented.

"Were there a bunch of people there?" I asked.

"Yeah, a decent crowd. They had book trivia going again. One of these days, you've got to come." He snickered. "I'm sure you would've helped us rock the erotic category."

*You have no idea.* "Sounds like fun. Maybe next time."

The barista pushed our drinks across the bar, and I wrapped my hands around the steaming paper cup.

"Gotta go. See ya later."

Murph raised his paper cup to me. "Thanks for the coffee, Faith."

"You're welcome." I checked my watch as I wove my way through the high-top tables and slipped through the door. Damn... no time for a nap. And if I wanted my application to take over Professor Middleford's classes to be taken seriously, that meant no more time to daydream about sexy bartenders or strangers' showers either.

# CHAPTER 9

## Dante

I GRUNTED and heaved the heavy bar up from my chest as Murph spotted me from above. Well, he primarily worked on spotting the few hot girls that stopped by to use the inner thigh machine, but he'd probably be able to catch the bar if I lost complete control. Maybe.

"Take it easy, man. You don't want to sprain anything." Murph eased his hands under the bar and moved it back to the rack. "You're going all out today. Was that a new record?"

"Something like that." I sat up on the hard bench. My mind wouldn't let go of the image of Faith standing in my bathroom in a towel the other night. Something about that chick got under my skin. Unable to distract myself, I'd decided to take advantage of my access to campus facilities and pound the thoughts out of my mind at the gym.

I stood up to let Murph take his turn on the bench. He grabbed the bar with his hands and tried to push up. "Um, maybe you can just take ten off each side?"

"Sure." I popped the clip open and adjusted the weight. As I leaned down to put the weights back on the rack, I caught a glimpse of a familiar head of dark red hair. Shit.

Faith sat at a leg press machine about ten feet away. She strained to extend her legs, her fingers wrapping around the handles at her sides. The heavy stack of weights she was working was pretty impressive. She had on a tiny little top with a loose tank over it and some clingy short black pants. While I stared, a drop of sweat rolled down the cleft between her breasts and disappeared into her hot pink sports bra.

"Fuck me," I grunted, adjusting the front of my baggy gym shorts.

"Hey, are you ready?" Murph asked, drawing my attention back to the chest press.

"Yeah, sorry." I put my hands under the bar and helped Murph ease it off the rack and down to his chest.

"Something catch your eye over there?" Murph struggled to push the bar up over his head.

"Just some girl I met the other night."

"A girl, huh? You get any?" Murph exhaled and did another rep.

I ignored Murph's question and let my gaze travel back to Faith. She grabbed a towel and wiped it across her temple, her neck, and then her chest.

"Jesus Christ," I growled, taking my glasses off for a moment and rubbing my hand across my face.

Murph lifted his head to follow my gaze across the room. "Shit, bro. Do you know who that is?"

I pulled my eyes away and glanced down at Murph. "Yeah, her name is Faith. She teaches in the English department with you, right?"

Murph laughed. "Don't even try to tap that, my friend. She's locked up tighter than Fort Knox. I've been working that for years. Nada, dude."

My eyes narrowed as I studied Murph's face. "She's a friend of yours?"

"Not exactly. We share an office. I've been shot down by

her more times than I can count. She's nice enough, but those waters aren't just cold, dude, they're fucking frigid."

I wasn't interested in swimming in any kind of water around Faith, much less the frigid variety. But why the hell was she popping up again? How many mornings did I meet Murph at the gym, and I'd never run across her before. I was pretty damn sure I'd have remembered.

Her skimpy little sports bra stood out like a beacon in a sea of testosterone-filled athletic shorts and stinky tank tops. Women usually worked out on the other side of campus in the new space with all the Nautilus machines.

"A little help here?" Murph groaned, and I pulled my attention away from Faith again, helping Murph settle the heavy bar back on the rack. "You working biceps today?"

"Nah, I think I'll run for a while." Faith had moved over to jog on a treadmill. I walked over to the machines and stepped onto the one next to her.

---

### Faith

I LOOKED OVER, a scowl on my face. Of all the empty machines in the room, and some guy had to pick the one right next to mine?

"Oh, it's you," I said, noticing Dante.

"Yeah, nice to see you again too." He pushed the button, increasing his pace.

I sped up, breaking out of my jog into a full-fledged run. Too bad we weren't outside where I might have a chance of actually outrunning him. The last thing I needed was more face-to-face time with the man who'd been haunting my dreams.

I'd tried declaring thoughts of Dante as off-limits, but my

head kept going there… again and again and again. And now here he was in the flesh—a distracting mountain of muscled, tempting, eye candy flesh.

"Thanks again for letting me use your shower the other night. I'll get your clothes back to you as soon as I have a chance to wash them."

"No rush. Sorry again about getting us locked in the storeroom."

"Don't worry about it." I glanced over at him, taking in the loose-fitting tank top. My gaze lingered on his well-defined biceps before roving down to his toned calves. What did the rest of him look like? No matter how much I tried not to, my imagination had been doing a pretty good job of filling in the details since I'd last seen him.

The sight of so much exposed skin on the machine next to me sent my pulse into overdrive. Beads of sweat broke out on my forehead, and I wiped them away with my towel.

"So, you come here often?" he asked, matching my pace.

"Really?"

"What?" He turned his head my way.

"Are you trying to pick me up with your best line?"

He chuckled, sending a rush of warmth to my chest. "No. Definitely not."

"Wow, you don't have to be so firm about it." I cringed as the word "firm" left my lips. Please don't let him crack a joke at my choice of words. Maybe my mind operated in the gutter, but I could twist just about anything into sounding like something dirty without much effort at all.

"Firm?" Brow raised, he nudged his speed up a notch.

I groaned. Nope, not getting away with that one. "I just meant—"

"Look, you made it pretty clear the other night you weren't pickupable."

"Forget it." Pickupable? My internal English snob stuck

her nose in the air, ready to dismiss the conversation altogether.

"Let's try again. I haven't seen you working out at the gym before." He lifted his chin, indicating the expectation of a response.

"I usually run outside, but I tweaked something last week and figured some weightlifting might help strengthen my legs."

"Well, that explains it." Dante nodded.

"Explains what?"

"Take a look around. See anyone else working out in a bikini?"

What a dick. I furrowed my brow and scanned the room. So what if I was one of only a handful of women in a room full of serious lifters? "It's a free country, right?"

"I didn't mean it like—"

"Hey, Faith, I see you've met my friend Dante." Murph walked over to the treadmills and put his hand on the front of my machine. Wonderful. Nothing could make this moment more awkward than adding another bundle of testosterone.

"Hi Murph. Yeah, we, um, actually met the other night," I said.

"The other night, huh?" Murph narrowed his eyes.

"She and her friends stopped in at the bar," Dante said.

Murph's frown lifted slightly at the corners. "Of course. Dante's new part-time job as an illustrious barkeep has him fighting off the babes. You've only been there, what, three weeks so far? How many desperate women have you had to turn down?"

Dante shot a dark look Murph's way. "Very funny, Murph."

I let my machine slow down before I hopped off. "I think I'd rather just run outside today. See you guys around."

Before either one of them had a chance to respond, I

picked up my water bottle and pulled my hoodie on over my head. It was like watching a cock fight about to take place. Murph was strutting his stuff, just begging for Dante to take him down a notch or two. Dante had shrugged on a dark and dangerous attitude.

It was time for me to go. I wasn't a betting gal, but if I had to put money down on one of them, I'd definitely back Dante.

Betting on Dante... that gave me an idea for a scene I'd been struggling with in my latest manuscript. I pushed through the doors of the gym and took a full breath of clean, fresh air into my lungs.

I'd damn well not let that guy get under my skin, but in my desperation to add word count, I'd eagerly take advantage of any new scenes he might inspire. As long as he stayed on the pages of my novel, where I could make sure he didn't get too close.

My feet struck the pavement as I turned toward home, eager to get my fingers back on the keyboard of my laptop... excited to explore a version of Dante I could control.

# CHAPTER 10

*Dante*

I SET the heavy box down on the floor in front of the refrigerator before sliding the bottles of beer toward the back of the shelf. It was slow for a Thursday night—a nice break from the typical non-stop routine. I was enjoying the rare peace and quiet. A cool rush of air reached me from the doorway, and I looked up as Murph and another guy walked in.

"Hey Murph. What's up?" I called out.

"Dude, where have you been, bro? Haven't seen you around." Murph approached the bar and stuck out his hand to catch mine in a handshake.

I gestured around me. "This place has been keeping me busy. I've been working every night for the past two weeks."

"That's too bad. Think you can get someone to cover for you on Halloween? We're planning a big bash, and it would be great if you could come."

"I don't know. I'll have to see. Might be pretty crazy around here that night."

"Yeah well, if you can make it, stop by."

"Sounds good. Did you guys want something to drink?"

"Yeah, pour us two of the stouts, will you?" Murph and his friend each took a stool at the bar and sat down to wait.

I grabbed two pints and pulled the handle of the tap, letting the beer fill the glasses to the top. I set one down in front of Murph and the other in front of his friend.

"Thanks, man. You two know each other?" Murph asked.

I shook my head and stuck my hand out to shake the other guy's. "Hey, I'm Dante."

"Oliver," he said, grasping my hand.

Murph took a long sip of his drink. "Oliver here is looking for a part-time job. Thought you might need some extra help around the bar."

"I can check. Wyatt mentioned something about hiring another part-timer. You have any experience?"

"A bit. I worked at a pub back in Christchurch for a couple of years."

"He's a Kiwi." Murph stuck his thumb out and gestured toward Oliver. "Fresh off the proverbial boat. Dude says the craziest fucking shit."

Oliver punched Murph lightly in the chest. "Yeah, nah, fuckwit."

"See what I mean?" Murph shook his head.

I grinned. "I like him already. Let me look into it. Why don't you stop by next week?"

"Chur, bro." Oliver raised his mug. "Sorry, I mean, thanks much."

"No problem." I grabbed a rag and began to wipe down the counter.

Murph leaned forward, placing his elbows on the bar. "I've been meaning to ask you something."

"Yeah?"

"You seen much of Faith lately?"

I paused and looked over at him. "Why do you ask?"

"She's kind of..." Murph seemed to struggle to find the right words.

"What? Special?" I asked.

Murph glared at me. "So, you've noticed, too?"

Damn. "Well, no, I mean, she's hot, but that's it." Murph obviously had a thing for Faith. The last thing I needed was for him to think I wanted in on the running.

Murph took a long sip of his beer. "Yeah, she's special all right. I'd appreciate it if you would, well... keep your distance. I've been working hard on her for over a year, and I think she's getting close, dude, really close to cracking."

In what kind of relationship would that be a good scenario—the girl close to cracking? "Wow, you must feel pretty great about that I guess."

"Yeah, yeah I do." Murph lowered his mug and gave me a pointed stare. "We're clear then?"

Clear? As mud. "I think you've got the wrong impression, Murph. I'm not interested in Faith. She's not exactly my type."

"What, not good enough for you?"

"Nah, it's not that. I'm just not really a relationship kind of guy. She doesn't seem like the one-night stand variety." More like the white picket fence in the suburbs, two-point-five kids, and a fluffy slobbery dog kind of gal.

Murph bobbed his head up and down in agreement. "You got that right. She's high class, douche bag. Way out of your league."

"Whatever. She's all yours, man." How did Faith feel about Murph? Would she even be remotely interested in him? Based on what I knew of her, which wasn't much, the guy didn't seem like a match.

Murph smiled and raised his mug at me again before lifting it to his lips and draining it. He set it down with a slam. "Great. I knew we'd see eye to eye on this." He threw a ten down on the counter. "Come on, let's go. Hey Dante, keep the change. I really hope you can make it to the party."

"Yeah, me too. Good luck with Faith."

"I don't need luck." Murph made a fist and pounded on his heart. "I've got words, dude. That chick is totally into words, and I am so gonna rock her world." He smiled and lifted his hand in a salute before he and Oliver turned toward the door.

I didn't know what to make of the whole exchange. Murph was turning into an ass. From what I could tell, Faith could take care of herself against any unwanted advances by that creep. I paused, washcloth mid-swipe. But what if she actually liked him?

A twinge of something prickled in my gut, but I quickly brushed it off. I didn't have the time or the desire to get involved with someone, not even someone like Faith Wainwright. Especially not Faith Wainwright.

I let myself think about her smart mouth for a moment, but that just got me thinking about what it might feel like to kiss her. Enough, already. I forced all thoughts of Faith out of my brain and walked through the back hallway to Wyatt's office.

A sliver of light escaped through the crack under the door. As I lifted my hand to knock, the rumble of Wyatt's deep laughter reached my ears. I paused, my fist in mid-air, as Lindsey said something too low for me to make out.

Damn, they must be at it again. I'd always liked Wyatt, but ever since he and Lindsey got married, he'd changed. She'd sanded away his rough edges, encouraged him to keep his fiery temper in check, and even had him talking about feelings and shit.

I was happy for Wyatt that he'd found his happily ever after. But the more time I spent around the two of them and their sugary sweet public displays of affection, the more alone I felt. Like something in my own life was missing.

Not wanting to interrupt whatever husband and wife moment they had going on, I took a step back. The distressed wooden floorboard creaked under my feet.

"Dante? You need something?" Wyatt asked.

Shit. "Just a quick question."

The office chair squeaked, light footsteps came toward me, then Lindsey pulled the door open. "Come on in. We were just going over the staff schedule for next week."

I followed her into the room and took a seat in front of the desk.

Wyatt patted his knee. "Come sit down, babe."

Lindsey stepped around the desk to cup her husband's cheek. "I'm going to head home. I've got to get that roast in the oven. See you in a bit?"

I looked to my left, intent on studying the beer sign on the wall. Out of the corner of my eye, I saw Wyatt's arms encircle his wife. I slid my gaze to the floor and shifted in the wooden chair as the unmistakable sound of lips meeting lips hit my ears.

"You know, I can come back later." I grabbed the sides of the chair and began to stand.

"No, I'm leaving." Lindsey gave me a teasing grin. "Sorry, I know how uncomfortable you get around the touchy feely stuff."

Wyatt planted one more kiss on Lindsey's lips and gave her a playful swat on the backside as she turned toward the door. "Just give him time. One of these days even Dante will be a sucker for the mushy stuff."

Lindsey wiggled her eyebrows. "We'll see." She grabbed her coat from the hook behind the door and blew a kiss to Wyatt, then disappeared down the hall.

"God, I'm whipped." Wyatt shrugged his shoulders while a dopey grin played across his face.

"Yeah, what the hell happened?" Back in high school, Wyatt had been voted the least likely to settle down.

"I got tagged, bro. That fat little cherub with the bow and arrow got a clean shot straight through my heart. Wouldn't have it any other way though."

I shook my head. "Not me, dude. That chubby little bastard gets anywhere near me, and I'll clip his fuckin' wings."

"Sometimes it's not up to us. You think I ever envisioned myself settling down?" Wyatt spread his arms wide. "I've got obligations now—a wife, a business— hell, I'm even entertaining the thought of starting a family one of these days. I'm tellin' you, you won't see it coming."

"Whatever. Listen, can we talk about schedules? This mentorship thing is kicking my ass, and I need to put in some extra time with my group."

"Sure thing." Wyatt shuffled the papers on his desk and pulled out a calendar. "Just mark down the nights you need off, and I'll work around it."

"Thanks." As I copied the dates I'd be working the late shift into my phone, I thought about what Wyatt said. Maybe someday I'd allow myself to think about opening my heart up to a woman again. Someday after I left Newbridge and started rolling in the dough. Someday, a long damn time from now.

# CHAPTER 11

## *Faith*

I SAT in my favorite study spot on the fourteenth floor of the library in the business reference section. I liked to hide out on this floor for two reasons. First, it was never crowded, so I could always count on securing one of the private study carrels with a door. Second, there was no thirteenth floor, so technically, the fourteenth floor was really the thirteenth.

It gave me some perverse pleasure to know I was sitting on the superstitious thirteenth floor. My lucky number had always been thirteen, and I liked to work on both my novels and my prep work here.

I wasn't leery of the number, but I was superstitious enough that once I found a system that worked for me, I stuck with it. So far, this corner study carrel had been the location where I'd done the majority of the writing on my most recent book.

Chewing on the tip of my pen, I pondered the current assignment for the intro to poetry class I was teaching. The students were supposed to write a love poem. I appreciated the greats: Elizabeth Barrett Browning, John Keats, Emily Dickinson, and even Edgar Allan Poe. But somehow the leagues of contemporary poetry I was supposed to teach were getting lost in my class. I'd much rather spend months dissecting Tolstoy or even my nemesis, Nietzsche, than try to help them pull apart a few lines of verse.

While I contemplated where to begin, my cell phone rang. Happy to have a distraction, I pulled it out of my bag and smiled as my agent's name and number lit up the screen.

"Hey Steph, what's up?"

"Great news, Faith. I know I should probably wait to call you, but I had to share as soon as I heard."

"What's going on?" I hadn't heard from Steph at all, except for a quick email saying she'd received my last manuscript and was looking forward to reading it.

"Your manuscript sold."

"Sold? What do you mean? You just got it a few weeks ago. Don't you want to see some edits or anything?"

"I'm sure it will need a little work, but I sent it out to a few editors last week and one of them made an offer. If you can commit to three more books in the next year, she'll make it worth your while with a nice advance."

"Nice? What does 'nice' look like?"

Steph clucked her tongue. "Nice is looking like mid-five figures. Hopefully, you don't have big plans over the next month or two?"

"Oh, my gosh." My mind rushed through a mental inventory of my to-do list. "Whatever you need, Steph."

"I knew I could count on you. I'm working out the details and will give you a call as soon as I hear something."

"Great. Thanks."

"Buckle up, Faith. I have a feeling this is going to be huge. You really nailed it. *Carnal Knowledge* will be out in a couple of weeks and they're talking about a late spring release for this one. We'll need to know what else you're working on so we can submit your book proposals for the next three. Can you throw something together and email it to me?"

Stunned, I forced myself to reply. "Sure. I'll send you something over the weekend."

"Fantastic. Talk to you soon."

Steph disconnected, and I sat momentarily paralyzed. When I'd sent in the manuscript for *Carnal Knowledge*, I had to wait a year before a publishing house acted on it and another eighteen months for it to go to print. How could they move so quickly on this one?

A four-book deal with a major publisher? With *Carnal Knowledge* scheduled to release in just a few weeks and four more on the way, I'd be set for quite a while.

As the realization of what had just happened hit me, the cold fingers of panic wrapped around my heart. What if I couldn't come up with anything to write about? What if someone figured out who I really was?

I closed my eyes and shook my head from side to side. Not going to go there. By the time I fulfilled my contract, I'd probably be close to getting tenured and would be putting an end to my erotic romance writing days.

Vowing to just enjoy the moment, I let out a high-pitched squeal.

---

### Dante

I SAT across from the group I was mentoring at a long table on the fourteenth floor of the library. They were supposed to be working on their project, although I seemed to be the only one who'd bothered to get anything done. Me and three female students.

The Entrepreneurial Leadership prof had assigned each

small group a struggling local business. The students were supposed to apply what they'd been learning in the program and come up with a business plan to help the merchant gain some traction and turn things around. The group I was mentoring was tasked with figuring out how to salvage the Sashay Salon.

Oh sure, we'd had our pick of businesses to work with. I'd tried steering them toward the sports bar, the laundromat, and when it looked like all three of them were going to veto anything that didn't have to do with women, even the women's consignment boutique. They ended up voting me down, saddling me with a freaking beauty shop.

Brittany smacked her gum and pointed the end of her pen at the new logo she'd designed. Swirls of pink ribbon on a white background with the words "Sashay Salon" in metallic purple in the middle. Made me want to hurl.

I didn't know much about salons or women, but I doubted that prissy, ultra-girly look would generate more business. I'd been arguing with her for fifteen minutes that there was such a thing as being too feminine. Bethany called for a truce so she could go get a power bar at the vending machine.

I got up to stretch my legs and visit the restroom. Working with these women got me frustrated as hell, and I needed to take a break before I said something I'd regret. As I walked down the hall toward the bathroom, music drifted into the hallway from one of the study carrels. I slowed down and glanced through the small window as I passed.

Well, I'll be damned. Maybe she actually was capable of having fun.

Faith's hands waved in the air and her hips gyrated as she danced to the music coming from her phone. A smug smile played across her lips and her eyes were closed.

I let out a loud laugh and quickly covered my mouth. She stopped moving abruptly, and her eyes flew open. I dropped down under the window to stagger past the doorway in a crouch.

As soon as I cleared the door, I stood up and ran down the hall. The door of the study carrel crashed open as I ducked into the bathroom. Maybe the ice princess was capable of having a good time. I'd have to figure out a way to see that side of her again. Seemed like I only ever got to see the pissed-off version of her. The fun version seemed a lot more, well, fun.

I took the long way back to the table. The team was still arguing over the damn pink and purple logo. I thunked a fist down on the table. "Black and silver, come on. The client said she's trying to attract both men and women. What dude is going to walk into a place that's decked out in freaking pink and purple bows?"

That sure shut them up. Bailey proposed a vote, and two to one, they voted on a black and silver color scheme. If every decision was going to take this long, we'd better start meeting five times a week instead of just two.

"What's next?" I looked around the table at the three of them.

"We need to allocate her advertising budget," Brittany said.

At that moment, a wad of paper sailed across the table and landed on the notebook in front of me. Four pairs of eyes looked up in search of the source of the paper wad. Faith stood about ten feet away. She had her bag slung over her shoulder and appeared to be on her way out.

Pissed off sure looked good on her. I leaned back in my chair and pushed my glasses up on my nose. "Hi, Faith. Fancy seeing you here."

"Are you following me?" she asked, the accusation hanging in the air between us.

"What do you mean? We're just meeting for their group project. Brittany, Bethany, Bailey, this is Faith."

For once, the women were speechless. They looked back and forth between me and Faith.

"No one's ever up here," Faith said. "The fourteenth floor is usually..."

As she struggled for the right words, I spoke up. "Your private dance studio?"

She glared at me, then whipped around and pushed through the door into the stairwell.

Brittany jabbed a hot pink fingernail into my chest. "You're in trouble, buddy. I don't know what that gal's problem is, but she sure is into you."

"What makes you think that?" I asked, removing her finger from my chest and nudging her hand back toward her lap.

"Did you see the way she looked at you?" Bailey asked. "Like she wanted to eat you for dinner."

"Yeah," Bethany agreed.

"Let's just get this done." I rested my elbows on the table and shuffled my papers around. Eat me, huh? I could think of a few parts of my anatomy she could wrap her mouth around.

Hmm, maybe these women weren't as bad as I thought.

# CHAPTER 12

## *Faith*

THE PARTY APPEARED to be in full swing by the time we arrived. I followed Jess and Robin up the sidewalk to join the stream of vampires, zombies, and other party-goers on the driveway.

"I can't see anything." Jess pushed her Catwoman mask up onto her forehead.

"Get it in gear, Pussy." Robin nudged her from behind. "If I'm going to survive this, I need a drink." The tight, low-cut top of her corseted pirate wench costume didn't quite contain all of her ample assets.

I stood on the driveway and lowered the hood of my red cape. I'd never been to Murph's before. He shared a house not far away from campus with a couple of other guys.

"Ready to go in?" Jess asked. She'd removed the mask, but I could still see the outline where it had pressed onto her skin.

"Sure. Let's do it." I'd let Jess and Robin talk me into coming to the party at the last minute, so I hadn't spent a lot of time on my costume. Jess loaned me a red cape, and since I had a tight red dress I'd worn to a formal a few years ago, I threw it on underneath. Tall, high-heeled black boots and a basket rounded out my adult version of Little Red Riding Hood.

"Thank God, more chicks!" A gangly hobo slung one arm around Jess and the other around Robin as we ventured into the house. As he led them through the foyer and into the kitchen, I followed behind. The scent of cheap beer and male B.O. assaulted my nose. Based on the way Murph looked down on so many things that had to do with the undergrads on campus, I'd expected him to have a bit higher standard of living.

"Ladies, so glad you could make it. What can I get you? Wine? Beer?"

"Three beers." Jess decided for us.

The hobo dropped his arm from around Robin's shoulder and focused all his attention on Jess. "Meow!" He snapped his fingers at two guys manning a keg in the corner. "Get this kitten and her crew some beers."

A few moments later, the hobo pressed full plastic cups of beer into our hands. I took a small sip.

"Who do we have here?" Murph appeared in the doorway to the kitchen wearing a tweed jacket and a derby hat with an unlit pipe clenched between his lips.

"Hey, Murph. Who are you supposed to be?" asked Jess.

"It's elementary, my dear Jessica," he said.

"A teacher?" asked Robin.

He pulled the pipe out of his mouth and frowned at her. "Not elementary, as in school—"

"How right you are, Mr. Holmes," I interrupted. "It surely is elementary. Sherlock, is it not?"

Murph turned his attention to me and gave me a warm smile. "Glad to see someone knows her Sir Arthur Conan Doyle."

I nodded, then took another sip out of my cup.

"That's an amazing crimson frock." His eyes raked over the ensemble I'd put together on such short notice.

"Thanks. Nice place you have here."

"Let me show you around." Before I could think up an excuse, Murph put a hand on the small of my back and guided me out of the kitchen and into the living room. "I'm so glad you could make it."

He propelled me to a sofa sitting in front of a giant TV. Cleopatra straddled what appeared to be some sort of creepy creature. They were so busy swapping spit, I couldn't tell whether it was a zombie or a vampire. A horror movie played on the screen, but there was no sound. Music blared through speakers from the corners of the room. Heavy metal rock from what I could tell. A small ache started at the base of my neck.

"What the—oh dammit." All of a sudden, Murph's hand disappeared from my back. "Excuse me for a minute, will you, Faith?"

I barely said "Of course" before he stomped off toward the sliding glass door leading onto a patio. I turned around to look for Jess and Robin and collided with a masked creature of some sort. The contents of my cup sloshed over the edge and spilled all over a nice-looking navy-blue suit.

A garbled "Agh!" floated through the mouth slit in the wolfish mask.

"I'm so sorry." I grabbed the edge of my cape and tried to dab up some of the beer.

"Nice move, Red." The wolf in the suit swiped at his pants.

"Do I know you?" Something about the voice caught my attention. He sounded familiar, but who could tell with that furry mask over his head.

"You tell me," Wolfman said.

I peered up into the mask. I caught the glare of a pair of

glasses. Him again! My heart sped up and my palms went clammy and cool. Murph would be back soon. Under the circumstances, hanging out with Dante for a few minutes seemed like the lesser of two evils.

"My, my, Mr. Wolf, what big eyes you have." I rolled my eyes.

"The better to see you with, my dear."

I smirked. "And what giant, enormous teeth you have." I reached a finger up and poked at a soft vinyl tooth on the mask.

"The better to nibble you with, my dear." I let out a sharp laugh and Wolfman extended his arm out to me with his palm facing me. "And the hands? Don't forget my enormous paws."

I wasn't sure why I did it, but I placed my hand palm-to-palm with his to play along. A strange buzz of energy pulsed between us. "Oh yes, what big hands you have."

He reached up and pulled the mask off his head. His hair stuck out like he'd just rolled out of bed and his cheeks sported a layer of stubble that appeared to be about twelve hours past a five o'clock shadow.

Dante gazed down at me, momentarily paralyzing me with those damn blue-green eyes, then wrapped his hand around mine.

He raised an eyebrow. "The better to paw you with, my dear," he whispered.

My face flushed. My thighs quivered. "Oh."

"What the hell are you supposed to be?" Murph's voice crashed through the intimate moment, and I yanked my hand away, embarrassed at the effect Dante's touch had on me.

Murph reached us and gave Dante a playful slug on the shoulder, bumping him away from me and positioning himself between us as an awkward third wheel.

"I asked what the hell you're dressed up as. An MBA

student on an interview?" Murph looked down at Dante's soaked suit.

Dante flashed the wolf mask at him. "Wolf of Wall Street. Get it?"

"Oh yeah. I get it. That's sick, dude." He wedged his body further in between us. "Faith, where were we?"

I needed to get away from Murph. I put my hand to my temple and took a small step back. "You know, I can feel a headache coming on. I think I'm going to head out."

Murph grabbed onto my arm. "Hey, no need to rush off. You can just lie down on my bed for a bit if you want."

"Smooth, dude." Dante let out a snort. "I've got to get to work. Come on, Faith, I can give you a ride home."

I looked back and forth between Dante and Murph. If I stuck around the party, I'd have to fend off Murph. But if I left with Dante? Did I really want to subject myself to being alone with him? The tremors running up and down my spine urged... yes.

"That would be great." I looked at Murph, but he was busy glaring at Dante. I gently pulled my arm away. "Thanks, I had fun."

I walked back to the kitchen to tell Jess I was heading home, then met up with Dante at the front door.

"Are you sure you don't mind?" I asked. It was just a ride home. Nothing more.

"Not at all. I need to get back to the bar anyway. I have to close tonight."

He opened the door for me and we stepped outside. The night was cool, but not too cold. A full moon illuminated the road in front of us, casting thick, dark shadows along the edges of the pavement. I shivered and pulled my cloak tighter around me. I wasn't sure yet if it was because of the chill in the air or my proximity to the big, bad wolf.

"It's a bit of a walk. Do you want me to go get the car and pick you up?"

"No. It's nice out. Thanks though."

"I haven't seen you at the gym lately."

"I've been jogging outside. I suppose once the snow starts falling, I'll have to find another way to get my exercise."

Dante let out a bark of laughter. "If you ever need to burn off some extra calories, I'd be willing to help."

I sighed. "Do you always relate everything back to sex?"

Dante shrugged. "Aren't you even the least bit tempted? Don't you ever take a break?"

"Of course, I do." I stopped in my tracks. "I do yoga, go for a walk, check out a movie,"—I gritted my teeth—"snuggle with my cat."

"Yoga, huh?" Dante turned back to face me. "You must be pretty flexible."

I opened my mouth to respond but decided against it. What was the point? He'd just twist my words around anyway, kind of like how my stomach was twisted into knots at his suggestion of a dual cardio workout.

We walked down the rest of the street in silence, eventually reaching his car at the end of the block. Dante jogged ahead to open the door for me.

"Thanks." I slid into the low two-seater.

He shut the door behind me, then walked around to the other side and got in. "You need to give me directions."

Sitting next to him in the enclosed space, my body flew into high alert. My pulse pounded in my temples, and my fingertips went numb. Just thinking about touching his hand sent a flock of butterfly wings beating against the walls of my gut. He wasn't part of the plan. Not trusting myself to look at him, I directed him back to my place with as few words as possible. He pulled into a spot and turned off the car.

"Thanks for the ride."

"Faith, I..."

I risked looking over at him. Shadows played across his gorgeous stubbled face, though his blue eyes burned bright in the darkness. My breath caught in my throat.

Dante started again. "Did you..."

I tilted my head and focused my eyes on his full lower lip. As I waited for him to speak, an urgent need to reach out and run my fingers over his cheek washed over me. I should go. Now.

"Dammit, Faith." His hand moved toward me, but he dropped it. He tilted his head one way and then the other like he wanted to say something more.

Before I realized what I was doing, my fingers wrapped around the front of his still-damp oxford, and our noses bumped. His hand sought out the tender spot at the base of my neck, and his lips smashed into mine. My first instinct was to push him away, but as his mouth parted and his tongue moved past my lips, I stopped resisting and melted into him.

# CHAPTER 13

## *Dante*

DAMN, she felt good. I hadn't expected to see her there. I hadn't even planned to be there myself. But Wyatt insisted since I was working the late shift, I shouldn't spend the whole night at the bar. With a few hours of free time and nowhere to go, I'd decided to check out the party at Murph's.

I'd been about to leave when I saw Faith walk in. A temptress in red—garnet cloak, ruby hood, crimson dress, cherry lips. I got stuck on the lips and hadn't been able to take my eyes off of her mouth. She didn't usually wear lipstick and those siren lips screamed at me...kiss me! So, I did. And I was still.

She shifted toward me and put her hand behind my head, pulling me closer. Her fingers played with the hair at the nape of my neck as her tongue swirled around mine. I tangled one hand in her hair and tugged her closer with the other. Damn stick shift. Maybe it was time to get an automatic.

Unbuckling my seatbelt, I twisted toward her, taking the gear shift in the abs. It was worth it. My lips roamed down her cheek and onto her neck while my hands traveled under the cape, searching for a way to get inside that damn red dress. I ached to feel her next to me, skin-to-skin.

She tilted her head back against the seat and moaned. The sound of her losing some control just made me hotter. I was so goddamn hard I felt like I would explode. I gave up on trying to find a zipper and moved a hand to her skirt. I edged the dress up and up, the slippery material sliding all over the leather seats. Her hands skated over the inside of my jacket, racing over my chest, and I paused to take it off, not an easy task in the confined space.

More, I needed more. Something deeper and darker than desire coursed through me—the need to totally possess the tight-laced professor. I threw my jacket into the back and loosened my tie, unbuttoning the top button of my shirt in an effort to get a little more air into my lungs. Every part of me was on fire.

She reached up to pull me toward her, her lips scorching the soft spot at the hollow of my throat. I slid a hand underneath her dress again, ran it up the length of her thigh, and felt her heat through thin silky panties. She parted her legs. I slipped a finger underneath the lacy edge, pushing her underwear out of the way, making contact with her sweet, soft skin. My finger found its way inside, surrounded with the slick heat of her.

She strained against my hand. "Oh my god, Dante."

Hearing my name rise up from the gravelly depths of her throat almost put me over the edge. With one hand making small circles in the depths of her core, I propped myself up with a knee on the center console so I could take a breast in my other. I managed to get a hand inside the front of her dress and rubbed her nipple through the flimsy material of her bra.

"Don't stop, please don't stop."

Her fingers fumbled with the button on my pants then slid into my boxer briefs and she wrapped her fingers around me. Hearing her so close to losing herself, I joined her at the brink. As she gasped and ground against me, a surge of pleasure welled up from my depths. There was no stopping it. I circled my finger inside her again and she clenched around me.

"Please, Dante, don't stop." Her whole body strained then shuddered as the waves of release washed over her and she came apart under my touch.

"Shit, oh Faith, shit, I'm going to—"

Fuck! I was coming in the palm of her hand. Dammit. I tried to pull away and bumped the steering wheel. The blaring horn disturbed the silence.

Faith sat up with a start, the magic totally and completely broken. She looked up at me in a daze. The streetlight cast a pale glow across her face through the steamed-up windows.

Damn, she was beautiful. So fucking gorgeous with messed up hair, swollen lips, and her dress bunched around her waist. Knowing I was responsible for her current state of disarray made me smile in utter satisfaction.

Her voice cut through the hormone-induced haze. "Would you mind removing your finger from my...uh..." Faith gestured to her lap.

Fuck! I slid my finger out from inside of her and she shifted in her seat to face forward. She looked at her palm, covered in my DNA. Reality rushed in, yanking me away from the rosy afterglow. I grabbed my suit jacket and handed it to her.

"Are you sure you want me to wipe it on this?" she asked, looking at the floorboard.

Good point. "Here, use my shirt." I leaned over and gave her the edge of my shirt to use as a towel. "Faith, I'm sorry—"

She looked at me. The heat had seeped from her eyes.

"No, I'm the one who's sorry. I didn't mean to give you the wrong impression."

I tried to make light of the situation. "That impression sure felt right to me—"

"No. Let's just pretend like this never happened, okay?"

Before I could answer, she opened the door and ran up the sidewalk to her apartment. She fumbled with her key for a moment then escaped inside.

Shit. What the fuck just happened? I was like a high school asshole trying to bag his first babe. She'd barely even touched me, and I couldn't control myself. Smooth move, dickwad.

I'd had plenty of hook-ups before, mutually satisfying encounters in which both I and whichever woman I was with enjoyed ourselves then left things on good terms. But this, with Faith, this kind of reaction was brand new. I'd never had someone run away from me. Should I go after her?

From the look she'd given me, she probably needed some space. Hell, I might need some space as well. It had been a damn long time since I'd gotten that worked up that fast. She'd made it clear she wasn't interested in fooling around. Besides, I needed to hurry if I wanted to take a quick shower before my shift at the bar. With one last look at her apartment, I turned the key and started the car.

### Faith

I SLAMMED the door behind me, leaning up against it and forcing myself to take calming, soothing breaths. Fleeing from the car had felt like walking on spaghetti noodles, trying to get to the door before Dante saw me completely and utterly lose my final hold on control. What just happened? For sure, I was attracted to him. How could I not be? He was the kind of guy that couldn't escape notice. The kind I wrote about. The kind I avoided as a matter of principle.

One look from him could make my blood pressure spike, my heart pound, and my head spin. But I never, ever, lost myself like that. Seriously, in a car? What was I, seventeen again, parked in front of my mom's house? What if one of my students had seen me? With my luck, they'd shoot a video and post it all over the college intranet.

I peered through a slit in the shades to scan the parking lot. Dante must have needed a moment to compose himself since his car still sat in the spot in front of my apartment. I jerked my hand away from the window. What if he thought I was spying on him?

Oh hell. He was probably used to this kind of thing. What was it Murph had said about him at the gym? He worked at a bar and most likely had his choice of one-night stands. I took a final deep breath, denying the urge to peek outside one last time. Who cared what Dante Bishop thought of me anyway?

But those fingers. And the feel of his mouth on my neck. Even recalling it now made me tingle in places where I hadn't felt any sensation for months. I didn't have time for tingles and botched hook-ups. I needed a cool shower, maybe even a cold one. Then I'd be able to forget all about Dante and his amazing touch.

Mr. Darcy wound around my feet.

"Hi baby." I leaned down to ruffle the fur behind his ears. "Mama was a bad girl tonight." Mr. Darcy purred. "Yeah, I was purring, too. But I won't let that happen again."

I stood and untied the red cape from around my neck. Back to work. I'd cool off with a shower then take advantage of my recent experience and channel any leftover desire into my book.

As I walked back to the bathroom, I stripped down, ready

to wash every last thought of Dante Bishop right down the drain.

# CHAPTER 14

## *Dante*

I MADE another loop around the fourteenth floor of the library. I was supposed to be meeting with my team to work on our group project, but I'd been trying to connect with Faith for the past two weeks to apologize for how I'd handled our intimate encounter.

Even though she seemed to like to study on this floor, I couldn't find her in any of the private study carrels. I'd cruised through a few times I'd been on campus, looking for her. Why should I even give a fuck? It's not like we were going to start dating or anything.

But still, I was embarrassed as hell at how I'd blown things and hadn't been able to get her out of my mind. I'd even driven by her apartment a few times. When I ran into Jess at the student center on my way over, she said Faith would probably be at the library now. That's why I'd grabbed the damn rose from the little floral shop and now paced up and down the halls like a crazed stalker.

I turned the corner and saw Brittany, Bethany, and Bailey sitting at their usual table. "Hey." I set my books down at one end and claimed my spot.

"Hi, Dante," said Brittany. "Who's the flower for?"

"Nobody. I, um, I just found it."

"Are you sure?" She leaned back in her chair and toyed with her pen, running it along her painted pink bottom lip while she watched me from under heavily made-up eyelids.

"Yep. Here, you can have it." I tossed the rose at Brittany. It skidded across the table and came to a stop right in front of her. The damn rose had been a stupid idea. I thought it would make a good peace offering, but fuck it. If Faith didn't want to be found, there were plenty of other women who *would* want to talk to me. And probably do much more.

"Wow, thanks. I can't remember the last time a guy gave me flowers."

"Yeah, well, it's not *flowers*, it's just one, and I didn't exactly give it to you."

"Still"—one side of her mouth lifted up in a seductive grin and she raised her eyebrows at me—"roses are the flower of love."

"Give me a freaking break," Bailey said. "Can we get back to work?"

"Gladly." I took off my jacket and tossed it over the back of my chair. I sat down and for the next hour, the three of us argued about how to allocate the marketing budget for the Sashay Salon. After much discussion, we finally came to an agreement and hashed out a plan.

"I think Tameka will be happy with this." I flipped the cover of my laptop down and shoved it in my bag. "Same time next Wednesday?"

"I can't make it next week," said Bethany. "That's the day before Thanksgiving. I'll be lounging on the beach with my own cabana boy bringing me piña coladas."

"Oooh, Mexico?" Bailey slid her notebook into her messenger bag.

"Yep." A dreamy smile played on Bethany's face. "The

folks are flying us all down. Next time you see me I'll be sporting a tan. Eat your hearts out, ladies."

"I won't be here either," said Bailey. "Can we hold off until the week after?"

"Sure. We can get together when everyone's back in town. How does that sound?" I stood and pushed my chair up against the table.

"Sounds good to me." Brittany shrugged into her puffy pink coat. "Aren't you heading home for Thanksgiving, Dante?"

"Yeah. It's just that home for me isn't that far away. Besides, I've got to work so I can't go too far," I said.

"That's a drag." Brittany put her hand on my arm. "Thanks again for the rose."

A flash of red caught my eye, and I looked up. Faith stood at the end of the bookshelf, her red coat wrapped tight around her, watching the whole exchange.

"Hey, Faith." I yanked my arm away from Brittany, grabbed my bag and jacket, and took a step toward her.

"Nice rose," Faith pointed to the rose in Brittany's hand.

"Thanks, Dante gave it to me."

"Yellow, huh? Ever read 'The Age of Innocence'? Wharton had a few things to say about yellow roses."

Wharton? What the hell was she talking about? Before I could reach her, she turned and walked away. Screw it. I wasn't going to let her run from me again. "Faith, hey, got a sec?" I jogged to catch up.

---

### Faith

THE YELLOW ROSE? I ripped off my knit cap and ran a hand through my hair. Where did that come from? I'd spent a good portion of my junior year studying Edith Wharton. My professor at the time had a hang-up about the symbolism of flowers in literature.

Dante took my arm, forcing me to stop. "Hold up."

I whirled around to face him. I hadn't seen him in a couple of weeks. God, he looked good. I lifted a hand to run it across the dark stubble covering his chin, but stopped myself at the last second and pushed my hair back behind my ear instead.

"Are you pissed at me?" His eyes darted over my face.

I looked away. "No. I'm not pissed at you. I'm pissed at myself. I'm embarrassed and mortified, okay? It has nothing to do with you."

Dante rolled his eyes and raised his voice. "It sure as hell does have something to do with me. You think you're embarrassed?" He put a finger under my chin and tilted my face up toward his. "Hey, look at me."

Why did he have to touch me? I lost access to all rational thought when his skin connected with mine. "What?"

My lower lip stuck out in a half pout. I'd tried to forget about that night in the car, the way his lips felt on mine, the way it made me feel to feel wanted. Trouble was, no matter how many times I pushed thoughts of Dante Bishop from my head, they always returned. Thanks to our little tryst, my writer's block had been obliterated, and I'd been able to outline the three books Steph needed by just picturing those blazing blue-green eyes and the way his mouth felt pressing into mine.

"I'm sorry. I've been trying to track you down for the past two weeks to apologize. That flower...I bought it for you. It was supposed to be a peace offering. Jess said she thought you'd be here studying. I couldn't find you, so I tossed it at Brittany."

"You bought me a flower?" I couldn't remember the last

time a guy had bought me flowers. It had to be in high school. Maybe a corsage for a dance or something.

"Yeah. What's the deal about the yellow rose, anyway?"

I flushed. "Nothing. It's just that the main character in the book buys a yellow rose for his wife's cousin, the one he wants to sleep with."

Dante's eyes widened. "The chick at the flower shop told me yellow roses mean friendship."

"Well, yeah, most people think they do now. But back in the late 19th century, it meant something different."

"Remind me to never send you flowers. I'd hate to say something I didn't mean." A smile played on his lips.

Warm, soft, kissable lips. Dammit. "Friendship, huh? Peruvian lilies would have been a better choice. You can never go wrong with those."

"I'll try to remember that next time I want to give a friend a flower. So, are you going or coming?" Dante's face flushed at his unintentional innuendo.

I smiled. "I just got here, if that's what you mean. Are you heading out?"

"Yeah, I've got to get to work. I was wondering, can we get together sometime?"

My heart skipped a beat. Together...I didn't have time for together. As much as my body ached for the touch of his hands and my mouth craved the taste of him, he wasn't part of my plan. I'd seen what happened when people gave in to all-consuming passion and blazing heat. It didn't last. Security, shared interests, common goals, those were the things I needed.

I shook my head. "I wasn't kidding when I said I'd like to pretend that night never happened. It won't do any good for us to get together. I just don't have time in my life for anything but work right now."

Well, work and the fantasy life I'd created for the two of

us on my laptop. He'd consumed my thoughts and thanks to the inspiration, I'd made it a quarter of the way through my next novel. Main characters Dante and Faith. I'd have to change the names later, but I was enjoying my erotic fantasy too much for the time being.

Although, I'd reached a point in the plot and was having some trouble. What if I let myself have one night with Dante? Just one to see if that would give me enough inspiration to finish my book and end my writer's block for good?

"Yeah, I don't know what I was thinking. I don't have time right now either. In fact, I've got to get to the office." Dante glanced at his watch. "Yep. Sorry, I've gotta go. See you around, Faith." He wheeled around and covered the distance to the elevator in just a few steps.

As I watched him go, my mind rapidly attempted to process the possibility of a one-night stand. Would one night be enough? Did I have enough nerve to even suggest it?

He didn't turn around, not even when the elevator door opened and he stepped inside. Maybe it would be better this way. The Dante in my head was much easier to control. I could make him do all kinds of things to me on paper without any of the emotional turmoil seeing the real Dante dredged up.

But somehow, my imaginary Dante didn't smell the same as the musky, male, touchable version. And my pretend Dante didn't make my heart skip a beat or cause my words to get caught up in my throat when I tried to speak.

Dammit. As the elevator doors slid shut, I swallowed the lump of apprehension in my throat.

"Hey, hold the elevator, will you?"

# CHAPTER 15

## *Dante*

I **THRUST** my hand between the elevator doors to prevent them from closing. The rubber edge ricocheted off my arm and the doors retracted. Faith stood front and center, shifting her weight from one foot to the other.

"Did you need something?" I asked, my mouth screwing into a frown. What could she possibly want now?

"Going down?" I cocked my head and waited.

She stepped into the elevator, then back out again. "I don't know. It's a dumb idea. Never mind."

"Okay." I released my grasp. I had a ton of work to do. Hanging out in the elevator on campus didn't fit into my plans. The doors began to close again.

Faith wedged her boot between them, and they separated briefly, then began bouncing against her leg in an attempt to close.

"What's going on, Faith?" I asked.

"I've never done anything like this before. It's just—"

"You've never ridden an elevator?" I shook my head, tired of her games. "Come on, it's easy. Step inside and push the button. Not much to it."

She let out a huffy breath as she took two steps forward.

"There, that wasn't too bad, was it?" I tapped the button to close the doors.

Faith kept her eyes trained on the speckled taupe linoleum tiles. Her voice came out quiet and breathy. I strained to hear her over the whir of the ancient motor.

"I thought maybe we could... I mean... would you..."

Jesus, spit it out already. For an English major, she sure had trouble speaking the language sometimes. I leaned down to make eye contact. A combination of uncertainty and fear flickered across her face.

Something was really getting to her. I caught her hands in mine. "Hey, what's wrong?"

"Nothing. I just... I don't know. I guess I've been thinking about what's been going on between us, and it's silly, really."

"Silly?" I let out a laugh. "Hot and twisted, maybe. But silly?"

Faith let my hand drop, then leaned against the wall. "It's just, I don't have time for a relationship."

"Yeah, that's not really my scene either." Where was she going with this?

She glanced up at me. "But I can't seem to get you out of my mind." Her eyes searched mine, begging me to laugh it off and send her on her way.

My heart thudded in my chest so loudly I automatically began to calculate the statistical probability that she'd be able to hear it. I opened my mouth to speak. But instead of blowing her off like I'd intended, I found myself saying, "I know what you mean. I was starting to think it was only me."

Relief washed over her face. "Really?"

Dammit. I'd already admitted it, so I nodded.

"So I've been thinking." Her cheeks tinged pink.

"And?"

"The, um, the hookup was pretty good between us, right?" Her gaze met mine. She looked away.

"Um, yeah. Better than good." I leaned forward, all ears. What exactly did she have in mind?

"Then how about we keep it physical? No attachment, no drama, no talking even. Just sex." Her shoulders lifted in a casual shrug, as if there would ever be anything casual about her when it came to getting it on.

I laughed. "Really? Just sex?"

Faith twirled a section of fiery hair around her finger and looked up at me through thick dark lashes. "Yeah, unless you don't think you can handle it."

My cock twitched. "Oh, I can handle it all right. I'm worried about you, though. You don't seem like the kind of woman who'd go for a sex-only arrangement."

In an instant, she raised up to her tiptoes, her mouth nuzzling the ticklish spot on my neck. I tensed beneath her, and she whispered into my ear, "People aren't always what they seem."

That was the understatement of the year. Faith Wainwright was definitely not what I'd expected. On one hand, what guy wouldn't kill for a gal like Faith for some friends-with-benefits action? On the other, I'd tried this kind of thing before, and a girl like Faith always ended up wanting more. I hadn't been so concerned about that in the past, but I'd grown up since then.

As strong as my attraction to her was—like taking a wrecking ball to the gut, over and over—there was something more between us. Something deeper than just the incredible chemistry, and it had me on edge.

Faith moved on to kissing my neck. Her fingers hooked the belt loops of my jeans and tugged me closer while her lips traveled up to meet mine.

My resolve flattened, as if it had been steam-pressed at the dry cleaner like one of my suits. Who was I kidding? If this hot chick wanted to use me for sex, who was I to deny her? I groaned and nudged her toward the corner, lowering my mouth to nip at her earlobe. If she was good with a sex-only deal, I'd be a dumbass to say no.

My fingers flipped the stop car button, bringing the elevator car to an abrupt halt.

Faith pulled back. "What, here?"

"Yeah, unless you don't think you can handle it."

Her eyes sparkled as I tossed her words right back at her. Challenge accepted. She yanked her backpack off her shoulders and let it crash to the ground. Next, the coat.

"Wait, won't someone wonder why the car stopped?" Her fingers paused on the zipper of her jacket.

"This building's so old, they're always having trouble with them. You chickening out already?"

Her teeth tugged on her bottom lip. Hell, she was all talk. I bent down to retrieve her backpack and hand it to her. As I stood, she let her coat fall to the ground, then whipped her long sleeve T-shirt over her head and pushed me back into the corner.

My gaze wandered over her flat stomach and toned arms. She was incredible, and she wanted me. I leaned down to kiss her again, a sense of urgency building with every flick of my tongue.

She maneuvered my shirt up, breaking our lip-to-lip contact just long enough to yank it over my head, and ran her hands over my bare chest. My skin prickled under her touch.

"Jeans...off," I mumbled into her neck. I undid her button with one hand and wriggled her jeans down her legs. The light flowery scent wafted off her skin. I slipped a finger under her bra strap and ran it up and down, edging closer to her breast with each pass.

Faith kicked off her boots, stepped out of her jeans, and flung them aside. She pressed into me, skin-to-skin. I couldn't get my pants down fast enough. Wrapping both arms around her waist, I whirled her around, putting her back up against the wall. Her mouth moved over every exposed part of me. Hands raced up and down my sides, fingers darted under the waistband of my boxer briefs. No way was this going down the same way as last time. I'd make sure of that.

Her fingers brushed against my crotch. My dick throbbed at the contact. I nestled it against her stomach. Let her feel how turned on she got me.

She moaned, pressing into me, lifting her leg to wrap around my waist. Her arms closed around my shoulders, pulling me into her, urging me on. As if I needed any encouragement.

My hands cupped her ass, and I lifted, resting her body on the handrail, lining her up, adjusting the angle for maximum dry-humping pleasure.

Her hips bucked against mine as the tip of my cock pushed into the damp spot on her cotton bikini briefs. I didn't know how much longer I could hold back. Her hands tunneled through my hair. My glasses bumped against her nose as she tilted her head and attacked my mouth from a new angle. I'd figured her for an uptight, repressed book-worm who got off on flowery prose and the Oxford comma. Thank fuck I'd been wrong.

She lifted her other leg and wrapped it around my waist, crossing her ankles behind my back and pressing up against my crotch, sliding up and down. The friction had me about ready to shatter. My hips automatically bucked against hers.

"Look what you do to me, Faith."

She pulled her hair away from her face and met my gaze with heavy-lidded eyes.

"You sure you want this?" I asked.

Faith's head tipped forward, a slight nod of agreement. "Yeah, but let's hurry."

I drew back, breaking contact, and reached into my bag.

# CHAPTER 16

## Faith

I WATCHED as Dante pulled a condom from his wallet. I was really doing this. The thought sent a thrill of anticipation from my core, down past weak knees, ending at the tip of my toes. He stood and ripped open the packet. The dim light of the elevator cast a golden glow over his frame, highlighting his broad shoulders, defined pecs, ridged six-pack, and tapered waist. My gaze followed his hands as he unrolled the circle of latex. Why was he taking so long?

In an effort to speed things up, I slid my panties down my legs and kicked them onto the discarded jeans. Rough hands gripped my waist. Dante's lips played against the curve of my jaw. His hips pushed into mine, and my bare ass smacked against the cold metal wall.

His lips nipped at the sensitive skin behind my ear, sending a shiver racing across my pebbled skin. I grabbed onto his shoulders, drawing him closer. A sense of urgency battled with my need to slow it down and savor each sensation. I'd need to be able to recall the details later. That was the whole reason I'd propositioned him in the first place—for research.

I closed my eyes, and the scruff of his whiskered cheek scraped against my collarbone. His head dipped lower, and he sucked the front of my bra, teasing my nipple into a peak, even through the thin fabric. The musky male scent of him enveloped me. I breathed it in, greedy, ready for whatever he had in mind.

His erection nudged into my abdomen. Eager to satisfy the need swelling inside me, I tried to compensate for our difference in height by pressing to my tiptoes.

"Not like that." His voice rasped; the grit in his tone making my toes curl. "Turn around. Grab onto the rail."

I spun around, compliant for a change. As my hands closed around the cool metal rail, he gripped my waist, pulling me toward him, stretching me backward. My breath caught in my throat as my gaze slid to the floor. His jeans pooled around his ankles. He nudged my feet farther apart. The sight of his bare legs so close to my backside made my legs quiver. He adjusted himself, and I felt him slide between my legs.

I leaned into him as his tip entered me. More, I need more.

His grip on my waist tightened. "Damn, you feel so good."

I bit my lip and rocked back, letting him bury himself inside me.

He pulled out, then slowly entered me again. The fullness of him inside me made me desperate to move. I increased the pace, ready to ride the wave as it surged and came close to cresting. His hand moved around to tease me where I craved his touch the most.

Pure pleasure rippled through me. He shifted, and I lost my momentum. My hands scrambled to press against the walls, propelling me back against him. A hot exhale warmed my ear. I tried to turn, needing him closer, frantic for the feel of his mouth on mine. His arm closed around my waist, and my hand shot out, slamming against the elevator panel. The elevator lurched.

"Fuck!" Dante's fingers fumbled with the button. The elevator stopped again.

Desperate for release, I focused on the feel of his finger as he stroked me to a climax. My body stalled, and for a glorious second, I hung, suspended in bliss. The strong arm around my waist held me up as my body shattered into pieces.

Dante grunted, pulled back one more time, and then let out a long, low groan as he reached his own release.

We stood still for several moments, his breath rushing across the expanse of my bare back, my clammy hands grasping the railing.

"You okay?" Dante asked, the gravel gone from his voice.

"Yeah, I, uh, wow." Not trusting myself to stand on my own yet, I waited for him to be the one to let go first.

"That was hot." His hand ran over my ribs, tracing the swirls of ink decorating the base of my spine. He gently pulled out and released me from his grasp.

I looked away as he dealt with the condom, then stepped into my underwear and jeans. "Where's my shirt?"

By the time I'd located my t-shirt, Dante had buttoned his pants and pulled on his shirt.

"Looks like the trip down might take a little while." He tipped his head toward the panel, and I noticed most of the buttons were lit up.

"Oh, crap. I'm sorry. My hand must have hit the panel."

"It's okay." He reached around me and bumped the stop button. The elevator shuddered, then began to move. "Your tattoo. I like it. What kind of flower is it?"

Before I could respond, the door opened, and a group of underclassmen entered the elevator. Dante stepped to one side while I stepped to the other to make room. I slipped my arms into my jacket and slung my backpack onto my shoulder.

The elevator stopped at the next floor, and another group got on.

"Jeez, who pushed all the buttons?" one of the under-classmen asked.

Dante's gaze met mine through the crowd of knit hats, ponytails, and baseball caps. Amazed that no one else seemed to notice the intense band of energy pulsing between us, I blushed and looked away.

As the elevator reached the ground floor and everyone filed out, Dante's fingers brushed against mine.

I looked up at him. "They're daisies."

His lips quirked up into a slight grin. "Why daisies?"

"Daisies symbolize loyal love, they—"

"You and your flowers." He lowered his head and swept his tongue over his upper lip. "You know I'm going to run my tongue all over that ink next time."

I raised my eyes, and his look dared me to deny him. A chill ran through me. "Is that a promise or a threat?"

"Both."

I didn't doubt he meant it. With a final glance at his teasing smirk, I turned and slowly walked away. The whole encounter had lasted less than ten minutes. But somehow, I felt as if my whole world had just shifted off balance. And I was a little freaked out about that.

Because I kind of liked it.

I STRUGGLED to keep my eyes open for the last five minutes of the Religion in Contemporary Literature class. Professor Wickstrom had asked me to sit in today, but his voice droned on and on. If only he could infuse his lectures with a little more enthusiasm. I patted my face with my hands, trying to increase the blood flow to my brain. Four more minutes.

"Before we wrap up for the afternoon, I have an exciting announcement to make. I want you all to mark your calendars. We'll have a special guest lecturer next month. Go on, write it down," he said, gesturing to a student in the front row with his pen. "Claire Kepner will be joining us to talk about her experience as a contemporary Christian author."

I let out an audible gasp. Professor Wickstrom must have mistaken my shock for excitement. "Glad to see at least someone is excited about this. It's not every day you're treated to a best-selling author's firsthand experiences. Faith, please prepare an introduction. You can introduce Mrs. Kepner that day."

"Oh no, Professor Wickstrom, I couldn't."

"You can, and if you want to stay in my good graces, you will."

I knew better than to argue with him. I'd let it go, for now. I snapped the cover of my laptop down and shoved it, along with the rest of my things, into my bag.

"You may want to wipe your nose there." Murph sidled up to me, rubbing the bridge of his nose.

"What are you talking about?"

"You had your nose stuck so far up Wickstrom's ass, I think you got something on it." He laughed at his own joke.

I let out an exasperated sigh. "Very funny." I slung my backpack over one shoulder and headed for the door. "What are you doing here anyway?"

"Wickstrom asked me to sit in." Murph caught up to me easily, taking one step to every two of mine. "So have you seen much of Dante lately?"

"Dante? Um, no. Why do you care?"

"I don't. I was just wondering. You two seemed chummy."

I reached up and adjusted my turtleneck, praying the fabric sufficiently covered evidence of my recent tryst with Dante. The thought of his body pressing against mine flitted through my head, and heat flushed my cheeks. "No. We're not chummy, not at all."

"Good. Then maybe you want to catch a movie with me later?"

"Come on, Murph. I told you, I don't date."

He looked down at his feet and kicked at something on the ground. "Can't blame a guy for trying."

We'd reached the student center, and I was eager to lose him so I could make a phone call in relative privacy. "Sorry, nothing personal."

"Yeah, see you around." Murph turned down another sidewalk. Probably off to harass some unsuspecting grad student. He was a nice guy, and I hated having to turn him down over and over again. But dating wasn't an option. How many times would I have to say no before he'd finally accept my answer?

# CHAPTER 17
## *Faith*

I PULLED out my cell phone and hit the speed dial. Mom answered on the second ring.

"Faith, darling. Let me guess. You just found out about the little visit I've planned for next month."

"Mom! You've got to cancel. How could you? Nobody here knows you're my mother. Why can't we just keep it that way?"

"Sweetie, are you embarrassed by me?"

Usually, Mom waited a few more minutes into the conversation before she played that card. "You know I'm not embarrassed. It's just that once people find out I'm your daughter they get all weird around me."

"Religion isn't weird, honey."

"Yeah, but they get all preachy and want to hold hands and pray and stuff."

"It would probably do you some good to hold hands and pray with some of your students and colleagues. Maybe we should hold an informal prayer rally while I'm there. Clem's trying to branch out with his ministry and reach a younger crowd. He's launching a new program against the media:

movies, books, television. The things they're promoting now, they're absolutely immoral."

"What kind of program?" My heart stalled. That's just what I needed—Clem taking on the publishing industry. I knew I wouldn't be able to keep up my writing gig for much longer, not if I wanted to keep my worlds from colliding. But I'd hoped to pay off more of my loans before I had to call it quits.

"He's talking about going into syndication. Reaching a broader audience and targeting America's youth. I think your idea of a prayer rally is a great way to get started. We could even kick off at Tempest. That's a great idea, Faith, I—"

"Mom, no! No prayer rally. No kick-off on campus. Please! Just having you speak here is going to be bad enough."

"She is clothed with strength and dignity—" Mom began.

"And she laughs without fear of the future," I finished. "I know, Mom, Proverbs 31. You've been quoting that to me since I was a little girl."

"Oh, Faith. I miss you. When an opportunity came up to see my baby, how could I say no?"

"I miss you too, Mom." I twisted a few strands of hair around my finger. "It'll be good to see you. I'm just not ready for everyone to make the connection yet. Marrying Clem was your choice, not mine. I never wanted to be thrown into the spotlight."

"I know, dear. It will all work out. I'll treat you to dinner after my lecture. How does that sound?"

"Sure. Sounds like fun."

"I'll have my assistant set it up and call you with the details."

"Sounds good. Love you, Mom."

"Love you too, honey. Bye."

I hung up first. I didn't begrudge my mother a second chance at happiness. How was she to know it would come in the form of Reverend Clement Kepner? Mom and Dad split up when I was five years old. I couldn't remember much about my father. Mom said he was the love of her life. He left one day, and according to her, he never looked back.

I used to make up stories about him when I was little. He was a photographer for National Geographic and was being held captive by an indigenous tribe in the Amazon. Or he was an award-winning journalist trapped behind enemy lines while reporting on a civil war in Africa. One day he'd ring my doorbell and tell me the thought of a reunion with me was the sole reason he'd been able to survive. I gave up my fantasies when I was about twelve.

When I was sixteen, Mom met Clem. She'd started going to a new church and was always inviting me to go with her. Clem had lost his wife to breast cancer a few years before and they gravitated toward each other like magnets. By the time I left for college, Mom was installed as the new Mrs. Clement Kepner, first lady of the Freebird Evangelical Christian Worship Center.

That was the main reason I'd chosen a college in the Midwest for my undergrad degree. Clem's life revolved around the church. Not only was he a pastor, he was a bona fide local Christian celebrity and the story of how he and the single mother had found a new chance at love propelled them both into a new stratosphere of fame.

Mom's writing career had taken off several years before that, but when she took the new last name Kepner, the shit hit the fan and she hit all the bestseller lists. Her inspirational romance novels and women's devotionals flew off the shelves. Mom was an international Christian superstar, and I was an unwilling bystander. I was happy for her, of course. But I didn't want any part of her new world, especially since I'd found a way to finance my education writing borderline erotica.

Mom would really flip if she knew about my secret part-time job. I'd fled a thousand miles away where I thought I'd be safe from the reach of Reverend and Mrs. Kepner. Evidently, it hadn't been far enough. Clem's celebrity was fairly localized, and he wasn't very well known outside of California. Mom, on the other hand, had hit a niche market when she started writing Christian inspirational romance novels and with thirty-five published romances and a handful of non-fiction books under her belt, she was the one I worried about.

Once my classmates found out who my mother was, I might as well throw in the towel. They'd never be able to look at me the same. It wasn't their fault. Mom's golden aura eclipsed my efforts at normalcy.

A few of my friends in the undergrad program in Illinois made the connection. Before, it had been all about football games, sunbathing on the quad, and checking out the guy's sand volleyball league. After, it was all about students trying to engage me in a Bible-quoting contest, apologizing for dropping a swear word, and invitations from complete strangers to join them at worship.

I shook my head, dislodging the memories and depositing my brain right smack dab into the present. With the immediate threat of exposure held at bay, I pushed away from the high-top table and picked up my bag, my eye on joining the line at the coffee bar. An afternoon jolt of caffeine would keep me going all night. As I whipped around, I smacked into something, sending my phone and bag skidding across the high gloss wooden floor.

"Oh my gosh! I'm sorry!"

I looked down onto a head full of thick, dark hair. Whoever he was gathered my items and shoved them back into my bag. I rubbed my arm where he'd bumped me, then squatted down and picked up my phone. We stood up at the same time and I cracked the top of my head on his very hard chin.

I grabbed my forehead and looked up. "You!"

A sheepish grin spread across Dante's face. "Sorry. It was an accident." He handed me the bag.

"What is it with you?" I asked, slinging the bag over my shoulder.

"Just luck that I keep running into you, I guess." He noticed a few more of my items under the table next to us and bent down to retrieve them. "You don't want to lose these." He handed me a lipstick and my case of birth control pills.

My face could have blistered from the heat flooding my cheeks. I snatched my pills and lipstick out of his hands and shoved them in my bag.

"Relax, it's not like I've never seen lipstick before." His smile proved he knew exactly what the little round case contained.

I gulped for air in an effort to steady my thundering heart and shaky hands. "I've got to get to a class."

"Yeah, I've got to get to my real job. I haven't seen you around lately."

"No, I've been tied up with stuff."

His eyebrows lifted. "Oh yeah? Get many ideas from that BDSM book?"

I swatted at his biceps. "Is that all you can think about?"

He grabbed my hand mid-strike and looked down into my eyes. I swallowed the nervous lump rising in my throat and met his gaze. My heart increased its tempo and my knees knocked together.

"It's not all I can think about. I do have some experience rock climbing though and am pretty good at a French bowline. You want to get together later?" He turned my wrist over in his hand.

I pictured him securing my wrist to a bedpost with a piece

of climbing rope. I took in a deep breath and yanked my arm away. "I can't. I have to figure out where I can go to get my monthly volunteer hours covered." As a Christian university with a commitment to social service, Tempest required students and staff to put in a minimum number of volunteer hours each month.

"You're running out of time, aren't you?"

"It's fine. I should be able to find somewhere in town to serve Thanksgiving dinner."

"Uh, no you won't. Those slots have been filled for months. But I know somewhere that would gladly take the help if you don't mind a bit of a drive."

"Oh yeah?"

"Check with the Hinkley Senior Center. It's about an hour and a half away. I know they'd be grateful for the help."

"If I can't find someplace closer, I'll look into it."

Dante shrugged. "Yeah, I'll be there. Think about it."

Think about it? I'd been doing nothing but think about him since our encounter in the elevator last week. I couldn't eat, couldn't sleep. The only part of me not suffering from Dante withdrawal was my imagination. My fingers couldn't type fast enough to keep up with the mental images playing through my mind. I'd sent some samples to Steph, who couldn't wait to get her hands on the whole thing.

Dante shifted his backpack on his shoulder and turned to go. "If you change your mind about later, you know how to find me."

I watched him walk away. Having had the opportunity to see him with his pants around his ankles, I could better appreciate the way his jeans hinted at the toned muscles underneath.

Ready to brave the cold on the quad on my way to my next class, I shoved my hands into my coat pockets. My right fist bumped against something. I pulled out a wad of paper and ripped off my gloves to smooth out the creases. As my eyes scanned the typewritten words, a wave of nausea swept over me, and the taste of sour bile rose in my throat.

There on the paper in front of me was the title page of the first draft of my most recent book, *Carnal Knowledge* by Chastity Austen. The words jumped off the paper and pierced my heart, sending sharp pains radiating throughout my chest. I staggered backward and dropped the page. This couldn't be happening. How did someone get something in my pocket without me noticing? As I bent down to retrieve it, I noticed a handwritten line on the back.

*I know who you really are, and I know what you've been up to.*

That was it. I flipped the paper over and even lifted it to my nose to see if it had any kind of distinct smell. The only one who'd seen my manuscript was Steph. I'd never even printed it. I crumpled the page and shoved it back into my pocket. Where would this have come from?

Someone knew my secret. My worst nightmare was coming true.

# CHAPTER 18

## Dante

AS I DROVE over the icy roads, the car slid again, and I turned into it, managing to keep control. The polar vortex had hit hard, bringing single-digit temperatures and heavy snow. Thanksgiving break meant fewer students on the roads, but driving in this weather was still a challenge.

I couldn't help but chuckle thinking about those poor kids from Texas who always ended up in ditches this time of year. Driving in snow wasn't something you just picked up; it was a skill you honed over time.

I was on my way to Meemaw's, my grandmother on my dad's side. She lived out in the middle of nowhere, surrounded by fields that were now just endless expanses of white. I slowed down as another gust of snow blew over the car, reducing visibility to almost zero. I'd been trying to convince her to move closer to town, but she was stubborn. "Your grandfather built this house with his own two hands. If you think some tract house in the city is going to cut it for me, you've got another think coming, my boy."

We made a good team, but she needed to stop pestering me about finding a nice girl to settle down with. She'd even threatened to fix me up with one of her bridge buddies' granddaughters over Thanksgiving. I'd bought some time by telling her I'd started seeing someone, though she definitely wouldn't understand or appreciate the nature of my "non-relationship" with Faith.

Meemaw was going to be pissed that I hadn't stayed in Newbridge. She'd warned me it was too dangerous to be out on the roads and suggested postponing our Thanksgiving. But I knew she'd been cooking up a storm, and I'd been dreaming about her homemade pecan pie for weeks. There was no way I was missing Thanksgiving on the farm.

After what felt like forever, I finally turned into the quarter-mile-long driveway. It looked like it had been freshly plowed, though it would need it again soon with the way the snow was falling. Her front door was always unlocked, so I let myself in.

I expected the smell of cinnamon and sweet potatoes or to hear her humming in the kitchen. But there was silence. Where the hell was she? I took out my cell phone and dialed the Withers, her closest neighbors. They were only in their mid-seventies, and if anyone knew where she was, it would be Mary Withers. She answered on the second ring.

After a long-winded conversation about her health and her granddaughter's new job in Chicago, I finally got a word in. She told me Meemaw had gone into town for dinner at the senior center. Classic Meemaw, telling me not to venture out while she braved the ten-mile drive in a blizzard. I thanked Mrs. Withers and, after another few minutes of pleasantries, managed to hang up.

Thirty minutes later, I pulled into the parking lot of the senior center. Meemaw's ancient light blue Ford pickup sat in the second row. She qualified for a handicap sticker but refused to use it, "in case one of the old folks needs it." There were only a few other cars in the lot; most of the "old folks" were sensible enough to stay home.

As I walked in, I braced myself. Being fifty years younger than the average attendee, I always seemed to catch everyone's attention. I put a finger to my lips to shush the gossiping ladies decorating tables with plastic cloths and made my way to the kitchen. Meemaw stood at the stove, stirring a giant pot of gravy. I snuck up behind her and covered her eyes.

"Guess who?"

She spun around and flung her arms around my waist. She'd been shrinking over the years, and the top of her head barely reached my chest.

"It's good to see you, my boy." Her eyes sparkled, and I could have sworn I saw her quickly wipe away a tear. "I thought I told you to stay put today." She stepped back, one hand on her hip, the other wagging a wooden spoon at me.

"So, I was supposed to stay home, but you thought it was okay to get out in this storm?" I asked.

"Well, who else was going to come in here and make Thanksgiving dinner for all these fine folks?"

I hugged her tighter. "Meemaw, have you ever considered taking a holiday off?" I knew the answer.

She scoffed. "Pshaw! Now, as long as you're here, make yourself useful. There are about forty pounds of potatoes that need peelin' over there." She waved the spoon toward a corner of the kitchen.

Shaking my head, I rolled up my sleeves and washed my hands in the big stainless sink. "Alright, Meemaw, let's get to work."

We fell into a comfortable rhythm, and as I peeled potatoes, I couldn't help but think about Faith. She'd gotten under my skin, and I wanted to know when we'd be able to see each other again.

It wouldn't be anytime soon. Right now, I needed to focus on Meemaw and making sure this Thanksgiving was as perfect as every other one we'd spent together.

---

### Faith

CLUTCHING THE STEERING WHEEL, my knuckles were as white as the sheet of snow blowing over the road in front of me. What was I thinking, trying to get out on a day like today?

It seemed like a good idea at the time. I needed something to distract me from the spiral of despair that had taken over since I found that stupid piece of paper. For the past week, I'd racked my brain, trying to figure out how someone could have gotten access to that page. Thanksgiving break couldn't have come at a better time. Most of the students had left campus for the holiday, and I didn't feel so threatened.

Dante had been right about not finding another place in town to complete my volunteer hours for the month. Desperate to make my quota, I'd called the Hinkley Senior Center and committed to an afternoon of serving turkey to seniors. Mom and I had always volunteered at a soup kitchen or homeless shelter on Thanksgiving. We cooked and served others, then went home for a feast of our own.

I'd been on the road for three hours and had no idea how much farther I had to go. I glanced over just in time to catch a sign, half-covered in snow. Great, five more miles. I let out a giant sigh and tried to lighten up on my white-knuckled grip on the wheel. I'd be there soon.

Twenty minutes later, I pulled into the parking lot of the Hinkley Senior Center. Not too many brave souls out tonight. A handful of other cars occupied a few spaces in the lot. If I'd driven all this way for nothing, I was going to be pretty disappointed.

I trudged through the knee-high drifts to the front door and pushed it open. A gust of wind sent it crashing into the wall and blew me, and a good amount of snow, into the room.

My hands scrambled to push the wet, icy hair out of my face. The door slammed shut behind me, and I looked out onto about two dozen of Hinkley's seniors, some of them frozen, forks in mid-air, in the middle of their Thanksgiving dinner. All conversation had come to a grinding halt. They stared at me, and I stared right back.

Movement in the kitchen caught my eye. Sailing through the swinging double doors, a red and white checkered apron tied around his waist, with his hands encased in oven mitts and carrying a giant pot, came Dante.

# CHAPTER 19

## *Faith*

"HERE COME MORE POTATOES." Dante stopped, set the pan down on the buffet, and squinted across the room. "Faith?"

Reassured I wasn't some turkey thief out to steal their meal, the seniors resumed eating and talking. A smiling older woman joined Dante, and they came toward me together.

"Faith, what the hell—" He looked at the older woman. "I mean, what in the world are you doing here?"

"You said they needed volunteers. I called and checked and told them I'd be happy to help."

"We sure didn't think you'd show up with this storm. Come on, sugar, you must be colder than a well digger's belt buckle. Let's get you some cocoa." The woman took me by the arm and propelled me toward the electric fireplace plugged into the wall. "Here you go. Sit a spell and let your toes thaw out."

Someone pressed a warm mug of cocoa into my hands as I sat down at a long table by the fake fire.

Dante had followed us and walked around to face me. "You should have told me you were coming."

"Are you going to introduce me to your lady friend?" the older woman asked.

Before I had the chance to turn that phrase over in my head, Dante put a hand to his brow and shook his head.

"Faith, I'd like to introduce you to my grandmother, Dolores Bishop."

My eyes widened in surprise. "Your grandmother?"

"The one and only." Dante wrapped his arm around the older woman's shoulders.

"I'm his Meemaw. Now tell me, how do you two know each other?"

My face flushed, and it didn't have anything to do with the heat from the fire.

"We, uh, we work on campus together," Dante said.

A smile crinkled the corners of Meemaw's eyes, and she patted my arm. "Dinner's about done now, sugar, but we'll fix you a plate and get something warm in your stomach."

"I'm sorry it took me so long to get here. You don't need to feed me. I came to help you."

"Don't you worry. There will be plenty to do." Meemaw touched Dante's arm. "Now go fix Faith and yourself a plate of food before Bugsy Divots eats all the potatoes." She put a hand up to her mouth and confided to me in a loud whisper, "He's got a thing for my taters."

"Yes, ma'am," Dante said.

"Dante will take good care of you, sugar. I'll be back in a flash, just need to go check on the next batch of rolls." Meemaw patted me on the shoulder then took off toward the kitchen.

I smiled and watched Dante walk over to the long table laden with food. It wouldn't kill me to spend an afternoon in the same building with him. It's not like he was going to grab my ass or come onto me in front of the senior citizen brigade. Plus, his grandmother sure was a hoot.

He came back a few minutes later carrying two paper plates piled high with a traditional Thanksgiving dinner with all the trimmings.

"I wasn't sure what you'd like." He set an overflowing plate down in front of me.

"It all looks delicious."

"Let me go grab silverware and some napkins. Do you want lemonade or iced tea?"

"Lemonade would be great, thanks." I leaned back in my chair and watched him walk away again, taking a moment to enjoy the view. A minute later he was back.

"Thank you," I said, as he handed me some plastic silverware and a napkin. He set my drink down next to me. "This looks wonderful."

"Yeah, just don't eat the Jell-O salad."

"Why not?"

"Mrs. MacNamara makes it." He scooted his chair in next to mine. "I think last year she put black beans in it instead of raisins. You just never know what she's going to throw in there."

"Thanks for the warning. Oh, and I really like your apron."

Dante reached back and untied the strings, then whipped the apron over his head. "Meemaw's a stickler for the rules. I'm surprised she didn't make me wear a hairnet."

"Now that I'd like to see." I smiled at the thought of him with a blue net over his head. He'd probably still look hot.

As we tucked into our meal, I looked around. The space was comfortable enough. Bookshelves lined the cheery yellow walls, stacked with paperbacks, puzzles, and board games. A giant television sat up against one wall, and long tables filled in the center of the room.

"It's like a rec room for seniors," Dante said between bites of stuffing and mashed potatoes. "Meemaw's been coming here for years. They have card clubs, sewing stuff, Bingo. Keeps her out of trouble." He glanced over at where Meemaw stood fidgeting with the food on the buffet.

I saw the love in his eyes. "She must be very special to you."

"She is. She raised me, pretty much by herself." He wiped the corner of his mouth with the paper napkin.

My eyes lingered on his lips. "So, you grew up around here, then?"

"Yep, about ten miles outside of town. I hated it at the time. Looking back, it was probably the best place for me."

"What do you mean?"

Dante fiddled with his fork. "Let's just say I went through a few years of soul searching. I caused Meemaw a lot of grief before I settled down." His gaze met mine as he stuffed an entire roll into his mouth.

I swallowed a bite of stuffing, forcing it past the lump in my throat. Those eyes, I could literally drown in them when he focused all his attention on me.

What kind of trouble had he caused as a kid? I pictured him shirtless, straddling a giant motorcycle. I'd let it go for now. Besides, I'd been the one to make the rules, and learning more about each other wasn't part of our agreement.

Meemaw finished messing with the buffet and walked toward us. "How is everything?"

"It's delicious. I'm so sorry I wasn't here to help with the cooking."

"Pshaw, don't you worry about it. I have a special job for you and Dante if you're willing to help?"

"Of course." It was the least I could do seeing as how I'd missed out on the entire meal prep process.

Dante smiled and shook his head, his mouth full of green bean casserole.

"Oh, you just stop that." Meemaw playfully slapped his arm.

He finished chewing and swallowed. "Be careful, Faith. She has a way of coercing unsuspecting people into doing her bidding."

I smiled and took a sip of my lemonade. Seeing this side of Dante, how playful and loving he was with his grandmother, cast him in a bit of a new light. "I'd be happy to help with whatever you need, Mrs. Bishop."

Meemaw gave Dante a triumphant smile. "See, my boy, not everyone thinks I have ulterior motives."

He raised his hands in surrender. "Okay, okay, what exactly is this special job you have for us?"

---

### Dante

I FOLLOWED Meemaw back to the kitchen. As soon as the swinging doors closed behind us, she whirled around and grabbed my arm.

"She's the one, isn't she?" she asked.

I studied her face before responding. Her eagerness to believe I might have actually brought a girl back to meet her filled her eyes with hope.

"Um, Faith's a—"

"Oh sugar, you don't have to tell me. I can see it for myself." She clucked her tongue and moved over to the stove to stir the gravy. "I'm proud of you, my boy. I know it's not easy for you to risk your heart again after what that Cheryl did to you."

"Meemaw, I—"

She turned and winked at me. "Faith seems like a lovely girl, and I can't wait to get to know her. We'll have plenty of time to chat later. Right now, I need the two of you to help me out with that little project."

Wouldn't do any good to try to dissuade her. Once Meemaw made up her mind about something, she'd dig in her heels and hold her ground. Besides, how was I to explain the exact nature of my involvement with Faith? It would be easier to just let her believe what she wanted for the time being. Faith would be on her way back to town soon enough anyway, so no need to get her involved in my little distortion of the truth. And if Meemaw thought I had something going, that would get her off my back for a while. Seemed like a win-win for everyone.

"All right, old woman. What do you need us to do?"

# CHAPTER 20

## Dante

TWENTY MINUTES LATER, Faith and I climbed into the old pickup truck, a stack of takeout containers balanced on the bench seat between us. Meemaw had tasked us with our own version of meals on wheels, delivering Thanksgiving dinners to those who couldn't make it to the senior center. I could never say no to her, and it seemed Faith had also fallen under her spell. As I turned the key, the truck rumbled to life.

"Where to?" I asked.

Faith consulted the handwritten list. "Looks like Mrs. Tierney is our first stop. It says the apartment over the drugstore?"

I watched as she studied the list, resisting the urge to reach over and tuck a strand of hair behind her ear. This girl did something to me, touched some part of me deep inside, a place I hadn't visited in a long, long time. She looked up and caught me staring.

"What?" She self-consciously wiped at her cheek. "Do I have food on my face or something?"

I laughed. "Nah. Let's get going. Knowing Meemaw, she'll have another job waiting for us when we get back."

We pulled out of the lot and took a left on Main. Mrs. Tierney was thrilled to see us and insisted we join her for coffee while she ate her meal. From there, we made a delivery to Mr. Sanders, who spent fifteen minutes showing me his collection of Civil War memorabilia. We only managed to leave after I promised to stop by the next time I was in town. The rest of the afternoon was a blur of stops, ending with a visit to Mr. Branson, my high school English teacher. He answered the door and welcomed us in.

"Well, Dante Bishop, aren't you a sight for sore eyes? Come in, come in."

"Hi, Mr. Branson. Happy Thanksgiving. Meemaw noticed you couldn't make it to the center, so she sent us over with dinner for you."

Mr. Branson took the container of food and ushered us into the kitchen. "Your grandmother is a powerhouse, Dante. I don't know where she finds her energy. If she's drinking from some secret fountain of youth, you've got to tell me about it." He transferred the food to a plate and put it in the microwave, then turned to face us. "Where are your manners, Mr. Bishop? Aren't you going to introduce me to your friend?"

"Sorry, Mr. Branson. This is Faith."

"The pleasure is all mine, Faith." Mr. Branson shook her hand.

"It's nice to meet you," Faith said with a sincere smile.

"You can call me Don," he told her. Looking at me, he added, "You still have to call me Mr. Branson."

I laughed. "Old habits die hard, huh?"

The microwave beeped, and Mr. Branson took his plate and grabbed some silverware from the drawer. "Shall we?" He walked into the dining room, clearly expecting us to follow.

We joined him at the table and sat down to keep him company while he ate.

"So, Mr. Branson, Faith's a professor in the English Department," I said.

"Just an adjunct," she added.

Mr. Branson raised an eyebrow and looked up from his sweet potatoes. "Really? Did Dante tell you I was his English teacher?"

"No, he didn't mention it," Faith said. "Was he a good student?"

Mr. Branson chewed a bite of turkey. "When he wanted to be." He gave me a pointed look.

"Aw, come on, Mr. Branson. You loved me. You always gave me A's in your classes."

Mr. Branson looked at Faith. "He had his moments. You should have him show you his poetry sometime."

My cheeks ignited. Leave it to Mr. Branson to remember the freaking poetry. I'd gone through a particularly angsty period during my junior year of high school, and when Mr. Branson gave the class a few poetry assignments, I'd found a release.

"Really?" Faith gave me an appraising look.

I picked at a hangnail on my thumb and tried to think of a way to change the subject. "So how about those Colts?"

For the next twenty minutes, Mr. Branson and I debated the possibility of the Colts making the playoffs. We finally got up to leave, and he walked us to the door.

"Tell your grandmother thank you for the meal. As usual, it was delicious."

"I'll be sure to pass along the compliment," I said.

Mr. Branson took Faith's hand. "It was a pleasure meeting you, Faith." He lowered his head and looked at her above his glasses. "The poetry, dear, ask him about his poetry."

She smiled. "I will."

I nudged her toward the door. "Take care, Mr. Branson. I'll see you around."

Mr. Branson put a hand on my arm. "That right there is a beautiful girl. Don't let her get away."

I removed his hand and gave him a handshake. "Is that the dementia talking, Mr. B?"

"Oh, be gone with you. Remember what I said." Mr. Branson shooed us through the door and back out into the snowy evening.

I opened the door, and Faith climbed up into the cab. "Poetry, huh?" The reflection of the streetlight sparkled in her eyes as she smiled at me.

"He must have me confused with someone else." No way in hell was I showing her that stuff, even if she did sound interested. I shut the door behind her and trudged through the snow to the other side.

When we got back to the senior center, Meemaw and her crew had all the tables cleaned off and the dishes washed. She and a handful of women sat at one of the tables playing cards.

"Good, you're back. Do you want to join us?"

"Not on your life, old woman." I turned to Faith. "She's a card shark. Don't let her suck you into a game."

"Oh, pshaw." Meemaw waved a hand at me. "It's just a friendly game of cards."

"Don't listen to her, Faith. How much has she taken you for, Mrs. O'Leary?"

"Just fifty cents so far," Mrs. O'Leary said.

"It's only a quarter a game, dear," Meemaw said.

Faith laughed. "High stakes, huh?"

"Ask her how she paid for her new sewing machine." I deposited a kiss on top of Meemaw's head.

Meemaw glowed. "Let's wrap it up, ladies. I need to get home. I promised this boy some homemade pecan pie." The women cleared away the cards, and Meemaw walked through the building, turning off lights.

"Thanks for a wonderful day, Mrs. Bishop. I'm so sorry I wasn't here to help out more," Faith said.

"Don't you give it another thought, sugar. You helped out plenty."

Faith gave her a quick hug. "I guess I'll just head out. Dante, I'll see you back in town."

Meemaw held her arm. "Just where do you think you're going, hon?"

Faith gave her a confused look. "Well, back to Newbridge, of course."

I snickered, and Meemaw snorted. "In this?" Meemaw gestured to the heavy snow still falling around us. "Get in the truck, sweetie. The only place you're going is home with us. Besides, I want to get to know you better if you're going to be spending time around my grandson." She waddled off toward the passenger side as fast as her short little legs would carry her.

"After you," I gestured toward the truck.

"But—"

"Don't bother arguing with her. You'll lose." I smiled to myself. As much as I'd enjoy seeing Faith go head-to-head with my grandmother, the outcome was predetermined, at least in my mind. "Besides, there's no way your car would make it back to the highway. The plows haven't even come through."

Faith bit her bottom lip. "I suppose I could come for the pie. Then we can see how the weather looks."

"Are y'all comin' or am I gonna freeze to death in this here parking lot and meet my maker?" Meemaw called from the truck.

I raised an eyebrow at Faith and pointed toward the truck.

"Well, okay, just for pie," she said, already taking cautious steps in the snow.

Sure, pie and who knew what else Meemaw had planned. She was known far and wide for her meddling, which was precisely why I hadn't mentioned a girl—much less introduced her to one—at least since junior year. One thing was for sure—it was going to be an interesting evening.

# CHAPTER 21

## *Faith*

I PUSHED BACK from the table. I thought I was full before, but now I felt stuffed tighter than the turkey I'd helped devour hours before.

"Worth the drive?" Dante asked.

"Oh my gosh, yes. I don't see how you can resist driving down here for dinner every night. Mrs. Bishop, that pie was delicious."

Meemaw beamed but waved away the compliment. "Some folks like sewin', some like readin' the news. My thing's cookin'. Always has been." She reached over and rested her hand on Dante's arm. "I just wish I had someone to cook for more often."

"I know, I know." Dante shook his head and stood up from the table. "I don't get here as often as I should." He reached in front of me to take my plate, and his hand brushed mine, sending a shiver up my arm.

"Oh honey, I don't mean nothin' by that. I just miss you, that's all."

"I know, Meemaw."

"Well, I don't know about y'all, but I'm just plum tuckered. I'm gonna turn in." Meemaw stood up from the table and pushed in her chair. "When y'all are ready for bed, Dante, you go ahead and show Faith to your room. The sheets are clean. You can take the couch."

"But—" I started to protest.

"Don't try to argue with her. I told you before, it won't do any good." Dante pulled Meemaw in for a hug. "Goodnight, old woman."

She wrapped her arms around him and swatted at his tush. "You be nice now."

"I'm always nice." He drew back and smiled at her, giving her a kiss on the cheek.

I felt like an intruder, watching the intimate moment between him and his grandmother. This glimpse at his softer side was both intriguing and a little disconcerting. So what if he's nice to little old ladies? He still wasn't part of the plan. No distractions.

Meemaw walked down the hall and disappeared through a doorway, closing the door behind her.

"Dante, I—"

"Look, Faith, I know you're not used to catering to the whims of a bossy old woman, but she will absolutely skin me alive if she wakes up in the morning and you're not here." He dunked the dirty dessert plates in soapy water and scrubbed what little remained of the pecan pie away.

I looked around. "I can't stay here."

Dante rinsed and stacked the clean plates in the drying rack. "If she thinks I let you drive home in this, I'll never hear the end of it. I'm not taking you back to your car. You'll have to wait till morning. Give the plows a chance to get out on the roads. I'll follow you home tomorrow."

I stifled a yawn. Meemaw's place looked so warm and cozy. The thought of braving the treacherous highways wasn't appealing. Even I could see it was smarter to stay put for the night. "Okay, fine. But where am I going to sleep?"

We walked into the TV room, and I looked over the choices. A single recliner faced the ancient television set, and a crocheted blanket draped over the back of a small, over-stuffed couch.

"You take my bed. I'll sleep out here," Dante said.

The thought of sleeping in Dante's bed sent a wave of heat through me. No, not here. I couldn't justify succumbing to more "research" at his Meemaw's house.

I looked him up and down, all six foot plus of him. "You won't fit on the couch."

"I'll be fine. It won't be the first time I've passed out with my feet over the edge. Are you tired? Do you want to watch TV for a while?"

"Sure." I sat down in one corner of the couch. Dante turned off the overhead light and flopped down on the other side, leaving the middle cushion empty between us. He put his feet up on the coffee table and grabbed the remote.

How did it come to this? If it was some other regular guy sitting next to me, it might almost feel normal. But being in Dante's grandmother's house? With the one man who'd managed to get under my skin not even two feet away? It was too surreal. *Just act normal. You only have to survive until morning.*

"What are you in the mood for?" he asked, flipping through the channels.

*Mmm, your fingers deep inside me.* Holy crap. Where did that come from? I cleared my throat. *Normal starts now.*

"Doesn't matter." I stretched my arms out and tucked my legs up underneath me. A little bit of tension eased from my body.

"We can always pick up where we left off last week." He reached over and ran a finger down the outside of my thigh.

"Come on, didn't hanging out at the Senior Center all day, talking about stuffing turkeys and mashing potatoes get you in the mood?"

I rolled my eyes. "No. And don't you dare start in on the stuffing jokes."

"Stuffing jokes?" A smug grin spread across his face. "What? Like, I've been wanting to stuff you all day?"

I groaned.

"Or how about, baby, I've got your stuffing right here?"

I couldn't help but laugh. "That's awful."

"Bad, huh?"

"Really bad."

He crossed the couch and straddled my lap, pinning me to the cushion with one muscular leg on either side of mine. My body immediately revved into hot and bothered mode.

"Enough with the stuffing jokes." His lips brushed my ear. "I bet there's some of that homemade whipped cream in the fridge."

My heart thundered. Dante and whipped cream. I licked my lips, imagining how it would taste if I smeared it all over his amazing body. His tongue rimmed the shell of my ear, making me struggle to remember why this was such a bad idea.

I slid my hands into the back pockets of his jeans, urging him closer.

"You smell so good." His hands cradled my head, tilting my face up to press his lips to mine.

The blare from the television's weather alert system pulled my attention away from the amazing things he was doing with his tongue.

"This is a test of the Emergency Broadcast System…"

I snatched the throw pillow and thumped it against his side. "Get off me. We can't do this—not in your Meemaw's house," I hissed. For crying out loud, the man had no shame.

He defended himself against the pillow, his laughs muffled. "I'm just sayin', she's a heavy sleeper. She wouldn't hear a thing."

I stole the remote and continued to channel surf, finally settling on *It's A Wonderful Life*.

"Okay, I give. If you'd rather hang out watching Jimmy Stewart make a play for Donna Reed than play with me..." Dante leaned back, putting his hands behind his head.

There was nothing I'd rather do in that moment than follow the trail of desire between us to see where it would lead. Whipped cream was just the beginning. I could imagine an entire night full of kissing and licking and touching and squeezing and tasting and...grrrrrrr.

I clamped my arms over my midsection and tried to focus on the movie playing out on the screen. No matter what I did, I couldn't avoid the undercurrent of awareness of the hard mass of muscle to my left.

Dismissing the urge to glance his way, I kept my eyes trained on the TV in front of me. Mary flirted with George Bailey at the school dance as the first sparks of romance ignited between them. Every part of me hummed, acutely aware of Dante's presence just a few feet away. How in the world had I ended up here, in this room, with him?

His eyes rested half-closed, and he looked like he was falling asleep. He sighed, and his chest rose and fell in a hypnotic rhythm. I wanted to lean over, bridge the distance between us, and put my head on his shoulder. His gray t-shirt stretched tight over his frame, and I could see the outline of his pecs underneath. My body remembered how it felt to be trapped under his weight in the car. Every last part of me ached to reach out and touch him, but I resisted.

Dante's head slumped down on his chest and his breathing deepened. I took off his glasses and set them down on the table. Without his glasses on, he looked so vulnerable.

Long lashes brushed his cheeks and I let my gaze wander over his nose, his lips, and the stubble over his upper lip, committing his face to memory.

As George and Mary clung together on the screen, I sat back on my cushion and struggled to keep myself from wrapping myself in Dante's arms.

# CHAPTER 22

## *Dante*

I OPENED my eyes and couldn't figure out where I was for a moment. The light from the TV reflected off the walls of the living room. Meemaw's. That's right, I was at Meemaw's.

I became intensely aware of a warm body snuggled up against me. I was on my back, stretched out the full length of the couch. Faith's head rested on my abs, her head just inches away from the one part of my anatomy that appeared to already be fully awake. Crap. Just being around her got me hard. The more I tried to mentally squash my desire, the more my body reacted on its own.

I shifted on the couch in an attempt to ease out from underneath her. Her body rolled slightly, and I wrapped my arm around her back before she slid to the floor. She gave a little moan in her sleep and burrowed deeper into my side. Her hand came up to rest under her cheek, with her forearm right on my crotch.

Hell. I ran through the starting line-up of the Colts in my head. Recited every NASDAQ symbol I could remember. It wasn't working. Her arm moved again, brushing against my hard-on. *Hold it together, Bishop.* She threw a leg over mine and ran her hand over my chest.

"Faith?" I whispered.

"Mmm."

"You awake?"

Her eyes blinked open. "What? Where am I?" She scrambled to sit up, but her legs were tangled in mine.

"Hey, it's okay. I've got you."

She propped herself up on an elbow and looked up at me. "What happened?"

"You fell asleep." I'd wanted to push that strand of hair back all day. I finally let myself brush it off her face and tuck it behind her ear.

"I'm sorry. Oh, I must be crushing you." She dragged her legs out from in between mine and stood up.

"It's all right. I kind of like it." I shifted to a seated position, took her hand, and pulled her back down on the couch next to me. She was rocking that sexy, bed-head, mussed up look and all I wanted was to pin her to the couch and fuck some sense into her.

I pressed her hand to my crotch. "Can you feel what you do to me? We can be quiet. Do you want to?"

"We're in your grandmother's living room," she whispered. Her head turned and our lips accidentally brushed. My mouth pressed down on hers and I leaned into her. I wasn't imagining it. She was kissing me back. As I buried my hands in her hair, her tongue responded to mine. I pressed my mouth to her neck, trailing kisses from her collarbone up to her earlobe.

"You feel so good," I whispered into her hair.

She writhed under me, sending my arousal level from excited to explosive. Her hands slid under my shirt and played across my ribs. I couldn't get close enough to her. Fuck. I wanted to be inside her, to completely fill her.

I pushed a hand up under her shirt and ran a finger under her bra. Her skin was so soft. The other pressed down between her legs and fumbled with the button of her jeans. Her legs kicked out at a throw pillow, knocking it off the couch and sending my glasses clattering onto the floor.

"Your grandmother," she said, her voice husky.

I sat up and shook my head to clear it. She laid sprawled out underneath me. Her shirt lifted up over her bra on one side and the button of her jeans was undone, showing a glimpse of red panties. What in the hell was it about this girl? I grabbed her hand and hauled her up off the couch, then flicked off the TV.

"Follow me." I held her hand in mine and tugged her down the hall.

Guiding her through the doorway to my bedroom, I pushed the door shut behind us. She whirled around and pressed against me, pinning me against the door. Whipping my t-shirt up and over my head, she attacked my chest with her mouth. Her kisses left a trail of fire in their wake, and I groaned.

I tangled my hands in her hair and resisted the urge to haul her harder into me. Her fingers made quick business of my button and as she pushed my jeans down my legs, I stepped out of them, lifting her up and carrying her the few short steps to my bed.

I deposited her on the bedspread and hovered over her on my hands and knees. She put a finger to my lips, and I kissed it. Then she trailed it from my lips, down my neck, my chest, and into my boxer briefs. Fuck. I wasn't going to lose it so easily.

I grabbed her hands up in one of mine and pinned them above her head. With the other, I lifted her sweater up and over her bra. Then I reached behind her and undid the hook, releasing her breasts. I played with one nipple, rolling it between my finger and thumb. As it hardened in my hand, I took it in my mouth, sucking and kissing and licking.

She closed her eyes and sighed. "Dante, oh god."

"Tell me there's not something between us, Faith." I raised my eyes to look at her. She couldn't deny it. Not with the way her body responded to mine. She had to feel it, too.

I could just make out the lines of her face in the dim light from my alarm clock. She didn't respond. I started working on the other breast and she moaned, making a half-hearted attempt to move her hands away.

I released her hands and lifted her sweater up and over her head. She pulled her arms free from her bra straps and pushed her jeans down. Panties to briefs, our bodies clashed together in a frenzied wave of heat. She rocked into me; the pressure on my dick making me crazy to possess her. Her hands roamed up and down my back as her mouth waged an assault on mine.

Damn, I hadn't seen this coming, not from her. Her nails raked my shoulders, and she opened her legs to me. I couldn't take much more. I pushed her panties down with one hand. She rolled on top and straddled me. I could just make out the edges of the swirly black ink rounding her hip and bleeding over onto her navel. I ran a thumb over the edge of her tattoo.

She was so fucking wet I could feel her through my shorts. Jesus Christ, who was this? Not the reserved fucking English prof. I reached a hand over to the nightstand drawer. I'd better have a condom. My hand fumbled around inside, and I felt a foil packet. I brought it up to the light of the alarm clock while she gyrated into me. Dammit, I'd have to hurry. I ripped it open and grabbed the familiar circle of latex.

"Let me." Faith took it from me and pushed my briefs down to my knees. She took me in her hands and expertly unrolled the condom onto my length. I'd been with girls who liked to take charge once in a while, but Faith didn't seem like the type. Coming from her, it was even more of a turn on. She raised herself up over me, then eased me into her, one slow inch at a time.

I groaned. Fuck. Not going to. She wasn't going to make me come. Two could play this game. I flipped her over on her back and she spread her legs, wrapping them up over my shoulders and hooking her feet behind my neck. She tightened around me, drawing me deep inside her and sending me to the edge.

I'd never been so frantic to possess someone before. I pounded into her, and she gasped. *She likes that, does she?* Her head whipped from side to side as her hips rocked into me. I pulled back and thrust into her again, sending her head bouncing into the headboard.

"Are you okay?" I slowed.

"Don't you dare stop." She grabbed a pillow and threw it behind her head. Her body crashed into mine in a frenzy, and she grabbed onto my arms, pushing her hips up against me and plunging me deep inside.

Hell, I couldn't stop if I wanted to. I continued to pound into her. She clenched around me, then shuddered as she reached her climax. The moment she finished, I let myself go, releasing everything into her.

My body completely drained, I collapsed on top of her.

# CHAPTER 23

*Faith*

I GRUNTED with the effort of trying to push Dante off. He was dead weight. What got into me tonight? Dante roused parts of me I didn't even know existed. I didn't regret it, and I'd enjoyed myself. But I had to get a grip. *It's just for research. I can end it whenever I need to.* I'd almost managed to wriggle out from underneath him when he flung an arm around me, drawing me tight against him.

"That was amazing." He nuzzled into me with his scruffy chin, dropping kisses on my ear, neck, and shoulder.

"I hope we didn't wake up your grandmother."

"She sleeps like a log."

I rolled away and turned to face him. The moonlight coming through the slats of the mini blinds washed over him, casting a bluish tone over his perfect naked body. We'd never managed to get under the covers, so he was sprawled out on top. I wanted nothing more than to run a hand over his back and the curve of his magnificent ass.

My fingers trailed over the dark ink on his hip. "Tell me about your tattoo."

He sat up and rubbed a hand across his chin. Grabbing a

tissue from the nightstand, he took care of the condom and walked over to the desk, depositing it into a trashcan on the floor.

"My Dad was a Marine. Killed overseas. When I turned eighteen, I wanted to join up. Finish the job he started, right?"

"Oh my gosh. I'm so sorry."

Dante walked over to the side of the bed, not embarrassed at all being fully naked in front of me. "They wouldn't take me. Crappy vision and all. I got his dog tag inked on my gut instead."

"That must have been really hard to grow up without a dad."

"Yeah, sucked."

"What about your mom?"

"My folks weren't ever an item. They met when they were both counselors at some summer camp in New York. When my mom found out she was pregnant, she came looking for him, but he'd already shipped out."

He sat down on the edge of the bed, and I rested my hand on his knee. "So what happened?"

"Meemaw took her in until I was born. She thought about making an adoption plan, but Meemaw said no grand-baby of hers was going to be raised by strangers." He lifted his eyes to meet mine, and a slight smile flitted across his lips.

"Your grandmother's an amazing woman."

"Yeah."

"And your mom? Do you still talk to her?"

The smile morphed into a scowl. "Nah. She sends a card once a year. Hell, if she doesn't want anything to do with me, I don't need her."

I could tell I'd hit on a sore spot. No wonder he came across as so guarded and aloof.

"How about you? Were you a daddy's girl?" he asked.

Where was my underwear? I glanced around the room. "My dad split when I was five."

"You mean to tell me we have something in common?"

"We're not supposed to be talking, remember? Just sex."

"Hey, you started it. Looking for these?" My panties dangled from one of his fingers, and I snatched them away. I pulled them on, followed by my jeans. He put an arm around me, turning me to face him, and ran a finger down my collarbone, then under my breast. My toes curled. Not going to go there again. For God's sake, we were in his Meemaw's house.

I turned away. "Look, Dante—"

He pressed up against me and caught my mouth up with his. I pushed against his rock-solid chest.

"I can't. This was um, fun and all, but I just can't."

"Can't what?"

"We agreed to keep it physical. I can't do grandmas and family secrets and sharing wounds from the past."

"So it's okay for you to ask me personal questions, but I can't reciprocate? Jeez, I'm just trying to get to know you a little better."

My face burned. As much as I appreciated the multiple "O's," he was getting too close. Sex was great. But a relationship, no. There was no time for a relationship.

"I don't want you to get to know me better." I yanked my sweater on over my head. To hell with my bra.

"Damn, what are you so afraid of? I'm just making conversation."

"Well, stop. If you want to call it off, fine."

"What are you trying to hide?" Dante stood bathed in the moonlight before me, a perfect specimen of the male species.

I needed to get out of there. Being that close to him was making it hard to think. A guy like Dante and a girl like me...it was all wrong.

"I'll just go out to the couch." I brushed past him and

escaped out into the hall. The wooden floorboards creaked as I tiptoed back to the living room and settled on the couch, snuggling under a homemade throw. What was he trying to do to me? The sex I could handle. But there wasn't room for him to start messing around in my head. The sooner I got back to Newbridge and away from Dante, the better off I'd be.

### Dante

THE SMELL of coffee roused me from a deep sleep. I woke up, fully naked in between the sheets. As I turned my head on the pillow, the scent of Faith's shampoo surrounded me.

So, I didn't dream it. I wasn't sure what I'd done wrong the night before, but it was obvious she couldn't wait to get out from under me. She'd seemed to enjoy herself. What the fuck? I rubbed my eyes and yawned. It was better this way, anyway. I didn't need the hassle.

I pulled on my clothes from the night before and walked into the bright kitchen. Sun reflected off the snow outside and streamed through the windows. Faith and Meemaw sat at the kitchen table, a carafe of coffee between them. I walked over to Meemaw and kissed her on the top of her head.

"Good morning, my boy. How did you sleep?"

I glanced at Faith, but she was busy studying the handle of her mug and wouldn't look up at me. "Great, I slept great. I must have really worn myself out yesterday." I turned to the cupboard and reached for a mug.

"Well, that's nice," Meemaw said. "I thought I told you to give Faith the bed? Poor girl, she probably didn't get a wink of sleep on that ole couch."

I looked over at Faith, still intent on her mug. She looked

up at Meemaw and smiled. "The couch was perfectly fine. Dante offered the bed,"—she glanced up at me and a slight flush danced across her neck—"but I insisted."

"Yep, she was pretty adamant about not sleeping in the bedroom." I sat down across from her at the table and poured the hot steaming coffee into my mug. Faith knit her brows into a frown.

Meemaw got up from the table and started hauling pans out of the cabinet. "What do you two want for breakfast? I've got some fresh bacon from that ole hog Bugsy finally put down."

Faith pushed back from the table to stand. "I really ought to be getting back, Mrs. Bishop." She looked over at me. "Do you think you could give me a ride to my car now?"

"Oh, so soon? I was hoping you could stay for a while." Meemaw set the giant frying pan on the counter and walked over to Faith. "I wanted the chance to have a nice long talk and get to know you better since you and Dante have become so close."

I studied her over the brim of my cup. "Faith doesn't appreciate conversation that much, Meemaw. She's all about just getting things done."

"Dante! Don't be rude."

Faith glared at me then turned to Meemaw. "I'm sorry. I just have a lot of work I need to get done this weekend."

"I understand, sugar. Dante, can you run her over to her car? You should probably follow her back—"

"Oh no, that's okay. I don't want him to miss out on any more time with you." Faith gave her a quick hug. "I'll be fine. I checked the weather report on my phone, and it said the highways are all clear now."

"Well, okay." Meemaw wasn't used to someone challenging one of her orders.

"Thanks so much for dinner yesterday and letting me

crash here. It was the nicest Thanksgiving I've had in a long time."

I scoffed and pushed back from the table, then padded back to the bedroom with bare feet and returned with my socks and boots. "Let's go, Faith. Wouldn't want to keep you here any longer against your will."

She thrust her arms into her jacket and opened the front door. I threw my coat on and snagged the keys to the truck off the hook. "Be back in a few, Meemaw."

We trudged through the deep snow to the driveway. I didn't bother trying to open the door for her. The sooner I got her out of my sight, the sooner she'd disappear out from under my skin. I fired up the truck and threw it into four-wheel drive.

My arm stretched across the back of the bench seat, and I looked over my shoulder as I reversed and turned the truck around. Faith scooted as far as possible to the other side of the cab, pressing herself up against the door.

"Careful you don't fall out." I removed my arm from the seat behind her and put both hands on the wheel.

"Hey."

"What?" I glared at her, not sure why I was so pissed off. If she didn't want to acknowledge the fucking fireworks that went off every time we were close enough to breathe the same air, it was fine with me.

"I'm sorry. I just can't get involved with anyone right now."

"It sure didn't seem that way when you had your ankles wrapped around my neck last night, telling me I'd better not fucking stop."

She gazed out the window as the snow-covered fields whizzed by. "Forget it. You wouldn't understand."

Like hell I wouldn't. I didn't want to get involved with anyone either. But there was something about her. Something that just wouldn't let me go. If she didn't want to acknowledge it, fine. I was better off without her anyway.

We rode in silence the rest of the way to the senior center. When we got there, she got out of the truck and quickly climbed inside her car.

Hell. I got out of the truck, grabbed the scraper, and began to brush the snow and ice off her windshield. Finished with the job, I leaned down to her driver's side window and she lowered the pane.

"Thanks." I could tell she was eager to go because she'd already thrown it in Drive.

"Yeah, see ya around." I patted her door, and she took off, slipping and sliding out of the lot until she hit the pavement on the road.

I climbed back into the truck and headed back to Meemaw's, hell-bent on getting the redhead with the gripping thighs out of my fucking mind.

# CHAPTER 24

## Faith

I SAT at my desk in the small office I shared with Murph. Not my ideal office mate, but adjunct faculty didn't have much say in which tiny, windowless box they got assigned. I needed to prepare lecture notes for my next class, but instead, I had opened up my latest steamy work-in-progress on the screen.

My night with Dante had unlocked a treasure chest of words from inside me, and over the weekend I found myself struggling to type fast enough to capture the story that flowed out of my fingertips onto the screen. What was it about him I found so inspiring? The ruggedly handsome good looks? His talented fingers?

When we first met, he'd claimed he had a gift for hitting the right spot. He hadn't been lying. But beyond the incredible, inspiring sex, he stirred up something inside me, something I wasn't sure I was ready to acknowledge.

My cell phone rang.

"Hey, Steph."

"It's new release day, Faith. How's my favorite author?

Any plans to go check out the bookstore this morning and see *Carnal Knowledge* on the shelves?"

"Come on, you know I'm incognito."

"When are you going to give up on that and embrace it? People love you. Your books are doing really well, and this latest one... whew... the gals in the office read it over the weekend and said their husbands wanted me to pass on their thanks. Steamy stuff, girl."

"Thanks. I just hope it clears enough to pay my rent for the next couple of months."

"I'm pretty sure that won't be a problem. Based on the reviews from your street team, it should be your best-selling book yet. They're all raving about it. Of course, all of them want to meet you. We're doing an author event in April in Chicago. That's not too far from you. Any interest?"

"I can't. You know I've got to keep it a secret. My job, my family... my future depends on it."

Steph sighed. "If you change your mind—"

"I won't. I've got a post ready to go for the blog. I'll send it over later today. Do you have any graphics you can add to it?"

Early on, Steph had come up with the brilliant idea to use an avatar as my profile picture. That way I could stay undercover and still have a way to connect with my readers.

"Yeah, I'll see what we can do. Good luck today, Faith. I'll keep you posted as the numbers roll in."

"Thanks. Talk to you soon."

I disconnected as the door crashed open and Murph stuck his head into the room.

"Hey, Faith, how was your Thanksgiving?"

I quickly switched screens. God forbid he catch a glimpse of my work in progress. He hung his coat on a hook behind the door and climbed over a stack of papers and books, flopping down in the chair behind the desk across from me.

"Oh, it was fine. How about yours?"

"Great." He set his coffee down and reached into his backpack for his laptop. "So is your application for taking over Middleford's classes ready?"

"Yeah, I worked on it over the weekend. I'm going to turn it in today. How about you?" I searched the pile of papers spread across my desk. "I know it's here somewhere."

Murph slid a big envelope from his bag. "Ready to go." He chewed on a fingernail while his computer booted up.

I continued to move papers around on the desk. Ah, found it. I placed the envelope on top of my keyboard so I wouldn't lose it again. "Whew, thought I lost it for a minute. Here it is."

Murph nodded. "So I was wondering if you wanted to go to the poetry slam at The Roastery next Sunday night?"

I glanced over at him as he spit a piece of fingernail toward the trash can. Ugh. Not a chance in hell. "Oh, I don't think I'm going to make it. Thanks though." When would Murph get the hint?

"I didn't mean with me. There's a big group of us going, and I just thought you might want to come."

"We'll see. I have a lot to do before winter break. If I get all my work done, sure, I might stop by." I fumbled for my earbuds. Maybe I could block him out with some tunes.

Before I got the cord untangled, a knock sounded at the door. We didn't usually get a lot of visitors during office hours, maybe an occasional undergrad looking for some help with an assignment, but otherwise it was pretty quiet.

"Come in!" Murph yelled.

We turned toward the door as Dante poked his head through. I let out an exasperated sigh. My stomach lurched at the sight of his stubbled cheeks, and I absentmindedly rubbed my hand along my jawbone where I still had a tiny bit of beard burn from our recent encounter. I'd been reliving our night together all weekend and had even written about it. The last thing I needed was to see him in the flesh.

"Hey, man. What's up?" Murph rose halfway from his chair and leaned across the desk for a manly handclasp/back-slap kind of thing.

Dante grabbed Murph's outstretched hand while his gaze darted from Murph to me. "Hey, Murph. How's it going?"

"Great, just great. I was just telling Faith here about my break. How was yours?"

I kept my head down, intent on my blank computer screen. *Go away, go away, go away!*

"It was okay. Thanksgiving was great. The rest of the weekend I just worked at the bar."

"Cool. What do you need, man?"

"I was hoping to talk to Faith for a minute."

My head shot up. What could he possibly want from me? No matter how great the sex was, as far as I was concerned, it was over. "I have to teach in a few minutes."

"It will only take a second."

"Oh yeah, what's going on?" Murph gave Dante a suspicious look. "Do you need to speak in private or something?"

"No. Murph, stay put. Whatever Dante has to say, he can say it here." My eyes challenged him to say anything personal in front of Murph. He wouldn't dare.

"Fine, if that's how you want it." Dante let his bag drop down to the desk. "I just wanted to return this." He reached in and pulled out my red lacy bra. "You left it the other night—"

"Oh, my god. Don't you think you could have given that to me in private?" I ripped it out of his hands and wadded it up as best I could, stuffing it in my top desk drawer.

Dante calmly zipped his bag back up and slung it over his shoulder. "I tried."

"What the fuck, man? I thought we had a deal?" Murph launched himself halfway out of his seat.

I pushed past Dante out into the hall, stumbling toward the bathroom. An army of angry hot tingles marched up my neck and spread across my face. I needed to splash some cool water on my cheeks. Unbelievable. I took a few deep breaths to calm the wave of anger rising in my gut. It wouldn't take long for Murph to tell everyone what happened. Gossip spread like wildfire through our department.

I hid out in the bathroom for about ten minutes, giving them enough time to get lost. When I got back to the office, they were both gone. Thank god. Reaching into my desk, I pulled out the bra and shoved it into my backpack

Dante's face flashed through my mind. Every milliliter of blood in my body rushed to my head as I recalled the look he'd given me when he plowed into me on the bed. My heart pounded, and I squeezed my legs together as my body remembered how he'd felt plunging deep inside of me.

No longer able to concentrate on work, I threw my things into my bag and decided to head to the classroom early. I could drop off my application on the way. Now if I could only find it again. As I rummaged through the pile on my desk, I saw a sticky note on the keyboard of my laptop.

*Headed to class and figured I'd drop off your application for you on the way.*

*Later,*
*Murph.*

Crap. At least I'd sealed the envelope so he couldn't read it on the way. With him gone, that was one less confrontation I'd have to worry about in the immediate future. I turned off my laptop and slid it into my bag.

I'd have to deal with Dante later. Right now, I had another crisis to handle. My mother's plane would be arriving soon. The fallout from the bomb Dante just dropped would cause some ripples. After everyone figured out my relationship with Claire, I feared I'd be doing disaster recovery from tsunami-level waves for months.

### Dante

I PUSHED through the throng of students coursing down the hall, embarrassed at the stunt I'd just pulled. It hadn't been necessary to dangle her bra in front of Murph. But she was so damn sanctimonious. It pissed me off that she'd gotten under my skin so bad.

How could she keep it so under control? An undeniable chemistry surged between us. Hell, I could practically see it crackle when I got near her. Yet she seemed to be able to turn it on and off at will. Damn.

Maybe it was just a physical thing. The guys at the office and at the bar had been telling me for weeks I needed to get laid. I guessed they were right. Whatever hold Faith had over me must be purely physical. Now that we'd consummated our combustible attraction a couple of times, I should be able to put her behind me and move on. Sounded good in theory. She probably wasn't going to let me get within a hundred yards of her now anyway, so I should be safe.

I walked across the snowy sidewalk to the student center. With about fifteen minutes before my check-in with my group's professor, I had time to kill. As I set my bag down on one of the mauve cloth loveseats in the main room of the student center, Jess waved at me from a table a few feet away.

I slumped down onto a cushion and scanned the room for another place to sit. It was too late. She'd already started my way.

"Hey, Dante."

"Hi, Jess."

"How was your break?" She reached the couch and gave me a smug grin as she towered over me.

"Um, it was fine. How about yours?"

"Pretty good. It was nice to see the family again. Did you do anything special?"

"No. Not really. Just worked a lot."

"I heard you might have seen Faith over the holiday?" The look on her face told me she already knew the answer to that question.

"Oh yeah? Who told you that?" Was Faith talking about me to Jess?

"I saw Murph in the hall a few minutes ago."

"Shit." I shoved my hands in my front pockets and glanced around the room for the giant douche bag. If Murph was still around, I'd pummel him.

"Faith didn't mention you guys are seeing each other."

"Oh yeah? Well, we're not. Listen, are you through interrogating me? I've got some work to do."

Jess gave me a small smile. "I suppose. Just..."

"What?" I asked, finally making eye contact.

"Faith needs to loosen up a bit. She's so wrapped up in planning for the future, she's not having any fun in the here and now. I think you'd be good for her. Let me know if I can help."

"Nothing to help with. She's made it crystal clear that I'm not part of whatever plan she's got going. Besides, I'm not interested." I picked up my bag. I could find somewhere else to kill the time. "See ya, Jess."

Jess's mouth screwed up and she brought a finger to her lips as if deep in thought. "I'll work on her."

I whirled around at her words, continuing to take steps backward. "Don't bother." I'd done just fine before I met Faith, and I'd be just fine now. I'd make sure of it.

# CHAPTER 25

## Faith

I STOOD and walked to the front of the room. As usual, a small crowd swarmed around my mother, everyone eager to get an autograph, a picture, or even just catch a few words. Claire's lecture had gone better than I expected. I'd stumbled through the introduction, but after she took her place at the podium, she'd held everyone captive for the rest of the hour. My mother had picked up a few traits from Clem and knew how to work a room. I stood at the edge of the fray, waiting for the crowd to disperse.

"So, she's your mom, huh?" Murph walked up beside me and gestured to where Claire stood, posing for yet another picture with one of my students.

"Yep." I held my notebook across my chest, my arms crossed over it, and rocked back and forth on my heels.

"You did a nice job of keeping that info to yourself."

Was that supposed to be a compliment? "Thanks."

Murph edged closer to me. "You did a nice job on the intro, too."

"Thanks again."

"That must be, uh, interesting having Claire Kepner as your mother."

I didn't know what he was after, but I refused to give him any more info about my private life. He'd already seen enough. "It has its ups and downs."

At that moment, Claire broke through the few remaining stragglers and walked over to us.

"That was fun. I always forget what a thrill it is to be up in front of a group." Her face glowed. The aftermath of being in front of a cluster of admirers was clearly good for her complexion. "Who's your friend?"

"Mom, this is Patrick Murphy. He teaches in the English Department with me."

Claire offered her hand. Murph grasped it in his and leaned down to kiss it.

"It's my pleasure, Mrs. Kepner."

"Well, aren't you a charmer?" Claire winked at him.

Murph let go of her hand and stood up straighter, the smile on his face showing his pleasure at the compliment.

"Hey, Mom, did you want to go grab something to eat?"

"Yes. Let's get you a real meal. Patrick, would you like to join us?"

I cringed. I'd been looking forward to having my mother all to myself.

"Sure, Mrs. Kepner, I'd really enjoy that." He grinned at me. "Unless you wanted to invite a certain illustrious bartender instead?"

My eyes bugged.

"What was that?" Claire asked.

I pasted on a smile. "Nothing. He's just trying to be funny. Let's go. You coming, Murph?"

Murph smirked. "I'd love to."

"Wonderful. Although you need to call me Claire. Mrs.

Kepner is what I would have called my mother-in-law had I ever had the chance to meet her."

"Claire it is. Ladies, shall we?" He gestured toward the door.

My mom sidled up to me and whispered, "Just a friend? He seems like a keeper."

I shook my head slightly as we walked out of the room. Murph trotted along behind us like a pleased puppy.

Dinner went well enough. Over medium-rare Kansas City strips, Murph talked about his career aspirations. He wanted to finish the year, then take some time to teach English overseas before settling into a PhD program. His ultimate goal was to teach college English at a prestigious university somewhere on the east coast and work on his great American novel. Him and every other person in the program.

My mother had found it a completely original and lofty goal and offered to put him in touch with some of her contacts in the publishing world when he was ready.

The two of them carried the conversation, and I interjected every once in a while. My mom let a few embarrassing stories from my younger days slip out and Murph responded appropriately, laughing at her recollections, but not enough for me to feel like he was laughing at me. When the bill came, he reached for the check.

"It would be my pleasure if you'd allow me to buy dinner for you both. It's not every day I get the chance to dine with two beautiful women."

Claire twittered. I couldn't believe my mom fell so easily for his obvious tactics. I rolled my eyes and sighed.

"Thank you, Patrick, for a lovely evening. If you need help or want me to put you in contact with anyone, just let me know." She pushed a business card across the table to him.

"Thanks. I really appreciate it." He smiled at me and slid the card into his wallet.

After the bill had been paid, it was finally time to go.

"Honey, my hotel is just up the street. Why don't you drop me off, and then you and Patrick can go do something fun together?" she said.

*She's been in town for less than eight hours and she's already playing matchmaker?* "But Mom, I can drop him off first and then we can spend a little time together."

"That would be lovely, but I've got an early flight, and I know you have lots of studying to do. I'll see you in a couple of weeks over winter break. We'll have lots of girl time then."

Wow, dissed by my mom. I sneaked a glance at Murph. His face lit up like a Christmas tree. We made our way to the car, and he sprinted ahead to open the door for her.

"What a gentleman. Most young men nowadays don't believe in chivalry." She gave me a pointed look before climbing into the car.

Most young men nowadays aren't conniving assholes, either. I wrenched open the door and slid my seat forward so Murph could climb in the back. Why did he have to tag along at dinner?

We stopped in front of the hotel, and the doorman opened the door for my mom. I hopped out and walked around the car to give her a hug. Murph climbed out of the backseat to say goodbye.

"Mrs. Kepner,"—she gave him a chastising look—"I mean, Claire. It was very nice meeting you."

"It was nice meeting you too, Patrick. It's good to know Faith has such lovely friends here. Take good care of my baby, will you?" She gave him a hug.

As they pulled away, Murph gave me a smug smile. "I'll just wait for you in the car." He climbed into the front seat and shut the door, finally giving us a moment of relative privacy.

"He's such a nice young man. Are you sure you're just friends?" my mother asked.

"Definitely. He's not my type." I knew exactly what my type was: tall, dark hair, talented fingers, in need of corrective lenses.

"The good ones are hard to find, sweetheart. Look how long it took me to find Clem. When you find a good man, you've got to hold onto him."

"Okay, Mom. If and when I find a good one, I'll keep that in mind."

"Oh, Faith. I miss you, darling. We'll have a great time together when you come home for Christmas." She drew me in close.

I wrapped my arms around her. "Love you, Mom. Thanks for coming."

"It wasn't as bad as you feared?" she asked.

The fallout had yet to be seen. I was sure someone would say something over the next few days. I wasn't embarrassed about who I was or who I was related to. It was just hard being thrust in the unwanted limelight my mother carried with her wherever she went.

"It's never bad. I'm proud of you, Mom. You've come a long way from a single, working mother trying to raise a daughter on her own."

"I wouldn't change a thing. Those early years were hard, but look how well you turned out." Mom kissed me on the cheek. "I'm proud of you too, honey."

I wondered how proud she would be if she found out about the book Chastity Austen had just released. With my writing career taking off, it was just a matter of time before I would need to pull the plug. If only I could only find out who'd left that page.

My stomach lurched and my palms went clammy at the

thought. I twisted my fingers together in an attempt to alleviate the pangs of panic clawing at my gut.

"Don't keep that boy waiting. Go have fun tonight."

Ugh. I had almost forgotten about Murph sitting in the front seat of my car. I glanced down at the passenger window, and he wiggled his fingers in a wave.

I gave my mom one last hug and watched her breeze through the revolving door and into the hotel. As I climbed back into the car, there was only one thing on my mind: how the hell to get rid of Murph.

"Your mom seems nice, so down to earth." Murph buckled his seatbelt.

"What was that bit about the bartender?"

Murph's mouth widened into a smile. A piece of steak or maybe salad was stuck between his two front teeth. "Well, it sounds like you and Dante are seeing each other. Doesn't your mom want to meet him?"

My hands wrapped around the steering wheel. "We are *not* seeing each other."

"What a relief. I didn't want to think you'd been lying to me about dating. So dating"—he curled his fingers into air quotes—"is off limits, but you're open to the idea of a fuck buddy? Damn, why didn't you say so? Where do I sign up?"

"Get out."

"I've been patient, Faith. You know Dante's all wrong for you. He'll sink his dick into anything. I think you owe me an explanation."

"I don't owe you a fucking thing. Get out of my car."

"You use that kind of language around your mom?" Murph gave me a long look. "You're going to regret this." He put one hand on the door handle.

"The only thing I regret is putting up with your crap for so long." I pointed at the door. "Go!"

A wicked smile slashed across his mouth. "Fine. Have it your way. But remember, you asked for it."

As soon as his feet hit the ground, I pressed on the gas. My tires squealed on the pavement and the door crashed closed behind him. Murph was all talk. I'd always thought of him as a pompous windbag, even if I had once considered him a friend.

No time to think about that now. I'd promised another few chapters to Steph before the end of the week. I turned the wheel and headed toward home. If I wanted to make my deadline, I'd have to get another couple thousand words down tonight. Too bad I'd turned my back on my source of inspiration.

# CHAPTER 26
## Faith

NO MATTER how hard I tried to force the words onto the screen, my writer's block had returned, rendering my efforts of stringing words together quite useless. I'd been sitting at my desk off and on for the past three hours and had written less than two pages. I played through the night at Meemaw's in my head over and over, desperately trying to force the words to appear.

I couldn't get past the look on Dante's face as I pushed past him into the hall the other day. He'd looked pissed and angry and, well... wounded. I needed to get past this if I was going to be able to unravel the story of my fictional Faith and Dante and turn it into my next novel. Steph had pretty much dismissed all my other ideas and was holding out for more of the Dante story. I glared at the blinking cursor on the screen for another full minute, then stood up and slammed down the cover of my laptop.

I whipped my sweatshirt off over my head and tossed it on the bed. Grabbing a long-sleeve T-shirt off a hanger, I threw it on and ran my fingers through my hair. I needed to talk to Dante and move on. Besides, what did I have to lose? People were already gossiping about us.

I grabbed my keys and made my way to the car. Ten minutes later, I turned into the parking lot of Tapped. *Here goes nothing.* As I pulled open the heavy door, I wondered if I was making a mistake. Too late for that. I stepped inside and walked back to the bar.

"What can I get you?" The bartender towered over the bar. Tall, dark hair, could have been a body double for Dante if it weren't for the dark brown eyes.

"Is Dante around?" I asked.

"Ah, he had to nick away. Something about an emergency meeting with his group."

"Are you new?" I couldn't quite place the accent.

"I'm Oliver. Nice to meet you." He thrust his hand across the bar.

I took his hand. "Hi. I'm Faith."

"The one and only, aye?"

"What?" I cocked my head. What was that supposed to mean?

"Nothing." He let go of my hand and flung a dishtowel over his shoulder. "Can I pour you a pint?"

"No, that's okay."

"Chur. He'll be gutted he missed you. You'll come back to visit me again?"

I nodded and pushed back from the bar and made a beeline for the door. It was a mistake to come here in the first place. What did I hope to accomplish with this little visit? As I walked back to my car, I noticed a guy heading toward me on the sidewalk. I looked down at the pavement as he passed.

"Faith?"

My head whipped up and we made eye contact. Those damn eyes.

"What are you doing here?" Dante asked.

"I was looking for you. The bartender said you weren't around."

"You must have met Oliver. He's new. I only catch about half of what he says. I was just on my way back from campus. Come on up." He made a move toward the staircase leading up to his apartment.

I took a deep breath. Now or never. My feet clattered up the steps behind him.

He led me into the room and set his backpack down on the floor. "Can I get you anything?"

"No, I'm fine." Being so close to him, I couldn't breathe.

"What's up with you? You told me you could handle things. Then you just walk away?"

"I shouldn't have come." I backed toward the door.

Dante's boots clomped across the room, and he slapped a palm to the door next to my head, leaning in and preventing me from leaving. "What do you want, Faith?"

His breath tickled my ear. My nipples tingled. Good question. What did I want from him? Sex. Inspiration for my book. But every time I got near him, my thoughts jumbled, my nerves jangled, and I lost all access to rational judgment.

My hands went to his chest. "I want to try again."

He traced the line of my cheekbone, and I closed my eyes, breathing in his scent.

"I don't know what that even means," Dante whispered, his lips barely brushing my earlobe.

Fisting his shirt in my hands, I pulled him away from the door and toward the couch. "It means I want to feel you." I nudged him backwards. "Inside me."

---

**Dante**

As I FELL BACK against the cushion, I pulled her down on top of me. I should say no. Tell her to get the hell out and leave me the fuck alone. She'd already invaded my mind. Every night I fell asleep thinking about how she felt underneath me. When I woke up, images of her teasing smile danced across the inside of my eyelids before I opened my eyes. Fuck, I'd jerked off so many times picturing the way she'd bent over in the elevator—I was surprised my cock was still attached.

As Faith's tongue traced the shell of my ear, my hands slid under her shirt and released the clasp of her bra. She moaned and shifted on my lap. My fingers skimmed over the soft skin of her ribcage.

"So, you want to give it another shot?" I asked.

"Yeah, if you're up for it."

I pressed my erection into her crotch. "I'm up for it all right. But we're going to play by my rules this time."

She rubbed against me. "What rules?"

My fingers darted underneath the waistband of her jeans. "You don't spook if I say more than a couple of words to you."

"Mmm." Her mouth nestled against my neck.

"And you can't just walk out on me again. I'm gonna need access to you at least twice a week."

"But only for sex. Not like hanging out or anything."

I smiled. "Only for sex. Don't worry, I won't try to complicate things by asking you out or something stupid like that."

"Fine."

"Should we shake on it?"

"Don't you think there's a better way to seal the deal?" Faith reached out to grab for the handle of her bag on the floor.

I dragged it close, and she felt around inside, pulling out a foil packet. I took it from her and ripped it open.

"Wait." Faith climbed off my lap and knelt down on the floor in front of the couch.

She tugged at my jeans, and I undid the button, then lifted my butt off the couch so she could slide them down my legs. She tossed them over her shoulder, then looked up at me and wrapped a hand around my cock. I sighed and let my head fall to the back of the couch.

She ran her tongue along the underside and took the tip into her mouth. Wet heat surrounded me. A surge shot straight to my dick, and I struggled to regain control. I wasn't going to let her finish me off this soon. She proceeded to stroke, suck, and lick, and I fought against the tide swelling inside until I couldn't stand it.

I grabbed the condom from the couch cushion and unrolled it onto my throbbing hard-on. She stepped out of her pants and shirt, and I yanked her down onto my lap, sinking inside her. Lotus Blossom finally achieved.

"So good, Faith. You feel so fucking good."

She wrapped her legs around me and slid up and down. My mouth searched out any part of her, depositing sloppy wet kisses on her neck, her shoulders, her arms. While her arms wrapped around my neck, I palmed her breasts, squeezing them together and letting my tongue travel the crease where they met. I took one nipple in my mouth and rolled the other between my fingers until they both hardened to points. Then I switched.

She shifted on my lap and picked up the pace. Her breath came faster. Her eyes closed and her legs squeezed around my midsection like a vise.

"I'm close, Dante. Really close."

I slid further down on the cushion for a better angle.

"Don't you fucking move," she ordered, and I shifted back. With her riding me, she was in complete control.

She clenched around me and pushed down while I moved

deeper inside her. As she reached her release, she threw her head back, and I rained kisses down on her neck and breasts. She looked so fucking hot. I loved knowing I could do this to her. Miss-Everything's-Under-Control. With a final thrust, I let myself go.

Sex only. With a side of minimal conversation. Yeah, for sure, I could handle it.

# CHAPTER 27

## *Dante*

I WIPED THE WET, soapy rag down the length of the bar. Most of the students had already left town for winter break. Faith would be flying out in a day or two. Sadly, there'd been no time for a repeat performance of last week's get-together. We'd have to wait until after the holidays to really get things going. I had plans to leave in the morning to head to Hinkley for a nice, cozy Christmas with Meemaw. The bar and my office would be closed over the next couple of days, so there wasn't really too much to keep me in town. I just had one more errand to run, and then I'd be free to start packing. I tossed the dishrag into the sink of bubbles.

"Hey Wyatt, I'm heading out."

A voice rang out from the supply closet down the hall. "Wait up. I have something for you."

I thrust my arms into my coat and pulled on my hat as Wyatt caught up to me by the bar.

"Here. Lindsey made some Christmas cookies for you." Wyatt passed me a round tin with a sparkly red bow on top.

"Wow. Thanks. She didn't have to do that."

Wyatt waved a hand. "Nah, she wanted to. You'd better

take them. She doesn't trust me to keep my hands off them. If I keep digging into the cookie jar, she'll make me start going to the gym with you."

"And that right there is why I'll never get hitched."

"Why, because you don't like cookies?" Wyatt smirked.

"No, dude. I don't like some chick telling me what to do, playing all those mind games. So what if you eat all the cookies? She doesn't trust you? That's bullshit."

Wyatt shook his head. "It's not like that, asswipe. She knows I'll eat all the cookies and then be pissed at myself afterward. So, she's helping me by making sure I get rid of them all first."

"Whatever." I grabbed my backpack and slung it over a shoulder.

"Just take the damn cookies, Dante. Some of us actually like having someone looking out for us."

"You're really happy, aren't you?" I gave him a playful punch in the arm. "Didn't figure you as the kind of guy who'd cut off his balls for a batch of snickerdoodles."

"You just don't get it. Get on out of here. Run home to Meemaw. She might be the only woman who'll ever give you a chance."

"Yeah, she's probably got a whole batch of sugar cookies just waiting for me." I tucked the tin under my arm. "And she won't care if I eat every last one."

Ten minutes later, I walked through the front doorway of the Sashay Salon, jingling the bell over the door and causing the customers to turn their attention my way. I always felt a little conspicuous walking in the door. Even though Tameka had agreed to change the color scheme to black and silver and started marketing to male clients, I was still usually the only guy in the place.

While I waited for her to come out from the back, I sat down in one of the chairs. The women had gone back to their chatting, and I picked up bits and pieces of their conversation.

"You should get a copy. It was an amazing read..."

"I didn't know a guy could be that romantic..."

The sight of Tameka coming from the backroom interrupted my eavesdropping. "Well, hi there, Dante. Thanks so much for stopping by."

"No problem. Looks like you're pretty busy, so that's a good sign," I said.

"Yeah, business has really picked up since I started working with your team. Y'all really know what you're doing."

I'd been apprehensive about taking on a salon with my group. Thankfully, we'd pulled together. If I could keep up the good work, I'd be able to get a kick-ass reference from the professor, which would go a long way in securing my move to a bigger company. Most of those jobs required some sort of teaching or training experience.

"We're happy to help. Do you want to talk here, or should we go in the back?"

She waved her hand at the chattering women. "Don't mind them, they're just comparing notes on their new favorite book."

"Oh yeah?" I asked.

"Some steamy romance." She laughed.

One of the customers whirled around in her salon chair. Strips of aluminum foil stuck out of her head like some glammed-up space alien. "It's not just a steamy romance novel, Tameka. It's a life changer. When Harrison goes all romantic on her and she finally realizes she loves him too—"

"Don't pay any attention. Next week they'll be onto something else. Let's chat in the office. It won't be so distracting."

I followed her down the hall to a small, cramped office. I spent the next half hour reviewing her financials and showing her how much her new marketing campaign had increased her business. When we were done going over the paperwork, she walked me back up to the front.

"You know, I wanted to get you something for the holidays to show you how much I appreciate all your hard work."

I smiled. "That's not necessary. We're happy to help. Besides, the team is getting graded, so just make sure you give their prof a good report."

"Oh, I will. Can I offer you a haircut, too?"

I ran my hand through my overgrown, shaggy hair. "I'm used to just stopping in at the barber every once in a while."

Tameka reached for a cape. "Trust me. It'll be quick and painless. Set yourself down in that chair right there, and I'll have you on your way before you even know what hit you."

Before I could come up with a quick excuse, Tameka's hand pressed on my shoulder, guiding me into the chair. The guys would never let me live it down if they saw me getting my hair cut in a freaking salon. I gritted my teeth and tried to make the best of it.

As Tameka secured the cape around my neck and reached for her scissors, tidbits of the ladies' conversation drifted to me. They still seemed to be talking about some book.

One woman put her hand over her chest and swooned. "That Chastity Austen really knows what she's doing. I couldn't put it down."

"Yeah, I tried looking her up to find out where she gets her ideas and stuff. There aren't any pictures of her on her website, just some graphics."

Space alien lady leaned over in my direction. "Do you read romance novels?"

Ha! I laughed. "Um, no. The last thing I read was a report on a potential new merger. Probably the furthest thing you can get from a love story."

An elderly woman on my right with skinny curlers lined up all over her scalp piped in. "That's the problem with men today, there's no more romance. Wham, bam, thank you ma'am. That's all they're interested in."

Space alien lady started in again. "You're absolutely right. Why, my granddaughter just helped me get set up on that dating website for seniors. That's all they want, those dirty old men."

I was caught in a damn crossfire. Not feeling up to defending the entire male population, I made eye contact in the mirror with Tameka. "Almost done?"

"Y'all leave him alone. This here is a good one. By the way, Dante, you seeing anyone?"

I never should have agreed to sit down in the chair. "Nope, no one special. You know, I really need to get going."

She picked up the clippers and flicked the button. "Just let me clean up the back here."

Curler granny raised her eyebrows at me. "You know, my granddaughter is probably about your age..."

"I really don't have time to see anyone right now. I work full-time, plus bartend on the side."

"Well, that's too bad. She's a real catch." She scowled at me and turned her attention back to the magazine in her lap.

"What do you think?" Tameka whirled the chair around so I could see my reflection in the mirror. She hadn't made a major change, just trimmed things up a bit.

I peeled the cape off my neck. "Looks great. Thanks a lot. I really appreciate it."

"Hey, honey, come over here." A woman across the room beckoned me over.

I took a cautious step toward her. Tiny silver pins covered her head, and she reeked of some strong chemical smell. She shoved her hand out from under her cape, thrusting a hard-cover book at me.

"Take it. See if you can pick up a tip or two."

I looked down at the cover. Two bodies pressed up against each other on a black background. Red letters blazed across the graphic—*Carnal Knowledge.*

I'd instinctively put my hand out, but when I caught a glimpse of the cover, I yanked it back. "Aw thanks, but I really couldn't."

"Young man, I want you to have it. I insist."

I looked over at Tameka, who gave me a nudge with her eyes.

I took the book. "Fine. Thanks."

As I shoved the book into my bag, I promised myself that I wouldn't set foot in this place again. From now on, I'd make one of the women deliver the paperwork. Should be their job anyway.

"You have yourself a nice holiday now, Dante," Tameka said.

"Thanks, you too." By the time I left the building and made it to my car, I'd already forgotten about the book with the red title sitting in the bottom of my backpack. The book by the author Chastity Austen.

# CHAPTER 28

## *Faith*

THE PLANE LANDED AT LAX, and as we taxied to the gate, I turned on my cell phone. Three missed calls from Steph? I hit the button to call her back, and she picked up on the first ring.

"Faith, where in the world have you been? I've been trying to call you all morning," Steph said.

"I'm on a plane. What's going on?"

"Your book, girlfriend. You've done it!"

I squished down in my middle seat. "What are you talking about?"

"*Carnal Knowledge* made it to the New York Times best-seller list!" Steph shrieked.

I held the phone away from my ear for a moment before Steph's voice could pierce my eardrum. The guy on my left shifted in his seat, scowling at me, and the woman on my right looked over. I put my free hand around my mouth as I spoke into the phone in an attempt to establish some privacy. "What?"

"You debuted at number ninety-eight. That's awesome, Faith! Traffic to your website is way up. You're going to need to make some social media posts later on today. Let's keep this momentum going."

"That's great, Steph. I'll log on as soon as I get to my mom's." My other books had sold fairly well, but I'd never made a list before. Part of me wanted to throw my arms in the air and shout out my accomplishment. The rest of me wanted to crouch down under the cushion of my chair and hide. A bestseller? Continuing to fly under the radar just got a tiny bit harder.

Other passengers in the rows ahead of me started to stand and grab their luggage.

"I've got to go. I'm about to get off the plane."

"Okay. Have a great holiday. I'll keep my eye on the list and let you know if you move up."

"Sounds good, thanks."

We disconnected, and the guy on my left finally stood up. I grabbed my bag and coat and followed the long line of passengers to the front of the plane.

As the escalator carried me down toward baggage claim, I scanned the crowd for my mother. She stood right outside the sliding glass doors, waving her arms, a big goofy smile plastered across her face. Clem paced a few feet behind her, cell phone glued to his ear.

I whooshed through the exit and let my mother envelop me in a hug. I drew in a deep breath. Donna Karan's Cashmere Mist and Mentos—the smell of home.

"Let me take a look at you," my mother said, stepping back and holding me at arm's length. "Have you been eating okay? You look thinner than the last time I saw you."

I laughed. "Three meals a day. I'm fine."

Clem hung up the phone and put an arm around my shoulder, giving me a half hug. "Welcome home, Faith."

"Thanks, I've been looking forward to it." Home? My mother and Clem had moved again since I'd visited over the summer, and I hadn't even seen the new house. I supposed home was where the heart was... and that meant with my mom.

"Let's get your bags." Clem took off toward the baggage claim. Mom and I followed, linked arm in arm.

I pointed out my rolling bag, and Clem grabbed it off the belt. "Is this all?"

"Yep, that's it," I replied.

"Oh, honey, where's your hang-up bag?" Mom asked.

"Mom, I'm only here for a week. What else do I need besides jeans?"

Clem gave my mother a pointed look. "Hon, didn't you tell her?"

She busied herself with her leather gloves. "Well, I guess I just didn't get around to it."

"What? What are you guys keeping from me?" I asked.

"We're going to a little party tonight," Mom said.

"A little party?" Clem put a hand to his chest. "Claire dear, it's black tie."

I waved my hands in front of me. "Uh no, I'll just order takeout and stay in. You two have fun."

"Oh, sweetheart, I knew you'd say that. That's why I didn't tell you about it," Mom said. "I have three dresses on hold for you at the boutique. I thought we could drop Clem off at home and head over for you to try them on."

"Aw, Mom, I don't want to go to some fancy party tonight." I felt like a four-year-old who'd been told she had to stop making mud pies and put on a dress.

She tucked her arm into mine and whispered into my ear. "It's important to Clem. Can you please do this for me?"

I sighed. "You could have told me about it, Mom."

She gave me the puppy dog eyes. I couldn't deny her when she pulled out all the stops like that.

"Fine. But there better be an open bar."

Clem laughed. "That shouldn't be a problem."

As we made our way out into the California sun, I held tight to my mother's arm. It was good to be home.

"You did tell her about Carter though, right Claire?" Clem asked.

I turned on my mom. "Carter? Who's Carter?"

Her hand fluttered to her chest. "Didn't I mention him, dear? I'm sure I meant to."

"Yeah, right." I'd been subjected to my mom's failed attempts at matchmaking before. "Who's Carter?"

"Just your plus one for the night, dear." We'd reached Clem's black Cadillac, and before I could come up with a killer reply, my mom climbed into the front seat and closed the door.

My plus one? Great, just great. A surprise black tie function and an unwanted blind date. Just the kind of evening I had in mind for my first night of winter break. What could possibly go wrong?

---

### Dante

I CAREENED into the Hinkley Memorial Hospital parking lot. I'd been on my way to Meemaw's when I got the call. What was the old bird thinking, trying to hang Christmas ornaments from the ceiling of the senior center? She'd fallen off a ladder and hit her head pretty hard on the corner of a table on her way down. The nurse on the phone said she'd passed out but was in stable condition, and I should try to get there as soon as possible.

I bolted through the revolving door and right to the information counter. "I'm looking for Dolores Bishop," I said to the woman behind the desk.

"You must be her grandson."

I nodded and pointed to the computer, frustrated that she didn't seem to be in much of a hurry.

She smiled at me and typed a few things on the keyboard. "She's still in the ER. Right down the hall and to the—"

I didn't wait around for directions. I took off down the long hall toward the ER. I'd been there often enough over the years to know my way around. A broken arm in fourth grade, a dirt bike wreck in seventh, jumping off the roof of the high school and earning a concussion in tenth... yeah, I knew how to find the ER.

I rounded the corner and came to a dead stop in front of the nurse's station. What the hell was *she* doing here?

The nurse on duty looked up with big brown eyes. "Dante?"

I hadn't seen her in years. Unless I counted the number of times I'd used her senior picture for target practice. The sight of her here in the flesh turned my blood thick and cold like the frozen pomegranate daiquiris I'd made popular at the bar. "Hey, Cheryl. So, you work here now?"

One hand fluttered up to her hair. Her lips spread in a nervous smile. "Yeah, I've been here since May."

No one told me she was back in town. Would it have mattered? "Where's my grandmother?" My heart pounded. If anything bad happened to Meemaw, well, I didn't even want to think about it.

"Oh sorry, let me show you where she is." Cheryl walked out from behind the tall counter and linked her arm through mine. "I'll take you to her. She had a pretty bad fall."

I came to an abrupt stop and yanked my arm away. "Why won't anyone tell me what's going on?"

"Come on, she's just right over here." Cheryl tugged on my arm, and I let her lead me to a small cubby. The curtain was drawn, and she eased it open, just enough for us to step inside.

The big hospital bed dwarfed Meemaw. Tubes stuck out of her mouth and arm. A giant white bandage covered half her head and the right side of her face had already turned ten shades of purple. An arsenal of machines whirred, buzzed, and beeped around her.

I covered my eyes, not wanting Cheryl to see me lose it. Dammit, I wasn't going to cry. "What happened? Why isn't she awake yet?"

"I'll have the doctor come in and talk to you." Cheryl stepped through the curtain and slid it closed.

I moved closer to the bed and carefully put my hand on Meemaw's. Thank God, she was warm. I'd expected her hand to be ice cold.

"Damn you, old woman. What have you done to yourself now?" I asked, willing her to open her eyes and chastise me for cursing.

I turned at the sound of the curtain sliding open. A man who didn't look that much older than I was stepped into the cubby. He offered his hand in introduction. "I'm Doctor Cain. You must be Mrs. Bishop's grandson. I believe you were listed as next of kin."

I shook his hand and nodded.

"Your grandmother had a pretty bad fall. She bumped her head and there was quite a bit of swelling—"

"That's what the nurse said on the phone. When will she wake up?"

"As I was saying, there was quite a bit of swelling. We thought it would be best to go ahead and keep her heavily sedated until the swelling goes down."

I nodded. "Wait. What do you mean heavily sedated?"

The doctor stepped over to the foot of the bed and picked up a chart. "Sometimes, in the case of a moderate trauma to

the head, it's best if we keep a patient sedated. It will mini-
mize your grandmother's discomfort and give her brain a
chance to heal faster."

This was a lot to take in. I ran my fingers through my hair,
wishing it was still long enough to grab a fistful and let out a
deep sigh. "What happens next?" I took in a ragged breath.

The doctor shrugged. "Rumor has it Mrs. Bishop is a
pretty tough cookie. She might be totally fine and just wake
up with a bad headache. I know it's hard to wait, but we're
doing absolutely everything we possibly can for her. The best
thing you can do is talk to her, sit by her bedside and hold her
hand. I'm sure she can hear you and has some awareness of
what's going on. I wish I could tell you more, but only time
will tell us what we can expect."

"Yeah, okay. Thanks."

"If you have any other questions, feel free to ask one of the
nurses to find me. I'll be around for the next couple of hours.
Once we get the paperwork done, she'll be moved up to a
room."

I stuck out my hand and the doctor grasped it in another
firm handshake.

"Take care, Dante." He stepped out of the curtain, leaving
me and Meemaw alone in the brightly lit room.

# CHAPTER 29

## *Faith*

I **TOOK** a sip of champagne as I waited in the personal shopper dressing room. My mother was arguing with the leggy blonde saleswoman at the front counter over which dress I should try on first.

It was pointless to start a fight about going to the party. Mom knew what she was doing all along. She was right. If she'd warned me about it ahead of time, I probably would have come up with some excuse to change my flight. Instead, I was on my second glass of champagne and had already consumed five of the decadent dark chocolates from the silver tray next to me.

"Ah, here we are." The blonde whirled into the room with a yellow concoction draped over her arms.

"Yellow?" I asked. "Won't I look like a giant lemon?"

Mom sat down on the edge of the couch next to me. "Oh Faith, it's buttercream chiffon, nowhere near lemon. Just try it on, for heaven's sake."

"Fine." I got up from the couch and set my empty glass down on the tray.

"Right over here." Blondie stepped into a large dressing

room and hung the dress on a giant hook on the wall. "Let me know when you have it on, and I'll help you fasten the back."

I nodded and let the curtain fall closed behind me. I whipped off my shirt and stepped out of my jeans, leaving my clothes in a heap on the floor. Stepping back, I studied the yellow dress with a critical eye. Buttercream chiffon, my ass. More like a giant helping of banana pudding.

I unzipped the back and climbed in, slipping the thick straps up onto my shoulders. Twirling around to face myself in the mirror, I took in my reflection. The flat front did nothing for my bust line and the wide, full skirt made me look like I'd gained twenty pounds in the last thirty seconds.

"I only ate five," I muttered under my breath.

"How's it going in there?"

"What are my other options?" I asked.

The curtain slid back and Mom gazed upon me in the mirror.

"Stand up straight. Chest out. Wipe that frown off your face." I struck my best runway model pose, sucking in my cheeks and sticking out a hip. She stepped closer, trying to fluff the skirt out behind me. "Maybe if we zipped it up, it wouldn't look so large."

Blondie stepped in, drawing the two sides of the back together and tugging the zipper closed. Now the fabric stretched tight across my middle, squeezing my breasts up and almost over the bodice. "Much better, Mom. Don't you think?"

Claire waved her hand in the air, signaling Blondie to take it away. "How about the pink one?"

"You've got to be kidding me. Pink?" I turned around as Blondie unzipped me. I took off the dress and passed it and the hanger through the curtain.

"Just try it on, Faith. It will look gorgeous with your hair."

Sounded like I didn't have much of a choice. Blondie entered with yards of pale pink fabric over her arm.

"First lemon, now cotton candy? Seriously, Mom, there's no way I'm even trying this one on."

My mother mumbled something, then a hand reached in, removing the offensive sugary pink dress. I shuddered to think what would come next. I vetoed sea foam green and a strapless apricot number. The lilac one wasn't so bad, but it was a tad too long, and they didn't have time to have it hemmed, so it was out.

"What's with all the pastels? It's almost Christmas, not Easter."

"Faith, you've got to settle on something. I told Clem we'd be home in about an hour. If you don't pick something soon, we won't have time to get ready," Mom said.

Blondie stood to the side, one hand tucked under her chin, the other tapping a private number on her lips. "If you're okay moving away from pastels, I might have just the thing." She spoke so quietly it was almost like she was talking to herself.

"Gladly!" I rolled my eyes. "Bring on the jewel tones." I pulled my arm from a periwinkle one-shouldered getup.

"Be right back." Blondie disappeared again.

Even she must be getting tired of this. Now if I could just get another glass of champagne. The bottle sat on a low table, not ten feet away.

"This next one has got to work," Mom said. "I don't care what it looks like, we'll take it."

At that moment, Blondie reappeared, a gray zippered dress bag draped over her arm. She stepped into the dressing room and hung it on the hook. She winked at me then left, taking the periwinkle nightmare with her.

I unzipped the bag. *Now this is what I'm talking about.* I wiggled into the strapless, satiny number. It fit like a glove. I opened up the curtain and Mom gasped. It hugged in all the right places, pushed up the right spots, and accentuated my tiny waist.

"This is the one," I said.

"Oh, honey. I did tell you that this party is honoring Clem, right? The board of directors will be there, along with most of his congregation. I'm just not sure red is the right choice."

"Mom, we've been here for almost two hours already. I'm done trying on dresses. I'd be happy to stay home—"

"Fine." She checked her watch. "We've got to get a move on. No telling what traffic on the 405 might be like at this time of day. I guess we'll take it."

A look of relief passed over Blondie's face, quickly replaced by a giant smile. "Do you need shoes? Accessories?"

I looked at my Converse sneakers in the corner. "I guess I'm going to need shoes, too. Sorry. If you'd told me we were going to a huge party—"

"Just pick something fast." Mom gathered her bag and jacket and moved toward the dressing room exit. "I'll meet you up front."

Ten minutes later, I met my mother at the front counter. Dress, check. Strappy black heels, check. Pearl and rhinestone accessories, check. While Claire paid the bill, I sipped another long-awaited glass of champagne.

"Thanks, Mom," I said as we left the store. "I feel bad you had to pay for everything."

"Don't be silly, dear. I love to treat you to nice things. Besides, I'm insisting you go with us tonight. You can't very well go in that." Claire gestured to my ensemble of jeans, hoodie, and sneakers.

"Yeah, what would the mysterious Carter think of me then?"

She clucked her tongue. "I don't like your tone, dear. Carter is a lovely young man. It won't kill you to just sit next to him for dinner. We needed another body to keep the numbers even."

God forbid I cause a dire situation like uneven numbers at a black tie dinner party. I'd just have to dump Carter off on some unsuspecting lonely woman when the dancing started and stake a claim to a seat near the bar. Surely, I'd be able to tolerate him through dinner. Maybe the night wouldn't be such a drag. Dressing up might even be kind of fun. I hadn't done that in a long time.

I opened the back door of my mother's Mercedes and hung the garment bag on the hook. Then I climbed into the passenger seat and gave her a half-hug over the center console.

Her eyebrows rose in surprise. "What was that for?"

"I'm just really happy to see you. Thanks for the dress and stuff. I'm kind of looking forward to tonight. It's been a while since I got all dressed up."

She patted my hand. "I'm sure we'll have a fun time." Then she put the car in drive and we rolled out of the parking lot. "By the way, did I tell you Carter is one of Clem's pastors-in-training? He's just finishing up the grad student program at USC."

"Really?" I shot my mother a look of disappointment.

She either failed to see it or chose to ignore the frosty glare as she accelerated onto the highway. "Oh no. Look at the traffic. I'd better call Clem. We're going to be late."

As she dialed on the car's Bluetooth speaker phone, I slumped down in my seat. Ugh. I should have known my mother had an ulterior motive. A pastor? I'd actually started to look forward to the evening. What the hell were we going to have in common?

# CHAPTER 30

*Dante*

I SAT in the stuffy hospital room. I hadn't left except to eat and take a piss for the past forty-eight hours. I'd met all the staff, fielded questions from Meemaw's cast of cronies, did my best to avoid the only woman who'd ever broken my heart, and got a good start on some serious facial hair.

Dr. Cain kept telling me there was no reason for me to stay, that Meemaw wouldn't wake up until they were ready to bring her back. But I knew how stubborn my grandmother could be and figured she'd wait until the minute I left to fight her way out of the drugs all on her own.

I wanted to be there when she woke. She'd do the same for me. Hell, she'd done so much more than that for me over the years. To think that I might not get the chance to tell her how much she meant to me. I ran a hand over my scruffy chin and rubbed my eyes.

For the past two days, I'd survived on strong coffee and bad cafeteria food. Tomorrow was Christmas Eve. Meemaw would be so pissed she was missing a holiday. The senior center would be fine without her, even though she was convinced they couldn't function in her absence. Several of her friends had checked in with me. I'd been told they were stocking her freezer at home with casseroles and lasagnas. As if she'd be able to eat a quarter of it.

I flipped on the television. Nothing but holiday-themed shows: how to cook your Christmas turkey or best gifts to give your parents. I didn't need any of that advice. My finger stilled on the remote as *It's a Wonderful Life* played on the screen.

Damn, that reminded me of the night I spent with Faith and the way she'd come on to me in my room. I'd enjoyed the whirlwind hook-up, no doubt about that. But I'd also gotten a glimpse at the woman behind the wall she'd put up.

Thinking about her made me wonder what she was doing at that exact moment out in California. Whatever it was, it had to be better than sitting bedside with a loved one. A little banter with Faith would surely take my mind off Meemaw, even if it was just for a few minutes. Sending her a text wouldn't necessarily violate our rules of engagement, right?

> Hey, hope you had a good flight. Just caught the end of It's A Wonderful Life and made me think of you. Merry Christmas.

I stared at the phone for a full two minutes. No response. Just as I was about to stand up and stretch, my phone pinged.

> Arrived safe but am being blindsided with a black-tie function tonight. Like my dress?

I clicked on the image and sucked in my breath. A picture of Faith rocking a satiny red dress filled my screen. Her breasts strained against the deep "V" neck and her lips puckered into a sexy kiss.

You're playing dirty. If I was there, that dress would be on the floor by now.

I'd hate to waltz across the dance floor naked.

Faith naked. Shit. My cock twitched to life.

Now you've got me all hot and bothered.

Too bad you're not here. I'd figure out a way to take care of that for you.

Fuck me.

Exactly. Gotta go.

I shifted in the hard vinyl chair, needing a distraction. Even though Faith and I had made up and figured out a compromise on our deal, she wouldn't be back until winter break ended. Wouldn't do me any good to spend the next week and a half with blue balls. Grabbing my backpack, I rummaged through, looking for something to work on or take my mind off my favorite redhead in that tempting red dress.

My hand closed around the book the woman at the salon had given me. I slid it out of the bag and took a long look at the cover. *Carnal Knowledge* by Chastity Austen. What the hell kind of name was that? Couldn't be worse than watching infomercials and reruns on TV. Maybe those women at the salon were onto something, and I could pick up a few tips or tricks. I kicked my feet up on the edge of the bed and flipped open the cover.

### Faith

Snowflakes fell from the sky, their delicate forms catching the light of thousands of twinkle lights woven through the fake pine trees. Stepping into the ballroom, I couldn't help but catch my breath at the magical atmosphere. Raising my hand, I reached out as if to catch a falling flake.

"Almost looks real, doesn't it?"

Startled, I turned around to face a tall, good-looking stranger. I tried to hide my embarrassment with nonchalance. "Yes, they do. It's amazing how they can do that."

"Special effects. It's all on a video loop." He gestured toward a large projector in the corner of the room.

"Don't I feel silly—" I began, but his grin stopped me short.

"You're Faith, right?"

"Yes." I tilted my head slightly. "Who are you?"

He extended his hand. "I'm Carter. Claire told me you needed a date tonight."

I rolled my eyes, already frustrated with my mother's meddling hand in this. "I bet she did. Nice to meet you, Carter." After shaking his hand, I turned away, scanning the room for the bar—a welcome sanctuary.

"Allow me to show you the way." Carter placed a hand on the small of my back, guiding me across the ballroom to the bar set up on the opposite side.

Reaching the tall counter, Carter turned to me. "What's your poison?"

"Just a glass of red wine would be great."

He signaled the bartender. "A glass of cabernet for the lady and Crown on the rocks for me."

As we waited for our drinks, Carter attempted to start a conversation. "So, Claire tells me you're teaching at a school in Indiana?"

I glanced up at him. "That's right. I'm an adjunct professor at Tempest, working on tenure. What else has she told you about me?"

A slight blush tinged his cheeks. "I've had the pleasure of spending quite a bit of time with your mother and Clem. I'm finishing up my JD and Masters of Philosophy over at SC. Clem has been serving as somewhat of an informal adviser to me."

"Interesting. Did you do your undergrad there too?" I found myself intrigued despite my initial reservations. He had a killer smile and looked pretty damn good in his tailored tux.

"No. I'm a Midwestern boy at heart. I got my bachelor's at the University of Kansas."

"So how did you end up in California?" I asked.

The bartender set our drinks down in front of us, and I wrapped my fingers around the stem of my wine glass.

"It's a long story. Let's just say there was a girl." The corners of his lips curled up in a bashful smile.

"Was?" I took a sip of my wine and peered at him over the rim of my glass.

"Yes, was." He picked up his drink. "Should we go check our table assignments? Looks like people are starting to sit down."

I glanced across the room. Most of the guests were settling at tables. We made our way back to the entrance and located our name cards. I'd be willing to bet my entire collection of Brontë sisters' books that my mother had arranged for the two of us to be at the same table.

He picked up his card. "Table three, how about you?"

I lifted the tented card and feigned surprise. "Well, would you look at that? Table three for me too."

Carter gave me another dazzling grin, and I took a good long look. Out here in the light of the hallway, I could make out his features better than I'd been able to in the dim ball-room. With sandy blond hair and a natural tan, I could see how he might be mistaken for a native Californian. His longer surfer hair alone made him look like he'd be more at home on the beach than on the plains of Kansas.

He offered me his arm. "May I escort you to our table?"

I linked my arm through his, willing to play along for a bit. Spending the evening chatting with Carter would be better than sitting back at the house... alone... fantasizing about Dante.

"Absolutely. It would be my pleasure."

# CHAPTER 31

## *Faith*

AS WE REACHED the large round table set for ten, I looked over at my mother and Clem seated at the table next to ours. They were right in front of the raised stage. When my mother saw me arm-in-arm with Carter, her face lit up, and she clapped her fingers together. As Carter slid my chair out for me, Clem gave me a sly thumbs up. I shook my head and sat down, scooting my chair close to the table.

"Do you mind if I sit next to you?" Carter asked, pulling out his chair.

"May as well. Looks like that's all part of their plan, right?" I jerked my head in the direction of my mother and Clem.

Carter laughed as he sat down. "Yeah, they've been prepping me for this for weeks. Your mom is really proud of you, Faith. She said you put yourself through school and know exactly where you're headed."

I put my napkin in my lap. "I'm trying. Hopefully, I'll be able to get tenure in the next few years."

"I love a girl with a plan," Carter said.

I choked on a sip of wine at the mention of the "L" word.

A few more people joined us at the table, causing our conversation to come to an end. As the servers brought out the salad, the woman on Carter's right started asking him questions. Her hand lingered on his arm as they spoke, and her laughter seemed a little forced, like she was trying just a little too hard.

Before I had a chance to give it too much thought, the gentleman on my left introduced himself. He was a pastor from a neighboring community and had nothing but good things to say about Clem and his church. When his wife found out who my mother was, she made her husband switch places with her. Through the rest of the meal, she quizzed me about Mom. As we waited for coffee and dessert, I excused myself to freshen up. Carter pushed back from the table and stood as I left.

"You'd better come back," he muttered under his breath. "If you leave me here alone to fend for myself, I might not ever forgive you."

I smiled and patted his lapel. "You look like you're doing a fine job."

He shook his head and sat down. I turned to go, and the woman next to him put a hand on his arm again. As I walked by my mother's chair, she reached out and clasped my arm.

"How's it going over there?" she asked.

"Just fine, Mom. Carter seems like a nice guy."

"Oh honey, he is. Did he tell you he's getting his law degree and his Masters in Philosophy? At the same time?"

"Yes, he did."

"He must be so smart. Clem just raves about him, don't you, Clem?" Clem mopped up the last bit of au jus from his plate with a dinner roll. His mouth clearly full, he just nodded in agreement.

"Yeah, he seems really smart. I'll be back in a few. I just need to go to the ladies' room."

"Okay, dear. Hurry, they're going to start the program right after dessert. Clem is being recognized. You won't want to miss it."

I nodded, turning toward the door. "I'll hurry."

"Oh, Faith?" I looked back at my mother. "He's very handsome too, don't you think?"

"Sure, Mom." I looked over at Carter and his eyes met mine. Great. He probably heard that whole exchange.

As I re-entered the ballroom and made my way back to our table, the program had already started. A man stood behind a clear acrylic podium on the stage, talking about how Christian values were under attack and how it was their job as leaders in the church to shepherd their congregations through these confusing times.

A slideshow played behind him, scenes from television featuring steamy love scenes, pictures from magazines with scantily clad women, and finally covers from some recent books. I took in a sharp breath as the cover of *Carnal Knowledge* flashed onto the screen. Sinking into my chair, I put my head in my hands and tried to still the pounding of my heart. A warm hand settled on my exposed shoulder.

"Are you okay?" Carter whispered in my ear.

I looked out at him from under my hands. "I just have a headache, that's all."

"Do you want me to go get you some aspirin or something?"

"No, I've got some here." I dug through my small purse and emptied two pills into my palm, then tossed them back with a large sip of water. It's not like a couple of pain killers would do the trick. Maybe if I chased them down with a liter of vodka, it would help numb the shock of seeing my book cover plastered across the screen.

The man on the stage went on to talk about Clem. How he was a warrior of faith and they were recognizing him for his leadership in the church. Everyone clapped, and then Clem stood and walked up the steps to the stage with Mom on his arm. My face blazed.

The screen showed an image of a large cross now; my book cover was no longer on display, although the visual was burned into my brain. Clem and Claire shook hands with the man, and then he handed them a plaque. The audience clapped, and I pounded my hands together along with the applause of the crowd.

Clem gave a short speech while my mother stood by his side, her loving gaze never leaving his face. More applause and then they came back down the steps and sat down at their table.

An announcement was made that the band would set up and start playing soon. Still not feeling quite myself, I forced myself to stand up from the table and walk over to where a small group congregated around my mom and Clem. I sensed Carter follow me.

"Look at this," my mother thrust the plaque into my hands.

"It's nice, Mom. Clem must be so proud," I said.

"Oh, he is." She beamed with pride. "He's been working so hard. It's so nice for him to be recognized by his peers."

I passed the plaque back to her as the band started to play *Walking in a Winter Wonderland*.

"Would you like to dance?" Carter asked.

Anything to get me away from my mother and Clem for a few minutes. "I'd love to."

Carter put his arm around my waist and whisked me out onto the dance floor. I'd taken ballroom dancing in high school and really enjoyed it. As Carter led me around the dance floor, I could tell he must have had lessons at some point as well.

"You're quite the dancer," I said to his chest.

"I've been to my fair share of sorority balls."

"Did you pledge at KU?"

"No," he glanced down at me as he twirled me around under his arm. "I never had time for it. Other priorities. How about you?"

"Same here," I said.

Despite the hiccup with the book cover, I was actually having a good time with Carter. In the past, when my mother tried to set me up with someone, it tanked early. So far, I'd managed to survive dinner and now dancing, and had yet to find a major flaw. Besides the obvious one—an erotic romance author and a pastor probably wouldn't make it long-term.

"What plans do you have while you're home on break?" he asked.

"Not much. I'm only here for a week. I need to get back and get a head start on some work for next semester."

"Your mother mentioned you take work too seriously and don't have enough fun." He twirled me around and caught me up by his side.

"She did?"

"Yes."

I spun away and back again, pressing up against him and swaying in time to the music. "What else did she say about me?"

"Let's see, that you don't date and don't cook. True?"

I smiled to myself. Mom definitely had me pegged. "True enough, I suppose."

The song came to an end, and I let my hand drop from Carter's grasp. The band launched into a slow song, and several couples moved onto the dance floor.

"Up for another dance?" Carter asked, opening his arms.

Why not? It was either dance with the smiling hottie in the tux or try talking the bartender out of a case of wine. I stepped into his embrace, and he wrapped one arm around me, settling one hand on the small of my back and catching my hand up with the other. I tucked my head to his chest and listened to his heart pound out its own beat. I breathed him in and let myself relax for a moment.

My mother was right about the no dating. But it wouldn't kill me to enjoy this beautiful man's company for an evening. Besides, I'd be heading back to Indiana in less than a week. What harm was there in sharing a dance or two with a relative stranger?

As we moved to the beat of the song, Mom and Clem waltzed by. My mother winked and gave me an exaggerated smile, apparently pleased with her matchmaking skills. I sighed. I'd let her enjoy her mini success, at least for tonight.

# CHAPTER 32
## *Dante*

I ALMOST DIDN'T HEAR Dr. Cain come into the room. I'd been immersed in the damn book for so long my butt had fallen asleep. Thanks to the constant, explicit sex scenes, other parts of me had become fully aroused. As the doc's rubber-soled shoes squeaked on the linoleum, I flipped the cover closed and tossed the book back in my bag.

"The swelling's gone down, and we've started to taper off the sedatives. Ready to see how your grandmother is doing?" he asked.

"Yeah, of course." I adjusted my crotch as I stood. Nothing like sporting a little wood in my ailing grandmother's hospital room.

The doctor stood over her bed, shining a pen light under her lids. "Mrs. Bishop, can you hear me?"

Meemaw's eyes fluttered, and my heart skipped a beat.

"Mrs. Bishop?" Dr. Cain moved the light.

She pushed his hand away. "Of course I can hear you. I hit my head. I'm not deaf."

I smiled as a wave of relief washed over me. She was back.

The doctor continued his exam. "Do you know what month it is?"

"May?" Meemaw asked, a twinkle in her gray-blue eye. "I'm just joking, Doc. It's December, or at least it was. I better not have missed Christmas. The senior center..." she flung the covers away and made a feeble attempt to get out of bed.

Dr. Cain stopped her, placing his hands firmly on her shoulders and guiding her back against the pillows. "Mrs. Bishop, you've been sedated for two days. You'll need to take it easy."

Meemaw's face took on a greenish tinge. "I don't feel so well."

I stood and grabbed her hand. "You had me really worried, old woman."

She met my gaze. "I'm sorry, my boy. I guess I'm just not as young as I used to be."

"You're going to be just fine, Mrs. Bishop. We'll just need you to take it easy for the next several days." Dr. Cain looked at me. "That means resting. No cooking, no big Christmas parties, and no more ladders."

"Got it, Doc. Thanks," I said, still holding Meemaw's hand.

"We'll keep her under observation for another night," Dr. Cain said. "Assuming all goes well, you can take her home tomorrow."

"Just in time for Christmas," I said.

"Oh, pshaw. They won't even be able to have Christmas at the center without me."

"That's not true," I said. "Mrs. Blake stopped by. She said she's got it all under control and that you shouldn't worry about a thing."

"Oh, Irene Blake. Sure, she's got it under control. She's been praying for me to stroke out for years so she could have a go at organizing a holiday meal."

Dr. Cain laughed. "I don't envy you, Dante. You're going to be busy trying to keep a handle on her for the next few days."

Meemaw continued, "Why, Bugsy told me he can't stand her stuffing. She uses a packaged mix. Can you imagine?"

"I'm sure it will be fine." Dr. Cain flipped the chart closed and slid it back into the slot at the foot of the bed. "We'll have you up and around in no time. You'll be back in charge well before the Valentine's Day dinner."

"You bet your sweet britches I will." Meemaw stuck out her bottom lip in a pout. "Speaking of food, who do I need to arm wrestle for a snack around here? I'm starving."

"I'll go get a nurse to find you something to eat," Dr. Cain said. "Keep an eye on her, okay?" With a final look at me, he left the room.

I set a Styrofoam cup of water down on the bedside table and tucked a straw into the plastic lid. "Do you want some water?"

"Bring it here." Meemaw reached out a shaky hand.

"You gave us all a scare. I'm glad you're going to be all right."

"How bad do I look?"

"Let's just say purple isn't your color."

Meemaw groaned. "Tell me, my boy, who came to visit me in the hospital? I want to know who my real friends are."

As I filled her in on all the news her visitors had shared, Cheryl stopped by with a tray of food.

"Here you go, Mrs. Bishop." She set it down on the table. "Soft foods without too much flavor. Doctor's orders."

"Cheryl Kincaid? Maybe I knocked my head harder than I thought." Meemaw pursed her lips and looked from me to Cheryl and back again.

"Cheryl's a nurse here at the hospital." I picked up the

plastic spoon and dipped it into the runny cup of Jell-O. "She's been taking care of you for the past couple of days."

Meemaw glared at Cheryl. "Never thought I'd see the two of you in the same room again."

Cheryl looked down at her feet. "I don't know what to say, Mrs. Bishop. What happened between me and Dante... well, that was a long time ago."

"Not long enough that I've forgotten how you broke my poor grandson's heart—"

"That's enough now." I lifted the spoon toward Meemaw's mouth.

"I thought they wanted me to get better." Meemaw scowled, taking the spoon from me and shoving it into her mouth. "This stuff is liable to make me feel worse."

I glanced at Cheryl's shocked expression and stifled a laugh. "She kind of calls it like she sees it."

"I remember." Cheryl smiled and grabbed the pitcher off the table. "I'll just go get you a refill on this."

After she'd left the room, Meemaw glanced over at me. "What's going on with you and Nurse Hatchett?"

"Nurse Hatchett, huh? Don't you think that's a little extreme, even for you?" I nudged the tray of food closer to her on the table.

Meemaw dipped her spoon into the bowl. "That girl is bad news, my boy."

"If I can get over it, so can you. Aren't you always telling me to forgive and forget?"

"Hmpf." Meemaw slid the Jell-O around in her mouth and swallowed. "I was talking about the time when Irene tried to pass off my famous checkerboard pie as her own recipe. That girl caused you so much pain."

"I said I'm over it." I sighed. I *was* over Cheryl Kincaid. It had taken me almost ten years and I still wouldn't consider the possibility of progressing beyond a casual fling with a woman, but for the most part, I'd patched my heart back together and forgiven her for screwing around on me with my best friend during my junior year of high school.

Meemaw wrinkled her nose. "Her grandmother stops in at the center from time to time. I thought she was running around with that no-good Jamie Casper."

"I wouldn't know. I've barely seen her since high school."

"Well, I'd steer clear of her."

"Trust me, I have no intention of starting anything with Cheryl. Now why don't you try some of these mashed potatoes?"

"You trying to poison me?" Her eyes widened. "I guaran-damn-tee you these came from a box."

"One serving of instant potatoes won't kill you."

"Fine." Meemaw scooped a tiny bit of potatoes onto her spoon and studied it before sliding it into her mouth. "How are things going with Faith?"

"Faith?" My cheeks flushed.

"Dante, surely you remember the sweet girl you got frisky with on Thanksgiving?"

My jaw dropped.

"Close your mouth, my boy. Anyone could see the sparks flying between the two of you." She pointed her plastic spoon at me. "Including Lorraine. And she's legally blind in one eye. Probably both, if you ask me."

"Things with Faith are, um, good. She flew home for Christmas."

Meemaw nodded and continued to slurp her way through her late lunch. My mind wandered to Faith. Just the mention of her name had me practically breaking out into a sweat.

Cheryl returned with the full pitcher of water. She set it down on the table and turned toward me. "If you want to run home and grab some clean clothes or something, I can sit with her for a while."

"Aw, that's okay," I said.

Meemaw sniffed the air. "A shower might be a good idea. How long have you been here?"

Cheryl sat down in the chair next to the bed. "He hasn't left your side since they brought you in, Mrs. Bishop."

"In that case, you'd better get out of here. Go on home and check on things for me, will you?" Meemaw narrowed her eyes. "It'll give Cheryl and me a chance to get all caught up. Make sure the turkey is in the fridge. I should have had that bird thawing days ago. You may even have to put it in a cold water bath... it'll probably never be thawed out in time to cook now."

"I don't think you'll be cooking any turkey for the next few days," I said. "Remember? Doctor's orders."

"Doctor, schmockter." Meemaw waved her hands at me. "Go on. Get out of here. Fill up the sink with cold water and let the turkey sit in it while you get cleaned up. If you don't want me to cook it, I'll walk you through how to do it yourself. I promised that old coot Bugsy some of my home-cooked bird, and there's no way my grandson is eating fast food on Christmas."

"I'd be happy to help you cook the turkey," Cheryl said.

I gulped, and Meemaw gave me a knowing glance. "Don't you have plans for Christmas?" She gave Cheryl the once-over with her eyes.

"My family's going out to my Granpap's in Rushmoor. I have to work that night, so I was just planning on cooking up a TV dinner."

Meemaw wouldn't hear of someone not having a home-cooked meal for Christmas, even if she was convinced Cheryl was up to no good.

"Let's get caught up a little before we make plans," Meemaw said. "Go on now. Fill up the sink. The whole thing's got to fit inside. Cheryl, hand me that paper over there, will ya? I'll make a list while you're gone," she said to me. "You can pick up the rest of the stuff we'll need from the store later."

I shrugged into my coat and grabbed my bag off the floor. I bent down to kiss Meemaw on the head. "So good to have you back, old woman. I sure was getting lonely with no one to boss me around."

Cheryl walked me to the door of the room. "I'm sorry. I probably shouldn't have invited myself over like that."

"Don't worry about it. She'll grill you for a bit, and by the time I get back she'll be insisting you join us for dinner. It'll be good for her to have something to focus on." *And I can prove to myself and her that you've got no hold on my heart anymore.*

She smiled. "Okay, then. Drive safe and I'll see you in a bit."

"Thanks." I walked down the hall and out into the cold, frozen parking lot. What the hell had I got myself into this time?

# CHAPTER 33
## Dante

"NOT LIKE THAT or you're going to get lumps." Meemaw sat on the edge of her kitchen chair, doing her best to direct me in the fine art of gravy making.

"Settle down. You're going to give yourself a heart attack." I lifted the spoon out of the heavy pan and licked it with my tongue.

Meemaw raised a fist and shook it at me. "Why, I'll knock you into next week—"

"How does the turkey look?" Cheryl opened the oven door and lifted the roasting pan out onto the counter.

Her attention temporarily redirected, Meemaw focused on the turkey. "That looks good, I suppose. Now just let it rest for a few minutes."

I mouthed a silent "thanks" to Cheryl. I hadn't been too excited about her joining us for Christmas, but after spending the entire day before trying to curtail Meemaw's activity, even I was glad for the distraction.

"I think we're almost ready." I poured the slightly lumpy gravy into the thermal gravy boat and set it down on the kitchen table.

"I do wish we were at the center right now," Meemaw said. "It's so lonely with just the three of us here."

"What are you talking about?" I asked. "There's more energy between the three of us than in the whole room of folks at the center. Besides, Cheryl brought a homemade pumpkin pie. You wouldn't want to have to share that, would you?"

"Hmpf." Meemaw always made homemade pecan pie for Christmas. Her nose had been knocked slightly out of joint, but that was probably good for her.

I plugged in the electric carving knife and proceeded to carve up the bird. "Smells good." When I was done, Cheryl and I sat down next to Meemaw at the small table.

Meemaw waggled a bent finger at us. "Join hands. Let's say our prayers."

I stuck my hand out for Cheryl to take. As our skin touched, I waited for that old familiar spark. Nothing. She had no hold on me anymore.

Our hands joining us in a circle, we listened to Meemaw say grace.

"Okay, let's eat." I couldn't drop Cheryl's hand fast enough before I reached for the platter of turkey.

"This looks delicious, Mrs. Bishop." Cheryl took the serving fork I offered and pierced a few pieces of meat.

"Well, I sure hope it's edible. It's nowhere near what I would have made if you two would've let me help." Meemaw stuck out her lower lip in her trademark pout.

"Looks good, smells good." I popped a bite of turkey in my mouth. "Tastes great."

Meemaw poked me in the arm. "Mind your manners, now."

I gave her a giant grin. "So, Cheryl, how late do you have to work tonight?"

"I go on at four and off at midnight."

"That stinks," I said. "Do you think it will be busy?"

"Depends on the weather. If the snow keeps falling like it has been, we'll probably have a few car accidents to deal with. We also usually get some folks who don't have anyone to spend Christmas with who stop by."

"What do you mean?" I asked.

"They just get lonely and come in. The cafeteria gives away a free meal on Christmas, so a lot of them just drop in for some food and conversation."

"They need to come to the senior center," Meemaw said.

"Oh, we send them your way." Cheryl took a sip of water. "Sometimes it's whole families though. It's sad to see the little kids who don't get anything for Christmas. We usually keep a stash of gifts at the nurses' station just in case."

"Isn't that sweet? Why, I've got some things I can send with you tonight," Meemaw said. "I bought some stuff to donate to that toy drive the police put on, but didn't get a chance to drop them off."

"That would be great, Mrs. Bishop."

I looked from Meemaw to Cheryl and back. When did she have time to go toy shopping? The capacity of my grandmother's giant heart never failed to surprise me. The fact she let Cheryl into her home, especially her kitchen, proved she had a heart of gold.

We worked our way through a third of the small turkey and half of the trimmings before I pushed back from the table. "I can't eat another bite."

"Me neither," Cheryl said. "It was delicious."

"It was fine," Meemaw said.

I gestured toward Meemaw. "She won't admit it, but she thinks it was the best Christmas dinner she's ever had."

Meemaw crumpled up her napkin and tossed it at me. "Oh pshaw. Your gravy was lumpy, and your stuffing didn't have near enough craisins in it."

I laughed out loud then stood up and began to clear the table. "Cheryl, can you help her into her recliner? I'll get started on the dishes."

"Sure." Cheryl stood up and offered her arm to Meemaw. "Let's get you settled and then I'll come back in to help."

My arms were elbow-deep in soapy water when Cheryl re-entered the kitchen. I hummed "Jingle Bells" under my breath while I scoured the remains of dinner from the plates and serving dishes. Cheryl began to rinse the soapy dishes stacked up in the sink.

"Thanks again for inviting me for dinner," she said.

"My pleasure. I think it was good for her to have some company. She really enjoyed it."

"And you?" She looked over at me, a crease furrowing the small space between her brows.

I lifted a soapy hand out of the dishwater and pushed my glasses back up on my nose. "Um, yeah, I suppose. Me too."

"Good." Cheryl bumped me with her hip.

I studied her face. She couldn't be hoping for another shot at things. "Look, I don't want you to get the wrong—"

"How's it going in there?" Meemaw's voice traveled from the front room. "Be careful with that turkey platter. Am I ever going to get to try that pumpkin pie?"

Rolling my eyes, I shouted back, "Hold your horses. We'll be done in a few minutes."

"You're lucky. She really loves you," Cheryl said.

"Yeah, I love her too. She's never let me down." I wiped my hands on a towel and reached for the pie on the counter.

"Dante, I—"

"You want to dish this up?"

Cheryl grabbed a knife and cut three slices of pie, then topped each one with a squirt of canned whipped cream. She set a fork on each plate and handed me one. We made our way out to the living room, where Meemaw watched an old Bing Crosby movie in black and white.

"Here you go, Mrs. Bishop." Cheryl set a plate down on the TV tray in front of her. "I hope you like it."

"I'm sure it will be fine." Meemaw let out a long forlorn sigh.

I took a bite and forced myself to chew and swallow. Did she say this was pumpkin pie? Didn't have much flavor to it.

Fork poised over her plate, Meemaw finished swallowing and opened her mouth to speak.

I cleared my throat and caught her attention. I shook my head, and she closed her mouth.

"This has a really interesting flavor," I said.

Cheryl's eyes lit up. "I'm so glad you like it."

"Mmm," I mumbled with a mouth full of tasteless, gelatinous dessert.

Meemaw let her fork drop to the plate in a clatter. "I'm just too full to eat another bite."

I stood up and took her plate. "I'll take it to the kitchen for you." I made it to the kitchen and scraped the remainder of my pie and Meemaw's into the trashcan before Cheryl had a chance to even look up. Some things would never change. She still couldn't cook for shit.

Cheryl brought her dessert plate into the kitchen. "I guess I'd better get going if I'm going to get to work on time."

Meemaw yelled from the front room. "Dante, go grab those packages for her. They're in the hall closet."

I found the bag of toys and carried it outside.

She followed me to the back of the car and popped the trunk. "Thanks for inviting me, I had a nice time today."

"Yeah, you're welcome."

"It was nice catching up. Sounds like you're doing really well over in Newbridge. I remember you always wanted to get the big paying job and all." She looked down at the ground. "I was wondering, would you want to maybe go out sometime?"

I sighed. I'd been waiting for her to bring up something like this. "I'm, uh, kind of seeing someone." Meemaw was already under the false impression Faith and I had something going on. Why not let Cheryl believe the same thing? If my little white lie got rid of any lingering ideas Cheryl might be having, what was the harm?

"Oh sure. I'm sorry, I didn't realize." Cheryl slammed the trunk then hurried to the driver side door. She climbed inside, turning the key over in the ignition.

I tucked my thumbs in the front pockets of my jeans as Cheryl backed down the drive. I wasn't sure what was going on with Faith and our strictly physical relationship, but the chemistry between us was hotter than anything I'd ever had with any other girl, including Cheryl. I didn't believe in giving someone who'd crossed me a second chance, and I sure as hell wasn't going to do anything to jeopardize another go 'round with Faith.

As Cheryl's car reached the end of the drive and made a right onto the main road toward town, I turned back toward the house. Meemaw stood at the front window, spying on me through the curtain. She should be taking it easy. I squashed all thoughts of Cheryl and Faith down for now and made my way into the house to do battle with my grandmother.

# CHAPTER 34

## *Faith*

"I'D GO with the light pink," Claire suggested.

We sat side-by-side in massage chairs, wrapping up our spa day with mani-pedis. I couldn't remember the last time I'd felt so totally and completely relaxed. A ninety-minute hot stone massage and hour-long facial had that effect on me.

"I don't know, Mom. Pink isn't really my color." So many choices. Maybe a different color for each toe? I considered a bottle of bright red. Little Red Riding Hood. Yep, this must be the one. I smiled to myself when I thought of dressing up as Red on Halloween.

Only two more days before I made it back to Newbridge and continued my "research" for my new book. I was looking forward to seeing Dante. Although, it wasn't really the seeing I was excited about... more like getting to feel his mouth on mine and the perfect way he felt inside me.

"What are you smiling about?" My mother's voice cut through the steamy recollection playing out in my mind.

I sat up in my chair. "Nothing."

"Oh, I thought maybe you were thinking about Carter." Claire lifted her eyebrows in an unspoken question.

"Mom, I told you already. Carter's a nice guy, but I'm not interested."

"He's quite a catch, Faith. Why, Clem says he can pretty much dictate his own future."

"That's great, Mom. But the thing is, I'm not looking for a catch right now. I don't have time."

Claire put her hand on my arm. "Don't get all upset. I'm just asking you to give him a chance."

She had been talking up Carter all week. It's not that I didn't like him. He was nice. Cute too. Once I earned tenure, I'd be giving up my career writing erotic romance, so long-term that wouldn't be an issue. On paper, we'd probably make a good match. But something was missing. I hadn't quite figured out what yet. But why lead the poor guy on?

"I'm leaving in two days. Even if I wanted to give him a chance, I'm running out of time."

"Nonsense." Claire stood up, waving her hands to dry her nails. "We'd better get going. I told Clem we'd be back in time for an early dinner."

I wiggled my feet into my flip-flops and followed her out of the salon. It had been a nice day. All week, all I'd wanted to do was spend some time with my mother. Finally, I'd had the chance.

We'd had lunch at a café we used to go to when I was little, then Mom had booked us for spa packages in the afternoon. She'd even splurged and arranged for a haircut, style, and makeup application for me. Having my mom to myself had been a real treat.

As we pulled up the hill and into the driveway, I noticed a black BMW parked in front of the third stall. Great, another one of Clem's disciples was probably hanging out inside. I didn't mind making small talk with Clem's followers, but I was ready to get back to my small apartment where I could inhabit my own space and not have to worry about slipping up and saying something that would expose me.

We walked through the door into the house, and I heard Clem's voice and then a man's laughter. As I rounded the corner, I saw Carter sitting on one of the barstools at the kitchen island. He stood up when he saw us come in.

"Well, Carter. What a surprise." Mom smiled and walked toward him, giving him a kiss on each cheek.

Carter turned to me. "Hi. Did you have a nice time today?"

I busied myself at the counter, reaching for a glass and filling it with water from the fridge. "Yeah, we had a great day. I didn't know you were coming over." I glanced at my mother, who stood next to Clem on the other side of the kitchen.

Carter smiled, then crossed his arms across his chest and leaned back against the counter. He looked pretty damn comfortable in my mother's kitchen. "I was just in the neighborhood and thought I'd stop by and see if you wanted to grab some dinner."

I shot a glance over at my mother. She smiled and shrugged her shoulders.

"Oh, I don't know. I think Mom mentioned something about having an early dinner here with Clem."

"Oh, you kids go on and have fun." Claire grabbed Clem by the arm and led him from the kitchen. "I think Clem and I are going to go out. Just the two of us."

Carter caught me rolling my eyes and laughed. "Looks like your mom just made other plans."

"Yeah, how about that? It appears I'm suddenly free for the evening." I didn't appreciate being blindsided with a dinner date, but I'd be gone in just a few days. What was the harm in having dinner together? "Let me just go freshen up a bit. I'll be back in a minute."

"Sounds good. I'll wait right here." He moved back toward the stool and settled in.

I jogged upstairs and set my purse down on the bed. Rummaging through the clothes I'd brought with me, I pulled out a fresh pair of jeans and a cami, then grabbed a light cardigan to wear on top. I picked up my phone and shot off a quick text to Jess.

> Surprise... Mom scheduled a date night for me with the pretty pastor.

> Don't do anything I wouldn't do.

> Yeah, right.

> What about Dante?

> Dante who? ;)

I was totally teasing. Carter was just a friend and Dante was... I wasn't sure exactly what to call him, but he'd definitely skipped way past the friend zone.

> If you're done with him, I'll take your sloppy seconds!

> Hands off, girl.

I almost followed that up by telling her he was mine. That wasn't entirely true, though. Our arrangement didn't include words like *mine*, or *ours*, and that was exactly how it needed to be.

I hadn't thought about him for at least two hours. When would I be done with him? I closed my eyes and remembered the last time we'd been together. Not in the near future. He'd been the perfect solution for writer's block, but I hadn't been able to type a single word since I'd arrived in California. I needed to get back to my muse.

Grumbling, I got up off the bed and entered the enormous bathroom. What did I want out of the evening ahead with Carter? He was easy on the eyes. Great at conversation. And I did enjoy his company. Secure future... stable family life. He was from the Midwest, for crying out loud. Plus, my mom loved him.

Sure, there wasn't the intense, overwhelming chemistry, but that never happened in real life. At least not with someone who seemed like such a logical match. I wasn't sure I'd ever warm up to the idea of being with a pastor, but he'd also have that law degree to fall back on. He was almost perfect on paper. Why couldn't I make my mom happy and give him a real chance?

He wasn't Dante.

Dante. With his piercing blue eyes and permanent five o'clock shadow. His talented fingers and wicked tongue. No, there was no way in hell Carter was anything like Dante.

I fanned my face and chest. I couldn't deal with another Dante right now. I wasn't even doing a good job dealing with just one. What exactly was going on between us, anyway?

The sex was inspiring. I had half of a completed manuscript to prove it. But was there something more to him than the incredible "O's" I'd grown so fond of? I pushed all thoughts of him aside for the night. I'd have a friends-only, G-rated good time with the safe, pretty pastor and save all thoughts of Dante for later...when I was alone and had time to do something about it.


CARTER MADE small talk as he navigated the BMW through the stoplights and slow traffic on the PCH. I half-listened as I rested my arm by the open window and let the cool late afternoon breeze flow over me. Back in Indiana, everyone would be tucked away indoors. If they had to go out, they'd have to bundle up in layers—long underwear, flannel shirts, wool socks, mittens, scarves, and gaiters.

A teen on a skateboard darted in front of the car.

Carter slammed on the brakes and laid on the horn. "He's lucky I had a chance to stop."

"So do you enjoy driving around the LA area?" I glanced over at him, his hands still clenched on the steering wheel.

He took in a deep breath and pressed on the gas. "I don't think I'll ever get used to the traffic. How can there be twelve lanes on the highway and all of them at a halt?"

"Yeah, you don't see that much in Newbridge. Think you'll ever move back to the Midwest?"

Carter reached over and squeezed my hand then put his own back on the wheel. "Once I'm finished with law school I'll be looking for a place to build my congregation,"—he glanced over and met my gaze—"and my family."

I closed my eyes and let my head fall back against the headrest. What exactly had my mom and Clem told him about me?

A few minutes later, the car stopped, and I opened my eyes.

Carter got out of his side and walked around to open my door. "It's probably been a while since you had fresh seafood. I thought you might enjoy dining down on the pier."

"Sounds great." I linked my arm through his and let him lead me out onto the dock as the sun dipped low on the horizon.

Shades of pink, purple, and orange blazed across the sky. I sighed. I could do without the traffic or the crowds of southern California, but I definitely missed the sunsets. We walked to the iconic restaurant at the end of the pier, and I leaned up against the wooden railing. "Can we finish watching the sunset before we go in?"

"Whatever your heart desires." Carter put an arm on either side of me and nestled up against me, his clean-shaven cheek pressed against mine. "It's beautiful, isn't it?"

I nodded, drawing my cardigan tighter around me.

"Are you cold?" He rubbed his hands up and down my arms.

"I'm fine. I always forget how much it cools off once the sun starts to set."

"Let's get you inside." He grabbed hold of my hand and gently tugged me toward the door.

# CHAPTER 35

## Faith

I RELUCTANTLY LEFT my post at the railing. Where was Dante tonight? It would already be pitch dark in Indiana. Had he watched the sunset while thinking about me? Doubtful. He was probably fighting off coeds who'd already returned to school from Christmas vacation.

I followed Carter into the restaurant and to our table overlooking the water. Candlelight flickered, the dim light darkening half of his face in shadow. "What are you in the mood for tonight?"

I took the menu from the server and scanned the wine and beer list. "I'll take a Honeyweiss, please."

"I thought maybe we'd share a bottle of Chardonnay." Carter nudged my menu to the side and smiled at me.

I shrugged. "Sure. Chardonnay would be lovely."

Was he going to order my food for me, too? Why was I being so bitchy? I shook my head, trying to shake my crabby mood away. A gorgeous, intelligent man sat right in front of me. Even though I wasn't interested in anything romantic happening, I could still enjoy his company for an evening and make my mother happy in the process.

I smiled and set my menu down. "Would you order for me, Carter?"

"I'd be honored."

The server returned with a bottle of Santa Maria Valley Chardonnay. She opened it and let Carter try it before pouring a glass for each of us.

Carter raised his glass and gestured for me to do the same. "I'd like to propose a toast. To new beginnings."

"To new beginnings." I lifted the glass to my lips and took a generous gulp.

When our server returned, Carter ordered salads and the catch of the day for both of us.

"Do you like oysters?" I asked.

He squinted at me. "I haven't tried them before."

"Do you want a half-dozen as an appetizer?" The server tapped her pen against her notepad.

"Sure, why not?" Carter smiled at me. "Let's try new things tonight."

Try new things, huh? Carter didn't strike me as the super adventurous type. What would he do if I pulled out one of the sex toys I'd mentioned in one of my books? He'd shit bricks, that's what.

I wasn't being fair. I hadn't actually tried any of them, either. All my knowledge came from extensive online research, but that didn't mean I wasn't willing to go there with the right guy.

An image of Dante slid through my mind. Eyes half-closed, jeans around his ankles, that look on his face like he always got right before he—

"Come again?" Carter's voice cut through my naughty fantasy, and I coughed. He was talking to the server.

"I asked if you want horseradish or Tabasco with your oysters."

Carter's brow furrowed as if this was the most important decision he'd make all day. "What do you think, Faith?"

"I like them both ways,"—I grinned and licked my lips —"hot and spicy."

The server nodded and walked away.

Carter didn't volley the conversation back at me, just cleared his throat and took a sip of water. "So, tell me about your plans for your career."

I launched into my standard reply. Publish in a few literary journals. Continue working toward a tenured position after that.

"I'm assuming at some point you want to settle down, start a family?" He took a roll from the breadbasket and spread a pat of butter over it.

"Eventually. I've still got several years to go before I'd want to settle down. Between teaching and publishing, I've got quite a bit on my plate."

"So where does the potential for a relationship fit in?"

I adjusted the cloth napkin on my lap. This was my chance to set him straight and make sure we were both on the same page. "I'm not looking for a relationship right now. Did my mother give you a different impression?"

"She said you'd say that. But she worries about you. I'd be willing to wait."

At that moment, our server returned and set our platter of oysters on the table between us. I bit my lip while Carter assured her we didn't need anything else.

His last comment had made me a little nervous. I needed clarification. "What do you mean by that?"

"Men have certain needs." He studied the platter of oysters.

Trying to avoid the direction the conversation seemed headed, I reached out and picked one. I shook the bottle of

Tabasco over it and raised the shell to my mouth, letting the oyster slide down my throat.

"Oh, my gosh. Delicious. Did you know some people say oysters are an aphrodisiac?"

"You're not making this easy for me." He took a sip of wine and attempted to pick up an oyster.

I selected one and passed it to him. "I'm not trying to make it hard."

"As I was saying, men have certain needs. I'm not proud to admit this to you, but I'm not pure."

Oh, my god. Where was he going with this? I avoided looking at him and took another large gulp of wine.

"I've been with a woman, Faith. She tempted me, and in my weakness, I succumbed. Clem saved me. I became active in the church and took a virginity pledge."

"So, you're a born-again virgin?" I poured myself another glass of wine and tried to digest Carter's revelation, especially why he thought he needed to share it with *me*.

He relaxed against the back of his chair, the oyster still perched awkwardly in his hand. "Wow. I was so nervous to talk to you about this."

"I think that's great. But I'm pretty sure we're not on the same wavelength here."

A look of concern flashed across his face. "What do you mean?"

I sighed. How much should I divulge? "I mean, I'm not exactly *pure* myself, but I don't feel like I need to talk about it with a relative stranger."

"I'd like us to be able to talk about anything." He lifted the oyster and tipped it into his mouth.

Immediately, his cheeks puffed out, and a strangled choking sound came from the back of his throat. A line of drool dripped from the corner of his clenched lips. He raised his napkin to dab at the edge of his mouth as his eyes bugged and his cheeks took on a greenish tinge.

"Carter, are you okay?"

His brows furrowed as his mouth gaped open. A horrible gagging sound ripped from his throat as the oyster and the remaining contents of his stomach splashed onto the stark white tablecloth.

I jumped out of my seat and away from the table. The diners around us stopped eating and looked on in disgust.

Carter wiped his mouth with his napkin. "I'm so sorry. I have a horrible gag reflex. If you'll excuse me for a moment."

I nodded and picked up my glass of wine, raising it in salute to the patrons around me. Then I tilted it back and drained it.

THE RIDE HOME didn't take long. Traffic had eased up and Carter maneuvered the car across multiple lanes on the 405. Conversation was minimal. After returning from the restroom, Carter had tossed a handful of twenties onto the table and led me out of the restaurant. He'd apologized profusely for ruining our evening.

I felt sorry for him for multiple reasons. First, the obvious. Puking in the middle of a nice restaurant would send almost anyone over the edge. He'd actually handled the whole situation better than I would have had I been the one to heave the contents of my stomach into the breadbasket.

Second, because there was no way in hell I was ever going to be the kind of girl Carter wanted and needed in his life. He was a good guy. A little too evangelical for my taste, but he would make some modest, virginal woman a wonderful, devoted, and loving husband someday. Everyone assumed I'd fit the bill. How could they not? I'd never done anything to show them otherwise.

I'd followed along with my mom and Clem, like a little lamb being led by the almighty shepherd. But that wasn't who I was. I didn't want to hurt anyone. Not Carter, Clem, or especially my mother. But this whole setup with Carter had gone too far.

What would they think if I told them about the books I'd written? And how would I ever explain the arrangement I'd proposed with Dante? Would my mother and Clem ever willingly welcome the illegitimate bartender into their fold?

The car slowed, and Carter entered the security code at the gate. A few turns later, he pulled into the long driveway and stopped the car. He walked around and opened my door, then followed me to the portico.

He paused before the stone steps leading onto the front porch. "I'm really sorry about the way this evening went."

I patted his arm. "It's okay. I had a good time."

"No." He wrapped his hand around mine. "I embarrassed myself and you. And now we're out of time. You head back soon, and I've missed my chance."

"Carter, I—"

My words were muffled as he drew me against his chest. "I won't ask for a kiss, Faith. I don't deserve one after the way I behaved tonight." His hand stroked my hair. "I think you'll come around. I'm a patient man. I'll be waiting." He pulled away and kissed the top of my head.

I stood motionless on the step as he walked back to the car and ducked inside. As he backed down the driveway, he lowered the window and waved. Stunned, I lifted my hand in response, then turned and slipped through the front door.

Wait a minute. He'd be waiting? Waiting for what? As the realization of Carter's intentions sank in, I staggered against the door and leaned into it for support. Unless I'd completely misunderstood, he seemed to think we'd made some kind of commitment to each other.

# CHAPTER 36

## *Dante*

I PULLED into the parking lot in front of Tapped and killed the engine. It was good to be home. The stress of not knowing what was going on with Meemaw had clawed at me all week. I'd made sure she was settled in and arranged for her friends to check in on her several times a day for the next few weeks.

What was I going to do if an offer from a division out east finally came? If I landed one of those jobs, it would mean up to ninety percent travel. I could never put her in a home. Not only would she flat out refuse to go, it would squash her spirit. I sighed and raked my hands through my hair, wishing I had someone to talk to about my problems.

As I climbed the steps to my apartment, I thought about Faith. I'd found myself thinking about her a lot over break. Too much, in fact. She'd gotten under my skin, burrowed in like some fucking wood tick or something.

If I wasn't careful, she'd suck the life force right out of me. I needed to focus on my job and my mentorship to secure that damn letter of recommendation. A transfer out east to a bigger division and a higher-paying job would guarantee my and Meemaw's future. I'd just have to figure out a way to convince Meemaw to come with me if the job panned out, and I damn well wasn't going to let my fuck buddy get in the way of that.

That wasn't fair. She'd made it perfectly clear she didn't want anything to do with me besides the free use of my body. It was my problem I was starting to let her get to me. Should I pull the plug on our arrangement before it even really began?

I opened the door to my apartment and flipped on the lights. The cushions on the couch sat askew. I hadn't fixed them after that night we'd reinstated her crazy sex-only plan. I dropped my bag on the floor and set my keys on the counter, then slid my coat off and walked over to the couch. Grabbing a cushion from the floor, I held it up to my face. The faint scent of her shampoo teased my nose, and I took a deep inhale.

I was turning into Wyatt, a fucking pussy-whipped pansy. Grunting, I tossed the cushion back onto the couch and exited my apartment.

Less than a minute later, I'd claimed a stool at the bar and watched as Oliver attempted to switch out a keg under the counter.

"Need some help with that?" I asked.

"Nah, bro. The fuckin' hose is just givin' me a bit of trouble. She'll be right in no time."

I smiled and shook my head. Hiring Oliver might prove to be a mistake; even after a few weeks, I could barely understand him. The girls seemed to like him, though. And Wyatt was a big fan of anything that brought more girls into the bar. More girls meant more guys, and more guys meant we'd sell more beer.

Oliver wiped his hands on his jeans and grabbed a pint glass. "So, what'll it be, mate?"

"How about a Honeyweiss?" Damn, that's what Faith always ordered.

"Right. Sweet-as."

"Sweet as what?" I asked.

"Aw, nothing, just sweet-as. You know, like cool."

"Whatever, dude."

Oliver set the mug down on the bar in front of me, and I took a long sip. As I turned on my stool to see if I recognized anyone, a hand clapped me on the shoulder.

"Dante, my man."

"Oh, hey, Murph." I eyed Murph over the rim of my glasses, not sure whether or not I should brace myself for an uppercut to the jaw or a handshake. Murph offered his hand, so I shook it.

As he settled onto the stool next to me, he signaled to Oliver, who automatically pulled a pint of Bud. "Thanks, bro."

"Have a nice break?" I asked.

Murph sipped the froth from the top of his glass. "Yeah, it was all right. How about you?"

"Fine. Glad to be back."

"I've been meaning to talk to you about Faith."

Damn, this again? "What do you need?"

Murph's eyes bored into mine. "Is there something going on between you?"

"No, not really." I sure as hell didn't need Murph busting my balls. Whatever crush he had on Faith, she definitely didn't seem interested in him.

Murph shook his head and smiled. "You're not fucking with me, are you? I was there when you tossed the bra at her."

"That was an isolated event." I shrugged. "You know me, I don't tend to stick around."

"Then you wouldn't be interested in a little dirt about her, huh?"

"What the hell are you talking about?"

Murph slid a copy of the newspaper across the bar to me. "Page three."

I took a swig of beer and flipped through the pages, my eyes scanning the headlines for whatever dumbass article Murph wanted me to see.

"Right there." His finger jabbed at the paper.

The words swam across the page, and I adjusted my glasses. Something about a little family reunion on campus. How famous Christian author Claire Kepner got to speak to her daughter's class. "What the hell?"

"Shit, bro. That's Faith's mom. Good thing you're not tapping that, my friend. Can you imagine? What kind of d-bag would stick it to the daughter of America's favorite Christian sweetheart? Her stepdad's the pastor of some wicked big evangelical church out in California, too. You dodged a bullet with that one."

I grabbed my beer and drained my glass. "Oliver, pour me another one?"

Murph swiveled around in his stool. "You've got nothing to worry about, though, right?" His eyes narrowed into slits.

"What's your big hang-up with her, anyway?"

"Nothing. I'm over it and moving on. Met this chick right before break, and we're hitting it off."

"That's great." I gripped the fresh beer and pushed off the stool. "See you around." Hopefully Murph would stop busting my balls about Faith now. But what the hell was with the article in the paper?

I made my way to the back office to check the schedule. I'd been hoping to start up where Faith and I left off as soon as her plane landed. But Wyatt probably had me working the late shift on New Year's Eve. Maybe I could sneak over before my shift started.

Oliver found me sitting at Wyatt's desk, beer in hand, shaking my head. "Are you pissed, mate?"

"Huh? No, I'm a little irked I'm scheduled for tomorrow night. It's New Year's Eve. But nah, I'm not pissed about it."

Oliver smirked. "Not pissed off, like mad. I mean pissed, like drunk?"

"Oh. Hell no. I'm not drunk. But if I have to spend any more time around Murph, I might need a few more pints."

"Yeah, he's a stirrer, all right." He mimed stirring a giant pot with a spoon. "Stirs up trouble?"

My mouth quirked into a smile. "Yeah, you're right. He's a stirrer for sure. Any chance you want to take my New Year's Eve shift?"

"Wish I could help you out, but I've got plans already."

I nodded, and Oliver disappeared around the corner. Shit. I'd hoped to have the night off so Faith and I could get together. I wanted to show her just how well I could handle her sex-only proposal, but now it looked like I might have to pull out. Maybe I needed to rethink our agreement anyway. I sure as hell didn't want to get caught corrupting a pastor's daughter.

But thinking about shutting down our arrangement made my heart squeeze. We were adults. We knew what we were getting into. We could handle it. And why would Murph try to shove a wedge between us unless he still had a thing for Faith?

With a slurry of unanswered questions spinning around in my head, I got up. My hand wrapped around the cold pint of beer, and I made my way out front. Murph had better be gone, or I might just have to invite him outside. I was done listening to what Murph had to say. From here on out, any digs at Faith might be best handled with a fist to the mouth.

# CHAPTER 37

## Faith

I READ over the email one more time. I'd been selected to take over Professor Middleford's classes. I rested my elbows on the laminate desk and cradled my head in my hands, gazing out the fourteenth-story window onto the snowy quad below. Good things were happening.

Being back in Newbridge, the words flowed again, and I wanted to get another chapter written before I'd let myself initiate a New Year's booty call. A tap sounded on the glass of the small study carrel window, and I turned around. When my eyes met Dante's, a slow smile spread across my lips. He must have taken that as an invitation and cracked open the door.

"Hey, you," I said. "How was your break?"

"It was okay. How about yours?"

"Fine. Too many parties to go to. I'm glad to be back."

"Yeah, I'm glad you're back, too."

I rose up out of the chair and snaked my arms around his neck. Instead of responding, he untangled himself and took a step back. Had he changed his mind?

"Is there something you want to tell me, Faith?"

He wouldn't make eye contact, just stared at the putty-colored wall.

"Um, I don't think so. What's going on?"

Dante pulled a piece of paper out of his pocket.

A sliver of panic sliced through me. Had someone left a page for him, too? I'd tried to put the threat out of my mind. What if Dante found out?

The paper crinkled as his fingers smoothed out the creases. "Murph stopped by the bar yesterday."

I swallowed hard. "Oh?" Dante passed the page to me. The damn article about my mom's visit to campus. Relief flooded my system.

"So, you didn't think you needed to mention the little fact that your parents are paving the moral high ground?"

I sighed and crossed my arms over my chest.

"What would Mom and Reverend Kepner think about our little arrangement? Did you fill them in on all the details after Christmas service?" he asked.

"That's not fair. I can't help who my mom is or who she chose to marry. I love my family, but that's not my life. I don't fit in there anymore."

"You didn't have to lie about it."

"Said the pot to the kettle, huh? You think I don't know that you told your grandmother we were officially an item? I got a Christmas card from her for crying out loud. She sent me her recipe for lemon crinkle cookies and told me how happy she is that you finally found a nice girl and that we'd make beautiful babies together."

Dante groaned and sucked in a deep breath. "She said that, for real? About the grandbabies?"

"She just wants you to be happy. You're lucky you have someone who loves you so much."

He nudged me with an elbow. "Looks like maybe we both fucked up a little."

I swatted at his chest. "No, you fucked up. Mine was a lie of omission. Not the same thing at all."

"Semantics. Are we still on or not? I have an hour before I have to start my shift."

I should call it off. Walk away and chalk this up to a botched experiment. Pull out my planner and figure out how to get back on track before Dante completely derailed me. But my fingers itched to tangle in his hair. My lips tingled, eager for the taste of his tongue.

So instead of kicking him out and getting back to my writing, I nodded.

His mouth quirked into a confident grin. "Come on, there's something I want to show you." He grabbed my hand and tugged me through the door.

## Dante

"WHERE ARE WE GOING?" She tried to keep up as I moved quickly through the shelves of books.

I reached the stairwell and opened the door, pulling her through behind me. One bare bulb above the door lit up the landing. I held onto the metal railing with one hand, my other still grasping hers. Then I began to move down the steps into the darkness of the floor below.

When we reached the landing, I slid a key out of my pocket.

"What are you doing?" she asked.

"Just wait." I unlocked the door and yanked it open. A blast of warm air blew past us into the stairwell.

"What's this?"

I nudged her through the doorway and let it slam behind us. "It's the thirteenth floor."

We moved through the dim room, past rows of mechanical equipment. The heavy air seemed to part as we passed, the tangy smell of machinery and neglect settling on our shoulders.

She stopped in her tracks, causing me to spin around. "But there is no thirteenth floor."

"Come on, even you know that's just superstition. One of the maintenance guys came in the bar over break and I asked him about it. Since the building is so tall, they put half the equipment in the basement and half of it here."

She looked around. "So, this is the real thirteenth floor?"

"I have to get the key back to him tomorrow." I ran my thumb over her wrist. Being so close to her... I'd missed this. "I thought it would be fun to check it out."

She slid her fingers over my palm. "Pretty cool, Dante."

I'd been looking forward to seeing her for over a week. Now that she was this close, I couldn't wait any longer. Grabbing her by the shoulders, I crushed my mouth down on hers. Her hands immediately went around my neck, drawing me tight against her. I fumbled with the edge of her shirt, yanking it loose from her jeans.

After fighting through four layers, my fingers finally rested on the soft skin of her waist. I urged her backward until we crashed into a tall metal gate. A loud clang rang out.

She drew back for a moment, and I listened to make sure no one would come because of the noise. Assured we were alone, my hands continued to explore under her shirt. Fuck, she felt good. She pressed against me, making me think she wanted me as much as I was dying to have her. Her desire turned me on so much I thought I would explode.

With her back against the metal cage, she lifted a leg and wrapped it around my waist, urging me even closer. My mouth moved over her neck, her cheek, her ear. In the dim light, I could just make out the heat in her eyes and the way her lips parted. Her hips rose up to meet mine.

I dropped my mouth to her collarbone, and she shivered. She smelled so damn good. As I unbuttoned the front of her shirt, I left a trail of kisses along her neck. Her shirt fell to the floor, and I lifted the edge of her tank top and pushed it up over her bra. She moaned and rocked against me. I wanted to make her scream out my name.

Her hands played in my hair as I knelt down in front of her. She kicked off her boots and watched me with half-closed eyes as I unbuttoned her jeans and slid them down one leg at a time. Her skin was so soft. With my help, her panties followed.

Naked from the waist down, her hands grasped the metal fence behind her, and she moved to a rhythm only she could feel. Still on my knees, I put both hands behind her, cupped her perfect ass, and brought her toward my mouth. She gasped as my tongue tasted her for the first time. I'd been looking forward to this for too fucking long.

It was worth the wait.

I took my time, teasing and flicking my tongue over her most sensitive spot. She writhed against me, her hands clutching the gate behind her head. My fingers slid in and out while my mouth taunted her. She was close.

She whimpered. "I'm close. Yeah, right there. Don't stop."

Stopping was the last thing on my mind. I was going to make her come so hard she'd be begging me for more. I picked up one of her legs and put it up over my shoulder. The angle of my oral assault shifted, and she moaned. The guttural sound came from the back of her throat, and she tightened.

I backed off. She wasn't going to get off so easily, not this time.

Her hand plunged into my hair. "Come on."

With one hand supporting her underneath, I slipped the other under her bra and rolled a nipple between my fingers. It hardened, and I moved my fingers over to the other one. I skimmed my tongue over her, and she gasped.

"Please. I need you...now."

"Ask me nicely," I teased.

"Just do it. Finish it, dammit."

My tongue stroked, and my lips gently sucked away her resolve. "Not until you say my name." I pulled back and met her eyes.

She put both hands behind my head and nudged me back into her. I slipped a finger inside. She was so wet. So incredibly, perfectly wet for me.

"Please, Dante," she whispered. She looked down at me through unfocused eyes.

As my fingers teased, in and out, I pushed my tongue inside her, swirling it around and sending her to the edge.

"Dante, oh god." Our eyes met and held. "Dante."

I sucked gently, and she writhed under my touch, my fingers sliding in and out as her orgasm gathered momentum. Then wave after wave crashed over her. She was so fucking beautiful when she came.

Finally, she lifted her leg off my shoulder and pulled away.

"Faith, that was—"

"Do you have anything?"

"What do you mean?"

"A condom. Do you have a condom?"

"Yeah. Of course."

"Give it to me."

I took the packet out of my pocket and handed it to her. She unbuttoned my jeans, yanking my pants and boxers down in a jerky movement. I was so fucking turned on, my cock sprang out of my pants, and she grabbed it in her hands, unrolling the condom down my length.

She turned around, putting her back to me, and looked at me over her shoulder. "Come on, Dante. Your turn."

I moved toward her, and she bent forward at the waist, grabbing the fence with both hands. I guided myself into her, feeling her clench around me.

"Oh Faith, shit, you feel so good."

She rocked back toward me, sending me deeper. I wasn't ready, and it caught me off balance. I grabbed her around the waist, driving deep inside. We found our rhythm. Every time I plunged forward, she rocked back, using her hands to push against the gate. Fuck. I couldn't hold back. I released into her, my knees so weak I had to tighten my grip around her waist to keep from collapsing.

"You done back there?" she asked.

Heat washed over my cheeks.

"Um, yeah." I backed away, taking care of the condom. By the time I turned around, she was already stepping into her jeans.

"Faith, I, uh—"

She planted a kiss on my cheek. "Good timing, Dante. I really needed a break. Same time tomorrow?"

I groped for my jeans on the floor, but she'd already reached the door. She gave a quick wave and pulled it open, stepping out into the stairwell and leaving me alone in the dark, wondering what the fuck just happened.

# CHAPTER 38

## *Faith*

MY KNEES WOBBLED as I climbed back up to the fourteenth floor. I supported myself by writing life-changing sex scenes. I'd just never experienced one myself. Until now. I still tingled and twitched in places I didn't even know existed.

That man had some serious skills. I leaned up against the door to the study carrel and tried to catch my breath. I'd better get it all down on my laptop before I forgot what happened. I smiled to myself. As if I could ever forget.

Although I was bound and determined that our little fling wasn't going anywhere, it sure was good for my writing. I could justify it based on the merits of research alone. Plus, it was good cardio. Yeah, I probably just burned at least five hundred calories on that little encounter.

Physically, whatever Dante and I were doing definitely agreed with me. Emotionally, I wasn't so sure.

I sat down at the desk and started typing. The Dante and Faith on my screen somehow found themselves in an abandoned warehouse and went through a similar encounter to what I'd just experienced one floor down. When I was done capturing it all on the computer, I felt like I'd just relived the whole ordeal. Obviously, I wasn't going to get much else done. Better to pack it in and head home.

As I shut down my laptop, my phone rang.

"Hey, Jess. How was your break?"

"Freaking awesome. I just got back. My ride fell through from the airport. Come pick me up?"

"Sure. I was just on my way home. I'll be there in fifteen."

I slid my laptop into my backpack. Something crunched in the bottom of the bag. Sticking my hand into the pocket, I felt around for the source of the sound. My fingers closed around a large, crumpled-up envelope. I'd forgotten I picked up the mail from my office before I left town. Hopefully, it wasn't anything important.

I undid the clasp and pulled a single sheet of paper from inside. The intimate details of my Halloween encounter with Dante flowed across the typewritten page.

No! I yanked my computer back out of my bag and paced the tiny room while it booted up again. When the login screen finally appeared, my fingers clicked on the keyboard.

I checked my recent documents. The last time I'd saved the manuscript, it had been on my hard drive. But wait, right there. For some reason, it showed another copy had been saved on a removable drive. I'd never saved a copy there.

Who the hell had access to my computer? I'd tried to put it out of my head, telling myself someone was just messing with me. But now, I couldn't ignore the fact that someone knew what I was hiding. The only question was, what would it take to get them to keep quiet?

I crumpled up the page and tossed it in my bag. Wouldn't do any good to obsess over it right now. I needed to get to the airport.

· · ·

JESS STOOD at the curb with two rolling bags behind her. Her breath floated out in clouds as she waited. As I came to a stop, she waved her arms in the air.

"Thanks so much for the ride." She caught me in a hug as I stepped out of the car.

"You're welcome. It's no big deal." We each grabbed a bag and heaved them into the trunk.

"How come I always forget how cold it is here? I hope you have the heat going."

We climbed into the car, and I turned the fan to high. "Tell me about your trip. You look fabulous." Jess had the kind of skin that tanned easily, and after a week of basking on the beach in Jamaica, she was rocking a killer tan.

"His name is Shanti. He plays the steel drums, and he's got moves like I've never seen before."

"So, you had a good time?" I asked.

"A great time. A mind-blowing time." Jess flipped down the visor and ran her lip gloss over her smile. "I'm still glowing."

"Yeah, I can see that." I was happy for her. Jess was the kind of girl who could have fun wherever she was. She lived in the moment and didn't spend much time thinking about the future. Wish I could try that for a change.

"Let's stop for a drink somewhere on the way home."

"I don't know, Jess." I needed to get home and try to figure out what to do about the pages that kept popping up.

"Come on, I haven't seen you in forever. It's New Year's Eve. Classes don't start until Tuesday."

Jess's voice took on the whiny tone meaning she wouldn't give up without a major fight. Easier to just give in. One drink. I'd still be home long before midnight. "Fine. Where do you want to go?"

"How about Tapped?"

"No. Pick somewhere else."

"What's wrong with that place? We drive right by it on the way home."

"It's just...I don't know. I don't like it."

"You don't like the bar, or you don't like him?" Jess asked.

I fiddled with the radio, searching for something besides Christmas music. The holiday was over, couldn't they move on? "It'll probably be crowded."

"Yeah, right. Most people aren't even coming back until the day after tomorrow." Jess pointed her finger at the window. "The turn is just up there."

"Fine." I figured I'd left Dante at the library less than an hour ago. Odds were, he probably had the night off and would be nowhere near the bar tonight. I took the turn and pulled into the lot. "Just one drink though, okay?"

Jess cast a sly glance at me. "I think maybe you like him."

"I don't. I mean, he seems like a nice guy, but that's it."

"Are you sure, Faith? When the two of you are together, I don't know, it's like static electricity or something."

I put the car in park and glanced over at her. "What do you mean?"

"I mean, I think your little one-night stand didn't get it all out of your system. There's something going on between you whether you like it or not."

"I changed my mind. Let's go somewhere else." Before I could start the engine again, Jess grabbed my keys and climbed out of the car.

"Meet you inside."

I sat in the parking lot until the heat seeped out and my toes went numb. "Dammit!" I slammed my hands down on the steering wheel, causing the horn to blare. Better get this over with. I climbed out of the car and followed Jess's footsteps through the snowy parking lot and into the bar.

Jess was right. It wasn't crowded, especially for New Year's Eve. In fact, only a handful of people milled around inside. I passed a couple of guys playing pool and a trio of girls shooting darts.

I made my way back toward the bar and found Jess sitting on a barstool talking to... aw, hell... Dante stood behind the bar. He was laughing and talking to Jess. As I approached, his mouth quirked up in a half-smile, and he winked.

"Oh, hey Faith," he said.

I sat down on the stool next to Jess and stuck out my hand. Jess tossed me the keys as a shit-eating grin spread across her sun-kissed face.

"Glad you could join me, Faith. Dante here was just telling me about his break."

"Oh yeah?" I asked, "What fun things did you do over Christmas?"

As soon as I sat down, he'd grabbed a pint glass and filled it up with my favorite brew. He set it down in front of me.

"Actually, I spent a lot of time in the hospital. My grand-mother had a fall."

My hand went to my chest. "Meemaw? Oh my gosh. Why didn't you tell me that earlier? Is she okay?"

Dante lifted an eyebrow at my concern. "We didn't do much talking earlier. Besides, she's fine now. She hit her head pretty hard, and they had to sedate her for a couple of days. She's back to bossing me around, though."

"Thank goodness." I took a long sip of my beer.

The group of guys playing pool yelled for Dante from across the room.

"Excuse me, will you? I'm on my own here tonight and need to get those guys another round."

"We can entertain ourselves." Jess waved him on. As Dante left the bar to go talk to the guys, Jess turned to me. "Okay, you're not telling me something. What the hell is going on with you guys? There's something, I can tell."

I put my head in my hands. "I know."

"So, you're willing to admit it?"

"You're right. We've been meeting on the sly. We're having rec sex."

"You're fucking?" Jess shrieked.

"Well, not right this second." I squirmed on my stool.

"Spill it, Faith. Now."

# CHAPTER 39

## *Faith*

MY HEAD SHOT UP. "Keep it down, will you?"

"Sorry! You just caught me off guard. You mean to tell me that the chick with the six-year plan goes on booty calls?"

"It's not just a booty call. We're having a monogamous friends-with-bennies fling."

"So, you're dating?"

"No. There's no emotional involvement. It's strictly physical."

Jess rolled her eyes. "Yeah, right."

"What? You don't believe me?"

Jess wildly shook her head back and forth.

"I used to play with Play-Doh as a break. Now I just—"

"Now you just play with Dante?"

I opened my mouth in shock, glanced over at Jess, and we both cracked up. Once I caught my breath, I answered, "Yeah, I guess I do."

"And?"

"And what?"

"What kind of a playmate is he?" Jess sat sideways on her barstool so she could give me her full attention.

"Attentive, aggressive."

Dante stood talking to the guys by the pool table. I hadn't noticed earlier, but he was wearing an untucked flannel shirt over a white undershirt. The sleeves were rolled up, and I caught a glimpse of his strong forearms. His jeans clung in the right places, and he hadn't shaved in a few days. I shifted on my stool. That stubble had felt pretty intense between my thighs.

Jess interrupted my thoughts. "Can I assume you're enjoying yourself?"

"Yeah," I sighed. "For now."

"Why the big secret? It's not like he's some fugly asshole who's just good in bed. I mean, look at him." We shifted our attention to the pool table. The guys must have talked Dante into shooting a few rounds, and as we gazed on, he stretched over the pool table, gliding the cue back and forth between his fingers, aiming to sink the eight ball in the corner pocket.

"You're right. He's the whole package. Smart, funny, good looking..."

Jess lowered her head and looked up at me. "Really? Good looking? I haven't even seen him naked, and even I can tell he's a total hard body."

Hard... so incredibly hard. "You have no idea."

I took another gulp of my beer. It felt good to finally talk to someone about him, like a little weight shifted off my shoulders. Could I trust Jess with the whole story?

"It's complicated. I don't have time for a relationship. I don't want to start something. I like my life the way it is."

"Sometimes things have a way of starting, even when you try like hell to prevent it." Jess raised her beer in a toast. "Here's to you. You go, girl. I hope you get exactly what you need out of whatever you want to call whatever it is that's going on between the two of you." She tossed back her head and polished off her drink. Then she turned on her stool and raised her glass toward Dante. "Bartender? Another round, please."

"Be right there," he called back.

I took another swig of my beer and set it down on the bar. "I take it you're not ready to go yet?"

"And miss out on watching you with your panties all in a wad? No way!"

Dante walked back behind the bar and filled up another glass for Jess. "How are you doing?" he asked me.

"Great, just great." I glanced over at Jess, but she was busy texting.

"Hey, Faith, good news." She looked up from her phone. "Jake's going to meet us here."

"I thought you guys broke up?"

Jess shrugged. "On again, off again. Even I can't keep up. He probably had to listen to his mom ask about me the whole time he was home for Christmas. She loves me, y'know."

I rolled my eyes. "I thought I was taking you home from the airport. Now it's turning into a party?"

"You got a problem with parties?" Jess asked. "Let's go shoot some pool." She grabbed me by the arm as she made an unsteady dismount from her stool.

I shrugged at Dante and grabbed my beer as Jess tugged me toward the pool table. The guys had wrapped up their game, and the table sat wide open. Jess racked the balls, and I studied the sticks lining the wall. I picked one, chalked it, and lined up to break. I got lucky, sending two solids and one stripe into the pockets.

"Solids, I guess."

"Freaking pool shark. I don't know why I even bother to play." Jess bent down to judge the angle she'd need to send the twelve ball into the side pocket. She lined up and took her shot, missing it by a good three inches. "Dammit."

By the time I had run the table, Jake arrived. I walked back to the bar, my empty glass in my hand.

"How about another?" Dante asked.

"I'd better not. I need to drive home."

"Aw, come on." Jess flung her arm around my shoulder. "It's New Year's. Jake here can drive us home, right?"

"Yeah, no problem."

I was about to protest, but before I could open my mouth, Dante slid another beer in front of me. This one in a tall glass mug with a handle. "A tall. On the house this time."

"Thanks."

"Let's shoot some darts. Come on, Faith." Jess grabbed her freshly poured beer off the bar and walked to the back of the room where the electronic dartboards lined the wall. She dug a few quarters out of her purse and slipped them into the slot.

The three of us played three games of cricket. I kept busting, so Jake won a round, and surprisingly, Jess won two.

Looked like Jake and Jess were definitely heading back on again. They were being pretty flirty with each other. Nothing like being a third wheel. I excused myself to the bathroom, then walked back to the bar to grab another round. As I waited for Dante to fill our mugs, Jess sent me reeling with a hip bump from behind.

"Hey, I just lost a bet, so Jake's going to drive me home."

"What do you mean?" I asked.

"He challenged me to another game. Loser does a strip tease for the winner."

"I guess things are back on again, then?"

Jess shoved her arms into her coat. "Looks that way. Things would never have worked out with me and Shanti. Jake's mom is Italian. She makes her own sauce. Jerk chicken just can't compete with that."

"Yeah, I see your point. I'm sure many relationships have been built on less."

Jess leaned into me, slurring her words. "You just get me. I lub you, Faith."

"I love you too, Jess. You sure you're okay? It's not even midnight yet."

"I'm fine. I'll get my bags out of your trunk tomorrow. Dante, you'd better give my girl Faith here a major dose of tongue when the clock strikes twelve."

Dante laughed. I took a step toward my friend just as Jake walked up and lifted Jess up under the armpits. He'd been a wrestler in high school and college, so he picked her up like she weighed nothing at all. "Come on, sweet cheeks. You owe me."

Jess smiled and waved at me as he carried her out of the bar.

"The happy couple leaves," Dante said. "And then there were two."

I looked around. Where did everyone else go? We were alone.

"Sorry, I didn't realize how late it was getting. Not much of a crowd for New Year's, huh?" I asked.

"The bar down the road is giving out free champagne and has a balloon drop at midnight. I guess we can't compete with that."

I bit down on my lip, suddenly nervous about being alone with him. "You probably want to close up. I should go."

"I'm in no rush. I have the day off tomorrow, and you probably shouldn't drive. Let me just clean up a little and I can run you home."

"That's really not necessary. I'll just hang out while you wrap up. I'm sure I'll be fine by the time you're done."

"Suit yourself." Dante turned on the TV over the bar.

The Times Square countdown showed forty minutes left until the New Year descended upon us. He busied himself behind the bar, stacking dirty glasses in the compact dishwasher and wiping down the counters.

"So, your grandmother is really okay?" I asked.

"Yep. She had me worried there for a while, but she's doing really well."

"Good."

"She asked about you." Dante tossed the dishrag in the sink and started refilling the napkin holders.

"She did?"

"Yeah. She doesn't know you like I do. She thinks you're a nice, sweet girl, committed to serving the greater good by cooking and serving turkeys to desperate senior citizens everywhere."

I snickered. "That sounds like an accurate description."

"How about a game of pool? I saw the way you ran the table with Jess. Think you can take me?"

"You're on." May as well. It would probably be a little longer before I could safely drive home, and technically, the place didn't close until two. I got up from the bar and moved toward the pool table.

Dante stepped out from behind the bar and walked to the front door. He flipped the outdoor lights off and locked the deadbolt. Then he muted the TV and turned the volume up on the stereo up as he passed. Jon Bon Jovi yelled at everyone to have a nice day.

"You want to break?" he asked.

"No, go ahead. I'll let you take the first shot."

I racked the balls, and Dante sent the cue ball slamming into the triangle, sinking a stripe. He proceeded to pocket two more before he miscalculated the angle on an attempt to put the nine ball in the corner, opening up the table to me.

I took my time, bending over and assessing my options before deciding to bank the two ball and put it in the side.

"Nice shot."

I looked at him over my shoulder, flipping my hair and leaning down in front of him, my full attention captured by the tricky combination laid out in front of me. He was pretty good at this. Better up my game. Three more solids fell in quick succession before Dante got to take another shot.

He sank the other four stripes and called the eight in the corner.

Stunned, I reached down to pick up a few of the balls and put them back on the table. "No fair. I need a rematch."

He shrugged. "Fine. But if you're going to flaunt yourself in front of me like that, I'm going to need something to drink."

"Winner breaks?" I asked, already racking the balls.

He stepped behind the bar and filled a highball glass halfway with a single malt scotch. "Sure, your rules this round." He walked around the table and leaned over to break, failing to pocket a single ball.

I sized up my options before I stretched over the table, lifted a foot off the ground and put a stripe in the corner. Then I proceeded to run the next four stripes before he got a chance to take a shot. He sank two solids, and I ran the rest of the table, pocketing the eight ball in the corner, right in front of him.

"Nice game, Faith."

"Thanks. I should probably get going."

"You can't leave it in a tie. Besides, it's almost midnight. We're one-to-one now. Don't you want to know who's the best?"

My competitive side wouldn't let me walk away from a challenge. "Okay, one more game."

"I think we need some new rules this round." He stepped over to where I stood against the table and set his glass down on the edge.

"Oh yeah, like what?"

"You've heard of strip poker, of course."

# CHAPTER 40

## *Faith*

I LAUGHED. "I am so not playing strip pool with you. Just forget it."

He took a slow sip of his drink. "Fine. I guess I'll just go down as the undisputed champion."

"What? It's a tie."

He put a finger up against my lips. "Shhh. I offered you a chance to redeem yourself. I guess we'll just never know who the real winner is."

"You've got to be joking." He really had to be joking. Anyone walking by would be able to see right into the bar. I might be up for another round, but I wasn't going to turn into an exhibitionist.

"If you're that confident, you shouldn't have anything to worry about. Hell, if you play like you did the last round, you'd barely lose a sock."

"But the window, anyone could see in."

"The bar's closed. Who would walk by the front window at this hour?"

A shiver ran through me. What if the person leaving pages for me caught a glimpse of Dante and me together?

"You can forfeit." He shrugged and walked toward the front windows, lowering the blinds.

"Fine, I'm in. What are the rules?"

"We go in order. One through fifteen. Every time you sink a ball, I have to take something off. Every time I sink one—"

"That's not going to happen. Who breaks?"

"As a show of good sportsmanship, you can go first."

"Good sportsmanship, my ass. I'm going to wipe the table with you." I pulled back and broke hard, pocketing the two and seven.

Dante cleared his throat. "I forgot to mention..." I looked over at him and a sadistic smile spread across his face. "If you sink a ball out of order, you have to take something off."

"But—"

"Rules are rules. And none of this one sock at a time thing."

I frowned then bent down to take off my boots and socks. The wood floor felt cold under my bare feet. He was going to pay for this. I lined up the one and sent it into the side pocket. "Shoes, please."

Dante shrugged and kicked off his shoes.

I banked the three, and it drifted to the corner, stopping less than an inch from the pocket.

"Tough break." He nudged me out of the way with his hip, easily sinking the three and gesturing to my sweater.

I glared at him as I peeled it over my head and tossed it at the table. No worries. I had on two other shirts along with my bra. Plenty to work with.

Two shots later, I stood in my bra and jeans. Damn him. He'd had a cocky grin on his face since we started. I was ready to give him a taste of his own medicine. I sank the six in the side pocket, and before he'd had a chance to remove his socks, I pocketed the seven.

"Nice work." He unbuttoned his flannel shirt, tossing it on top of the pile of my discarded clothing.

I looked over at him and could see his chest muscles move underneath the tight white tank. *Focus, dammit.* The eight was a challenge. I barely squeaked it by the ten ball. He took off the tank top, and I didn't look up.

Instead, I walked around the table, trying to figure out how to get a shot on the nine ball. The best I could do would be to set it up so he didn't have a clear shot, either. I wedged it up against the side, making his shot difficult, if not impossible.

"What's it going to be, Faith? The bra or the jeans?"

"Ha. You won't be able to make that."

He raised his eyebrows at me.

"You make that shot, and I'll take them both off. You miss, and you take off your pants."

"You've got yourself a deal, sweetheart." He lined up, and I moved to a spot just opposite of his aim. I leaned down, resting my hands on the edge of the table, letting my cleavage fall directly in his line of sight. He took the shot and missed.

"Dammit. You're cheating."

I shrugged, enjoying the sight of Dante slipping out of his jeans. The only thing standing between me and the sweet taste of success was a snug pair of boxer briefs.

"You play hard."

"Looks like you're the one playing hard." I gestured toward his crotch.

"Yeah, you'd better not sink another one, or you might get an eyeful."

I sized up my options. My little stunt had worked, but left me in a bad position to get a shot as well. I struck the cue ball, sinking the ten and then the nine. Dante gestured toward my bra. "I like the red one better, anyway."

"In your dreams." I undid my jeans and kicked them off, revealing my pink cotton bikini briefs with purple hearts all over them.

"I like your panties." He bent down to line up his shot. "Although I'd like them better on the floor." My mistake gave him a clear shot on number eleven, and he sank it with ease.

"Shit." I shrugged out of my bra, crossing my arms and covering my breasts with my hands.

"Now we're getting somewhere." He moved toward me, and I darted to the opposite side of the table. He lined up his shot and missed.

"You did that on purpose," I said, arms still crossed.

"Your shot, doll. Here." He handed me the stick, and I reached one hand out to take it, keeping the other in place. "I don't think you're going to be able to hold the cue like that, Faith."

"Can't you close your eyes?"

"Close my eyes? I'm pretty sure we're way past that."

"Come on."

"After the way you came in my mouth today, sweetheart? Now you're shy?"

I groaned and dropped my other hand. Although he was beyond aggravating, he was right. We really were past the formalities. I'd never felt so uninhibited and free with anyone before. He got me so worked up. And based on the way things were going, he'd be taking care of that desire in a matter of minutes.

This was so going in my book. Just looking at him standing up against the side of the pool table in nothing but his underwear, I wanted to run my hands down his chest, grab onto his perfectly sculpted ass, and drive him deep inside me. I was getting wet just thinking about it.

For my next shot, I'd have to stretch all the way across the table. I hiked one leg up and rested my knee and thigh on top of the table in an attempt to extend my reach.

"Think that's going to help?" Dante asked.

"I'll do anything for a couple extra inches." I winked at him and smiled.

He laughed.

As my breasts grazed the felt on the table, my nipples hardened. I drew the cue back to strike the ball as Dante came up behind me, pressing his erection into the dampness of my panties.

"Hey, that's cheating." The moment he connected, my hand slipped, causing my shot to go wide.

"Just helping you out with those last couple of inches."

Neither one of us moved. The pressure on my backside held me firmly in place. The pressure, crap, the exquisite pressure. I pushed back against him, and he reached out, fondling my breast and sending a wave of pleasure crashing through my core.

"It's your turn."

He moved away, and I put my foot on the ground. I took a deep breath and turned around to face him. He took a step toward me, and I backed up, my butt hitting the edge of the table. My hair fell over my breasts, and he moved closer. As he pushed it back over my shoulders, his fingertips grazed my bare skin.

"No fair covering up."

"It's your turn. I got it all lined up for you. All you have to do is nudge it in."

"Just nudge it, huh?" He pushed his crotch up against mine, making contact.

I closed my eyes, enjoying the feel of him. "Yeah, just a little nudge."

"Like this?" He pushed harder, and the edge of the pool

table pressed into my backside while his hard-on bumped into my front.

"Yeah, just like that." I reached my hands behind me, taking some of the pressure off by raising myself up on the edge of the table, giving him easier access.

"What if I don't want to nudge it?" He pushed harder against me. "What if I want to sink it all the way in?"

# CHAPTER 41
## *Faith*

THE PRESSURE, don't let it stop. I was going to come, and he hadn't even touched me skin-to-skin yet. I tried to pull back, but he wouldn't let up. He dropped his head, taking a nipple in his mouth, running his hands over my breasts, my stomach, and my back. I moaned and pressed into him. He lowered me so my back laid on the table, and I stretched out and drew my legs up. I heard the rip of the packet, and he was back, sliding a finger under the edge of my panties.

"You're so wet for me, Faith. Are you always this wet?"

I moaned, stretching my hands above my head and scooting up so I sprawled out along the full length of the pool table. He slipped my underwear off, and I opened my eyes in time to see him climb onto the pool table and hover over me. The briefs were gone. He was primed, and I was ready.

"Okay?" he asked.

I opened my legs to him, and he placed a palm on the table on either side of my face, lowering himself down into me, one glorious inch at a time.

"You're so tight." He settled deep inside and paused for a moment.

I let him fill me but couldn't hold still for long. I had to move. Sandwiched between the hard slate of the pool table and Dante's body, my options were limited. I wrapped my legs around his waist, drawing him even further into me. He tried to find his rhythm but kept pulling back.

"It's too hard. We've gotta move."

I propped myself up on my elbows. "I don't really think it's possible for you to be too hard."

He cracked a grin. "Not me. The table. My knees are killing me. The pool table is a much better idea in theory."

"Are you bailing on me?"

"Not a chance. Hold on, I'll find something." He hopped off the table and ran behind the bar. He was quite a sight with his condom-covered cock flopping up and down as he ran across the room.

I let my head fall back as he grabbed something behind the bar and raced back to me. He stopped about ten feet away.

"You're so incredibly beautiful. Just look at you, sprawled out on the table like that. I've got to get a picture of this."

"Don't you dare. Get your ass back over here before I climb down and go home."

Dante returned, a wad of bubble wrap in his hands. "Here, lift up your butt. I'll slip it underneath you."

I hiked my rear in the air, and he pushed the bubble wrap under me, then climbed back onto the table. "Where were we?"

"I think we were somewhere around here." I lifted my hips up to him. He slid inside, pushing me back toward the table.

As my butt settled on the bubble wrap, the small pockets of air burst underneath me, making popping sounds.

"Geez, Dante. Is this the only thing you could find?" I looked up at him.

His eyes were closed, and he rocked into me, causing more pops to explode onto my ass. I started to giggle. He looked like he was concentrating so hard. He thrust into me. *Pop, pop, pop.*

I bit my lip to keep from losing it. Then I flung an arm around his back, trying to pull him down onto me so I wouldn't keep landing on the bubble wrap. He flipped me over ,so I was on top. I straddled him, popping more bubbles with my knees.

He smiled up at me and lifted his hips. "Come on, concentrate. Work through it."

I pushed my hips into his, making a wide circle with my pelvis. Ah, the spot. There it was. I ignored the pops and focused on the feeling. If I could just follow it. His hands roamed over my naked body as I glided up and down. I found my groove and made it to the edge. I was close, so close.

Right before I let myself go, he sat up, settling me on his lap and changing the angle. The friction shifted, and I lost it for a moment. Then all of a sudden, it was back, even stronger than before. I flung my legs around his waist and wrapped my arms around his neck, pulling his mouth into mine. His lips found my neck. He was leaving marks, and I didn't even care. He kept pounding into me until I couldn't take it anymore. I let myself go, and my orgasm washed over me, leaving me weak and super sensitive in its wake.

Dante wasn't done. I propped myself up, then slid back down onto him, clenching as I raised up again. Lift, clench, slide. Repeat. He strained against me, and I watched his face as he reached his climax and released into me.

I loved the power I felt. The fact that I could make his body feel this. It was incredible. He opened his eyes and smiled at me. His glasses sat crooked on his nose, and I reached up to fix them. As I did, he shifted his weight, and a few more bubbles popped. I laughed so hard I snorted.

"Okay, I'm sorry. In hindsight, bubble wrap probably wasn't the best choice."

I couldn't catch my breath. "That's...ah...oh my gosh, Dante..."

He lifted me up and deposited me onto the bubble wrap. *Pop...pop...pop.* I melted into a puddle of hysterical laughter as he stood up from the table.

Finally, I took in a deep breath, and the wave of giggles subsided. "That was so freaking funny."

He stepped into his jeans. "I'm glad you found it so amusing."

I crawled off the table and walked over to him. Standing on my tiptoes, I planted a kiss on his chin. "It wasn't amusing. It was hot." I pressed my cheek against his chiseled chest and hugged him around the waist. I hadn't laughed that hard in forever. This guy...he was really getting to me.

He kissed my forehead. "Happy New Year, Faith."

"Damn, we missed it." I looked at the TV screen and saw they were counting down to the next time zone.

"Don't I get a New Year's kiss?"

"You want a kiss? After all that? Wasn't there enough kissing between pops?"

His arm went around my waist, and he tilted my face up to his. As he moved in, his eyes searched mine. I closed my eyes as our lips met. This wasn't the crushing, scorching, frantic kiss I'd come to expect from him. His tongue tentatively sought mine. His lips were tender, tasting, testing, questioning, demanding more from me than his body had over the past several hours.

He pulled away first. "Want to stay over tonight?"

The moment passed.

"I can't. I've got to go." I untangled myself from his arms

and searched for my clothes. Jeans on the floor. Underwear flung over the back of a barstool. Shirt...damn, what did I do with my shirt? I got dressed, making sure I put on every article of clothing. No need to repeat that scene in the office again.

Dante gathered the bubble wrap off the pool table and tossed it in a large trash can against the wall. "Do you need me to drive you home?"

"No. I'm fine now. Thanks for, uh—"

"The game of pool?"

"Yeah. Although we never finished. I guess you forfeit."

"I don't think so. I'm pretty sure I had you."

"You had me all right. But you still lost the game."

"No fair. Want to go again?" he raised one eyebrow at me.

"Not tonight. I don't think my ass could take another round on that table. Maybe some other time."

"Sure. Some other time then." As we talked, I walked toward the door. He unlocked it for me and stepped back. "Drive safe."

"Thanks." I stood for a moment in the awkward silence. Should I hug him? Give him a kiss goodbye? Nah. A high five? Aw, forget it. I opened the door, walked through it, and let it close behind me. It would be so easy to climb up the steps to his apartment and crawl under the covers with him. If I was going to be honest with myself, that's what I wanted.

I stopped and looked back toward the door just as the lights went out inside. It would be better if we kept it physical. Less messy and easier to handle when we went our separate ways.

Turning toward my car, I sure hoped I'd be able to walk tomorrow. Two hard rounds in a row might leave me with some temporary collateral damage. I needed to pace myself with Dante. I had enough material now to almost finish my book and would probably be up all night trying to capture our strip pool session on my computer.

Being around him, I'd been able to temporarily forget. But as I pulled my hood over my head and forged through the snowy parking lot to my car, the writing on the page came back to me. Was someone watching? And how long would it be before I needed to tell Dante?

For the time being, there wasn't anything I could do but keep an eye out. Obviously, whoever it was, was trying to freak me out. Since they hadn't gone public yet, there must be something else they wanted.

I started the car and rubbed my hands in front of the vent, waiting for the cool air to switch to warm. Dante Bishop sure was full of surprises. It would be awhile before I could play pool again without fantasizing about him sinking his balls right into my pocket.

# CHAPTER 42

## *Dante*

I SLID a chair out from under the table and set my briefcase down. The girls were back in town and back to their group meetings. They were deep in conversation, though I couldn't tell what they were talking about. Not that I cared.

My mind was preoccupied. I hadn't seen or spoken to Faith since we rang in the New Year together last week. My day job had grown more demanding over the past few days. I was ramping up to take on new projects and bigger clients, making it even harder to find time to spend with my favorite distraction.

Before I had a chance to settle in my seat, Brittany threw her hands up. "How can you even think that, Bailey? He's perfect for her. She's just too stupid to see it."

"Oh, I think she sees it," Bethany said. "How can she not? She's just protecting herself. She's been so hurt before."

"What the hell are you talking about?" I asked, eager to get the meeting over with so I could get back to work.

"It's this book." Brittany tossed a hardcover book on the table.

My cheeks burned. I grabbed my bag and felt around

inside for my copy of *Carnal Knowledge*. Satisfied they hadn't found me out, I played it off. "What's the problem?"

Brittany continued. "It's this couple. They have hot, amazing, mind-blowing sex, and she won't let him get close to her. Finally, he starts romancing her, pulling out all the stops, and she—"

"Don't tell me. I haven't made it that far yet." Bailey covered her ears with her hands.

"Wow, that good, huh?" I'd started reading it at the hospital. They were right, it had some pretty incredible sex scenes. I'd put it down when Meemaw woke up and hadn't looked at it since.

"It's amazing," Bailey said. "I can't wait until her next book comes out."

"What makes him this book so special?" I asked.

Brittany grinned. "You want to borrow my copy?"

"No." I shook my head, dismissing her suggestion with what I hoped was an acceptable and believable level of disdain.

"Okay." Brittany leaned back in her seat. "If you change your mind—"

"Can we go ahead and get started?" I asked. "I've got to get back to work."

Brittany grabbed the book off the table. "Fine. What have you got?"

We spent the next forty-five minutes going over the holiday sales figures for the Sashay Salon. I opted not to mention my free haircut. We divided up some tasks for the next week and wrapped up.

I walked out, making sure to pass the study carrel Faith usually used. It was empty. Where could she be hiding out these days? Things seemed to be going well between us. Hell, if she didn't want to be found, I wasn't going to start looking. I had enough to keep me busy with work, my side gig at the bar, and trying to get home to check on Meemaw a couple of times a week.

As I left the library, I saw Jess talking to some girls in the lobby. She said her goodbyes and caught up to me.

"Hey, Dante," she called out.

"Hi. How's it going?"

"Pretty good. Just wrapping up a study session with some undergrads. Were we ever that naïve?"

I laughed. "You're probably only a couple of years older than them, you know."

"Yeah. But in their case, I think a couple of years makes a world of difference."

I slowed my pace to match hers. "So, have you seen Faith around?"

Jess glanced over at me, a sly smile spreading across her lips. "You two still seeing each other?"

I cleared my throat. I didn't like talking about my love life with Jess, but if I wanted to find out where Faith had been hiding, it was worth a shot. "I just haven't seen her around for a while."

"I talked to her the other day. She's sick. I think she got a bad cold. She's had a sub covering her classes."

"Oh." That explained it. I didn't know much about Faith, but I knew she was serious about her career. If she was too sick to make it to class, she must be in bad shape. Maybe I should stop by.

We'd reached the doors, and Jess turned to head left while I needed to go right.

"She sent me a text saying she's running out of tissues. Maybe you could bring her a box."

Tissues, huh? At least I could stop by tomorrow after work to make sure she was okay. "Maybe I will. Thanks."

"Any time. Good luck."

I hunkered down against the cold and trudged across the

quad to the parking lot. I'd better get a move on, or I'd be late for my day job. They'd be announcing promotions and new assignments in the next month or two. If I wanted to fast track, I needed to make every moment, every effort, every project count.

Tameka had given me a raving review for the work I'd been doing in the salon with my team from Tempest. Now, if my current clients could be as generous with the praise, I ought to be in good shape.

Maybe I could find a stretch of land outside of DC or somewhere in upstate New York where Meemaw would feel at home. It would put her closer to whatever new office I'd be working from. I could have the best of both worlds. The one thing I hadn't quite figured out yet was how Faith might fit into those plans.

THE BAR HAD BEEN UNUSUALLY quiet for a Thursday night. I powered through my shift and made my way upstairs to my place to heat up some leftover Chinese food. I was always too wired to go straight to bed when I got done working. It was two in the morning, but I didn't have any meetings the next day, so I planned on working from home.

Faith had been on my mind all night. Hell, all week. It didn't help that Meemaw kept calling and asking when I would bring Faith down for another dinner. She probably just wanted to make sure Cheryl didn't try to sink her claws into me again. Like I'd ever let that happen.

This whole thing with Faith had me on edge. I was used to being in complete control, never letting anyone get close. But Faith had somehow breached the razor wire I'd erected around my heart, and I found myself wanting to be a little bit more to her than just a twice-weekly booty call.

I yanked the copy of *Carnal Knowledge* out of my backpack

and sat down at the table to dig into my leftover chow mein. If Brittany was right and the guy eventually turned on the charm and won the girl over, that's the part I wanted to find

I got a little distracted when I came across the sex in the mailroom closet. Yeah, that part was pretty good. How many women read this kind of stuff? Did they get as turned on as I did just by reading a couple hundred words on a page? Based on the heated conversation between the women this afternoon, that had to be a yes.

As I shoveled forkful after forkful of noodles into my mouth, my eyes devoured the inner workings of a woman's mind. It was awesome stuff, and I knew Faith wouldn't be able to resist it. But was I willing to try? Something more than just great sex existed between us, whether she was ready to admit it or not. It wasn't like I was looking for a long-term commitment.

If Meemaw had taught me one thing over the years, it was to take my chances when they came up. My dad provided a perfect example of that. Meemaw's words played through my head. "You never know how much time you have left, my boy, but you can choose who you want to spend it with."

The whole ordeal with her being in the hospital had thrown me for a real loop. Meemaw wasn't going to be around forever. As much as I didn't want to think about that, it was a fact. Maybe it was time for me to open up a sliver and think about letting someone else in. I'd been protecting myself for so long though, would I even know how?

I got up, put my dirty dishes in the sink, and grabbed a notebook and pen. If I was thinking about launching an assault to win Faith over, I'd have to take some very good notes.

# CHAPTER 43

## *Faith*

I ROLLED over and looked at the clock. Almost noon. I'd been fighting a cold all week, but today was the worst. My head hurt, my nose was rubbed raw from hundreds of tissues, and every muscle in my body ached. I'd been spending most of my waking hours trying to figure out how to handle my new identity crisis. It seemed like only a matter of time before another page turned up, and I still didn't know the best way to handle the situation.

Mr. Darcy hopped up on the bed and walked around in circles, finally settling in next to my side. "Hey, buddy. I'll get up in a minute."

The cat purred and curled up into a ball. I stretched my arms over my head, then slowly sat up in bed. Wadded-up tissues littered the floor, and my nightstand held an assortment of half-full water glasses and abandoned mugs of tea.

I couldn't remember the last time I'd felt so awful. I lifted the edge of the comforter to fling it off. Somehow, today it weighed a ton. Freed from my layers of blankets, I shifted my legs over the side of the bed and felt around on the floor for my slippers. There was one. My other foot tapped around on the carpet but couldn't find the match.

As I stood up, a wave of dizziness washed over me, and I grabbed onto the nightstand to steady myself. Every part of me hurt. I gently shook my head to rid it of the pounding sound between my ears. Shaking, I released my grip on the nightstand and managed to stand.

The pounding continued. Someone was actually banging on my door.

"Oh, crap. I can't deal with this."

"Faith?" The knocking continued.

I shuffled my one slippered and one bare foot toward the front door. *Shuffle, whap. Shuffle, whap.*

*Knock, knock, knock.* "Faith?"

"I'm coming." I tried to yell, but it came out more like a croak. Reaching the door, I peered through the peephole. Dante stood on my stoop with two brown paper bags in hand. I slumped against the door for support. "Go away."

"What? Faith, are you in there?" The knocking paused.

I couldn't let him see me like this. My voice cracked as I tried to speak louder. "I said go away."

"Jess told me you're sick."

"I feel like crap. Go home."

"I've got tissues." He pulled a box out of the bag and waved it in front of the peephole.

Tissues, eh? I'd run out of tissues on Thursday and had been wiping my nose with toilet paper and paper towels for the past thirty-six hours. The tissues were tempting.

"Just open the door, and I'll slide them inside," Dante said.

He *would* have to tempt me with Kleenex. Desperate for the little square box of pillowy softness, I turned the deadbolt and tugged on the handle, cracking the door about six inches.

Dante slid the tissues in as promised, then wedged his boot in the doorway so I couldn't push it closed.

"Come on. I don't want you to see me like this." My voice sounded muffled, even to my own ears. That's what having a head full of green snot would do to a gal.

"I'm not going away. I don't care what you look like. I'm coming in." He gave the door a slight push, and I had no energy to resist.

I stepped out of the way, and Dante pushed through the door and into my stuffy, dark apartment.

"Jeez, how long have you been like this? You look like shit."

"Thanks. You're already making me feel so much better." I shuffle-whapped over to the couch and curled up into a ball, then yanked a fuzzy blanket over my head.

Dante set the bags down on the table and walked over to sit down on the side of the couch. He slid the edge of the blanket back to put a cool hand to my forehead. "Have you taken your temperature lately? You're burning up."

"I ran out of medicine last night. You shouldn't even be here. You'll catch the crud."

He stood up and walked over to the kitchen. The sound of cabinets closing and drawers opening filtered through the blanket. I peeked out to see him fill a plastic cup from the tap. Then he brought the cup of water and a bottle of pills over to me.

"Lucky for you, I brought some ibuprofen. Here, take this."

I propped myself up on an elbow and managed to swallow the pills he held out.

"Let's get you back to bed."

"No." I grabbed onto his arm. "No movement."

"Okay. Then you just stay here." Dante continued to talk, but I tuned him out. As I drifted off to sleep, he might have said something ludicrous about making me soup, but I must have been already dreaming. Dante making soup. What could be more ridiculous than that?

---

### Dante

"A ROUX, MY BOY," Meemaw's voice carried across the kitchen. I looked up to make sure Faith hadn't woken up on the couch.

"But the flour's getting all brown." Meemaw had been trying to walk me through making her homemade creamy chicken soup for the past half hour, and I'd already thrown away the first two attempts.

"Stir it faster. Just keep whisking."

"The whisk is the beater thing, right?" I asked. "I don't think she has one of those. I'm just using a spoon."

"Oh, child. I should have tried harder with you. Where are you exactly?"

"I'm at Faith's. She's got a horrible cold, and I wanted to make her some soup."

"That poor girl. Step away from the stove. I can be there in a little over an hour."

That's all I needed, Meemaw busting in and taking charge. I groaned. "No, that's not necessary. If you can just tell me again."

"All right. We'll go through it one more time." Meemaw started from the beginning once more, and I did my best to follow along. By the time she'd covered the whole recipe, I had something that kind of resembled soup bubbling on the stove.

"Thanks, Meemaw. I owe you one."

"Nonsense. You don't owe me a single thing, you know

better than that. By the way, I saw that Cheryl the other day in town."

"Oh yeah?"

"She asked about you."

"There's nothing going on between me and Cheryl." I glanced over at the couch where Faith laid curled into a ball. I pressed the button to take Meemaw off speaker, just in case.

"You might want to tell *her* that, Dante. Now, I don't want to get involved in your business—"

I let out a loud laugh. "Since when?"

Meemaw clucked her tongue through the phone. "I know how you young 'uns are nowadays. No one gets married anymore. Y'all just string each other along—"

"I thought you didn't want to get involved in my business?"

"That's right. You're a grown man now. I just don't want to see you get hurt again."

"No one's getting hurt, Meemaw. There's nothing going on between me and Cheryl. I told her that on Christmas."

"You'd be a fool to get involved with the likes of her. Why, she can't even make a decent pie."

Meemaw's standards, although somewhat questionable, were pretty clear. Made me wonder if Faith could bake.

"You're still stirring, right? Don't let it boil. Keep it at a simmer. I don't know how in the world you manage to feed yourself without me. I told that Cheryl things were getting serious between you and Faith. She's such a nice girl. I can tell she really likes you too."

"Oh yeah, how?"

"It's the way she looks at you, sugar. I've spent eighty-two years on this earth watching love blossom between folks, and I think you're onto something with her."

I wasn't ready to think about my feelings for Faith, much

less talk about them with my grandmother. "Don't you need to get to the senior center for bingo?"

"That's right," Meemaw said. "Good luck with your soup, hon. Tell Faith I hope she's feeling better real soon. If she's all stuffed up, she should rub some oils on her chest. Just mix a little coconut oil or lotion with peppermint or eucalyptus."

"Okay, Meemaw, I'll tell her. Thanks again."

"Or that Vicks Vapor Rub. You can't go wrong with the Vicks."

"Got it. You don't want to be late for Bingo."

"All right now. I'll talk to you soon."

"Love you, old woman."

"Love you, too."

I disconnected and turned my full attention to the stove. Time to taste my concoction. I dipped a spoon into the pot and held my breath. Not bad for a first-timer. Now to find the bowls.

# CHAPTER 44

## *Faith*

I SETTLED the blanket over my shoulders and shuffled into the kitchen. I'd been trying to fall back asleep, but Dante's conversation had grabbed my attention. Listening to Meemaw coach him through the soup recipe, not once, not twice, but three times, secured my opinion that his grandmother must possess the patience of a saint.

Hopefully, whatever he'd made was edible. It would be a shame if Meemaw wasted all that time. Dante stood with his back to me. A creamy yellow broth bubbled on the stove as he pulled cabinet doors open, standing up on tiptoe to peer at the top shelves.

"The one next to the fridge," I said.

He whipped around. "Hey, when did you get up?"

"Just a minute ago. I needed to stand up so all this crap could drain out of my head." I tried drawing a breath in through my nose but failed. "I'm really stuffy."

"Yeah, I can tell. Meemaw says I should rub some oils on your chest."

I rolled my eyes. "I haven't showered in three days. I'm pretty sure you don't want to go anywhere near my chest."

"I don't know," Dante moved toward me and drew me into a hug. "Three days isn't that long."

I let myself lean up against him. He felt solid...safe. I should kick him out, but I didn't have the energy. Besides, he'd already seen me at my worst when I answered the door. It's not like I needed to impress him. That was one of the benefits of a sex-only arrangement.

His lips grazed the top of my head, and I pulled back to look up at him. "What's that for?"

"Jeez, Faith. Can't you let me be nice to you for an afternoon?"

I shook my head and turned away. Being nice to me would only make things more difficult, especially when I had to confess there was someone threatening to expose my alter ego. "This isn't part of our arrangement. Sex means sex. No soup, no kissing. No being nice."

Dante found the bowls and filled them with the steaming soup. "I know you don't feel well, so I'm going to ignore that. Now sit down and eat your damn soup."

I wobbled to the table and dropped into a chair. Dante set a bowl and spoon down in front of me then sat down across from me.

As I dipped my spoon into the bowl, I peered over at him. I felt stale and stinky, and he looked so fresh and healthy. If I were looking for love, he'd be on the short list. I already knew he was amazing in bed, not to mention what he could do on a pool table.

Although my taste buds weren't exactly working and I couldn't smell a thing, the soup was hot, and it looked delicious. So now he could cook, too? Too bad I wasn't in the market for a boyfriend.

After a few spoonfuls, I pushed back from the table. "Thanks, Dante. The soup was great. You should go now. Don't you have stuff to do?"

"I don't have to go into the office today, and I don't work at the bar until later tonight. I'll just clean up the mess in the kitchen. Do you want to go lie down?"

"Yeah." I dragged my heavy limbs over to the couch and buried myself under the blanket. Mr. Darcy hopped up next to me and turned in circles before nestling up against my stomach.

Dante sat down on the edge of the couch. "I almost forgot. This was tucked into your door when I got here." He handed me a large manila envelope.

I reached a shaky hand out to get it.

"Need some help?" Dante made a move to take it back from me, and I yanked it away.

"Thanks, I've got it."

He stood up and went back to the kitchen as I slid a single typewritten sheet from the envelope. The familiar lines detailing the scene at Meemaw's blurred as tears leaked down my cheeks. I turned the paper over. The back was blank. I folded the paper up and put it back in the envelope, then slipped it underneath the couch cushion. Who was doing this and what could they possibly want?

I took in a ragged breath and dabbed at my eyes with a tissue. My hand glided over Mr. Darcy's silky fur, eliciting a soft purr as Dante moved around my kitchen, washing dishes, putting ingredients away, and humming to himself. I tried to fight the wave of utter exhaustion dragging me under. It was no use. I closed my eyes and drifted into a dreamless and troubled sleep.

---

**Dante**

I FINISHED DRYING the stock pot and found a place for it in the cabinet. Faith sure hadn't been very excited to see me. Not exactly what I was expecting. When I'd made my list of how to win her over, I'd hoped for a different reaction. In the damn book, Harrison made homemade pasta for Eleanor and felt a crack in her hard exterior, like she'd let him in a bit. Not so with Miss Hardass over there. Evidently, she would be a tougher nut to crack. I still had a few more items on my list. I'd just have to wait for the right moment for my next attempt.

Why I was actively pursuing her remained somewhat of a mystery to me. I still wasn't ready to go all-in on a relationship, but maybe taking it a little beyond our just sex agreement wouldn't kill us. I'd probably be moving on in a few months. As long as I didn't get too close, I could still keep my heart in check.

I grabbed my bag and moved toward the living room. Curled up into a little ball, Faith didn't even take up half the couch. I plopped down on the vacant end and pulled out my laptop. Mr. Darcy stretched then walked over to nudge underneath my arm. I ran a hand down the cat's back.

Faith may not want me here, but I'd brought enough work to keep me busy through the afternoon. As she stretched out her legs in sleep, I slid her blanketed feet onto my lap. She might not like it, but I wasn't going anywhere, at least not until the end of the semester.

# CHAPTER 45
## *Faith*

"YOU GUYS ARE LIKE A COUPLE," Jess said, swinging her backpack onto her shoulder as she stood up from a table at the student center.

"No, we're not," I said. I finally felt well enough to get back to my teaching schedule. That cold had knocked me out for a week, and I still wasn't operating at one-hundred percent. Jess and I had met for lunch during a break in classes. She couldn't seem to understand the relationship, or lack of one, that Dante and I shared. "We're not in a relationship. It's just sex."

Jess raised an eyebrow. "Just sex? He's over at your place all the time."

"Yeah, just for sex."

"You mean to tell me that you guys are doing it every night of the week?"

I crumpled up my sandwich wrapper and moved toward the trash can. "He only comes over twice a week. Wednesdays and Saturdays."

"Really? You told me you couldn't meet up on Friday because Dante was coming over after work."

Damn, she'd been paying attention. "Okay, you're right. He came last Friday, too."

"Yeah, if you ask me, he's coming a lot more than he should be if you're not technically seeing each other."

"Very funny. By the way, I'm coming a lot now, too. It's a mutually beneficial arrangement."

I smiled and hugged a textbook against my chest. Dante and I had reached a very comfortable point in our arrangement. The only wrinkle in my life was that the damn pages of my manuscript kept showing up. I'd found one slipped under my office door and another one on the windshield of my car. I'd been working on a plan to come clean about my secret, but every time I tried to bring it up to Dante, I froze. Besides, I only had a couple thousand words more to go. If I ended things with him before my manuscript was complete, I feared the writer's block would set in again.

"Whatever floats your boat. But I'm warning you, I don't think you can keep this up forever."

"As long as he can keep it up for now."

Jess rolled her eyes.

I laughed. "Forever is the last thing on my mind. Now stop worrying about me and tell me what you and Jake are doing tomorrow night for Valentine's Day."

---

### Dante

I KNOCKED LIGHTLY on Faith's door. Stopping by her place after closing the bar on Saturday nights had become a habit—one I had no intention of breaking. I turned the doorknob. It was unlocked.

"Honey, I'm home," I called out.

"Not funny." She sat in bed, her back resting against a stack of pillows and her nose buried in a thick book.

I draped my coat over the back of a kitchen chair. A vase of long-stem red roses occupied the center of the table. Who the hell sent her flowers? I wanted to slide the card out of the envelope and take a peek. As far as I knew, I was the only one enjoying her nighttime company. Could she be seeing someone else? What the hell?

Playing it cool, I set my bag down on the floor and covered the distance to the bedroom in a few long strides. I placed a kiss on the top of her head and sat down next to her. "What'cha reading?"

She marked her spot and put the book on the nightstand. "Doesn't matter."

"I brought you something."

She cocked her head. "What, like a present? What's the occasion?"

I pulled the wrapped package out from behind my back and handed it to her. "You must be the most unromantic woman on the face of this earth. It's Valentine's Day."

She reached for the package. "We don't do commercialized made-up holidays. Not part of the deal."

I made a move to take it back. "I guess I'll return it then."

"Not so fast. I mean, you already bought it and all." Her fingers fumbled with the red satin ribbon. She ripped the paper and lifted the top off the small box. "What did you do?"

"Remember that day we met on the sidewalk?"

"Yeah. Outside the library. You told me about your favorite sex position." She lifted the delicate silver chain out of the box. A small silver charm dangled from the end. "What's this?"

"I know how much you like flowers." Why was I suddenly so embarrassed? It was cheesy. Dammit, she'd probably bolt again. "Never mind, it's stupid." I tried to grab it out of her hand, but she yanked it away.

"Not so fast. It's a lotus blossom, isn't it?" She twisted the silver charm back and forth in her fingertips.

I shrugged. "Seemed fitting. You know, your love of flowers, my love of sex."

"Get over here, cheeseball." Her arms snaked around my neck, and she pulled me down to her, finding my lips with her own.

My body responded like a well-trained machine. I nudged closer to her on the bed as she parted her lips, and my tongue tasted the minty flavor of her toothpaste.

It was two-thirty in the morning. I loved that she always waited up for me. Wyatt used to mention how nice it was to have someone waiting for him when he closed down the bar. I had given him crap about that, but now I was starting to appreciate the feeling of knowing someone would be there when I finally locked up and called it a night.

"Do you like it?" I asked, moving my lips to her earlobe.

"Of course I do. Put it on me?" She held it out to me, and I secured the necklace around her neck.

"It's not too much?"

"Shhh." She reached out a hand and turned off the lamp. Straddling my thighs, she whipped her pink flannel pajama top over her head and tossed it on the floor.

I peered up at her. A sliver of moonlight came through the blinds, covering half of her body in a ghostly shadow. She put a hand on either side of my head and hovered over me. "Get naked."

I wanted to resist, force her into talking about the growing connection between us and find out who sent her those fucking flowers, but my body betrayed me, and my desire won. I wriggled out of my jeans as she unbuttoned my shirt. She stood up from the bed long enough to step out of her pajama bottoms, then reached for something in her night-stand drawer.

"I've got a little something for you, too," she said.

"Oh yeah?" I slid a sheet over my naked body and watched her move around the bed in the dim light.

"How do you feel about being tied up?"

Holy shit. She always seemed to surprise me. I got hard at the mere suggestion. "Yeah, I could go for that."

"Good, give me your wrist." Faith placed my hand up against the bedpost and secured it with some kind of fabric. She crawled over me to the other side, making sure to brush her naked chest against mine on the way, and did the same to my other hand.

"Now what?" I licked my lips in anticipation of what she had in mind.

"Feet, too."

She reached under the covers and dragged one foot over to the bedpost and tied it up, then did the same on the other side. The sheet tented at my crotch. Obviously, I was more than ready for whatever she had planned.

Faith pulled the sheet back and trailed kisses from my cheek to my ankle then back up the other side, intentionally ignoring my obvious need.

This chick, fuck, what she did to me. Blood raced to my crotch, and I throbbed with desire.

Faith crouched between my legs. She licked my cock from my balls to my tip, then blew out a soft exhale. I shivered as her breath hit me. Smiling, she leaned down and took the tip of my cock into her mouth, running her tongue around the rim of my head and sending waves of pleasure radiating out to the rest of my body.

I wanted to twist my fingers into her hair. A tug against the restraints sent the headboard clattering into the wall.

Faith made eye contact. "Careful. You'll wake up my

neighbors." She bent her head and took me into her mouth again, this time easing further down. I bucked my hips up to meet her mouth, and she drew back.

Once my body stilled, she went to work again, drawing my full length inside her mouth. Her wet heat enveloped me while she ran her nails up and down my inner thigh. She cupped my balls, and her fingers danced under, over, and around them.

Every time I moved my hips, she paused until I became still. I strained against the ties on my hands and feet, and she stopped. She drove me fucking crazy. I wanted to yank her up and crush my mouth down on hers, roll her over and slam inside her, go down on her, and make her scream my name.

The intensity of my need built upon itself until it had nowhere else to go. She slid me in and out of her mouth, humming when I hit the back of her throat, brushing her breasts up against my inner thighs and wrapping her hand around the base of my cock. I'd be a total douche if I didn't warn her I was about to explode into her mouth.

"I'm going to...it's coming..."

She looked up at me and smiled... so fucking hot with her lips wrapped around my cock and her eyes daring me to hold back. Relentless, she drew me deeper into her mouth and increased the pressure of her hand around the base of my dick.

Holy fuck. I tried to resist, but it was no use. My legs shook, my butt cheeks squeezed together, and I came like I'd never come before. She sucked me off until the last bit of my orgasm left me drained. Only then did she sit up and wipe the back of her hand across her mouth.

"How was that?" Faith asked.

"Get these fucking ties off my hands and feet, and I'll show you." My voice came out more like a snarl. If that's how she wanted to play tonight, I was all over it.

Faith released one foot, then the other, rubbing my ankles as she slid the restraints off. "I don't know. I kind of like you like this."

I twisted on the bed. "Now!" She looked pretty damn pleased with herself.

"Okay, just a sec."

She barely had time to untie me. Released from my restraints, I flipped her over onto her back. "Your turn."

# CHAPTER 46
## *Faith*

I WAS THRILLED at how the tie-up experiment had gone. I'd been meaning to try it out to make sure I'd captured the right movements and sequence of events in the scene I'd been playing out in my head. I only had a couple more chapters to go, and Dante's reaction proved I'd gotten it right when my fictional Dante and Faith tried it out in my book. I hadn't counted on this turn of events, though. Seemed like Dante wanted to give as well as receive.

I let him fasten one arm to the post, then the other. I even moved my legs to make it easier for him.

Dante paused beside the bed. I smiled up at him, delicious anticipation coursing through my veins. But instead of kneeling down and racking my body with pleasure, he leaned down and grabbed his jeans. Wait a minute. He wasn't leaving, was he?

"What are you doing?" I asked.

"You had your turn." He slid a leg into his pants. "Now it's mine."

"Yeah, but—"

"No buts." He tugged his jeans up over his hips and sat

down near the foot of the bed. "Since I can't get you to talk about us, I figured I'd take this opportunity to force a conversation."

I groaned. "Dante, there is no us. I've been perfectly clear about that. We both agreed, no strings."

He wrapped his large, capable hands around my foot and dug his thumb into the instep. Wow, that felt good. Not as good as if he'd been rubbing another part of my anatomy, but I'd play along with him... at least for the time being.

"Is the pressure okay?"

"Yeah, that feels great. Although, I'd feel better if you used your skills about three feet higher on my body."

Grinning, he continued to work on my foot. "Patience. So about us—"

"No. I'm not taking part in this conversation."

He moved his attention to my other foot. "Then I'll talk, you listen."

I closed my eyes, not that he'd be able to tell in the inky darkness, but it was the only act of defiance available to me in my current compromised position.

"Who are the flowers from?"

His thumbs circled my heel. Holy guacamole, he had great hands. "What flowers?"

"The roses sitting on your table. Are you seeing someone?"

My mouth went dry, and I eyed the outline of the bottle of water on my nightstand. "Of course not. They're from a friend."

"You're the one who's been teaching me about the symbolism of flowers, remember? Pretty sure red roses aren't for friendship."

"They're no big deal. Some guy my mom's pushing on me sent them. He's all the way out in California."

"So, you *are* seeing someone else?"

My stomach started to tighten. "I'm not even seeing you. I told you, I don't date."

"This guy out west, he's mom-approved?"

Dammit, I'd meant to hand the flowers off to Jess before he saw them. I'd told Carter I wasn't interested, tried to let him down easy. It wasn't my fault he sent me some dumb flowers. Okay, gorgeous flowers. Now Dante's nose was all out of joint, but the flowers didn't mean a thing. He was the one I wanted to spend Valentine's Day with, even though I couldn't admit it to him.

"My mom thought we'd hit it off. We didn't. No big deal."

"But he sent you flowers."

"Yeah, so what?"

Dante let my foot fall back to the bed. "Whoever he is dropped some serious dough on those roses."

"What's your point?"

"My point is, when a guy gives a girl flowers like that, he expects something in return."

I pictured Carter earnestly spilling his heart over oysters at the marina, and then spilling the contents of his stomach over the table. "I promise you, it's not what you think."

Dante shifted closer to me on the bed, and my body rolled toward him. "And what do you think I think?"

"I think you think too much." I groaned. "Can't you just let it go?"

"Whatever's going on between us, it's more than just sex." Dante's hand came to rest on my thigh, sending a zing of anticipation to where I wanted to feel his touch the most. "I mean, the sex is great, don't get me wrong, but there's something more."

I hummed to myself, trying to drown him out—a childish move, but maybe it would work. I'd never admit he was right. My plan didn't have room for a relationship, at least not until I became a tenured professor. Maybe it was time to call things off.

"Just untie me. Now, please."

Dante continued, "Try telling me you don't have feelings for me."

"I don't have feelings for you," I growled through gritted teeth as I bit my bottom lip. A little white lie, no big deal. "Are you happy?"

"You're lying."

A sharp laugh broke free from my chest. "How can you tell? You don't know me at all."

That was the problem. No one knew who I really was. I didn't even know myself anymore. I'd spent so long hiding under the layers of my mother's cloak of fame, I wasn't sure I could ever break free. At least not without hurting the people I loved.

Scratch that. I loved my mom and even Clem. But if I came out of hiding as Chastity Austen, the person I might end up hurting the most was sitting right next to me. And love? I didn't love Dante Bishop.

Did I?

"You think I don't know you?" His fingers fiddled with the tie on my ankle. "Your favorite beer is Honeyweiss, but only on tap."

I rolled my eyes. "You got me. Yep, you really know me."

"And you're superstitious and love the number thirteen." He released my other foot.

"I flat out told you that."

He walked around the bed and untied my wrist. "You're stubborn as hell and would do anything for your friends."

I blew a raspberry.

"You've got a wicked sense of humor, have a talent for handling Meemaw, and never fail to call me on my bullshit." He climbed onto the bed and hovered over me as he untied the other wrist. His thumb brushed over my lower lip. "You always bite your lower lip when you lie."

"You're wrong, Dante." I rubbed my wrists and bit my lip.

His mouth covered mine, and he nipped at my bottom lip. "You're lying, Faith."

I mumbled into his neck, "I don't want to talk anymore. If you want out, just say so."

He drew back, and I could just make out the edges of his face in the dim light coming in from the parking lot outside my window. "I don't want out, Faith. I want you."

I took in a deep gulp of air, suddenly feeling bare and exposed, and pulled the sheet over me. What was wrong with me? Wasn't this what most women wanted?

Dante cupped my face in his hands and traced the outline of my jaw with his finger. "What do you say, Faith? Want to ditch the rules and try this thing for real?"

Images crowded my brain... holding hands while walking across the quad, doing prep work together at the library, driving down to Meemaw's for a Sunday dinner. *Don't lose focus. Guys like Dante don't stick around. Remember your dad?*

My teeth pressed into my bottom lip. "No, I want to keep things the way they are." The safe way. Where I finished my manuscript and we'd go our separate ways in a couple of months.

He took my hands in his. "You're scared. I get it. But we'll figure it out together. Someone once told me, that all it takes is one moment of courage to change your life forever."

"Who told you that?" I'd written that exact statement into *Carnal Knowledge*. Could Dante possibly be reading my book? No way. An erotic romance would never find its way onto his bookshelf.

"Doesn't matter who said it. The point is, take a chance. What have you got to lose?"

"Are we done here?" I pulled the sheet tighter around me

and sat up. He had no idea what I had to lose. I could lose it all: my family, my teaching job, my career. If I let him in, if he got close enough, he'd figure out my secret and everything could disappear.

"So that's it then?"

"I guess so."

"Unbelievable. You're right, Faith, I guess I don't know you at all." He stood from the bed and scrounged around the floor for the rest of his clothes.

I fisted my hands in the sheets. Every ounce of my being wanted to call him back to bed, wrap my arms around him, and let him love me.

He was right, he knew me better than anyone.

And that's exactly why I had to let him go.

# CHAPTER 47

## *Faith*

I SAT on a low couch in the Student Center, trying to finish my lecture notes. Dante's words from the night before made it impossible to concentrate. My phone buzzed, a welcome distraction, and I looked at the screen as I answered.

"Hi, Steph. What's up?"

"You're moving up the list, Faith. *Carnal Knowledge* just hit the top twenty."

I'd wished for success, but now that it was knocking down my door, I wasn't sure I wanted it anymore. "That's awesome. Thanks for letting me know."

"When do you think you'll have that new manuscript done? We want to follow this up with something epic."

I slid my laptop out of my bag and flipped the screen open. Another page of my manuscript sat on top of my keyboard. How the hell? As my eyes skimmed the print, I relived my interaction at Dante's apartment, all of it captured on the page in front of me.

The contents of my stomach revolted, and I ran for the nearest restroom.

"Are you there? Faith?" Steph's voice sailed through the phone.

I barely reached the bathroom before my nerves emptied my stomach. I'd have to call Steph back.

My cheeks cooled with the help of cold water from the tap. I rinsed my mouth and wiped it off with a scratchy paper towel. What was I going to do?

As I stepped out of the bathroom, I saw Jess at one of the tall tables by the coffee bar. I swung by the couch where I'd left my things, then made my way over. I could use a friendly face right now.

Jess looked up from her book as I approached. "Hey, how's it going?"

"Not good. I just got some really bad news."

"You look like shit. Want to talk about it?" Jess patted the stool next to her.

"Not yet. I need to figure out what I want to do about it first."

"You sure?"

"Yeah, thanks though. How are you?"

Jess rolled her eyes. "Same old, same old. Jake and I are off again. He needs space."

"When are you going to cut those ties for good?" I leaned against the stool, wishing my life was a lot simpler.

"Wait. Is that you, giving me relationship advice?"

"Good point."

Jess leaned forward. "Speaking of relationships, how are you and Dante?"

I shrugged, hoping she'd drop it. "It's complicated."

"Sounds serious to me."

"I've told you. There's no relationship."

"That's what you keep saying—"

"I keep saying it because it's true!" My head started to pound, and I stood. "I've got to get to class."

"We're still on for tonight, right?" Jess asked.

"Tonight?" I racked my brain, trying to remember what Jess might have talked me into this time.

"Yeah, the poetry slam."

I sighed. "I really shouldn't."

"No!" Jess slapped her palm down on the table, and a couple of people around us looked over. "You promised. You canceled on me last time."

I raised my hands in surrender. "Okay, okay. Pick you up at eight."

"That's better. See you tonight." Jess settled back down on her stool and took a sip of her coffee.

I gave a wave and made my way out of the building. Things were happening so fast. If someone wanted to flush me out, I wasn't going to go down without a fight. I needed a plan. If I could just figure out who'd been leaving the pages, I might get an idea of how to handle it.


Mr. Darcy meowed as he wound his way between my legs. I opened the pantry and scooped some food into his bowl, wishing for the thousandth time I hadn't promised Jess I'd go to the poetry slam tonight.

"Here you go, baby." I bent to rub him behind the ears, just how he liked it, eliciting a wave of purrs. Grabbing my coat and purse off the counter, I made my way through the door and out into the cold, dark night.

A few minutes later, I turned into the parking lot of Jess's complex. Jess lucked out and scored one of the brand-new townhouses on the edge of campus. The downside was she had to share the two-bedroom unit with another gal.

Still, her place was much nicer than mine and twice the size. I didn't mind my cozy studio, though. I needed the privacy and wasn't ready to give up Mr. Darcy since pets weren't allowed at her complex.

Jess bounded out the front door and over to the car. She wrenched the door open and hopped inside. "I didn't think you'd show. Ready for tonight?" She rubbed her hands together and blew into them.

"I suppose." I put the car in reverse and eased out of the lot. The Roastery wasn't far, just a few blocks over. I found a spot on the street and left the warmth of the car for the cold sidewalk.

"Come on, this will be fun," Jess said, already a few steps ahead of me.

I followed her into the dim interior, and the smell of high-quality coffee washed over me. Burlap coffee bean bags stenciled with poetry verses hung on the walls. Yellow lights from a raised dais against the light brick wall created a golden sheen that lit up the edge of the crowd. Jess recognized someone and wound through the tables to the far side of the room. I trailed behind.

"Hey, guys," Jess said, reaching a group of tables. Several small round tables had been pushed together and people clustered around them. As I stepped up behind Jess, a few people shifted over, making room for us to sit down at the edge of the group.

I scanned the faces, recognizing most of them as colleagues. Great...Murph. He caught my eye from the other side of the table and raised his mug toward me in recognition.

I ignored him as I sat down to study the coffee bar menu. Caffeine. Yes, caffeine would help.

The server came around and took orders. I put mine in for an extra-large chai latte and sat back to wait for the show to start. Jess started up a conversation with a guy on her right. I recognized him from the fiction writing seminar I'd taken a couple of years ago. He had an interest in sci-fi, if I recalled correctly.

"I was hoping you'd be here tonight," Murph said. With no one on my left, it didn't take long for him to pull up a chair.

Great, just great. "Yeah, I needed a break, and Jess really wanted to come."

"Did you bring anything?" he asked.

"What?"

"To slam? It's a poetry slam, remember?"

"Oh, yeah. No, I don't have anything." If I didn't engage, maybe he'd return to his seat. I scanned the crowd. How many of these people had a poem prepared? My last attempt had taken me a week, and I'd only come up with a few measly lines.

Murph's mouth spread into a wicked smile. "I have a little something I've been working on."

A voice rang out over the speaker system. "Hi, everyone. Welcome to The Roastery and our much-anticipated poetry slam." Our server had stepped onto the small stage and spoke into a hand-held microphone. Hoots, hollers, and applause broke out.

Murph got up from the table and moved back to his original seat as the woman on the stage continued to speak.

"It's an open mic format. Just make sure you state your name when you come up on stage. We need three judges. Anyone want to volunteer?" She put her hand up to shade her eyes from the lights and looked out over the crowd.

Jess grabbed my hand and pushed it up in the air.

"Hey, what are you doing?" I asked, trying to tug my arm down.

"Great! That's one. How about two more?" the woman on the stage asked. Two more hands went up, and the server motioned for them to come over to the stage. "If my judges will head over to the table in front of the stage, we'll get started."

"Thanks a lot." I pushed back from my chair and grabbed my mug. "I've never even been to one of these things before. What do I know about judging?"

Jess shrugged her shoulders. "You looked like you needed a little extra fun tonight, plus I didn't want you to cut out early. I'm sure you'll do great."

I joined the other two judges at the table in front and sat down. The server explained that after each performance, we needed to hold up a sign with a score. Each performer could rate from zero to ten, with ten being the highest. Sounded simple enough. I settled in, ready for the first victim.

A short, wiry guy sporting multiple facial piercings and lots of ink took the stage. He launched into a dramatic telling of losing his virginity, complete with body motions for all the actions. He finished, and the crowd broke into enthusiastic applause.

My initial reaction was to give the guy a three, but I didn't want to be too harsh. When I bent down to write my score on the paper, I sneaked a look at the judge to my left. Hmm, he gave ink guy a six.

I jotted down a seven, and in unison, we raised our sheets to show the crowd. Ink guy hopped up and down on the stage, apparently psyched to score a whopping twenty points. That wasn't too bad. Judging should be relatively easy.

Three more slammers followed, each giving a more dramatic performance than the last. I continued sneaking looks to my left and right, trying to keep my scores in line with the other judges.

As I readied myself for the next performance, Murph took the stage. He stated his name and bent his head down low, the yellow lights making his hair look more orangey than usual.

. . .

*You...*
*You with your good girl looks,*
*you haunt me*
*You with your good girl smarts,*
*you taunt me*
*What would they say, what would they do*
*If they knew, if only they knew*
*You're a tease, just to please*
*Make me hot, that's your shot*
*Can't eat, without a chance*
*Dish it out, just a glance*

MURPH LOOKED RIGHT at me and continued...

*It's a front, a façade*
*Not a lady, just a broad*
*Taking us all for a ride*
*Tearing me up inside*
*What to do, what to do*
*Tell the truth, but to who*
*Would it hurt, being true?*
*Screw it, Fuck you!*

I gasped. *He knows. It's him and he knows.* A coldness gripped my heart, sending ice water surging through my veins.

Murph took an exaggerated bow and leered at me, his white teeth glowing in the incandescent light. I fought off a sob. Wouldn't do me any good to break down in front of an audience. All I wanted was to get out of there.

I pushed back from the table and staggered to my feet. Murph strutted around the stage like a freaking rooster. I stumbled through the tables, reaching for my coat and purse on the way out.

Jess grabbed my arm. "Hey, Faith, wait! What's going on?"

"I've got to get out of here." The walls pressed in on me, and my lungs struggled to take in a breath. I yanked my arm away from Jess and rushed toward the door. Dante... I needed to get to Dante before he found out about this from Murph. He had to hear it from me. It was time to come clean.

I crashed through the door into the cold winter night, with Jess still calling my name.

# CHAPTER 48

## *Dante*

"YO, Dante! There's somebody at the bar asking for you." Wyatt's voice carried through the back hallway to the storeroom.

"Be there in a sec." I lowered the box crusher in the storeroom and waited for it to finish its cycle. Ever since that night I'd been trapped with Faith, I always made sure to check the door before letting it close behind me.

The machine stopped, and I made my way back out to the bar. The place was hopping, even for a Friday night. Maybe Faith had stopped by. A wide smile spread across my face. Maybe she'd given some thought to going public and wanted to stop hiding behind her stupid "sex-only" rule.

I rounded the corner. Cheryl balanced on a stool at the bar. What the hell was she doing here? "Hey, what's going on?"

She wore her nurse's scrubs under her winter coat and gave me a shaky smile. "Is there somewhere we can go to talk?"

I cocked my head. "Why? What's going on?"

She squinted and looked around. "Maybe somewhere quiet?"

"Um, yeah, sure." Whatever was bothering her, she'd driven almost a hundred miles to get it off her chest. The least I could do was give her five minutes of my time. "I live upstairs. Come on up and we can talk there."

As I left the bar area, I called out behind me. "Back in five, Wyatt."

Cheryl hopped off her stool and followed me through the bar and up the stairs to my apartment.

"Can I take your coat? Get you something to drink?" *Please say no.* I was eager for her to get to the point of her visit.

Cheryl shook her head and raised her eyes to meet mine. "I wanted to come tell you in person."

"Tell me what?"

She put a hand on my arm. "It's Meemaw."

"What about her?"

She drew in a jagged breath and looked away. "This is harder than I thought it would be."

I clenched my jaw. Through gritted teeth, I asked, "What about Meemaw?"

Her eyes filled with tears. "She didn't suffer, Dante. It happened so fast. There was nothing we could do to save her."

I stood shock-still. No. This had to be a mistake. I'd just talked to her earlier this afternoon. She'd been on a tirade about the spring flower show at the senior center. I collapsed into a chair and cradled my head in my hands. "No."

Cheryl walked around behind me and put her hands on my shoulders. "I'm so sorry. I wanted to tell you in person. I wouldn't let them just call you with the news."

"She's gone?" I squeezed my eyes shut tight, waiting for her to confirm the news. I needed to hear her say it.

"She had an aneurysm. It burst. There was nothing anyone could do. She didn't feel any pain." Cheryl turned my body to face hers.

As my tears started to fall, I rubbed at my eyes. Cheryl tried to put her arms around me, but I turned away. "I can't believe it."

"I know. I'm so sorry. Do you want to head home tonight? They're waiting for you. You can still see her and say goodbye."

I yanked off my glasses and wiped my cheeks with the back of my hand. My voice husky from the raw emotion, I replied, "Yeah, just let me throw some stuff in a bag."

It couldn't be real. Still, I got up from the table and felt around for the duffel bag under the bed. Without a conscious thought about what I'd need, I swept a random assortment of clothes from the shelves and tossed it all into the bag, then made my way to the bathroom. I grabbed my toothbrush and a couple of other toiletries, then zipped up the bag and threw it over my shoulder.

Cheryl stood by the front door. "Ready? I can drive you back if you want. I don't think you should be alone right now."

"Yeah, sure. Just let me stop in at the bar and let them know where I'm going."

I held the door open for her, and we stepped out onto the stoop. With my pulse racing, I turned and locked the door. Cheryl hooked her arm through mine as we made our way down the steps. At the bottom, she drew me into a hug.

"I'm so sorry, Dante. I'll go get the car." She took my duffel and slung the strap over her shoulder as I went into the bar.

Inside, I found Wyatt wiping down the counter. He looked up as I approached. "Everything okay?"

I shook my head. "No. I've got to head out. Meemaw passed away."

Wyatt's face fell. "Oh, man. I'm really sorry to hear that. Is there anything I can do?"

"Yeah, just hold down the fort. I don't know how long I'll be gone."

"Take all the time you need, Dante. We'll manage here."

I nodded and headed back outside, the weight of the Meemaw's pressing down on me, making it hard to breathe. Cheryl sat behind the wheel with the motor running. I climbed in, and she reached over to squeeze my hand as we pulled away from the bar.

### Faith

I PULLED into the parking lot of Tapped and turned off the engine. I'd tried coming up with a plan on the short drive over and still had no idea what I was going to say. Maybe something along the lines of "Guess what? All that sex we had? It was so great I wrote it all down and someone's been reading about it. You don't mind, do you?"

What would Dante do? Would he get angry? Break a beer mug or two? That would be better than the simmering silent treatment. Either way, it would be bad, that much I was sure of. I rested my head on the steering wheel and took in a few deep breaths. Best to just get it over with.

I unbuckled the seatbelt and was about to get out of my car when Dante and some woman came out of his apartment and walked down the steps. I slouched down low in the driver's seat and watched as the woman put her arms around him and wrapped him into a hug. Dante hugged back, then they separated, and he went into the bar. Probably just a good friend. No need to jump to conclusions.

I kept an eye on the woman who walked over to a car, threw a bag in the backseat, then pulled up on the side of the building and stopped. A few seconds later, Dante strode out of the bar and I watched in disbelief as he climbed into the passenger seat and the car turned out onto the road.

Looked like Dante had gotten tired of waiting for me to shift into relationship gear and found someone new. Sure as hell didn't take him very long. Well, that would make things easier in the long run. He was probably doing me a favor.

Then why did my heart feel like it was caught in a vise? And why was I finding it hard to breathe? I took in a few jagged breaths and turned the key in the ignition. What a shit day.

### Dante

I WALKED through the senior center in a daze. Gnarled hands reached out to clap my back or grab my arm as I passed. Everyone wanted to offer their condolences and tell me what a wonderful person my grandmother had been. Her voice ran through my head. *They sure went all out, didn't they, my boy? Real silverware for the luncheon and the minister even wore those purple vestments I like so much.*

I almost smiled. Pushing through the doors into the kitchen, I noted Meemaw's nemesis, Mrs. Blake, standing in front of the oven, hot mitts in hand. *I bet that's her signature shepherd's pie. Do you know she uses instant potatoes on top? Instant potatoes! At my luncheon?* I ran my hands through my hair. If this kept up, I'd have to go get myself checked out at the psych ward.

Mrs. Blake turned and smiled. "Dante. Your grandmother sure will be missed around here."

"That's what I hear, Mrs. Blake. Thanks for coordinating the luncheon."

"It was a lovely service."

"Yes, it was."

"Of course, Dolores probably would have had something to say about the music. That organ player can't keep up. They don't even let her play at mass anymore. I don't know how she's allowed to play..."

Mrs. Blake continued to complain about the organist while I waited for a break in the conversation so I could escape. "I see someone I need to talk to over there. Thanks again, Mrs. Blake."

"Mmm hmm." She turned to grab an industrial-size box of instant mashed potatoes and I almost laughed out loud. Maybe Meemaw really was talking to me still.

I made my way back to the dining room where Cheryl stood, orchestrating the buffet. A rainbow of Jell-O salads clustered at one end of the table, and the men hovered around the lemon bars and cookies, waiting for the first person to be brave enough to take one.

"How are you holding up?" Cheryl asked, placing her hand on my arm.

"I'm okay. Thanks for helping out today."

"It's my pleasure. Your grandmother was well-loved, Dante. They're really going to miss her around here."

*They'll miss me all right, like a hole in the head.* I blinked hard. "Yeah, they'll miss her. I think I'm going to head back to her place. I've got to get back to the office tomorrow and want to get a head start on packing stuff up."

"Do you want any help?" Cheryl's hand rubbed my arm.

"No, that's okay. I think it's something I need to do by myself." I appreciated Cheryl's help over the past couple of days, but I still wasn't interested in anything beyond friendship with her.

There was only one person I wanted to see right now—Faith. But I hadn't wanted to call her. I didn't know if she'd be willing to drop everything and come running if she knew about Meemaw. I kind of thought she would, but I didn't want to know for sure. What if this was the kind of thing that crossed the line for her into a relationship? I was afraid to ask her to come because I was afraid she'd say no.

"I can stop by later if you want company." Cheryl seemed hesitant to let me go.

"I'll be okay." I clasped her hand in mine, removing it from my arm. "I really appreciate all you've done. I'll see you around." She let her hand drop to her side as the corners of her mouth tugged down into a frown.

I wheeled around and made my way through Meemaw's friends. As I exited through the doors of the senior center out into the parking lot, I took in a deep breath of the crisp cold air. Alone. Finally.

I'd been holding it together over the past several days as people stopped by to share a memory, tell a story about how Meemaw had helped them over the years, or drop off a casserole. I'd unloaded twelve pans of food just now at the senior center and had three more dishes back at Meemaw's place.

Her friends meant well. I'd be willing to bet half of them had a freezer stocked full of casseroles, just waiting for the next person to drop dead.

Meemaw always used to say that when you got to be her age, every day was a gift. She'd lost so many friends over the years, she said she had to keep making new ones as fast as the old ones were dying.

I rubbed my hand across my eyes as I climbed up into the old Ford. As I turned the key in the ignition, it lumbered to life. I pulled out onto the highway and headed toward home, where a house full of memories and the treasures of an eighty-two-year-old woman waited for me to pack them away.

# CHAPTER 49

## *Faith*

I CHECKED my watch for the tenth time in the past five minutes. Murph usually stopped in our office around this time of day. I'd been trying to figure out how to handle the atomic bomb he'd dropped on Friday night at the poetry slam. He had to be the one leaving the pages for me. No one else would have had the opportunity to get near my laptop and copy the file.

It had to be Murph.

I'd just confront him, find out what he wanted, and ask him to stop. It had to be that easy. Maybe I could grade some papers for him or prep his next month's lesson plans. Whatever he wanted, I'd figure out a way to fix this. The alternative wasn't an option.

Just as I was about to give up on him making an appearance and make the mad dash to teach my next class, the doorknob turned. A shock of red hair appeared in the crack of the doorway, followed by the rest of him.

I squirmed in my chair as Murph entered the office, a giant smirk on his face. "Well, hi there, Faith. Or should I say Ms. Austen?"

I gritted my teeth and blew a blast of air through my nose. "Spill it. How did you get your hands on my stuff?"

He moved around my desk and plopped down in his chair, putting his feet up on his desk and leaning back with his hands behind his head. "It was actually quite easy with us sharing an office and all. You really should password protect your computer."

"I did password protect my computer."

He scoffed. "Yeah, but then don't write your password down and keep it on a sticky note in your top desk drawer."

I wanted to launch myself across the desk and strangle him, especially since he made a good point about my substandard method of securing my computer. But still, that didn't give him any right to go snooping around in my stuff. Best to get right to the point.

"How long have you known?"

"I suspected. That day you left your computer here while you went to class? I did a little digging and came across the first manuscript."

Hot pinpricks danced across my cheeks. "Go on."

"But that day Dante stopped by with your lingerie…" He paused and let his feet drop to the floor. "When you stormed out and Dante followed you, I hit the fucking jackpot. I figured I'd be a nice guy and turn in your application. Imagine my surprise when I walked over to your desk to grab it and saw page after page of porn about you and Dante written on your screen."

"That was private. You had no right to look—"

"And Dante had no right to pursue you." Murph leaned over his desk toward me. "I knew you were both lying. There had to be something going on between you. Did you think I was too stupid to figure it out?"

I narrowed my eyes. "Why leave me the pages? What do you want?"

"You cut right to the chase, huh?"

"I just want to get this over with."

He examined his nails. "I did have a little proposition in mind."

"Like what?"

His giant mouth leered at me, his glowing white teeth on full display. "Like turn down the offer of taking over Middleford's classes, and I give you back the flash drive holding all of your manuscripts and promise not to say another word."

"The classes? You've been putting me through hell over taking over Middleford's classes?"

"That stupid job is my ticket to reducing my student loans. Not to mention edging you out of the tenure track." Murph crossed his legs and examined his thumbnail. "As of right now, you're their top choice."

"And if I don't?"

Murph grinned. "I leak it to the paper. I'm sure everyone on campus would love to know they're rubbing elbows with a bestselling erotic author, especially the President of the University. And what about all the moms and dads who are paying for their kids to get a Christian education? The Dante and Faith stuff is scorching hot. Oh, and I still have your mom's email address. It was so nice of her to give me a card." He sneered, waiting for me to respond.

"You're an asshole."

Murph shrugged. "It's up to you. Tell you what, since I'm such a nice guy, I'll let you think about it overnight. You can even drop by if you want. Say my place, tomorrow night, nine o'clock? You know how much I love that red lingerie."

"Like that would ever happen."

Murph shrugged his shoulders. "Fine. Stop by, email, call, text. You've got a lot at stake here. Your job, the reputation of your dear, loving mom and stepdad." He lowered his voice,

"Plus, you don't want to be the one to break Dante's heart, do you?"

My heart surged in my chest. What would Dante think when he found out? It looked like he'd moved on, but still, I didn't want him to think I'd just used him. Sure, it had started off that way. But now? How exactly did I feel about him now?

Murph stood, grabbed his backpack, and leaned over my desk. "Nine o'clock. I'll be waiting." Then he opened the door and stepped out into the hall.

I jumped out of my seat and pushed the door closed behind him, then collapsed back in the chair and cradled my head in my hands. What should I do? Sure, the extra money from taking over Middleford's classes would be nice, but was it worth it?

And what would prevent Murph from leaking it, anyway? He was enough of a slime ball to take the added classes and still smear my secret all over the paper just for spite. I wished I had someone to talk to, someone who could help me sort out the mess I'd made of my life.

I ran through the possibilities. There was Jess... but she wouldn't understand what a big deal it would be for me to claim the identity of Chastity Austen. She'd think it was cool as hell. Dante wasn't an option. Robin wouldn't get it, either. Why hadn't I tried harder to make more friends?

That just left one option. I gathered my things together and grabbed my bag. It was time to pull out the big guns.

It was time to call my mother.

I SLUMPED in the corner of the couch. I'd put off calling my mother for hours, hoping I'd come up with an alternate solution. Procrastination had been good for my apartment—my kitchen sink sparkled, I'd cleaned the bathroom from top to bottom, and there wasn't a single item of dirty laundry left in my hamper. But I'd stalled long enough. Sooner or later, I had to figure out what to do.

One hand held my phone to my ear, the other wrapped around a short glass about two inches full of peach schnapps. It was either that or tequila. Without a stocked liquor cabinet, my options were limited. I took another sip of liquid courage and let it burn down my throat while I waited for my mother to pick up. She answered on the third ring.

"Hello, honey. What a wonderful surprise."

"Hi, Mom. Are you busy?" *Please say yes.*

"No, darling. Clem just sat down to watch the game, and I was about to dig into a new book. Why aren't you out somewhere exciting tonight?"

"I teach an early class tomorrow."

"I wish you'd have more fun. You're so serious all the time, dear."

I stifled a groan. "I have fun. I even went to a poetry slam the other night." Not that it had been a fun evening out with friends. More like a personal attack by someone I thought I could trust.

"Well, good. I'm glad you're getting out."

"So, Mom, I was wondering if I could talk to you about something?" I took another small sip of my schnapps, trying to tamp down the apprehension trying to claw its way out of my chest.

"Sure, sweetheart. What's going on?"

I hesitated. Once I spilled my guts to my mother, there would be no turning back. But based on the way things were going, she was bound to find out sooner or later. It was probably best if she heard it straight from me.

I'd had all day to think about it, to try to get my thoughts in order. But now, with my mother waiting on the other end of the line, my mind went blank. All the bullet points I'd jotted down and memorized flooded from my brain.

"Faith? What is it?"

I let out a long breath. "Mom, there's something I need to tell you."

# CHAPTER 50

## *Faith*

"ARE YOU OKAY? YOU SOUND FUNNY." Concern laced through my mother's tone.

I adjusted my position on the sofa. "I'm fine, Mom. There's just something I need to let you know before you hear it from someone else."

"My God, are you pregnant? Faith, how could you? How far along are you? Who's the father? Is it that Patrick I met a few months ago? What about Carter, dear? He really cares about you, you know. Oh no, is Carter the father? He doesn't seem like the type that would engage in pre-marital—"

"Mom." I tried to get her attention without success.

"You and Carter will have such beautiful children. We'll have to have a wedding right away though. People will talk, but—"

"MOM!" I yelled into the phone. She paused, and I quickly shouted, "I'm not pregnant."

Silence.

"You're not?" Claire asked. "So, I'm not going to be a grandmother?"

"Well, maybe eventually someday. Listen, I'm trying to tell you something important."

"Thank goodness. That would look really bad in the press. Well, if you're not pregnant, what is it? Do you have cancer? Oh my gosh, my poor baby—"

"Mom, stop. I'm not pregnant, and I don't have cancer. I've been writing erotic romance to put myself through school. I've been using the pen name Chastity Austen and one of my colleagues found out. He tried to blackmail me to keep it a secret, and I actually thought about doing what he wanted just to keep him quiet."

I paused to take in another deep breath, eager to get it all out.

"Can you believe that? I was so afraid you'd be disappointed in me. I just wanted to let you know before you hear it from someone else." The words flew out of my mouth like a run of verbal diarrhea. Way to go. Couldn't give her just a little at a time? Had to spill it all at once?

The silence coming from the other end of the line was deafening. I waited a few moments for her to respond.

"Mom?"

"I'm processing, Faith. How long has this been going on?"

"I started writing my freshman year. My first book got published when I was a sophomore, and I've been releasing two or three books a year since then." I hated springing this on her, but I wanted to be the one to tell her, and I needed some advice.

"Chastity Austen? I think I've heard that name."

I cringed. "Yeah, my most recent book hit the New York Times bestseller list."

"That book that's getting all the press?" She gasped. "Oh, Faith. That's you? Clem wrote a whole sermon about how modern fiction is corrupting our youth. He mentioned that book in particular."

"Yep, that's me. I'm sorry. I just kind of fell into it. I know it's embarrassing for you and Clem, but I'm actually pretty good at it. I wanted to be the one to tell you."

Silence filled the airwaves between us.

"Mom, are you there?"

She clucked her tongue. "I'm not sure what to think about this yet. You say you've been putting yourself through school this way? I told you Clem and I would have been happy to cover your tuition. I just don't understand, honey."

"Yeah. Between the writing, scholarships, and my teaching position, I've paid off about three quarters of my undergrad tuition."

"Writing about sex."

I groaned. "It's not like it's, jeez Mom, it's—"

"I know firsthand how hard it is to make it as an author. But we need to talk about the subject matter. Your books... a lot of people think they're immoral."

"Oh, Mom. They're stories and people like them. They might have a lot of sex, but I'm not writing about anything illegal."

"I don't know how I feel about that yet. Clem's going to blow a gasket. Do you have any idea how embarrassing this is going to be for him? His youth outreach program is just taking off. How's that going to look when the press finds out his own stepdaughter is making a living writing porn?"

Telling her was a mistake, but what did I expect? "First or all, it's not porn. They're love stories. My heroines aren't afraid to go for what they want, to stand up for themselves in and out of the bedroom."

"I'll have to call Clem's new publicist. Maybe she can figure out how to spin this for him. I just don't know, Faith. I'm going to need some time to work through this. Marcy's a genius, but this might be a stretch, even for someone with her talent."

"What about you, Mom?"

"What about me, dear?"

"How's this going to reflect on your career? You write inspirational romance and devotionals. Is it all going to be ruined because of me?" That was my fear. I didn't want to be the cause of everything my mother had worked so hard for blowing up in her face.

"Oh, honey. If there's one thing that's good for publicity, it's scandal. Even in the world of inspirational fiction. There may be some major fallout, but I'll survive."

"So, you're not mad?"

"Mad? No. I'm absolutely livid. Why didn't you come to me before? If I'd have known you wanted to write, I might have been able to steer you in a different direction."

A tear slid down my cheek. "I'm so sorry, Mom. I love writing my books, and I'm not going to change my stories. The only regret I have is making a mess of things for you and Clem. I should have told you sooner."

"Yes, you should have. Did you tell Carter about this? That poor man. He has such high hopes for your relationship."

I stood and paced the narrow width of my living room. "There is no relationship with Carter. Don't you see? We'd never work. He has no idea who I even am."

"Honestly, Faith. I don't think I have any idea of who you are either. Is this what you want? To come out to the world as an erotic romance author?"

"I don't know what I should do. Do I try to hide? Deny that I'm Chastity Austen? I'm proud of my books but I don't want to make things worse for you." I felt faint, like my legs were about to buckle out from underneath me.

"What do you want to do, Faith?"

"I'm not sure. I thought I wanted to work on publishing in literary journals and gain tenure at a college somewhere."

"And now?" Mom asked.

"I don't know. Everyone's going to find out I've been hiding behind a pen name. I love writing. I just thought someday I'd write literary fiction, not romance novels."

"There's nothing wrong with romance novels, honey."

"Oh, I know. It's just some of my colleagues will probably look down on me, and I don't want to cause trouble for you and Clem." Most of the people I worked with turned their noses up at genre fiction. I used to be one of them until I started reading romance and realized how much I craved a satisfying happy ever after.

Since I'd been writing, I'd learned a lot of readers felt the same way. The world was a dark enough place. If I could provide a little light along with a happy ending, that felt like a worthy calling to me.

"It's too late for that. As for your co-workers, how many of them have paid off a good part of their student loans by publishing? They can make fun of you, dear. And you can laugh about it... all the way to the bank."

I smiled at her last comment.

She continued. "Did I ever tell you my first attempt at writing was a mainstream romance?"

I didn't even try to contain my surprise. "It was?"

"Sure. As a single mother, dreaming of her knight in shining armor, I had all kinds of story ideas running through my head. I wrote three hundred and fifty pages of dribble and even sent it out to agents."

"What happened?"

"Nothing. I had a little interest, but no one wanted to sign me on as a new author. When one of them mentioned offhand they were seeing a new trend develop in inspirational romance, I tried my hand at that."

"And the rest is history," I said.

"Pretty much. I needed a way to support us. I think things turned out okay."

I took in a ragged breath. "Not if I've gone and ruined it all for you. I didn't mean to let you down."

"You need to figure out what you want to do."

"Does that mean you're not going to disown me?"

"Give me some credit, sweetheart. You're still my baby girl and I'm proud of you. But I'm also disappointed that you didn't trust me enough to tell me what was going on, and I'm going to need some time to work through it."

"I'm so sorry, Mom."

Claire sighed. "Can I offer one piece of advice?"

"Of course."

"Don't let anybody push you around and make your decisions for you. If you're ready to own it, you need to be the one calling the shots."

"Thanks. I love you."

"I love you, too."

I disconnected and let the phone drop to my lap. Then I took another sip of my drink while I contemplated my next move. If I was going to come out as Chastity Austen, I wanted to do it in style.

# CHAPTER 51

## *Faith*

"HELLO?" I woke to the sound of my cell phone buzzing on the nightstand.

"Where are you?" Jess's voice blared in my ear.

"I'm at home. In bed." I glanced at the clock. "It's one in the morning. What's going on?" I tried to suppress a giant yawn but failed.

Jess growled through the phone. "Is there something you've been meaning to tell me?"

"Like what?"

"Like the fact you've been writing sex scenes all year?"

I sat up straight, suddenly wide awake. "Who told you?"

"So, it's true?"

"Well, yes, kind of, I mean, no. I write erotic romance. It's fiction." First my mom, now Jess. My heart seized, like someone had wrapped a fist around it and squeezed tight.

"Well, you're not going to fucking believe this. The paper found out you're Chastity Austen and they're running a story about it."

"What paper?"

"The school paper. Someone came forward with an

excerpt from your latest novel and they're printing it. The article says they have a source who knows the name behind Chastity Austen, and they're going to release her identity."

"Murph." I groaned and fought off the initial onset of a panic attack.

"What's he got to do with it?"

"He found my manuscript on my computer and tried to blackmail me over it. Wants me to turn down taking on Professor Middleford's classes and told me I had until nine tonight to make a move or he was going to out me."

"I'm on my way over. Be there in ten."

I rubbed the sleep out of my eyes. The fragile barrier I'd constructed between my two worlds had come crashing down around me. By the time I splashed some cold water on my cheeks and ran a toothbrush over my teeth, Jess's fists pounded on the door.

"What the hell is going on with you?" She pushed past me into the living room and kicked her feet up on the coffee table. "You're some superstar author? What else have you been hiding from me?"

"Nothing." I perched on the edge of a kitchen chair. "I didn't mean for things to get out of hand."

"What's the big deal? I mean, besides who your mom is. Does she know?"

"Yeah, I told her today. But I haven't had a chance to talk to Dante yet."

Jess hopped off the couch and walked to the fridge. She rummaged around inside and pulled out a beer. "What's Dante got to do with anything? I thought you two were off?"

Heartburn. The flash of heat rising from my gut to my throat had to be from heartburn, right?

"The stuff Murph found on my computer... it's pretty much a detailed account of everything Dante and I have been up to for the past several months."

Jess took a swallow from the longneck. "So? Nobody will be able to tell, right?"

My fingers twisted together, and I studied a scuff on the worn kitchen floor. "I kind of used our names in my rough draft."

"You're fucking kidding me."

I met her gaze. "I wish."

"So, everyone is going to know about the late-night booty calls?"

I nodded.

"His favorite sexual positions?"

Coming from Jess's point of view, things sounded worse than I'd imagined.

She shook her head. "You'd better hurry. I just ran into one of the editors as I left the library and she said it's already at the press."

I fisted my hands and dug them into my stomach in an attempt to break up the massive knot growing inside my gut. "I can't believe it. I knew this would blow up in my face, but I thought I'd have more time."

I'd meant to get to Dante earlier that day, even walked through the library looking for him. As nine o'clock drew closer, I'd grabbed my keys a few times with the intention of heading to the bar to confess everything. After several failed attempts, I still hadn't found the courage to try to talk to him again.

Seeing him hugging that girl in the parking lot and leaving with her... it felt like he'd driven a spike through my heart. What did I expect? That sex would hold his attention? Well, maybe. How many times had he tried to get me to admit there was more between us? Every time, I'd shot him down. Too concerned about my freakin' six-year plan. Look at how that was turning out.

If only I'd had a chance to get to him before he'd moved

on. I'd been too scared to call or text ,and he was obviously already over me since I hadn't heard a word from him in the past week.

Jess's voice turned my attention back to the conversation at hand. "You need to tell him, Faith. If he sees it in the paper..." her voice trailed off.

"Yeah, I know. I'm going to head over there now."

She stood and tossed her empty bottle in the recycle bin. "Come here."

I shuffled over to her open arms and allowed my friend to give me a hug.

"Good luck. Call me and let me know how it goes, okay?"

We broke apart.

"Sure." I couldn't imagine it going well. I followed Jess to the door and closed it behind her, then retreated to the bedroom to grab a sweatshirt. *Doesn't matter what I look like. After tonight he won't ever want to lay eyes on me again anyway.*

With what felt like the weight of the world on my shoulders, I braved the cold March night and headed toward the bar.

---

### Dante

I SCRAMBLED TO A SEATED POSITION. I'd fallen asleep on the couch again. A loud banging noise on the front door jarred me out of a dreamless sleep. I squinted my eyes against the glare of the TV and staggered to my feet. Drawing one of Meemaw's knit blankets over my naked shoulders, I peered through the peephole.

Faith? What was she doing in Hinkley?

I opened the door and without a word, she wrapped her arms around my waist. It was good to see her. I didn't even mind the way her cold jacket felt on my bare skin. I pulled her into the room and held her close.

She spoke into my chest. "Why didn't you call me?"

"I didn't know if you'd come," I mumbled into her hair.

She drew back and looked up at me, tears spilling over the edges of her beautiful green eyes. "How could you think I wouldn't come?"

Overcome by the look in her eyes, I scooped her up and carried her back to the bedroom, depositing her in the center of my bed.

"Dante, I—"

I put a finger to her lips. We could talk later. Right now, I didn't need the comfort of her words. I wanted to lose myself in her. Make the stress and tension of the past few days melt away.

I unzipped her coat as she kicked off her boots, sending them clunking to the floor. She wriggled out of her coat and peeled her sweatshirt over her head. I knelt down on the bed next to her and crushed my mouth against hers as my hands ran over her stomach, cupped her breasts, and plunged under the waistband of her pajama bottoms.

She wrapped her arms around my neck, pulling my weight down on top of her.

I needed this.

I needed her.

I shivered as our bare skin connected. Then she arched into me, and I slipped a finger inside her panties. She was wet. As my finger slid back and forth, just how I knew she liked to be touched, she rocked hard against my hand.

I drew back, and she grabbed at my fingers, trying to push them back between her legs. I rolled off her and ran a hand up her side, feeling her skin prickle with goosebumps. This woman... what she did to me... how could she get me so hard, so fast?

Her hand groped for me through my thin flannel pants, then slid up and down my length.

I propped myself up on an elbow, watching her writhe against my leg. She opened her eyes and met my gaze. Without breaking eye contact, she slid her pants down and kicked them off the edge of the bed. My hand laid still on her stomach. She took it to her lips and sucked my pointer finger into her mouth, running her tongue around it. My need surged and my cock grew even harder.

She gave my finger a playful nip then skated my hand down, over her breasts and back between her legs. With her finger on mine, she slid them both inside her.

Holy fuck. Just when I thought things couldn't get any hotter, she kept surprising me. I watched through heavy lids as she pressed into me, grinding against our hands. I slid my hand away, leaving hers where it was, and she continued to work herself into a frenzy. Her breathing quickened, and she moaned. I was right there with her. She watched me watching her and smiled.

I couldn't stand not being inside her for a second longer. I reached for the nightstand and ripped the packet open with my teeth. Nudging her legs apart with my knees, I pinned her to the bed with my body as I lowered myself into her.

This was what I needed. The stress and tension of the past week eased away. She wrapped her legs around my waist, raising her hips up to meet me as my body rocked into hers, over and over again.

She tightened around me, and her body shuddered with her climax. I grunted, groaned, and released myself into her. She clenched around me, draining me, and I collapsed on top of her.

Our bodies glistened with sweat from our efforts, and I tugged the blanket over us so she wouldn't get chilled. I threw a leg over her hip, curled her up against me, and nestled my cheek into her neck.

"I love you, Faith," I whispered into her hair.

She didn't respond. I couldn't tell if she'd already fallen asleep or maybe hadn't heard me. It didn't matter. She was here and that could only mean one thing.

She was ready to be together.

For real.

# CHAPTER 52
## *Faith*

TEARS ROLLED down my cheek as I listened for Dante's breathing to even out. *I love you?* I hadn't been expecting that. My heart swelled until it came close to bursting.

I didn't deserve a man like Dante. I'd wanted to warn him about the article. I'd gone to the bar to find him, but they told me he'd been in Hinkley all week. That his grandmother died, and he had to make arrangements and wouldn't be back for a few more days.

Before I knew it, I'd turned onto the highway and ninety minutes later I'd been knocking on his door. He'd looked so relieved to see me, I didn't want to tell him right away. And then he'd kissed me and any idea I'd had about telling him the truth fled from my brain as the hormones rushed in.

I couldn't stay. When he found out I'd been using him to research my manuscript, it would wreck him, especially after the loss of his grandmother. I couldn't bear it.

Lifting his arm, I squirmed out from underneath him. He stirred.

Trying to be as quiet as possible, I tiptoed around the bed, gathering my clothes and boots. Maybe I could find a pen and paper in the kitchen and leave him a note. Telling him in person had been my intent. But I couldn't go through with it.

At least if I left a note, he'd see it before someone else had a chance to get to him. As I passed through the doorway, a floorboard creaked.

"Hey, where you going?"

I paused, mid-step, at the sound of his voice. The bed groaned and his feet thudded to the floor. I turned around as he encircled my waist with his arms.

"Come back to bed?"

I let my cheek rest against his chest for a moment and breathed in his familiar scent. It would be so easy to climb back under the covers and pretend like everything was fine. For half a heartbeat I considered it. But I needed to come clean.

In a few hours, Dante would know the truth. Although it would be the hardest thing I'd ever done, it might make it easier for him if he heard it straight from me. The chance to escape without having a major breakdown disappeared.

"We need to talk."

His hands cradled my head and tilted my face up toward his. "Can it wait until morning?"

"No, unfortunately it can't. Why don't you get dressed, and I'll make a pot of coffee?" That would give me a few minutes to figure out how to begin.

"Something happen? Is your family okay?"

The concern in his voice pulled at the edge of my resolve. I needed to get this over with. But as soon as I came clean it would be over. Dante wasn't the kind of guy to forgive and forget. Drawing it out was only making it harder. But every second I stalled gave me one more moment with him, with how things could have been if I hadn't screwed them up so bad.

"They're fine." With a deep sigh, I broke our embrace. "Just give me a sec and meet me in the kitchen, okay?"

He pressed a kiss against my temple, and I battled the impulse to wrap my arms around his shoulders and cling to him. Instead, I closed my eyes, savoring the way his lips felt on my skin. This would probably be the last kiss of his I'd ever feel.

"Okay, be out in just a minute." He turned toward his dresser and began to rummage through a drawer.

I made my way to the kitchen, stepping into my pajama bottoms and pulling my sweatshirt over my head as I went. By the time Dante joined me in the kitchen, I was fully dressed except for my coat. The pungent smell of fresh-brewed coffee permeated the air and the dark liquid flowed through the ancient countertop machine. I poured a cup for each of us and sat down across the table from him.

Dante scooted his chair closer to mine and put a hand on my knee. "Is it the *L* word? Too soon?"

He leaned back and tunneled his fingers through his hair. "I didn't mean to throw you. I've just been thinking, with Meemaw passing and everything. Life's relatively short, you know? I know this isn't what you wanted. But I'm not sorry I said it." He put a finger under my chin and tipped my head up to make eye contact. "I love you, Faith."

His eyes revealed everything... hope, happiness, love. A smile played at the edges of his mouth, encouraging my lips to lift and return the sentiment. This was it. This moment. I committed his face to memory, one square millimeter at a time. As the moment dragged on without a response from me, his smile tugged down. His brows knit together, and the hope dissipated.

I shook my head and focused on his feet. "I can't."

"What do you mean?" The tone in his voice shifted from an undercurrent of nervousness to confusion.

"I'm so sorry. I never meant for this to happen."

"For what to happen? Why do I feel like I'm out of the loop here?" He made a move to take my hand, and I jerked it away.

I needed to spill it, fast. That would be the only way I'd have the nerve to get it all out. I took a deep breath in through my nose and opened my mouth to let the betrayal begin.

"I'm a writer. Our sex-only arrangement was a research project. I needed to get past a bad case of writer's block and you were the perfect inspiration."

I dared a glance at his face. Confusion flickered behind his eyes.

"I write erotic romance. Everything we did...everything... I wrote about it."

"I don't understand."

I put a hand up to silence him. "It gets worse. I used our names. Eventually, I was going to change them, but someone found out and tried to blackmail me. They leaked it to the paper and there's going to be an article tomorrow."

"An article in the paper?"

I nodded.

"About us having sex?"

I cradled my head in my hands. "Yes."

"They can't print that."

"I don't know exactly what they're printing. I just know that someone leaked it that I've been writing as Chastity Austen, and it's all coming out."

"Chastity Austen? That book everyone's talking about?"

"Yes."

"So that's all this is for you? Research for your book?" Dante stood and walked to the sink, turning his back to me.

I moved to stand behind him, desperately wanting to reach out, run my palm down the smooth skin of his back and press up against him. "That's how it started. But then I fell for you…hard. I didn't want to, but I did."

"And now my sex life is going to be public? New Year's Eve at the bar? The elevator? You wrote about everything we did together? In private?"

The anger in his tone crushed my heart. "I never meant for anyone to see it with your name on it."

"But you were still going to publish all that shit? Doesn't matter whose name you put on it, that was between us." He turned and pushed past me to the living room. "I think you should go."

I followed him toward the door. "Dante, I—"

"Fucking unbelievable. I fell for you. I fell so fucking hard. Should have known better."

"I'm sorry."

"No, I'm the one who's sorry. Damn. You got me good, Faith. You're right. I don't know you at all."

I shrugged into my coat. He wouldn't look at me. I tried to touch him, put my hand to his chest one last time, but he turned away. So much had been left unsaid. How could I make him understand? As I'd gotten to know him, I'd grown to appreciate how few people he let in. By the time my heart had caught up with my need for inspiration, the pages had started to appear. Now it was too late.

Before I'd fully stepped out onto the stoop, he slammed the door behind me. My fingers tightened around the front of my coat, and I somehow made it behind the wheel of the car before the wave of tears crashed over me and spilled down my cheeks.

I took a final look at the front of the house. The curtain fell back in place and the lights went out. As I turned onto the highway, the first pinks and oranges of dawn bled across the sky.

# CHAPTER 53

## Dante

I SLIPPED through the next few weeks in a daze. By day, I stumbled through my time at the office. By night, I worked at the bar. There was nothing in between. The article in the paper hadn't been that bad. But then a website published several of the steamy scenes—the thirteenth floor, the pool table—unedited and in full detail.

For the first couple of weeks, I'd been approached by a variety of girls. Faith was good at what she did, and I had to admit, she made me sound damn good on paper. In the beginning, I let them down easily. A smile, a shrug of the shoulders. As their advances became more brazen, my attitude sharpened.

I'd lost track of how many times I'd been propositioned as I walked across campus. I even caught a girl stuffing her underwear into my mailbox. Those chicks wanted me to do to them everything Faith wrote about in her books. The guys wanted my advice. I was so sick of this shit. I'd been spending as much time as I could down at Meemaw's. By the end of the month, I'd have everything sorted and ready for the estate sale.

There was just one problem. I missed Faith. She'd called, left messages, sent texts, she even made me a batch of Meemaw's lemon crinkle cookies. I'd eaten every last one and damn if they didn't taste just like the old woman's. Meemaw would have been proud—turns out Faith *could* bake. I'd done everything I could possibly think of to get her out of my head. I drank. Then I stopped drinking and started running. I was in the best shape of my life thanks to daily workouts at the gym.

I couldn't stand it anymore and couldn't wait to put as much distance between us as possible. In a few weeks, I'd be packing everything I owned into my car and driving halfway across the country to my new job in Baltimore. I just needed to survive a bit longer, and I'd be out of there. Somehow, the thought of moving farther away from her made me feel worse, not better.

I yanked an earbud from my ear. I'd hoped no one would bother me if it looked like I was listening to music, but Murph wasn't necessarily known for paying attention to even the most obvious social cues.

"Hey, Murph, what's up?"

"Do you need a spot, bro?" Murph asked.

"Sure." I laid back on the bench and waited for Murph to get in position.

"Saw you got a bad break, man."

"Yeah. Didn't see that one coming." I took in a big breath and extended my arms, raising the bar over my chest.

"I tried to warn you about that bitch."

I cut my eyes to Murph's face and grunted as I lowered the weight and pushed the bar up, completing one rep. "Watch it."

Murph smiled a lopsided grin. "Still got it bad for her, huh? Dude, you're pussy-whipped."

I ignored the comment and focused on the weight. My

arms and chest burned from the effort. I'd been numbed by Faith's betrayal. It felt good to feel something, even if it was pain. I had started to think I might never be capable of feeling anything again.

"What are you going to do?" Murph asked.

"Who says I have to do anything?" I squinted up at him.

"No offense, bro, but I read that shit. It was hot. If I was getting off like that with some chick, I'd be banging it until she shut me down."

I struggled to get the weight back up onto the stand. If I kept pushing myself like this, I wouldn't even be able to lift a beer mug tonight. Murph grabbed on and helped guide the bar to a resting position.

"Well, that's probably just the beginning of the difference between you and me." I sat up slowly and wiped a towel across my brow.

"Dude. Did she tell you I found that shit on her computer? She offered to fuck me to keep it quiet. Like I'd want to put my dick in your cum dumpster. What a cu—"

Instinct took over. Before I realized what I was doing, I jumped off the bench and wrapped the towel around Murph's neck, pulling it tight with both hands. "It was you! Take that back, you piece of shit."

Murph gagged and sputtered, sending a dribble of spit down his chin as his hands came up and scrambled to pry the towel away. The usual clank of barbells and raucous back-ground voices came to an abrupt halt. As I released my grip, I looked around the weight room. All eyes were on me. Just like they'd been all week. Murph's face started to regain a natural color, and I clapped him on the back.

"Get the fuck away from me." Murph slapped at my hand.

With every eye in the place boring into my back, I grabbed my water bottle and keys and made my way to the door. Shit.

I couldn't even get away from her at the gym. I saw her everywhere I looked.

I'd done exactly what I promised myself I'd never do again—put my trust in someone. Faith had played me like a fucking fiddle. She'd blindsided me, pulled the rug out from under me, taken my heart to the cleaners. I'd never be able to live it down, thanks to the diligence of the paper and the worldwide web. My mistake would go down in everlasting history.

I needed to get my mind off her once and for all. I needed to get wasted. Maybe even laid. And I knew just the place to go to make both of those things happen.

I WRAPPED my fingers around the stem of the last clean wine glass and hung it upside down from the rack over the bar. I'd been scheduled for the early shift on a Saturday afternoon for a change. I caught a glimpse of pink from the corner of my eye and looked up to see Brittany coming through the door. As she made her way through the tables of men watching the Blackhawks take on the Red Wings, all of their eyes followed her from the doorway to the bar.

"Hey, Brittany. How's it going?"

"So this is where you hide out when you're not meeting with us at the library?" She lifted one butt cheek onto the edge of a stool.

I set a paper coaster down in front of her. "What can I get you?"

"Well," she drew out her l's, making the word last ten times longer than it should have. "Semester's almost over. I was kind of wondering if you might be interested in dinner sometime. You know, like a last hurrah."

She was decked out in all pink, like some frosted cotton candy concoction. Tight raspberry pink jacket over a snug bubble gum pink tank top. Even the purse she plopped down on the bar was pink. Pink overload.

I fought the urge to shield my eyes. "Dinner, huh?"

"Yeah, the meal after lunch. Most people eat it in the evening, say, around seven?"

I smiled. "I'm not opposed to dinner, but I don't date."

"Oh, I thought maybe you'd changed your position on that, after all of the stuff in the paper." A gleam caught her eye and she leaned over the bar, giving me a glimpse of the ample cleavage spilling out of her lacy, pastel pink bra. "We don't exactly have to date, Dante. In fact, we don't even have to have dinner."

She was a good-looking girl. Blonde hair, blue eyes, a cross between a busty Julianne Hough and a platinum Katy Perry.

"Tempting." I grabbed a rag and wiped down the counter, forcing Brittany to remove her hands from the bar and sit back down.

"But?" she asked, raising a well-groomed eyebrow at me.

"But I've pretty much sworn off women for a while, especially the ones I mentor, you know?"

"I get it. Just between us,"—she cupped her hand around her mouth as if divulging a huge secret—"what she did to you was wrong. Leading you on like that. See, with me, what you see is what you get."

I swabbed the rag further down the bar, away from Princess Pinky Pie. "I'm flattered, but I have to pass."

What the hell had gotten into me? There wasn't an official rule about not dating a student, and she was offering me exactly what I'd always been after... sex with no strings attached. Only now that didn't seem like enough anymore.

"Fine. If you change your mind, you know where to find me." She stepped down off the stool and sashayed her tight, Pepto-Bismol-covered ass right out the front door.

I let out a groan and took out my frustration on a particularly stubborn spot on the bar as a vision of Faith lying on my bed in her red lacy bra cavorted through my mind. So much for getting laid. At least I could still get rip roaring wasted. I snagged a bottle of Jack from behind the bar and grabbed a plastic cup.

"I'm taking five, Wyatt." I stomped down the hall to the office and slumped into a chair.

Wyatt pushed the door open and walked around the desk while I poured an inch of the dark amber liquid into the cup.

"You want to tell me what's going on here?" Wyatt asked.

"Care to join me for a shot of this fine beverage?"

Wyatt sat down and propped his elbows on the desk. "When are you going to get your head out of your ass?"

"I guess that's a no. Bottom's up." I chugged the Jack and poured another.

"Still haven't talked to her?"

"Who, Faith? We're toast. As in stick-a-fucking-fork-in-it, over with a capital 'O.'"

"I think you're blowing this out of proportion."

"Oh yeah? Lindsey ever publish a detailed account of every time you buried yourself balls-deep inside her?"

Wyatt reached for the bottle and the cup. "Give me some of that."

"See? Just the thought is driving you to drink."

"She did apologize."

I slammed another shot. "She left me a few messages. Hardly an earth-shattering apology." I reached for the bottle again, but Wyatt grabbed it first.

"Why don't you slow down on the shots? Look, I know what happened to you back in high school. I was there, remember? But Faith didn't cheat on you. She made a mistake."

"Oh yeah? Well, some mistakes are too big to forgive." I

jerked the bottle from Wyatt's hand and poured another inch into the cup.

"You think you're the only one who's ever been blind-sided? Hell, Lindsey and I had some issues early on," Wyatt said.

"Coulda fooled me. The two of you... you're like syrup and pancakes... sticky, sweet, and completely smothering."

Wyatt slapped his hand down on the desk, and I jumped in my seat. "I screwed up. Lied to her about something so stupid. I almost lost her." He moved around to lean up against the desk, leveling his gaze at me. "If she hadn't forgiven me... I don't know where I would have ended up."

Leave it to Wyatt. He hadn't been such a pussy back in Hinkley. But there was a tiny bit of truth to his words. Faith hadn't cheated. She just failed to tell the complete truth. Had I been too quick to bail on her?

"I don't know, Wyatt. I'm pretty sure I'm not the forgive-and-forget type."

"Then find a way. I know you. This chick really got to you. I'm not saying she's the one, but there's a strong possibility. You don't want to spend the rest of your life wallowing in shit when you could have done something about it." He grabbed the bottle and headed back out to the bar.

I steepled my fingers and pressed them to my forehead. I was driving myself crazy. I'd have to talk to her. I promised myself the next time she called I wouldn't automatically send it to voicemail.

Maybe she'd actually say something worth listening to.

# CHAPTER 54

*Faith*

THUNDERSTORMS BLEW across the upper Midwest, causing multiple cancellations and flight delays. I checked my phone one last time. The flight to Chicago showed a thirty-minute delay. Oh well. Jess and I were already on the way to the airport. I'd just settle somewhere in the gate area and try to get some writing done.

"So you still haven't heard from him at all?" Jess asked.

"Not a word," I said.

"Have you tried to call him?"

"I've left messages, but he hasn't called back. I'm going to give him some space."

"That's probably a good idea."

Jess had been right. The article ran in the paper, and the English department had contacted me. Even though I'd always received fantastic reviews, I'd been relieved of my teaching responsibilities. They couldn't suffer the embarrassment of having my name associated with both the highbrow University program and my erotic romance novels. Whatever. With the publicity from the article, sales of *Carnal Knowledge* had skyrocketed. I'd have enough to pay back a nice chunk of my student loans even without teaching.

This trip to Chicago couldn't have come at a better time. Steph had been pressuring me to attend the author event, and I figured it would be as good a place as any to go public with my identity. I just hoped I didn't lose my nerve.

"You sure you're ready for this?" Jess pulled up at the curb next to the departure sign.

"As ready as I'll ever be." I grabbed my bag and opened the car door. Turning to Jess, I said, "Thanks for everything."

"Don't mention it. Have fun in Chicago."

I rolled my eyes and grimaced. "No turning back now."

"It'll all work out."

As I stepped up onto the curb and closed the car door behind me, I hoped Jess was right. While I entered the airport and made my way through the long security line I let my mind wander to Dante.

He hadn't so much as sent me a text since I'd left him at Meemaw's. I couldn't really blame him. His name had been plastered all over the Tempest paper and the internet. The local paper had even picked it up and printed a small story.

It would be good to get away for a few days. If Jess was right, things would settle down soon. There would be a new scandal to cover, and the news of our fling would take a back-seat to outrage over the student center approving a fast-food chain or another professor getting caught in an affair with a student. I'd be old news by next week. At least I hoped so.

I reached the gate just in time to hear the gate agent announce they were expecting a break in the bad weather and might be able to take advantage of a small window to take off before the next round of storms came through.

Determined not to board without a bottle of water, I walked over to the small gift shop. As I waited in line to pay, my eyes scanned the two shelves of books. There on the bottom shelf, two from the end—a small stack of my books sat in between two other best sellers. I always got a thrill when I saw my pen name in print.

When I got back to the gate, the flight attendant made the boarding announcement over the loudspeaker. I'd forgotten to check in early and claim an aisle seat, so I found myself squashed into a middle, between a young mother with an infant at the window and a stuffy-looking, suited businessman on the aisle. Didn't look like I'd get much writing done. I smiled at the mother, then pulled my headphones out of the bag. I turned on my music and closed my eyes.

Jagged cries woke me from an uneasy sleep. The man on my left had claimed the armrest and as his head bobbed up and down, grunts and snores escaped from his mouth. The mother balanced the screaming baby on her lap while she tried to grab something from her bag on the floor.

"Here, let me take her." I tugged my headphones off and reached for the red-faced baby girl.

"Are you sure?" the mother asked, already passing the tiny baby over.

"It's no problem." Actually, it could be a big problem seeing as how my experience holding babies was limited to one time in high school. One of my friends got pregnant our senior year and I visited her in the hospital after she'd delivered. That baby had been quiet and sleepy. This one was a ball of fiery energy and looked like she was about to spontaneously combust.

I grasped the baby under the arms and held her away from me. The child stopped wailing. She cocked her head and looked at me, blue eyes taking me in.

"Wow, you have a magic touch," the mother said.

She sounded surprised, although she couldn't have been more shocked than me. "I don't know about that," I said.

The woman pulled a bottle out of the bag at her feet and

dumped some powder into it, shaking the water inside to form a milky liquid.

"Here, I can take her now." She reached for the baby.

As I passed the baby back, she started to scream again. The passengers in front of us craned their heads over the seat to see what the commotion was all about. The mother flushed and wiped at her eyes.

"Why don't you let me feed her while you take a break?" I asked, reaching for the bottle.

The mother offered it up with no resistance. "Thanks. By the way, I'm Maria."

"Hi, I'm Faith." I nestled the baby in the crook of my arm as the child grabbed for the bottle.

"Just lift her head a little bit," Maria said.

I adjusted the baby and she latched onto the bottle with surprising strength.

"Wow, she must be really hungry," I said.

"Yeah, that's all she does. Eat, sleep, poop, repeat. Seems like I never have time for much else anymore."

"Babies are hard work."

Maria rummaged through the diaper bag. "I've started this one book four times now. As soon as I really get into it, it's time to change a diaper or make up another bottle." She laughed. "Don't get me wrong, I love being a mother, I just don't have time for anything else."

"I'm sure it will get easier as she gets a little older," I said, gazing down at the baby.

"Have you ever read this author?" Maria asked, pulling out the book.

"Who is it?"

"Chastity Austen. If you like romance novels, you'll love her."

I blushed. I'd been planning on going public at the event anyway, may as well practice. "Um, I actually wrote that."

"I thought you said your name was Faith?"

"Chastity Austen is my pen name."

"You're joking, right?"

"No. I haven't really told anybody about it yet but I'm going to an event this weekend so the cat's kind of out of the bag now."

"Oh my gosh, you're the only reason I still have a husband."

"Really?" Where was she going with this?

"Yeah. It's not easy finding the energy to be romantic with my hubby now that we've got a baby. Your books... I'll just say they're inspiring. After I finished the first one, my husband bought me the rest for my birthday."

I laughed. "Hey, if you want to come to the book signing tomorrow, feel free to stop by. It's at the convention center downtown."

"I can't wait to tell my sister. Would you sign my book?"

"Um, sure."

She dug through her purse for a pen, and I scrawled my signature across the front page while I propped the bottle under my chin. First time for everything. I'd better get used to the attention if everything was going to go according to plan.

Turning the conversation back to the baby, I asked, "What's her name?"

Maria spent the rest of the flight opening up and bragging about little Maddie. By the time the flight attendant made the announcement to prepare for arrival, I'd learned more about motherhood than I'd ever cared to know.

After the plane landed, we said our goodbyes. Maria promised to stop by the next day and bring her sister and friends along. It would be nice to see a familiar face in the crowd, even if we had just met.

Inspired by my run-in with my first fan, I wrapped my

fingers around the handle of my rolling bag and made my way down the jetway and out to the curb. I was ready to claim my alter ego.

# CHAPTER 55

## Dante

I EASED to a stop by the curb and looked up at the new sign for the Sashay Salon. One more meeting with Tameka, and then she'd be on her own. I got out of the car and stepped through the door.

"Hey, Dante. Thanks for coming by." Tameka stood behind her new sales counter, one of the suggestions my team and I had made for her interior remodel.

"Hi, Tameka. How's business?"

She came around the counter and pointed at my bag. "You probably know better than me. Tell me, how am I doing?"

I smiled. "Want to talk in the back?"

"Sure." She led me to her small office and sat down behind the desk.

I slid a file out of my bag. "The salon is doing great. Business is up over two hundred percent since we started working with you last fall."

"I can't tell you how much I appreciate your help. You and the girls."

I smirked, recalling some of my teammates' ideas. Thank God we'd vetoed the pink motif. "We really enjoyed working with you. I just wanted to come by and drop off our final report." I'd managed to avoid the salon since the haircut incident but wanted to be the one to bring over the last bit of paperwork. I laid a stapled packet down on the desk and Tameka picked it up.

"I don't know what would have happened to this place if y'all hadn't come around." She gave me a warm smile. "You sure have made a difference."

"Thanks for the great review. I'm sure it came into play when the board was considering my promotion."

Tameka nodded. "It was my pleasure. You deserved it. Now, how are you doing, Dante?"

"I'm great." I shrugged. Everything was falling into place for me, so how could I be anything but fantastic? "I took a promotion with a branch of our firm out of Baltimore. I'll be moving in a couple of weeks. I'm really looking forward to it."

"Mmm hmm," Tameka hummed. "But how are you doing?"

I furrowed my brow. Didn't I just tell her? "It's a great career move. I'm excited about it."

"And Faith?"

I groaned and rubbed my hands across my stubble. "Even you know about that, huh?"

"Have you talked to her?"

"Look, that's old news and not really anyone's business."

Tameka's eyebrows lifted. The look she gave me reminded me of the one Meemaw had used when she knew I wasn't owning up to something.

I shifted in my seat. "I just, well, Faith and I aren't seeing each other anymore."

Tameka stood up and walked around the desk, then sat down on the edge, facing me. "You've done such a great job for me. I don't know what I would've done without your help."

"And the team..."

"We both know those girls didn't do much. You're the reason I'm still in business." Tameka pointed a long purple nail at me. "I just hope you find the happiness you deserve."

"Thanks. I'm sure I will. Did you want to go over those papers or just look them over when you have time?"

Tameka shook her head. "You should talk to her."

"With all due respect, you really don't know anything about us." *Us.* As if Faith and I were ever an *us.* An *us* required commitment. An *us* required honesty. An *us* required two people to actually feel the same way about each other.

"Well, I may not know a lot about you or a lot about Faith." Tameka shook her head. "But I know a good story when I read one and whewy, that girl is into you, my boy."

My boy? Holy shit. Meemaw had stopped talking to me in my head. Was she now channeling herself through Tameka? I shook my head to clear it as Tameka stood up.

"If there's nothing else, then I think I'll just head out." I'd had to listen to enough people tell me what they thought I needed to do about Faith. It was time to move on. Time to leave Faith and Newbridge and all the bad memories behind. I stood and grabbed my bag.

The weird moment passed as Tameka led me to the front of the salon.

"The Phil & Piper Morning Show" blared from the television hanging on the wall. I glanced over as I passed by and almost crashed into a manicure station. Faith sat on a red sofa opposite the two hosts. A screen behind her displayed the covers of all her books.

I hadn't seen her since that last night at Meemaw's. Her hair seemed longer, the fiery red strands falling over her shoulders. She looked thinner and the dark smudges under her eyes weren't quite concealed with whatever makeup she'd slathered on. Maybe she was having trouble falling asleep, too.

I shoved my hands in my pockets and waited for someone on the screen to start talking.

Phil spoke first. "We're here this morning with bestselling contemporary romance author, Faith Wainwright. She's in town for a book-signing event that gives local readers a chance to meet their favorite romance authors. Thanks for joining us, Faith."

Faith's hands nervously played with the book in her lap. "Thanks for having me."

"Faith, you've had quite a year," Piper said. "Most of your readers know you as Chastity Austen. Your latest release has been climbing the bestseller lists, right?"

Faith cleared her throat. "That's right. Like many other authors, I've been using a pen name."

"Nothing wrong with Faith Wainwright. Why bother with a pen name?" Phil asked.

Faith turned her attention his way. "In my case, I wanted to distance myself from my parents." She lifted one leg and crossed it over the other.

"You're speaking of your mother, Claire Kepner, and step-father, Clem Kepner, correct?" Piper asked.

"That's right." Faith turned her head toward Piper while she uncrossed her legs and scooted closer to the edge of her seat. Why was she putting herself through this? Obviously, she hated the spotlight. Was she that hungry for fame?

"But recently someone thrust you into the spotlight. A colleague or co-worker?" Piper lifted her morning show mug up from the table and took a sip.

"I was blackmailed by another faculty member. He found

out my true identity and leaked my current work-in-progress to the paper. Can I just say something real quick?"

Phil shifted in his seat. "Um, sure. I suppose. Go ahead."

Looked like Faith might be going off script. She glanced around and the camera zoomed in on her face. Her fingers went to the chain suspended from her neck and she fingered a charm. The lotus blossom. My heart stalled in my chest.

She cleared her throat and looked directly into the camera. "I just want to say I'm sorry. To my mom and stepdad for causing them any embarrassment. I know it won't be easy for them to come to terms with my chosen genre. But I especially want to apologize to the person I hurt the most. I've tried saying I'm sorry, but you won't take my calls. I never meant for things to go this far." She looked down at her lap and paused. The camera zoomed out to catch Phil and Piper whispering to each other.

I scoffed and shook my head. Leave it to Faith to botch her first big interview. I took a step toward the door.

"Wait." Tameka's hand went to my shoulder. I shrugged it off while I looked back at the TV.

The camera zoomed in on Faith. Her eyes welled with tears. "I never meant to fall in love, but I did. I love you, Dante. I'm so sorry. Can you forgive me?"

Tameka took in a sharp breath and grabbed my shoulder again. The camera zoomed out. Piper handed Faith a tissue.

Phil attempted to regain control of the set. "Well, thanks, Faith, for sharing your story with us. We hope you find your own happily ever after. Remember, you can get your copy of *Carnal Knowledge* signed this weekend at the convention center or head out to see her next week at the local bookstore in Newbridge, Indiana. Next up, how one young man is saving the planet's oceans, one plastic bottle at a time."

The screen went dark for a moment, then a commercial for diapers started. I sighed.

Tameka's hand fell from my shoulder. "Promise me you'll talk to her, okay?"

I cocked my head. "Yeah, sure."

"Keep in touch, Dante. Good luck with your big job."

"Thanks. Let me know how things go here."

Tameka winked at me as I passed through the door and back onto the street. Shit. Maybe it was time to talk to Faith. But what the hell would I say to the woman who still held my heart in her hands?

# CHAPTER 56

## *Faith*

I PAUSED, pen poised over the title page of my book. "Who do you want me to make this out to?"

"Lynne. L-y-n-n-e."

I scrawled the Chastity Austen signature I'd been practicing over the page and handed the book back to the woman in front of me. "Thanks for coming today."

I'd been signing autographs at the independent bookstore just off campus for over an hour. I shook my hand and grabbed a sip of water as the next reader stopped in front of the table.

I was ready to get out of Newbridge and move on with my life. I wasn't sure yet where I was headed, but it was time for a new start. After the conference in Chicago, I'd decided I was done with teaching. Those women, and their husbands, needed my stories. And I needed to tell them.

Since I'd gone public as Chastity Austen, my book sales had exploded, and Steph was at auction for another multi-book deal with a couple of major publishing houses. I was eager to see where my writing career might go.

Surprisingly, my mother had come around and encouraged me to step back from teaching and work on my writing career. She'd also gently hinted that maybe somewhere on the east coast would be best. Her publicist was still working out how to spin the fact that her daughter was a bestselling novelist of erotic romance. Clem hadn't been quite as supportive, and definitely lacked my mother's enthusiasm. Mom said he just needed time.

Robin tossed her book down on the table. I stood and gave her a hug. "Thanks so much for coming."

"Are you kidding? I wouldn't miss it! I haven't talked to you in so long. Have you figured out where you're moving yet?"

I scrawled my signature again. "Not yet. I still have a month or so before my lease is up."

"Wow. Living on the edge from the girl with the six-year plan. Who would have thought?"

I laughed. "Yeah, it's a change for sure, but I kind of like it." Worrying about what would come next had plagued me for so long that this freedom from planning was a welcome change. I only had one regret—Dante. I'd finally had the guts to admit to myself that I'd fallen for him—hard. If only I'd handled things differently. If only I'd been willing to admit that I'd had feelings for him all along—things might be different right now.

But I was starting a new chapter in my life, and he obviously didn't want to be a part of it. How could I expect him to forgive me and give me another chance? I'd hoped he'd seen the episode air last week from Chicago. But it had been eight days and there had been no word. I didn't blame him. If roles had been reversed and he'd been the one to let me down, I wasn't so sure I'd be so willing to forgive and forget either.

I handed the book back to Robin. "Stick around if you want. I'm here for another fifteen minutes and then Jess

wants to go out for one last drink before we all go our separate ways."

"You got it." Robin winked at me and moved over to
where Jess stood, nuzzling into Jake. They were back on
again... at least for the moment.

The next person stepped up and slid a hardcover copy in
front of me. My eyes remained on the table.

Pen poised, I flipped open the first page. "Who do you
want me to make it out to?"

"Asshole."

"What?" My heart froze. All the blood drained from my
face and pooled in my feet at the sound of his voice.

"I've been a real prick."

My gaze traveled up to meet his. The air whooshed out of
my lungs while my heartbeat thundered in my ears.

He held one hand behind his back and brought it around
to set a long tissue-wrapped package on the table. With
what felt like everyone else's eyes in the entire bookstore on
me, the only one I could see was Dante. I peeled the tissue
away.

A bouquet containing every kind of flower imaginable sat
in front of me. Red roses, orange Peruvian lilies, pink carna-
tions, striped amaryllis, white calla lilies, lavender asters,
ivory freesia, purple iris, yellow tulips, and white daisies—he
remembered the daisies.

It wasn't too late.

I looked up. Dante shrugged then gestured toward the
flowers. "I want it all, Faith. The love, the friendship, the
loyalty. I'm sorry about—"

His words were lost as I stood up and launched myself
over the table at him to press my lips against his. His arms
wrapped around my waist and he pulled me into him. The
crowd applauded and whistled as the kiss deepened and our
tongues tangled.

He was here. I clung to his shirt, aware of the rock-solid feel of him under my hands. What did this mean?

Dante drew back and looked down at me, catching my gaze with his own. "We really did a number on each other, huh?"

I didn't want to let go. "I never meant for this to happen. Everything got a little out of control."

"A little?" He tucked me even tighter against him. His chuckle vibrated through his chest.

"Okay, a lot. A lot out of control. I'm so sorry. I should have been up front with you in the first place. And once I knew someone found out about my pen name—"

"Murph."

"You knew?" I pulled back to meet his gaze.

"Not until recently. We exchanged words. I don't think he'll be bothering you again. You should have told me."

I nodded against his chest. "I know. But I was afraid if I told you, you'd want out."

"I never wanted out. I might have suggested you change our names."

My hair fell around my cheeks as I shook my head. "I was so stupid."

"Hey"—he leaned down to kiss my cheek—"we both were. I should have pushed for more sooner."

"So, what do we do now?"

His finger slid along my cheek. "Rumor has it you might be looking for a place to live?"

"I still have a month left on my lease. Haven't figured out where I want to end up. My mom suggested I stay away from the west coast."

"Ever been out east? I rented an apartment overlooking the river in Baltimore. Thought maybe it might be fun to take you out on a boat sometime. You ever done it on the water?"

My heart fluttered. "First time for everything, right?"

"No more secrets."

I nodded against his chest and inhaled his intoxicating scent. "No more secrets, I promise."

His lips crooked into a perfect grin. "You prepared to shake on that?"

"Isn't there some other way we can seal that agreement?"

Dante growled into my ear, sparking a dormant need I'd stuffed away inside. "Damn straight there is. You've got three minutes to wrap this up and head home with me or else I'll bend you over that table and take you right here."

A delicious chill ran up my spine as I glanced over at the table in question. I pushed away from him long enough to catch Jess's thumbs-up and announce to the people left in line, "Book signing is over for tonight. If you still want me to sign, just leave your copy with your name and number over there and you can pick them up tomorrow afternoon."

"You forgot to sign mine." Dante held his copy out to me.

I took it, not sure what to write. How could I sum up in just a few words how much he meant to me?

With the weight of his delicious gaze resting on me, I scrawled my signature and handed it back to him.

Dante glanced at the page. "From one asshole to another?"

"Hey, we were both to blame. Let's not let it happen again, okay?" I tucked the bouquet of flowers against my side.

"You got it." Dante wrapped an arm around my shoulders and pulled me up against him as he guided me toward the door. "I've been meaning to ask. Did you finish it yet? How does it end?"

I shook my head, breathless, still reeling from the fact he'd shown up and was willing to give things another try. "How does what end?"

He stopped and turned to face me, circling my waist with his arms. "The story of Faith and Dante, the one you've been working on. The story of us."

I tugged his mouth down to mine again and whispered, "It doesn't end. This is just the beginning."

I HOPE you enjoyed **Betting on the Bad Boy**! f you didn't get enough of Faith and Dante, you can snag a free bonus scene through this link: https://dylanncrush.com/Bad-Boy

Or by scanning the QR code below:

## Also By Dylann Crush

**Betting on Forever Series**

*Betting on the Bad Boy*

*Betting on the Bartender*

**Mountain Men of Mustang Mountain Series**

*January is for Jackson*

*March is for Miles*

*May is for Mack*

*July is for Jonas*

*September is for Shaw*

*November is for Nate*

**Whiskey Wars Series**

*Drinking Deep*

*Tasting Temptation*

*Sipping Seduction*

*Drowning Desire*

**Cowboys in Paradise Series**

*Kiss Me Now, Cowboy*

*Make Me Yours, Cowboy*

**Tying the Knot in Texas Series**

*The Cowboy Says I Do*

*Her Kind of Cowboy*

*Crazy About a Cowboy*

**Lovebird Café Series**

*Lemon Tarts & Stolen Hearts*

*Sweet Tea & Second Chances*

*Mud Pies & Family Ties*

*Hot Fudge & a Heartthrob*

**Holiday, Texas Series**

*All-American Cowboy*

*Cowboy Christmas Jubilee*

*Cowboy Charming*

**The Love Vixen Series**

*Getting Lucky in Love*

**Standalone Romances**

*All I Wanna Do Is You*

# About Dylann Crush

*USA Today* bestselling author Dylann Crush writes contemporary romance with sizzle, sass, heart and humor. A true romantic, she loves her heroines spunky and her heroes super sexy. When she's not dreaming up steamy storylines, she can be found sipping a margarita and searching for the best Tex-Mex food in the Upper Midwest.

Although she grew up in Texas, she currently lives in a suburb of Minneapolis/St. Paul with her unflappable husband, three energetic kids, a clumsy Great Dane, a lovable rescue mutt, a very chill cat, and a crazy kitten. She loves to connect with readers, other authors and fans of tequila.

You can find her at www.dylanncrush.com or join her reader group on Facebook, Crushin' It Crew.

facebook.com/dylanncrush

instagram.com/dylanncrush

pinterest.com/dylanncrush

bookbub.com/authors/dylann-crush

goodreads.com/DylannCrush

tiktok.com/@dylanncrush